PRAISE FOR

The Sil

'A short, sharp, electric shock of

'Races along. In a word: FRAUGHT' *Weekend Gold Coast Bulletin*

'Highlights of Haas's cinematic thriller include a cross-country junket, quick reversals, lightning violence and a surprising denouement . . . Lean work, with every word counting and adding up to more than most authors land in twice the space' *Kirkus*

'Well written, fast-paced, and engaging . . . fans of James Patterson and Jeffrey Deaver will enjoy' *Library Journal*

'Moody, gloomy, but curiously gripping' *Literary Review*

Hunt for the Bear

'A straight-out thriller that moves at an arrow's pace' truecrimereport.com

'Haas takes his title character – and the reader – one step further by yanking down the barrier between antihero and audience . . . a nifty modern riff on pulp-fiction' *Las Vegas Weekly*

'Impossible not to like . . . Recommended to fans of the Dexter novels, as well as readers of Barry Eisler's John Rain novels, or Lawrence Block's stories about Keller the killer.' *Booklist*

'Absolutely one of the best reads I've had this year . . . Haas is a guy whose work I'll pick up any time he publishes.' Hitfix.com

Derek Haas

Derek Haas is the author of *The Silver Bear*, the Barry Award-nominated *Hunt for the Bear* and *Dark Men*. Derek also co-wrote the screenplays for *3:10 to Yuma*, starring Russell Crowe and Christian Bale; *Wanted*, starring James McAvoy, Morgan Freeman and Angelina Jolie; and *The Double*, starring Richard Gere and Topher Grace. He lives in Los Angeles.

DEREK HAAS

THE SILVER BEAR TRILOGY

THE SILVER BEAR | HUNT FOR THE BEAR | DARK MEN

MULHOLLAND BOOKS
HODDER

The Silver Bear © 2008 Derek Haas
First published in Great Britain in 2008 by Hodder & Stoughton
An Hachette UK company

Hunt for the Bear © 2009 Derek Haas
First published in Great Britain in 2009 by Hodder & Stoughton
An Hachette UK company

Dark Men © 2011 Derek Haas
First published in Great Britain in 2011 by Mulholland Books
An imprint of Hodder & Stoughton
An Hachette UK company

These three books first published as *The Silver Bear Trilogy* in paperback in 2012

1

A CIP catalogue record for this title is available from the British Library

Paperback ISBN 978 1 444 73239 9
eBook ISBN 978 1 444 74244 2

Typeset in Times by Hewer Text UK Ltd, Edinburgh
Printed and bound by Clays Ltd, St Ives plc

Hodder & Stoughton policy is to use papers that are natural, renewable and recyclable
products and made from wood grown in sustainable forests. The logging and manufacturing
processes are expected to conform to the environmental regulations of the country of origin.

Hodder & Stoughton Ltd
338 Euston Road
London NW1 3BH

www.hodder.co.uk

THE SILVER BEAR

Derek Haas

For Chris, who pulled.
And for Kristi, who pushed.

I

The last day of the cruelest month, and appropriately it rains. Not the spring rain of new life and rebirth, not for me. Death. In my life, always death. I am young; if you saw me on the street, you might think, 'what a nice, clean-cut young man. I'll bet he works in advertising or perhaps a nice accounting firm. I'll bet he's married and is just starting a family. I'll bet his parents raised him well.' But you would be wrong. I am old in a thousand ways. I have seen things and done things that would make you rush instinctively to your child's bedroom and hug him tight to your chest, breathing quick in short bursts like a misfiring engine, and repeat over and over, 'It's okay, baby. It's okay. Everything's okay.'

I am a bad man. I do not have any friends. I do not speak to women or children for longer than is absolutely necessary. I groom myself to blend, like a chameleon darkening its pigment against the side of an oak tree. My hair is cut short, my eyes are hidden behind dark glasses, my dress would inspire a yawn from anyone who passed me in the street. I do not call attention to myself in any way.

I have lived this way for as long as I can remember, although in truth it has only been ten years. The events of my life prior to that day, I have forgotten in all detail, although I do remember the pain. Joy and pain tend to make imprints on memory that do not dim, flecks of senses rather than images that resurrect themselves involuntarily and without warning. I have had precious little of the former and a lifetime of the latter. A week ago, I read a poll that reported ninety percent of people over the age of sixty would choose to be a teenager again if they could. If those same people could have experienced one day of my teenage years, not a single hand would be counted.

The past does not interest me, though it is always there, just below the surface, like dangerous blurs and shapes an ocean swimmer senses in the deep. I am fond of the present. I am in command in the present. I am master of my own destiny in the present. If I choose, I can touch someone, or let someone touch me, but only in the present. Free will is a gift of the present; the only time I can choose to outwit God. The future, your fate, though, belongs to God. If you try to outsmart God in planning your fate, you are in for disappointment. He owns the future, and He loves O. Henry endings.

The present is full of rain and bluster, and I hurry to close the door behind me as I duck into an indiscriminate warehouse alongside the Charles River. It has been a cold April, which many say indicates a long, hot summer approaching, but I do not make predictions. The warehouse is damp, and I can smell mildew, fresh-cut sawdust, and fear.

People do not like to meet with me. Even those whom society considers dangerous are uneasy in my presence. They have heard stories about Singapore, Providence, and Brooklyn. About Washington, Baltimore, and Miami. About London, Bonn, and Dallas. They do not want to say something to make me uncomfortable or angry, and so they choose their words with precision. Fear is a feeling foreign to these types of men, and they do not like the way it settles in their stomach. They get me in and out as fast as they can and with very little negotiation.

Presently, I am to meet with a black man named Archibald Grant. His given name is Cotton Grant, but he didn't like the way 'Cotton' made him sound like a Georgia hillbilly Negro, so he moved to Boston and started calling himself Archibald. He thought it made him sound aristocratic, like he came from prosperity, and he liked the way it sounded on a whore's lips: 'Archibald, slide on over here' in a soft falsetto. He does not know that I know about the name Cotton. In my experience, it is best to know every detail about those with whom you are meeting. A single mention of a surprising detail, a part of his life he thought was buried so deep as to never be found, can cause him to pause just long enough to make a difference. A pause is all I need most of the time.

I walk through a hallway and am stopped at a large door by two towering black behemoths, each with necks the size of my waist. They look at me, and their eyes measure me. Clearly, they were expecting something different after all they've been told. I am used to this. I am used to the disappointment in some of their eyes as they think, 'give me ten minutes in a room with him and we'll see what's shakin'.' But I do not have an ego, and I avoid confrontations.

'You be?' says the one on the right whose slouch makes the handle of his pistol crimp his shirt just enough to let me know it's there.

'Tell Archibald it's *Columbus*.'

He nods, backs through the door, while the other studies me with unintelligent eyes. He coughs and manages, 'You Columbus?' as if in disbelief. Meaning it as a challenge.

I ignore him, not moving a centimeter of my face, my stance, my posture. I am in the present. It is my time, and I own it.

He does not know what to make of this, as he is not used to being ignored, has not been ignored all his life, as big as he is. But somewhere, a voice tells him maybe the stories he heard are true, maybe this Columbus is the badass motherfucker Archibald was talking about yesterday, maybe it'd be best to let the challenge hang out there and fade, the way a radio signal grows faint as a car drives further and further down the highway.

He is relieved when the door opens and I am beckoned into the room.

Archibald is behind a wooden desk; a single light bulb on a wire chain moves like a pendulum over his head. He is not a large man, a sharp contrast from the muscle he keeps around him. Short, well-dressed, with a fire in his eyes that matches the tip of the cigarette stuck in the corner of his mouth. He is used to getting what he wants.

He stands, and we shake hands with a light grip as though neither wants to make a commitment. I am offered the only other chair, and we sit deliberately at the same time.

'I'm a middleman on this,' he says abruptly, so I'll know this from the get-go. The cigarette bobs up and down like a metronome as he speaks.

'I understand.'

'This a single. Eight weeks out, like you say.'

'Where?'

'Outside L.A. At least, that's where this cat'll be at the time.'

Archibald sits back in his chair and folds his hands on his stomach. He's a businessman, talking business. He likes this role. It makes him think of the businessmen behind their desks in Atlanta where he used to go in and change out the trash baskets, replace the garbage with new dark plastic linings.

I nod, only slightly. Archibald takes this as his cue to swivel in his chair and open a file door on the credenza matching his desk. From the cavity, he withdraws a briefcase, and we both know what's inside. He slides it in my direction across the desk and waits.

'Everything you requested's in there, if you want to check it out,' he offers.

'I know where to find you if it's not.'

It's statements like these that can get people into trouble, because they can be interpreted several ways. Perhaps I am making a benign declaration, or possibly a stab at humor, or maybe a little bit of both. But in this business, more often than not, I am making a threat, and nobody likes to be threatened.

He studies my face, his own expression stuck between a smirk and a frown, but whatever he is looking for, he doesn't find it. He has little choice but to laugh it off so his muscle will understand I am not being disrespectful.

'Heh-hah.' Only part of a laugh. 'Yeah. That's good. Well, it's all there.'

I help him out by taking the case off the desk, and he is happy to see me stand. This time, he does not offer his hand.

I walk away from the desk, toward the door, case in hand, but his voice stops me. He can't help himself, his curiosity wins over his cautiousness; he isn't sure if he'll ever see me again, and he has to know.

'Did'ja really pop Corlazzi on that boat?'

You'd be surprised how many times I get this one. Corlazzi was a Chicago underworld luminary responsible for much of the city's butchery in the sixties and seventies, a man who redefined the mafia's role when narcotics started to replace liquor as America's drug of choice. He saw the future first, and deftly rose to prominence. As hated as he was feared, he had a paranoid streak that threatened his sanity. To ensure that he would reign to a ripe old age, he removed himself to a gigantic houseboat docked in the middle of Lake Michigan. It was armed to the teeth, and its only connection with land was through a speedboat manned by his son, Nicolas. Six years ago, he was found dead, a single bullet lodged in the aorta of his heart, though no one heard a shot and the man was behind locked doors with a bevy of guards posted outside.

Now, I don't have to answer this question. I can leave and let Archibald and his entourage wonder how a guy like me could possibly do the things attributed to the name Columbus. This is a tactic I've used in the past, when questions like his are posed. But, today, the last day of the cruelest month, I think differently. I have six eyes on me, and a man's reputation can live for years on the witness of three black guys in a warehouse on the outskirts of Boston.

I spin with a whirl part tornado and part grace, and before an inhale can become an exhale, I have a pistol up and raised in my hand. I squeeze the trigger in the same motion, and the cigarette jumps out of Archibald's mouth and twirls like a baton through the air. The bullet plugs in the brick wall above the credenza as gravity takes the cigarette like a helicopter to a gentle landing on the cement floor. When the six eyes look up, I am gone.

2

Lateral bursts of wind prick the side of my face as I walk into my building. By the time I hear the story again, the scene in Archibald's warehouse will have taken on Herculean proportions. There will have been ten guys, instead of three, all with their guns drawn and trained on me. Archibald will have insulted me by saying, 'There's your case, bitch,' or some other endearment. I will have danced around bullets, mowed down seven guys, and walked on water before the cigarette was shot out of Archibald's mouth. Advertising doesn't hold a candle to the underworld's word of mouth.

My apartment does not reflect the size of my bank account. It is eight hundred square feet, sparsely decorated, with only the furniture and appliances necessary to sustain me for a week, the longest I stay most of the time. I do not have a cleaning service, or take a newspaper, or own a mailbox. My landlord has never met me, but receives a payment for double rent in cash once a year. In return, he asks no questions.

On my one table, I open the case carefully and spread its contents in neat stacks. Twenty dollars to a bill, a hundred bills to a band, five hundred bands in the case. This up front, triple when the job is complete. Underneath all of the money is a manila envelope. The money holds no allure for me. I am as immune to its siren's song as if I had taken a vaccine. The envelope, however, is my addiction.

I slide my finger under the seal and carefully open the flap, withdrawing its contents as though these pages are precious – brittle, breakable, vulnerable. This is what makes my breath catch, my heart spin, my stomach tighten. This is what keeps me looking for the next assignment, and the next, and the next – no matter what the cost to my conscience. This . . . the first look at the person I am going to kill.

Twenty sheets of paper, two binders of photographs, a schedule map, an itinerary, and a copy of a Washington, D.C. driver's license. I savor the first look at these items the way a hungry man savors the smell of steak. This mark will occupy my next eight weeks, and, though he doesn't know it, these papers are the first lines written on his death certificate. The envelope is before me, the contents laid out next to the money on my table, the end of his life now a foregone conclusion, as certain as the rising sun.

Quickly, I hold the first paper to the light that is snaking through my window, my eyes settling on the largest type, the name at the top of the page.

And then a gasp, as though an invisible fist flies through the air and knocks the breath from my lungs.

Can it be? Can someone have known, have somehow discovered my background and set this up as some sort of a joke? But . . . it is unthinkable. No one knows anything about my identity; no fingerprints, no calling card, no trace of my existence ever left carelessly at the scene of a killing. Nothing survives to link Columbus to that infant child taken from his mother's arms by the 'authorities' and rendered a ward of the state.

ABE MANN. The name at the top of the sheet. Can this be a mere coincidence? Doubtful. My experience has proven to me time and time again that coincidence is a staple of fiction, but holds little authority in the real world. I open the binder, and my eyes absorb photograph after photograph. There is no mistake: this is the same Abe Mann who is currently Speaker of the House of Representatives of the United States of America, the same Abe Mann who represents the seventh district of the state of New York, the same Abe Mann who will soon be launching his first bid for his party's nomination for president. But none of these reasons caused the air to be sucked from my lungs. I have killed powerful men and relish the chance to do so again. There is more to the story of Abe Mann.

Twenty-nine years ago, Abe Mann was a freshman congressman with a comfortable wife and a comfortable house and a comfortable reputation. He attended more sessions of congress than any other congressman, joined three committees and was invited to join three more, and was viewed as a rising star in his party, enjoying his share of air time on the Sunday morning political programs. He also enjoyed his share of whores.

Abe was a big man. Six-foot-four, and a one-time college basketball star at Syracuse. He married an accountant's daughter, and her frigid upbringing continued unabated to her marriage bed. He stopped loving her before their honeymoon ended, and had his first taste of a prostitute the Monday after they returned from Bermuda. His weekdays he spent at the state capitol as a district representative; his weekends he spent anywhere but home. For five years, he rarely slept in his own bed, and his wife kept her mouth sealed tight, fearful that intimate details of their marriage would end up sandwiched between the world report and the weekend weather on the five o'clock news.

Once elected to serve in the nation's capital, Abe discovered a whole new level of prostitution. There were high-quality whores in New York, mind you, but even they paled in comparison to the women who serviced the leaders of this country. The best part was, he didn't even have to make polite enquiries. He was approached before he was sworn in, approached the first night of his first trip to Washington after the election. A senator, a man he had seen only on television and whom he had never met in person, called him directly at his hotel room and asked if he would like to join him for a party. What an incredible time he had had that night. With the stakes higher, the women so young, so beautiful, and so willing, he had experienced a new ecstasy that still made his mind reel when he thought of it.

Later that year, after he had settled, he grew fond of a hard-bodied black prostitute named Amanda B. Though she argued against it, he forced her to fuck him without a condom, satisfying his growing thirst for bigger and bigger thrills. For about six months, he fucked her in increasingly public locations, in increasingly dangerous positions, with increasingly animalistic ferocity. Each fix begat the next, and he needed stronger doses to satisfy his appetite.

When she became pregnant, his world caved in. He crawled to her in tears, begging for forgiveness. She was not frightened of him until she saw this change. This change meant he was more dangerous than she had anticipated. She knew what would happen next: after the tears, after the self-flagellation, after the 'why me?' and the self-loathing, he would turn. His internal remorse would eventually be directed outward; he would have been made to face his own weakness, and he would not like what he had seen. And so he would destroy that which made him feel helpless. Even in the altered state that cocaine had made of her mind, Amanda B. knew this as surely as she knew anything.

But she liked the way the baby felt inside her. She liked the way it was growing, swelling her stomach, moving inside her. Her! Amanda B., formerly La Wanda Dickerson of East Providence, Rhode Island, formerly inmate 43254 of the Slawson Home for Girls, her! Amanda B.! *She* could create life as well as any uppity wife of a congressman, any homemaker in a big house on a big lot next to a big lake. Her! As good as any of them.

So she decided to hide. She knew he would come for her, and when he did, she would be gone. She had a friend back home, a john who had proposed to her when she was fourteen. He still called, long distance and not collect either! He would take her in, would hide her from the congressman when he came looking. If she could just get to him . . .

But she didn't make it to Rhode Island. Instead, she ended up in the hospital, her nose bleeding, her lungs exploding, her heart beating holes into her chest. The police had found her seven-months-pregnant frame in the basement of an abandoned tenement building during a routine drug raid, a rubber cord tied around her bicep, a needle sticking out of her forearm. She was checked into the hospital as Jane Doe number 13 that day. The next day, she went into labor and gave birth to a four-pound boy. Social Services took him from her before she had held him for more than a minute.

Congressman Mann saw her for the last time two months later. Having seen the error of his ways, having rededicated his life to his country, his wife, and his God, he had her forcibly escorted from his front yard as she screamed louder and with more vehemence than she had ever screamed in her life. Ten days after the police report was filed, she was found dead in an alley behind a Sohio gas station, a knife handle sticking at an awkward angle from her neck. The policeman on the scene, a sixteen-year veteran named William Handley, speculated the wound was self-inflicted, though the coroner thought the circumstances of the death were inconclusive.

It took me two and a half years to put all that together. I did not ask the clay's question of who is the potter until I had achieved adulthood, not believing I would survive long enough to care. Then, after killing my eighth mark in three years, achieving a level of professionalism few have matched, I started to wonder who I was. Where did I come from? Who could possibly have sired me? The past, for which I had held no deference, reached out its huge, black paw and batted me right in the face.

So I clawed and scratched and exercised the necessary patience and restraint, and slowly put the jigsaw puzzle together, starting with the edges and working my way toward the center. A newspaper story connected to a hospital report connected to a police record until it all took shape and became whole. Once the puzzle was complete, I decided to dismiss the past once and for all. The present would be my domain, always the present. Every time I had tried to befriend the past, it chose to have no amity for me. Well, no more. I would bury my mother, Amanda B., so deep I would never find her again. And so I would my father, Congressman Abe Mann of New York.

And then, here is his name at the top of the sheet. Seven black letters printed in a careful hand, strong in their order, powerful in their conciseness. ABE MANN. My father. The next person I am to kill, in Los Angeles, eight weeks from now.

Can this be a coincidence, or has someone discovered my secret past and put the jigsaw puzzle together as I had? In my line of work, I can take no chances with the answer. I have to react quickly, waste as little time as possible, for if this does prove to be just another assignment, I'll have to compensate for each minute missed.

I, too, have a middleman. Pooley is the closest thing to friend or family I have, but we prefer the noncommittal label 'business associates.' I take one more glance over the documents, stack everything back in the case, and head out the door.

A hotel a block away provides me with quick access to taxicabs whenever I need them. The rain diminishing, I make my way over to where the hotel's doorman can hail me a car. The driver feels like chatting me up, but I stare out the window and let the buildings slide by outside like they're on a conveyer belt, one after the other, each looking just like the one before it. Stymied, the driver lights a cigarette and turns up the radio, a daygame, a businessman's special, broadcasting from Fenway.

We make it to Downey Street in SoBo, and I have the driver pull over to a nondescript corner. I do nothing that will cause him to remember me; I pay a fair tip and move up the street quickly. A day from now, he won't be able to distinguish me from any other fare.

I buy two coffees from a Greek delicatessen and climb the stoop to a loft apartment above the neighboring bakery. I am buzzed in before I can even juggle the styrofoam cups and press the button. Pooley must be at his desk.

'You brought me coffee?' He acts surprised as I hand him one of the cups and sit heavily in the only other chair in the room. 'You thoughtful bastard.'

'Yeah, I'm going soft.'

I hoist the case onto his desk and slide it over to him.

'Archibald's?'

'Yep,' I answer.

'He give you any problems?'

'Naah, he's all bluster. What I want to know is: who's he working for?'

This catches Pooley off guard. Ours is a business where certain questions aren't asked. The less you know – the fewer people you know, I should say – the better your chances of survival. Middlemen are as common as paper and ink, another office supply, a necessity to conduct business. They are used for a reason: to protect us from each other. Everyone understands this. Everyone respects this. You do not go asking questions, or you end up dead or relocated or physically unable to do your job. But those seven letters at the top of the page changed the rules.

'What?' he asks. Maybe he hadn't heard me right. I can't blame him for hoping.

'I want to know who hired Archibald to work as his go-between.'

'Columbus,' Pooley stammers. 'Are you serious?'

'I'm as serious as you've ever known me.'

This is no small statement, and Pooley knows it. We go back nearly twenty years, and he's seen me serious all my life. This breach of professional etiquette has him jumpy. I can see it on his face. Pooley is not good at hiding his emotions, not ever.

'Goddammit, Columbus. Why're you asking me that?'

'Open the case,' I say.

He looks at it suspiciously now, as if it can rise off the table and bite him, and then back at me. I nod without changing my expression, and he spins the case around and unhinges the snaps.

'In the envelope,' I urge when he doesn't see anything looking particularly troublesome.

He withdraws the envelope and slides his finger under the flap as I did. When he sees the name at the top of the page, his face flushes.

'You gotta be shitting me.'

Like I said, Pooley is practically my brother, and as such, is the only one who knows the truth about my genesis. When I was thirteen and he was eleven, we were placed with the same foster family, my sixth in five years, Pooley's third. By then, I could take whatever shit was thrown my way, but Pooley was still a boy, and he had been set up pretty well in his last home. He had an old lady for a foster mother, and the worst thing she did was to make him clean the sheets when she shit the bed. Not a particularly easy job for a nine-year-old, but nothing compared to what he had to survive at the Cox house after the old lady passed away.

Pete Cox was an English professor at one of the fancy schools outside Boston. He was a deacon at his church, a patron at the corner barbershop, and an amateur actor at the neighborhood theatre. His wife had suffered severe brain damage four years prior to our arrival. She had been in the passenger seat of a Nissan pickup truck when the driver lost control of the wheel and rolled the truck eleven times before it came to rest in a field outside Framingham.

The driver was not her husband. The last person who could substantiate their whereabouts was the clerk at the Marriott Courtyard Suites . . . when they checked out . . . together.

Subsequently, his wife occupied a hospital bed in the upstairs office of Pete's two-story home. She was heavily medicated, never spoke, ate through a tube, and kept on living. Her doctors thought she might live another fifty years, if properly cared for. There was nothing wrong with her body, just her brain, jammed in by. the door handle when it broke through her skull.

Pete decided to take in foster children, since he would never have children of his own. His colleagues felt he was a brave man, a stoic; they certainly would have understood if he had divorced his wife after the circumstances of the accident came to light. But not our Pete. No, our Pete felt as though his wife's condition was a consequence of his own sin. And as long as he took care of his wife, as long as he showed God he could handle that burden, then it was okay if his sin continued. And grew. And worsened.

Pete liked to hurt little boys. He had been hurting little boys on and off since he was eighteen. 'Hurting them' could mean a number of things, and Pete had tried them all. He had nearly been caught when he was first learning his hobby after he had sliced off the nipple of an eight-year-old who was selling magazine subscriptions door-to-door. Pete caught up with him in the alley behind his cousin's apartment – just luck he had been visiting at the time! – and invited the kid to show him his sales brochure. With the promise of seventeen subscription purchases, which would qualify the kid for a free Sony Walkman and make him the number-one salesman in his Cub Scout den, Pete got him to step behind a dumpster and take off his shirt. He had the nipple off in no time, but he hadn't anticipated the volume of the child's scream. It was so loud, so visceral, so animal, it excited Pete like a drug; yet, at the same time, windows were going up all over the block. Pete booked it out of there, and no one ever came looking for him. He promised himself to be more discreet the next time. And the next time. And the next.

By the time we came to live with him, Pete had hurt hundreds of children all over the country. He had thought his wife to be his savior, the only woman who had really, truly cared for him, and for a while after they were married, he had stopped doing what he did to little boys. But an addiction is tough to put away permanently; it sits in dark recesses, gathering strength, biding its time until it can unleash itself, virgin and hungry, again. It was a week after Pete had fallen off the wagon, had done an unmentionable thing to a nine-year-old, when his wife had had her accident. How could he not blame himself for her fate? The Bible spends a great deal of time explaining the 'wages' of sin, and what were his wife's infidelity and her crumpled brain but manifestations of the evil he had committed on that boy? So he took care of her, and four years later, signed up with the state to be a foster parent.

I don't need to shock you with the atrocities Pooley and I endured in the two years we lived in the Cox house. Rather, to understand the relationship we now share, I'll tell you about the last night, the night before we were sent to finish out our youth at Juvenile upstate.

I was fifteen then, and had figured out ways to make my body stronger, despite Cox's best efforts to keep us physically emaciated. When he went to work, I put chairs together and practiced push-ups, my legs suspended between them. I moved clothes off the bar in the closet and pulled myself up – first ten times, then twenty, then hundreds. I bench-pressed the sofa, I ran sprints in the hallway, I squatted with the bookcase on my back. All of this while Pete was gone; everything put back and in its place before he returned. I tried to get Pooley to work his body with me, but he was too weak. He wanted to, I could tell, but his mind wouldn't let him see the light at the end of the tunnel, so much had been taken out of him.

On this day, the last day, Pete had given his students a walk. He had not felt good, had started to come down with something, and when the dean of the department told him to go on home and rest, Pete decided to take his advice before he changed his mind. This is why he entered his house not at four o'clock like he usually did, but at two-fifteen. This is why he found me surrounded by books all over the floor, the bookcase lofted on my back, my taut body in mid-squat.

'What the fuck?' was all he could muster, before his eyes narrowed and he came marching toward me.

I tossed the bookcase off my back like I was bucking a saddle, and looked for the easiest escape route, but there wasn't one, and before I could move, his arms were around me. He hoisted me off the ground – I couldn't have weighed more than a hundred and twenty pounds – and threw me head-first into the wall. Instead of cracking, my head ripped through the plaster into a wooden beam. Dazed, I pushed away as fast as I could, shaking wall dust from my hair, but he was on me again, and this time, he held me up in a bear hug. His face was both angry and ecstatic, and he squeezed until I couldn't breathe and my eyes went bleary with tears. I think he would have killed me. I was getting too old to bully and he knew I was building up resistance. It would have been safer to kill me. To go ahead and finish this here and now. He still had one more little boy he could torture.

From up the stairs, Pooley found his voice. 'Let go of him, you stupid motherfucker!'

This got our attention, both of us, and distracted Cox enough to make him drop me. From *my* mouth, he was used to hearing such language, such resentment, such fury, but not from little Pooley. We both jerked our heads simultaneously and looked up the stairs.

The door guarding Mrs. Cox stood open. The padlock that usually kept it firmly closed was somehow forced, wood scrapings cutting claw scratches into the wall. Pooley stood just outside the door, his tiny body shaking, drenched with sweat, a glass shard in his hand, blood dripping from the end in large red drops.

Pete's face metamorphosed so dramatically, it was like someone had flipped a switch, turning from acid rage to sudden confusion and trepidation. 'What'd you do?' was all he could manage, and his knees actually wobbled.

Pooley didn't answer; he just stood there, trembling, his face strained, blood and sweat mingling on the carpet at his feet.

'What'd you do?' Pete shouted a second time, his voice marked with desperation. Again, Pooley didn't answer.

Pete launched for the stairs and ascended them in five quick steps. I was close behind, prepared to tackle him with everything I had if he went for Pooley. But he didn't. He took two more steps toward his wife's open door, peeked into the room fearfully, as though hands might suddenly reach out and grab him, and then collapsed inside.

I got to Pooley as tormented wails began to waft from the open door. 'Come on,' I said.

Pooley's eyes continued to stare off into space.

'Let's get out of here,' I added. The urgency in my voice snapped some life back into his face and his eyes settled on me.

'I had to,' he said weakly.

'I know,' I offered.

I put my hand on his arm, and he let the shard drop to the floor. The blood caught it, and it landed sideways, red flecks marring the beauty of the glass. We stepped over it and walked down the stairs. I picked up the bookcase again and heaved it into the living room window, somehow knowing instinctively the front door had been double bolted before Pete turned and found me there.

We climbed out of the window and tasted the air outside for the first time in over a year, just as the loudest wail rose from the dark upstairs. 'I'm sorry! I'm so sorry! I'm so sorry!'

All those months Pooley had been silent, pretending to be resigned inside himself, he had really been watching, studying, understanding the motivations of our Pete. Taking his beatings in silence, letting me take mine, but watching, waiting. Twice he had overheard Pete in Mrs. Cox's room, pouring out his penitence to her mindless eyes. Twice he had heard Pete begging for forgiveness, only to increase his savagery two hours later. So Pooley began to figure out that Pete needed her there to continue doing what he did to us.

He needed someone who wouldn't judge him, but would sit passively and let him forgive himself so he could do it again. While I trained, trying to make my body stronger so I could one day fight back, Pooley cracked a mirror in the back bathroom, sharpened a shard on the side of the bedroom headboard, and waited. When Pete came home early and found me getting stronger, he knew he could wait no longer.

The police picked us up before we had gone a mile. We were indicted for killing Mrs. Cox, and my descriptions of our treatment seemed to fall on deaf ears. I had a petty-crime juvenile record in my past, and Pooley was done talking to adults for a long time. I can't say I blamed him; he saved my life, after all. Nor was I surprised when we were convicted. But because of some of the oddities that came out of Pete's mouth when he talked cryptically to the judge about swift, painful discipline – lending some credence to what I had said about our treatment – we were tried as juveniles and sent upstate to finish out our youth.

So Pooley was the first assassin I had known. When I decided to begin this life professionally – or you might say it was decided for me – he was a natural to be my middleman, though he wasn't my first.

3

Pooley agrees the coincidence surrounding my father is too odd to let pass without some digging. Since I need to head west without delay, he'll handle the shovel for me. We agree to speak again when I call next week from the road.

My rule is eight weeks out. I will not agree to complete a job in less than that time, and, as such, have turned down quite a few assignments, even when offers for more money have been dangled like grapes. I can flawlessly plan and execute a job in less time; of that, I have no doubt. But assassinating a target takes psychological preparation, and shortchanging yourself in that area can lead to debilitation long after the mark is in the grave.

I open the folder again and this time, study the contents without flinching. He will be traveling by bus, a 'whistle-stop' tour crisscrossing the country, culminating in Los Angeles at the Democratic National Convention. His path is strategically haphazard, planned randomness, with stops in most of the major television markets surrounding battleground states and enough small towns peppered in so that no economic demographic will feel slighted. Three thousand miles and a million handshakes in eight weeks. I will follow the same route, and will wait for him in the Midwest, allowing him to catch up, before I follow him the rest of the way to California.

The next morning, a rental car is parked out on my street with no paperwork to sign, no instructions to receive, the keys on the floorboard under the steering column. A beige car, a sedan, with nothing to distinguish it from the millions of other cars sprawling across American highways at any given time. With only a small duffel tossed in the back seat and a larger case lodged in the trunk, I head west, the sun at my back.

When I pull over to eat lunch at a small roadside dinette with the provocative name SUE'S NO. 2, I am approached by a prostitute. I had grabbed a booth in the back of the restaurant in order to avoid contact with the local denizens of this somewheretown, but this girl could care less where I sat. She homed in on me as soon as the bells jingled on the door.

She is dressed in a skirt that stops well above her knees and a white halter that exposes the baby fat around her middle. Her hair is stringy blond with burgundy roots and hangs away from her head like a web. She possesses a crooked nose but an uncommonly pretty mouth with perfectly straight teeth. Her eyes are sharp and intelligent.

'Hey there, mon frer,' she says, plopping down in the seat across from me. My guess is she cannot weigh more than a hundred pounds nor be older than seventeen.

I don't say anything, and she proceeds, unfazed.

'Here's what I'm thinking. I got dropped off in this shithole town, and I need a lift outta here.' This comes out between smacks of bright purple gum and the smell of grapes left too long on the vine. 'So I'm prepared to grant you favours in exchange for a lift.'

'A lift where?'

'Wherever it is you're headed.'

'What kind of favours?'

She drops her chin and looks at me from the tops of her eyes like I don't have the sense God gave me. Just then, the waitress approaches. The girl waits for me to order, and before the waitress can disappear, I find myself asking her if she's hungry.

'Fuckin' starvin', man.'

The waitress takes an order for steak and eggs and hash-browns and bacon if they have any left over from breakfast. Oh, and some orange juice and some milk and that'll be it. The girl's eyes are merry now; there is a break in the storm clouds. I don't normally talk to people, but it's been an abnormal week and those merry eyes stir something inside me I thought wasn't there.

'How'd you get here?'

'This nut-rubber wanted some company for his ride over to Boston. He wanted me to jerk him along the way.' Hand gestures for emphasis. 'I gave him what he asked for and when we pulled over here to get something to eat, he split as soon as I stepped out of the car.' Matter-of-factly, as though she were telling me about her day at school. 'Stiffed me, too, the bastard. It's gettin' to where there's not any honest people around.'

'How old are you?'

'I lost track.'

I swear she's seventeen. 'What's the last age you remember being?'

'Let's not talk about me. Let's talk about—'

But she's interrupted by the food. We both eat in silence; I because I enjoy it, she because she can't get the breakfast into her mouth fast enough. The food is flying up to her face like a power shovel at full steam, and she is as unembarrassed as a hog at a trough. She devours all of hers, and when I proffer half of my plate, she attacks it.

After I've left money for the tab, she asks, 'So how about that ride?'

'What do you think?'

Smiling now with those beautiful ivory teeth, she puts one finger in her mouth. 'I think I've got a pretty good shot at taggin' along with you.'

She's asleep in the passenger seat, and I am pissed. Pissed I let my guard down, pissed I've committed a cardinal sin, pissed I've ignored every professional instinct in my ken to allow her to share this car with me. I can still kill her, can still pull the car down one of these farm-to-market roads, roll the tires against some deserted brush, and pop, pop, dump the body where it won't be found for weeks. She won't be missed, that's certain. Except, goddammit, people saw us at the diner, the waitress, the old man in coveralls at the counter, the couple in the booth at the far end of the joint. They saw her lock in on me, and they saw us leave together, and they saw us get into my beige sedan. People noticed. They noticed, goddammit. What is happening to me?

Bad luck. The name at the top of the page was bad luck, and now picking up this girl-whore is as black bad as it can get. My stomach is queasy with the blackness. I must be slipping.

'So, where are we headed?' She puts her bare feet up on the dashboard in front of her and blinks groggily.

'Philadelphia.'

'Yeah? Good. That's where I came from.'

'Originally?'

'Naah,' she snorts, finding the question funny. 'Originally I'm from a little hovel outside of Pittsburgh that you've never heard of. Recently, I'm from Philly.'

'That's where you . . . work?'

She snorts again, not at all self-conscious about the way it makes her sound like a sow. 'Yeah, work. Working girl.' She pauses thoughtfully, and then, as though she's struggling with the weight of her question, 'What do you think about that?'

'About what you do?'

'Yeah. I'm curious. You seem like a normal dude. What's a normal dude think about a working girl?'

'I think it can't be too good of a way to make a living.'

'You got that right, buddy. You certainly got that right.'

'So, why do it, then?'

'I don't know. I can tell you one thing, I'm rarely lucid enough to sit and think about it. You got any liquor in here?' She tries to swivel in her seat to look in the back, but when she reaches for my duffel, I grab her with my free hand and spin her around hard.

'Owww. Shit, man! I'm just looking to see if you got anything to drink!'

'I don't.'

'Well you don't have to be a cocksucker about it.' She's showing me the same mouth that can use words like 'hovel' and 'lucid' can spew vitriol as well. And she's testing the envelope to see how far she can push it. Was the way I spun her around portentous of a beating to come? Did she get a rise out of me with the severity of the way she pronounced cocksucker, the way she paused right before the word, collecting her breath and then pounding that first syllable like she hit it with a hammer? COCKsucker! We drive on in silence. I can tell she'd rather pass the time talking than pouting, but she wants me to make the first move.

After two minutes, she gives up. 'I was just looking to see if you had something to drink.'

'I don't.'

She decides to get off the subject. 'You like music?'

'I like silence.'

This seems to do the trick, and for a few minutes more, the only sound in the car is her nasal breathing, in and out, in and out, like wind through a cracked window.

'I need to pee,' she says suddenly, nodding at the approaching exit where a Texaco sign pokes just above the tree line.

I throw up my blinker and guide the car toward the exit. As we approach, I can't help but notice a farm road running directly behind the service station, leading off into obscurity. Maybe I can get away with it, with a little extra time. If I can find some soft earth, I can dig a little hole to hide her body, and it'll be months, maybe years before anyone finds the remains. But it's broad daylight and I don't know this road and any dumb farmer could happen along at just the right time.

By the time I've rejected the temptation, she's opened the door. I watch her ask the attendant where the restrooms are and he hands her a giant block of wood with a key attached and points around to the back of the building. I watch him watch her all the way out the door, and when he catches me observing him, he quickly looks back down at the binder he had splayed on the counter.

What am I doing here? I should just gun the car and forget I ever saw this girl, but for some reason, I'm paralyzed. What is it about those teeth and that mouth? What do I see in them?

I turn off the ignition and head into the convenience store portion of the station where the clerk gives me a once-over and shuffles his binder down below the counter. I move to the drinks stacked like bricks up to the ceiling in the back of the store and withdraw a six-pack of Budweiser. For someone whose every move is performed to draw the least amount of attention – domestic over import in rural Pennsylvania – I realize I've already attracted notice just by parking the car and having this girl ask for the bathroom key. The clerk's once-over wasn't because he was worried I'd shoplift something from the store; he wanted to know what kind of man would pick up a girl like that. And he is going to remember who it was and what the man looked like when and if he is asked.

This is how it happens. In the game I play, you cannot give in to temptation, even if temptation is merely to hold a conversation with someone, to connect with another human being on a superficial level. And once you give in to temptation, even if you only do it one time, then the dominoes start to topple until the entire floor is covered with a dark blanket.

I pay for the beer and the clerk only grunts at me without meeting my eyes when he hands over the change. Maybe this isn't so bad. I've done a thoughtful thing for this girl, and the clerk is back looking at his binder before I even leave the store. Maybe I can pull this off, talk to this girl, gain some insight into her world and what she imagined she would be doing with her life. Find out where her life took the left turn instead of the right, where she missed the exit and eventually got lost and discovered that her map was terribly inaccurate.

Maybe I can learn about someone for once, someone whose life had been like my mother's, with no hidden motives.

In the car, I slide back behind the wheel and put the six-pack on the seat so the girl will see it when she returns. It's as simple as that, buying her breakfast, giving her this six-pack of beer, and that smile will come to her lips again, and she will lean back in her seat, and she will be warm and rosy, and she won't have to say things like cocksucker and pee and we can have a normal conversation like normal people.

A moment exists in time – a flash of a moment – right before you realize how fucked you are. You can't explain it scientifically, but a shiver settles on the back of your neck as though someone placed an ice cube there. The fine hairs on your neck stand erect like they've been jolted with electricity. A rush of heat flashes through your body and your muscles all contract in unison. This happens instantaneously, when your mind hasn't quite caught up to your body's impulse. It is what I felt when I happened to glance in the back seat.

My duffel. She had reached for my duffel and I had immediately seized her arm and jerked her around hard. Therefore, there must be something valuable in the duffel. She must have taken it while I was in the store.

I bolt from the car and around to the bathroom, knowing instinctively the clerk's eyes are riveted on me. Nothing. Just a key stuck in the open door of a filthy bathroom and no trace of the girl or my bag. Behind the Texaco, a thick growth of trees, a country road leading to oblivion, and no sign of the fucking girl. Pandora has climbed out of her box.

My breath escapes quickly, four quick bursts, and then I'm off into the woods. I don't even know what goddamn name to call her, to call out, so I just stay quiet, a determined expression now blanching my face. I have to improvise, to hunt her quickly. How long will the clerk look at that rental car parked in front of the store before he calls the police with a declaration that something a little strange is going on down at the Texaco? He saw the girl. He saw me. He saw her go around to the back and then he saw me spring from the car after her. Had I even shut the door of the car? I'm not sure. Son-of-a-bitch, how had I let this get so out of hand?

I have five minutes, maybe ten to find her before the clerk ventures out to see if we're in the bathroom together. After that, who knows? Another five minutes to call the police? I'm fucked. That's all there is to it.

Trees everywhere, and then, a clearing, and I catch a glimpse of her just as she crosses into the growth about a tenth of a mile from where I stand. She caught sight of me, too, and I spot a panic in her face usually reserved for wild prey. Maybe she's seen what's in the bag and she's spooked. But she hasn't dropped the duffel either; I can see its yellow flash caught against her dark skirt.

I close the distance in no time. She's skittish, and she makes a mistake, turns and trips over a dead oak stump. Her hands go up as my footsteps crunch through the dead leaves, on her back, arms bent, scrambling, scratching the air, trying to get me off before I'm even there.

And then my foot comes down on her neck, twisting her face into the dirt so that those pretty teeth are smeared with earth.

'No, mister. Please. I don't want it. I didn't mean to . . . I didn't mean . . . I didn't mean . . .'

Fighting with everything she has, every inch of strength she can muster, her arms wailing at my shin, beating my pants leg, her eyes desperate with fear.

And then I step down harder until I hear the bones in her neck crack like wood.

The forest is silent in the peculiar way nature seems to go mute when a living creature is killed. I hesitate to say 'innocent' creature, because if she hadn't been so stupid, if she hadn't been so goddamn reckless, she'd still be alive and we'd be chatting on our way to Philadelphia, making a connection, talking about the normal things normal people talk about and her mouth would be smiling and sipping on a beer rather than silent and gaping and half-filled with muck, and leaves, and decay.

Or maybe the woods aren't silent at all. Maybe my ears are ringing so loudly all other sounds are drowned out. I am breathing hard and a bead of sweat has rolled from my eyebrows to the tip of my nose, but the silence is implacable, as thick as cream. Underneath my boot, the girl remains still, her energy as used up and wasted as her life.

I will need a little luck. I prop the girl on my shoulders as though I'm carrying a wounded soldier, and hurry back through the woods toward the convenience store. A little luck, a little luck. That's all I'm asking. My footsteps are firm, finding solid ground again and again, weaving in and out of the trees, the back of the store looming larger and larger through the brush. Her weight is slight, and her body bobs up and down on my shoulders, light as a backpack. Thirty feet, twenty, and no sign of the clerk. Just stay at your counter, friend. Keep marking in your binder, counting up that inventory, and you'll soon forget about us, just another couple of customers amidst a constant string of travelers.

I break through the tree line and I'm back at the store, the block of wood still dangling from the doorknob like a pendulum. In a quick step, I'm in the room with the body on my back and the block of wood in my hand and the door shut tight. Almost there. Stay with me, luck.

The smell in the bathroom is horrible, and stains splotch the walls like a foul mosaic. It doesn't take me long to work myself up. The stench, the agitation, the degradation of killing in this animalistic manner, her body propped across the sink, her head facing me, her lips curling back away from her teeth in a sneer that is accusatory and mocking and hopeless. I double over and retch until I can feel the pulse thick in my ears.

He knocks as I finish my second heave.

'Are you okay in there?'

Luck is a funny thing. I open the door, carrying the girl in my arms, quickly, out into the open. 'Do you have a hose?' I say, and his eyes immediately go over my shoulder to the bathroom, his nose curling.

'Awww, shit.'

'Sorry, man. She got sick.' I smooth the girl's hair with my supporting hand.

He doesn't even look at us, shaking his head. 'Don't worry about it,' he says, resigned, and passes me to survey the mess in the stall.

I don't wait for him to give us a second look. I am around the building and into the car before he can even hook up the hose, my bag and the whore's body laid to rest in the wide back seat.

4

I wash myself the best I can at a highway rest stop. I buried the body a hundred yards inside a thick growth of trees off of a deserted farm-to-market road with nothing but a tyre iron and my bare hands. It was a messy operation. Messy because I don't know the land, don't have time to do it the right way, don't have time to plant the body deep enough so it won't be found for decades. And yet I am not worried. If a hiker or the landowner stumbles upon her corpse, I did take the few minutes necessary to make it difficult to identify.

I am still blanketed in dirt when I enter the brick courtyard of the Rittenhouse Hotel. I pass through the lounge, only slowing for a hasty check-in, and then up to my room, fending off assistance with my bags from dueling bellboys. Just get me to my room, get me to a shower, let me wash off the grime and the smell of this day gone sour.

The room is enormous, with a large window overlooking Rittenhouse Square and the city. More furniture stands in this room than I've owned in my entire life. I would not choose to live this way, but this is where Abe Mann will be staying in a few weeks, and I need to forget who I am and get my mind right. For the first time on this job, I will get my mind right.

To hunt a human being, it is not enough to plot from afar, externally. An assassin must understand his prey by storming the target's mind the way an army storms enemy territory. He must live, sleep, eat, breathe as the target does, until he has merged with the target, until they are one. To kill a man, he must become the man, so that he can live as himself beyond the man.

The water is a blessing, as purifying as a baptism. Just relax, relax, re-lax, and this day, and everything in it, will be just like the soap washing down the drain. Gone and forgotten.

But no. The girl hides right behind my eyes, popping out like a child playing peek-a-boo whenever I close the lids. I've killed people without blinking, without feeling a twinge of remorse, and yet this girl continues to haunt me like an itch under a plaster cast.

'That's right,' she says. 'You and me. We're stuck together. Scratch-scratch.'

I shake my head, and the water in my hair sprays the shower curtain. But I do not open my eyes. I like the way she looks. I actually like looking at her, I giggle to myself. And then for the first time, I think my past has finally caught me, my defenses are being stormed by a battering-ram of life I've tried so desperately to shake. I thought if I ran fast enough, if I shirked the past off my back the way I bucked that bookcase in Mr Cox's living room, it would be too heavy and slow to catch me. But it's here, in this shower, in full force, pissed off and angry and bringing madness along for the ride.

'Tell me about your mother,' the girl says, so close to my face I can smell the dirt in her breath.

'What's that supposed to mean?' I mumble, although I can't be sure if it's aloud or in my head.

'I want to understand,' she says, floating, swimming, just on the other side of my eyes. 'Tell me about your girl. Tell me about Jake.'

Then the water runs hot, a surge of searing heat, and the spell is broken. I jump back from the stream and wait for it to cool a little. Finally, it tapers back to a nice tepid temperature, and I rinse quickly, towel off, and collapse on top of the bed. I feel my eyes close, searching for the dead girl.

* * *

I did have a girl once. For just a few months, a long time ago. She had honey-blond, shoulder-length hair and a chocolate lab named Bandit. She had bright, cheerful eyes that were amplified behind thick black glasses and a single-bedroom apartment above a bookstore in Cambridge. She was smart, engaging, lithe, and alive. Her name was Jake.

We met after my release from Waxham Juvenile Corrections and right before my new term started, the bondage that began when I shook hands with a fat man named Vespucci. The handshake with that dark Italian ended things forever, but before that, right before that, was the only period in my life where I felt normal. The only period where I believed, if only for a few fleeting months, I could make it, could whip life, could become a 'new' man, like the priest, Father Steve, always repeated at Waxham.

'You came in here dirty, debased boys, but you can leave here as new men. The blessed waters of forgiveness will cleanse you, make you new men, but only if you bathe in a pool of repentance.' And I wanted to believe it, every word. For someone who had been a dirty, debased boy all his life, who didn't know his mother or father, I thirsted to be a new man the way a desert traveler thirsts for just one drink of water. For once, just one time, I wanted to be a new man drinking a clean glass of water.

When I was released, I hurried to Boston, where Father Steve secured me a job loading cases of beer into trucks. Apparently, Father Steve's brother hadn't received the same telegram from God that had found Steve, and he had prospered as a beer distributor. The siblings were cut from the same cloth, though, and Father Steve's brother helped 'new men' get on their feet, get closer to that cool glass of water, even if lugging stacks of beer was the only way he knew to get them there.

A couple of weeks after taking the job, I received the first paycheck of my life. Me, orphan, foster child, ex-convict, me, with a check for four hundred and seventy-two dollars made out in my name. I wrote to Pooley as soon as I got home. We were sentenced to serve until we were eighteen, and since I was older, I had gotten out a couple of years before him. Receiving a letter was one of the few joys a boy could have at Waxham, so I sent him one just about every day. He had to know I had made it, there was something to look forward to, something to dream about in the darkness of that damn rat cage. He had to know I had received a paycheck, was opening a savings account, was waiting for him when he got his release.

It was on the way to the bank to cash my new check that I met her. I didn't know how to open an account, but Father Steve's brother had explained to me how easy it was, how glad the banks would be to hold my money each week. I was wearing a clean shirt, and my pants were only slightly dirty. I felt good.

She grabbed me by the shoulder and spun me around. 'Louis?' she had said. My instinct was to watch out, to protect myself, so seldom had I let someone touch me. But for some reason, as firm as her grip had been on my shoulder, I didn't feel threatened.

'Oh, I'm sorry,' she said. 'I'm so sorry, I thought you were my brother.'

I felt a smile coming. Her laughter was real, exposed, infectious. 'I'm sorry,' she finally finished, catching her breath, and then her hand extended toward me. 'From the side, you looked exactly like my brother. I'm Jake.'

'Jake?'

'Jacqueline. Jake. I like Jake better.'

I nodded, grinning like a madman, and shook her hand. Damn, did it feel soft. 'I do too.'

Her eyes narrowed, still smiling, and she examined me almost with affection. 'I swear. From the side, I thought Lou had come to town.'

'Yeah?'

'It was uncanny. I was just heading in to have a coffee, and bam, there goes Lou, walking right past me.'

'Except it was me.'

'Yep. From the side, the spitting image. Man, that's something.'

The way she said 'something' – she sort of lifted up on her toes and then rocked back on her heels – I melted like candle wax.

'Say, you want to go in and have that coffee with me?'

Somehow, I found my voice. 'Yeah. I'd like to.'

I'd never had coffee in my life.

Every day for a week, we met at the frog pond and watched the tourists take their shoes off and wade in the ankle-high water. She talked a lot, and I loved to hear her husky voice tickle my ears like a feather. God, that girl could talk, and I would have done anything to stay there, my head in her lap, watching the tourists pass by.

'My philosophy is this. We don't owe anything to our family, to our parents, just for conceiving us and putting a roof over our heads for so many years. The question becomes, do you like these people? Do you want to spend time with them, have a coffee with them, eat dinner with them? If the answer is "no," then so be it. Why should you waste your time with them if you don't even like their company? What society deems appropriate is contrary to rudimentary truths. Life is precious. Life is fleeting. Life is fragmentary. It's here today and *whip!* it's gone before you know it. One second you're a little girl asking if you can please, please, please get the Barbie easy-bake oven for Christmas and the next minute you're twenty-one and you have nothing in common with these people you call mom and dad. They don't understand anything about you. You are speaking a foreign language to them. So why do you care about them at all?'

I just stared up at her chin as it bobbed up and down in the rhythm of her words, and it didn't matter what she was saying, the voice wafted down and covered me like arms. A couple walked by holding hands and smiled at us and I thought, *my God, that couple is us. We are them.* For once, for the first time in my life, I felt loved.

I didn't see Vespucci coming. There was no portent of evil rushing my way, no accumulation of dark clouds on my horizon. As I said, things were good. I had been loading beer for several months, piling the cases onto pallets, spreading shrink-wrap around the cases, and hauling the pallets onto the trucks. It was difficult but fulfilling work, the kind that exhausts and exhilarates at the same time. I was good at it, my arms having grown strong in Cox's living room and the weight room at Waxham.

The way it worked was one shipping boy was assigned to one truck driver on each load, working until the truck was filled and ready to depart. Then the next truck would come in, get loaded, and take off. There was no order to the trucks, and we would work with nearly all the drivers in the course of a week. The aspiration of the shipping boys was eventually to get to drive the trucks, which meant greater pay and at least part of your day in the air-conditioning or out of the rain. When a driving vacancy occurred, Father Steve's brother promoted from within based on driver recommendations. This meant all the shipping boys busted their asses for all the drivers, so coveted were those recommendations. It was a good system.

One of the drivers was Hap Blowenfeld, and every shipping boy looked up to Hap the way some people look up to movie stars and ball players. He was larger-than-life, with perfect hair, a quick smile, and pearl white teeth. He had huge arms, could load a truck faster than anyone, and bought a six-pack of Coke for the shipping boy who helped him each day. The day you got assigned to Hap was like winning the lottery, and if you got him twice in one week, you were the envy of every other shipper in the crew.

'What's your story, Buck?' he asked me after I had worked there a couple of months. We were loading Budweiser, and it was hot outside. We hadn't said much to each other, both concentrating on stacking the cases on to the wooden pallets. I wasn't much of a talker, and the question caught me off guard.

'No story,' was all I could mumble.

Hap looked up with the hint of a grin, his arm leaning on one of the beer cases. 'I'll let you in on a little secret. I spent my time in Juvenile too.'

I didn't say anything.

'That's right,' he said, starting to lift the cases again. 'Five years in a place called Skyline Hall in Sacramento for choking a kid to death. I grew up on the West Coast, in Arcadia, outside Los Angeles, went to school with mostly Mexicans. Well, this one bean-eater stole my daddy's billfold, and I didn't like that too much. I didn't know I'd kill't the poor bastard until someone pried my fingers off his throat.' He stopped and wiped his head with the back of his hand. 'I was thirteen years old. I thought I was gonna play college football.'

I didn't know what to say, and for a moment we resumed loading the crates onto the pallets and the pallets onto the truck in our comfortable rhythm. I was beginning to think maybe Hap's story was all in my head. He broke the silence again.

'So what's your story, Crackerjack? And don't go soft on me.'

Hap wasn't the kind of guy I was prepared to lie to, so I just spread it out before him like I was unfolding a map, starting with my first venture inside the Cox house and finishing with my release from Waxham. Before I knew it, my story was over, the truck was completely loaded, and Hap and I were leaning against the back bumper sipping Coke out of bottles through pharmacy straws.

'You didn't kill him?' Hap asked, gnawing on his lower lip a little bit.

I shook my head side to side.

'But you wanted to.'

'Yep.'

'I'd've liked to get my hands on that sum-bitch.' He stared down at his hands, as though he could see it happening, what Cox's throat would look like caught in his massive fingers, squeezing the neck until it caved in on itself.

Hap looked at me sideways. 'You think you had it in you to finish him?'

'If I could've, I would've.'

Hap grinned. 'I'll bet you would. I just bet you would.'

He drove off a few minutes later, and I went to get my next assignment, feeling a slight pull in my chest.

A week later, I had completely forgotten about my conversation with Hap when a Cadillac limousine pulled alongside me while I was walking home from work. A dark window slid down and an olive, moon-shaped face stared out at me. I thought this man must have mistaken me for someone, the way Jake had mistaken me for her brother. A fat hand extended out the window toward me.

'Vespucci,' the face said, the hand waiting in anticipation.

I shook it, unsure what to say.

Then a second face filled the window behind Vespucci's, with a broad grin and a wink aimed in my direction. 'Get in, Buck,' Hap said, as the door opened my way.

The car was bigger than anything I had seen before, like the inside of the empty beer trucks, and I sat facing the dark Italian and Hap. Their eyes studied my face like they were trying to read a book; what exactly they were hoping to find in my expression, I had no idea. Waxham had taught me to suppress my emotions, to make my face as blank as fresh paper, and for a long moment we rode in silence, measuring each other.

'You some kind of orphan?' the dark face asked in a thick Italian accent.

'Yes.'

'Yes, what, kid?' Hap corrected, his face urging me.

'Yes, sir,' I said, not wanting to disappoint Hap.

'Good. Dat's good, kid. What's your name?'

I answered him and he laughed. 'You get a new name starting today. A new name when you work for me.'

I had no idea what this man was talking about.

'Work for you?'

'Dat's right. Starting today.'

I looked at Hap, and he just nodded at me, smiling, like he had done me a great favor.

The car pulled up alongside an abandoned warehouse, a large building in a part of town I had never visited. The building took up a city block, and was probably once teeming with factory workers and sweat and life, but now just stood blank and forgotten, like an old man put to rest in a nursing home. The windows in the upper stories looked shattered, and natty birds flew in and out intermittently. On the side of the building, 'Columbus Textiles' was printed in faded block letters.

'But first, a test,' Vespucci said. 'To see what kind of . . . possibility . . . you might have.' He seemed to linger over the word 'possibility' like it tasted sweet in his mouth and he was savouring it. 'Let's go.'

Inside the warehouse, dust settled over what little furniture had been left behind when the company packed up and moved. The place had once been used to make textiles, and inoperative looms and abandoned sewing machines lay dormant on the tops of forgotten tabletops. The main room was huge, like a cathedral, and a small desk had been recently pushed to the middle of the floor. On top of the desk lay a pistol.

'What is this?' I asked, puzzled, searching for answers in the faces of the men who'd brought me here. If those faces held answers, I wasn't experienced enough to read them.

Just then, another door opened on the other side of the enormous room. Three men approached us, their hollow footsteps clomping over the concrete floor, but in the dim light of the room I couldn't make out their features. One of the men, though, had a hauntingly familiar gait, a way of walking as unique and identifiable as a fingerprint.

'What is this, Hap?'

Then a voice I had tried to forget so many times reached out and punched me in the gut like a fist. 'Yeah,' said Pete Cox, representing the middle of the trio who approached. 'What the fuck is this? These two fellas promised me there was something I'd . . . want . . . to . . . see . . .'

His eyes found mine, and for a moment he was as surprised as I was. He said my name, then repeated it, dumbfounded, like he was waking from a dream. Then he looked over his shoulder at the two men flanking him, their eyes as hard as concrete. 'What is this?' he repeated, weakly.

'This,' said Vespucci in a rough growl, 'is a test.'

'A what?' said Cox, like he didn't hear the man correctly.

'A test for the boy you liked knocking around so much, tough guy.'

Cox's eyes settled on the pistol resting on the desk and he started backpedaling, his feet moving almost involuntarily. But the two men closed on him, and held him firmly by the elbows so he could no longer move.

'Hey, wait, what's this . . . ? What's this all about? He . . . he killed my wife. Did he tell you that?' His voice sounded shrill.

Hap spat on the ground. 'He told me everything I needed to know.'

I still couldn't find my voice . . . this clash with my past jarring me as though I'd been shell-shocked. Here was Mr. Cox, the man who had caused an enormous abyss in my childhood, standing before me. The only item positioned between us was a pistol.

Vespucci spoke. 'In ten seconds, my men and I are going to leave this place and lock the door behind us. On that desk is a pistol. Somewhere in this room are the bullets that can be fired from that pistol. I will open the doors again tomorrow morning and only one of you will come out. If there are two of you standing here when I open the door, I'll cut you both down. Only one walks out tomorrow morning.'

I looked at Mr. Cox's face with what must have been a feral snarl and I could almost feel him reeling back, looking for an escape route.

'You must be joking. I can't . . .' he started to protest, but every man in the room besides us turned on their heels and headed for the exits, leaving the sentence to die in the air, unfinished. We both stood silently, as two sets of doors swung shut and were bolted behind us. Neither of us flinched, nor twitched a muscle; we just stared at each other.

Then as the weight of the silence threatened to crush us, he leaped for the gun. My legs took over, and I tackled him before his hand could grip the weapon. We smashed into the desk, overturning it, and the gun skittered across the floor.

His hands went for my face, trying to claw my eyes as we both fought for leverage. He was still bigger than me, and his legs straddled mine, so I couldn't gain my balance, while his hands continued to scratch at my face. The only thing I could do was ball my hands into fists and start driving my knuckles into his rib cage, his kidneys, one, two, three times, again and again. He may have had a weight advantage, but I had learned a great deal about dirty fighting in the exercise yard at Waxham. I must have caught him under a rib, because suddenly he gasped for breath and fell over sideways.

I sprang up, my eyes a bit blurry from the pressure, and stumbled toward the gun. He caught his breath and stood to follow, just as I scooped up the weapon.

As I held it up, he sneered, 'Lot of good that will do you without the—' But before he could finish that thought, I pistol-whipped him across the face, smashing him so hard his mouth filled with blood and he fell to the floor in a heap. He started to rise, so I smashed him again harder, putting all my weight behind it, and this time he stayed down. Faint whimpers came from his throat and quickly died in the large, hollow room.

Fuck the bullets. I headed for an old rusty sewing machine that looked like it hadn't been used in decades. It must have weighed over fifty pounds, but it seemed light as a feather as I hoisted it onto my shoulder and marched back toward the whimpering heap on the floor.

He looked up as I stood over him, gore splashed all over his lips, his gums, his teeth. 'Wha-what are you doing this for?' he sobbed.

'For Pooley,' I said, and smashed the sewing machine down on top of his skull.

I sit in my hotel room in Philadelphia watching Abe Mann outline his vision for America on television. This is how he will sit, I imagine, a few weeks from now, watching himself say the same things by rote, over and over. How he's for working families, and lower taxes, and cutting tax breaks for the rich. How he's for a woman's right to choose and a stronger military and jobs staying home instead of going overseas. The same fast-food dish served up stale by politicians every few years.

His voice is throaty; it arrives from deep down in his lungs. It is one of the reasons he has been so successful in politics: he is well-practiced in *how* he speaks, even if he doesn't believe *what* he is saying. And he has a new handgesture: an open palm, the fingers splayed, shaking at an angle as he punctuates the key words in his speech. It is a variation on the thumb-point, or the crooked index finger. It gives him a certain authority, like an old Southern preacher at the pulpit. I find myself making the same gesture with my hand, watching him without listening, the way he does while he speaks.

The phone rings, and it is Pooley on the other end when I answer.

'What did you find?'

'Very little, so far. Archibald Grant has disappeared; no one has seen him in days.'

'Then whoever hired me has tossed his middleman.'

'Looks that way.'

My mind is racing. 'What next, then?'

Pooley blew out a long breath. 'I'm going to dig some more, see if I can't find a trail from Grant to someone else.'

'You sure you want to do that?'

'Hey . . . why should you be the only one who gets to climb out from behind a desk?'

I smile. 'You be careful.'

'You got it.'

I am on the road again, back in my element, the present. I am heading to Ohio, what they call a battleground state, where Abe Mann will spend an unprecedented three days on his tour . . . Cleveland, then Dayton, then Cincinnati. Electoral votes in this state have swung an election in the past, and glad-handing is necessary and expected. I try to imagine what Abe Mann will be feeling at this point in the campaign. Fatigue? Irritation? Or will he feel renewed, as I do now? Back in the present. Yesterday behind me.

In Cleveland, I eat lunch at a restaurant called Augustine's. It is upscale but strives to be better than it is, like a scarred woman who puts on too much rouge to cover her blemishes. The food is bland and tasteless. A young couple at a table next to me is talking about the upcoming election, and without turning my head I can hear every word they say. Or rather I can hear every word *she* says, since she is dominating the conversation.

'I consider myself socially liberal but economically conservative. Winston Churchill once said, "If you're young and a conservative, you have no heart. But if you're old and a democrat, you have no money." ' The man across from her chuckles. 'But I'm being serious here. I feel like we pay way too much in taxes, and for what? More Washington waste?'

'So you're voting Republican?' the man asks.

'No, I'm still undecided. I want to hear what the candidates have to say at their conventions and then . . .'

Her voice continues on and on, like a comfortable hum, and it strikes me that this woman is the same age Jake would be. Now, I know I shouldn't turn my head, I know I definitely should *not* make eye contact, but there is something in her voice that washes over me like warm water. I stick out my index finger and clumsily knock my fork off the table, toward the woman's voice. We both reach for it at the same time, and for a full second, we look into each other's faces. I don't know what she finds in mine, but in hers I see what might have been.

5

My first paying job for Vespucci was to kill a woman. He was waiting in my apartment on a Sunday afternoon, after I had spent the day walking around the Harbor with Jake. His face was grave, serious.

'Do you know what a fence is, Columbus?' He had been calling me 'Columbus' since the door swung open at the abandoned Columbus Textile warehouse the morning after I had brained Mr. Cox.

'No, sir. Not any other way than what I think it is.'

'I am a fence. A fence is a middleman. A go-between. Do you understand?'

I looked at him with what I am sure was a blank expression.

'I am hired by certain people for the purpose of assassination. They give me a target's name. It is my job as the fence to find out as much information about the mark as I can. Then I, in turn, assign the job to one of my professionals. The professional never meets the client. That is my job. Do you understand?'

'I think so.'

'Good, Columbus. You are . . . a quick learner.'

'And I'm your professional?'

He chortled a little. 'Not yet, no. You are . . . how should I say . . . an understudy, like in the theater. You will learn your role and be ready to fill a position as necessary. You will be paid only if you kill a mark. And once you're paid,' he said, a broad smile appearing across his face, 'well, then, I suppose you are a professional.'

I moved to the kitchen and took down a box of crackers from a shelf. But I only fidgeted with the box, turning it over and over in my hands like a pig on a spit.

'What if I'm not interested in being one of your professionals?'

He cleared his throat, covering his mouth with his fist, and the smile left his face. 'God gave you free will. I do not presume to take that away from you. However, I have looked into your eyes, Columbus. I have seen the orphan childhood; I have felt your hands turn into fists. You are a killer. A . . . how is it . . . a natural killer. The warehouse didn't make you a killer. You were one before you ever lifted that sewing machine above your head. I only helped show you what you are.'

I set the box of crackers down on the counter in front of me. There was a ringing in my ears, and I'm not sure if it was fear, or the fact I had heard the sound of truth delivered by this dark Italian in my kitchen.

'Hap saw something in you . . . saw this quality. He saw it . . . instinctively. He thought you could do this job after one conversation with you.'

'He works for you, then?'

'I have many people who work for me.' He studied me for a moment, appraising me. 'I have a feeling. I have a feeling I would have found you anyway. There is a level to . . . how do you say . . . to fate? Yes? It causes paths to cross in ways we cannot understand.' He stopped, waving his hand, like he had stumbled down a dark road and now wanted to reverse direction. He handed me a manila envelope, the kind you might find in any office storage closet. A ten-by-thirteen plain manila envelope, heavy and rigid. 'Read this,' he said, 'then we'll talk. Tomorrow, perhaps.'

With that, he put on his hat and shuffled toward the door.

I spent hours poring over the contents of that envelope, exhilarated, like a person entrusted with a singular and dangerous confidence. The first sheet held a name printed in big black letters across the top: Michael Folio. There was an address: 1022 South Holt Ave., and a description: six-two, 200 pounds, medium build, sandy hair, wire-frame glasses, no tattoos, no birthmarks. And there was more: 'Michael has a facial tic that causes his upper lip to curl at the right corner. He has no relatives except a sister who lives in British Columbia, Carol Dougherty. She is married to Frank Dougherty, a plumber, and has two kids, Shawn, ten, and Carla, eight. They have not corresponded with Michael in over seven years.'

The next page gave a detailed description of Michael's office: 'He is a litigator in the law firm Douglas and Thackery. His office is on the fifth floor of a five-story office complex known as The Meadows. The firm has 25 employees. They are: Carol Santree, receptionist . . .' This type of thing. The third page provided a blueprint of the office with a seating chart as to where exactly each employee sat. The fourth page gave a chronological list of precisely where Michael had been over the last thirty days: '8 A.M., target leaves house, moving West on Holt. He stops at Starbucks on corner of Holt and Landover. 8:15 A.M., leaves Starbucks continues west on Holt, follows until he reaches Highway 765, then turns north.'

This description continued for the next thirty pages or so. It began to dawn on me the time and energy and man-hours it took to compile the pages I held in my hands. Why would I need to know that working in his office was a junior partner named Sam Goodwin? That Michael frequently ate his lunch alone at The Olive Garden? That the route he took to get to the cleaners involved a shortcut on Romero Street? But the answer was obvious . . . so I, as the assassin assigned the task of killing Michael Folio, would best be able to plan my attack and my escape. Since I know that when he finishes his meal at The Olive Garden, eighty-seven percent of the time he uses the bathroom on his way out the door, I could plan to wait and ambush him in the men's room stall. Since I know that he hasn't spoken to his niece and nephew in seven years,

I could pretend to be a friend of theirs and 'bump' into him next to the dry cleaners. Gain his trust and get invited into his home. The possibilities were endless, but only because I had this file Vespucci had meticulously labored over.

That's when the addiction began. I studied those pages as though I was reading scripture, each line read and read and read again until Michael Folio's life was committed to memory. I found myself thinking of little else, waiting for the phone to ring.

We were eating lunch when I saw him. Jake had ordered breadsticks and salad and was picking away through her meal, while I was waiting on the pasta I had ordered.

'I'd like you to come home with me for the holidays,' she said, looking at me through the tops of her eyes.

'I thought you weren't interested in seeing your family.'

'I didn't think I was. And I don't know why, but they *are* my family and for some inexplicable reason I feel compelled to see them over the holidays. Maybe there's something to be said for nature and nurture and all that sociological bullshit we studied my freshman year. If you don't want to go, you don't have to . . . I'd understand.'

'Why wouldn't I want to go?'

She smiled. 'I don't know. I just assumed you wouldn't want to . . .'

'You still don't have me figured out, do you?' I said.

'Every time I think I do, you throw me a curveball.'

She settled into her food again, and I looked at the door, and that's when I saw him. Michael Folio. The man from the envelope. The man who was going to die as soon as Vespucci gave the word. He waited at the hostess stand, then held up one finger, and the hostess nodded and led him toward a booth halfway between the bathroom and the table where Jake and I sat. I had purposely picked a table so I could sit with my back to the wall. That way, I would have a view of the entire restaurant.

Jake started talking again, but I didn't hear what she was saying because a buzzing nested in my ear as I watched Michael Folio – not just a picture on top of a sheet of paper but a living and breathing human being. He sat down and studied his menu.

Jake turned her head to see what had gotten my attention. She probably thought I was staring at a woman, but when she saw a man in a suit and tie, she said, 'You know him?'

I shook my head. 'What?'

'That man . . . you looked at him like you knew him.'

'Did I?' I laughed. 'I blanked out wondering where the hell my food was.'

That did the trick. She went back to talking about her family, and my food arrived, and I twirled the noodles around my fork and tried to concentrate, but every few seconds my eyes drifted to the breathing dead-man seated alone in the middle of the restaurant.

Finally, I excused myself and walked toward the bathroom. I had to pass by his booth on the way, and I glanced down at him as I went, but he didn't notice. He was reading a copy of *Sports Illustrated*, engrossed in an article.

Inside the bathroom, I stared at myself in the mirror, trying to get my body to stop shaking. This was a new sensation; I felt electric, like a brewing storm. I splashed some water on my face, was rubbing my eyes, when the door to the bathroom opened.

I half-expected to see Michael Folio come through the door; in fact, I had planned my trip to the bathroom to coincide with the waitress bringing him his bill. But instead of Folio, it was Vespucci's large figure who shuffled through the door. His eyes glowered at me, like they wanted to pick me up and throw me across the room.

'What're you doing?' he spat in a hushed tone.

'Nothing. I—'

'You were to do *nothing* until I gave you the command. What you are doing here is not nothing!'

'I'm doing my homework, in case you called.'

'Homework? Don't bullshit me.'

'That's all I was doing.'

'Who's the girl?'

'What? She's just a girl I know.'

'You like her?'

'She's just a girl, Mr. Vespucci.'

'We'll talk about this later. Pay your bill and go home.'

I knew this was not open for discussion. I nodded, shimmied past him, and headed back to the restaurant. As I passed Folio's booth, I noticed he was gone. Jake looked at me concerned as I approached our table.

'What's wrong?'

'I'm not feeling well.'

'Oh, I'm sorry. Do you think it was the pasta?'

'I don't know. We just need to go.'

She stood up, sympathy on her face. 'You just head to the car. I'll get the check.'

She drove me home while I pretended to feel queasy. It wasn't difficult, since I was thinking about how upset Vespucci had been, how his eyes had flashed when he entered the bathroom. She dropped me off and I protested against her coming in with me . . . saying I needed to be alone and get this worked out. Reluctantly, she let me go, and I noticed it was several minutes before her car moved away from the curb.

Vespucci didn't come that night, or the next day, or the second night. I talked to Jake a couple of times and told her it was nothing but a stomach flu, that I would be fine, that I just felt weak and begged off meeting up with her for a few days. She wanted to take care of me, and I think she was saddened that I refused her succor. I think this might have raised the first questions in her mind as to where our relationship was going.

I more or less had the radio on all day, just background noise to keep me company as I waited. Which is why at first I didn't process the report about the litigator who had been shot while sitting at his desk on the fifth floor of the Meadows Office Complex in the northern part of the city. The reporter's words were just a dull hum when the name 'Michael Folio' broke through the clutter. I leapt up like I was on fire and raced to the radio, turning the volume up as loud as it would go. The reporter was talking about another D.C. sniper, right here in Boston. Police were speculating that the bullet must have come from a neighboring rooftop and had caught the litigator just above his right ear as he sat reading a briefing at his desk. His assistant had heard the sound of glass shattering and had rushed to his office, only to find him lying facedown on his desk in a pool of his own blood. There was no more news at this time.

Just then, my door opened and Vespucci showed himself inside. He nodded at the radio, 'You heard?'

I nodded back.

'Who was the girl?'

'A girl I've been seeing.'

'Get rid of her.'

'Why?'

'Don't ask me why. You know why without me telling you.'

He dropped a new envelope on my counter and sat down on top of a bar stool.

'Mr. Vespucci . . . what I do on my own time is my business . . . now I don't mind—'

He cut me off. 'You think you are the first one to do this job? To be a professional?'

'I don't—'

'There are reasons why I picked you. Number one. No father and mother. Number two. No father and mother. Do I make sense? Yes?'

I stood there, smarting.

'Relationships are weakness. In this line of work, you can have no weakness. Or, I assure you, your weakness will be discovered and exploited.'

'By whom?'

'By whom?' he snorted. 'I forget what a babe you are. You are now in the business of killing men. Women and children too, if that is your assignment. When you do this job, you make enemies. Enemies in law enforcement, enemies in the families of the person you kill, enemies who are rival assassins. Yes. That's right. I am not the only fence in this country; not even in this city. There are others who will do whatever they can to stop you from continuing to do what you do. And they will find this girl and exploit her. I promise you that.'

'She's the first girl—'

'What? Who cared for you? Who made love to you? Bah. Let me tell you this, Columbus . . . she is nothing but a weight on your chest, pushing down on your breastbone, crushing the wind out of you. You *must* let her go. Tell her you will never see her again. I can give you no better advice than this.'

'I understand.'

'We're in agreement, then?'

'I said I understand.'

I said it passionately too, and he stared at me for a long time, measuring me, trying to read my thoughts. I diverted my eyes and picked up the envelope.

'What's this, then?'

'Your next mark.'

'Will I get a chance to prove myself this time?'

Vespucci stood up. 'That is not up to me.'

'Who is it up to, then?'

'To God, I suppose. Study the contents of that envelope.' He made it to the door. 'And forget this girl, Columbus.'

He didn't wait for my reply as he shuffled out into the hall.

The name at the top of the page in the second envelope was Edgar Schmidt, a police detective. I did not get the call to kill him, but read about his death on the front page of the *Globe* three weeks later. The third envelope contained the name Wilson Montgomery, a pipefitter who had dealings with the mob. He died a week later, though I never found out how. The fourth envelope was devoted to a man named Seamus O'Dooley, a nightclub owner. He was gunned down in the alley behind his establishment.

I studied all of these files with undiminished intensity. In fact, each time I wasn't called in to complete the mission only served to make me more focused on the next file.

But I didn't forget the girl, despite what Vespucci ordered of me. I wanted to please him, but I wasn't about to cast off the only part of my life that had ever meant anything. So when the holidays rolled around, Jake and I took off in her little Honda for New Hampshire.

Her family met us at the door. Her father, Jim, took my hand and warmly pumped it as he guided us into the house. In the fireplace, warm flames licked the screen that kept the embers at bay. The house was rustic, like many of the homes dotting the New England countryside, and the inside was filled with wooden Western-style furniture. A brown leather sofa took up most of the living room, and the home felt as warm as the fire. It was a home, a real home, something I'd never experienced.

Her mother, Molly, studied my face, a broad smile on her own, and said, 'Well, don't just stand there, Jim, grab his bag. We're gonna put you in Louis's room. It gets a little cold at night, but we'll throw some extra blankets on your bed and you'll be snug as a bug.' It seemed that once Jake's mother opened her mouth, she couldn't stop the onslaught of words tumbling from it.

Jake smiled and rolled her eyes when Molly wasn't looking, as if to say 'I tried to warn you . . .'

The food covering the dining table was enough to feed a dozen people: peaches wrapped with prosciutto, a warm pear-and-endive salad, a honey-baked ham with a brown-sugar crust, baked beans, and no less than three pies waiting on a side table: pumpkin, key lime, and buttermilk chess.

'Jake tells us you work for a distribution company?' Jim asked when we had stacked our plates.

'Yes, sir. It's just a start until I can earn enough money to begin school.'

'Oh?' Molly said, more of a comment than a question.

'Yes, ma'am. I didn't—'

Jake rescued me. 'Mother—'

'What? I didn't say anything.'

I looked at Jake and nodded, like I had this under control. 'My parents died when I was an infant, and I was raised in foster homes, though not by parents you would call "loving." So if I want to go to college, it's up to me to pay for it. And I don't believe in owing the government a nickel, so, like I said, I'm just building up my account.'

Jim cast a stern eye at his wife, then looked back at me. 'Well, I think that is not only a refreshing attitude but an admirable one.' He deftly changed the subject . . . 'Well, what did you think of the drive into Nashua? Jake always likes to come in the back way, but I've been saying for years the Interstate can slice twenty minutes off . . .'

'Jesus, Daddy, you're embarrassing me!' she squealed happily and tossed her napkin at him.

The conversation stayed in the mundane, and Molly didn't let anything dampen her ability to dominate a conversation. Her sentences ran together without punctuation . . . I'm not even sure she took breaths. But I loved every minute of it . . . the food, the conversation, the family, and Jake's hand that made its way under the table to mine. She squeezed it in three pulses, as if to say 'I love you,' and I believed she did, believed it like I had never believed anything. And I started to think, we could be like this, Jake and me, thirty years from now, talking over a table to our own child and her new boyfriend. We could be having a meal like this.

I left the light on next to my bed so I could read the latest file Vespucci handed me before I left. He had been in the hallway when I returned from a hard run, and I didn't invite him in. I don't know why I didn't, or even if he gave a shit. He just waited for a second, studied my face, and when I didn't extend the invitation, he turned and left. I had the feeling he knew I was still seeing Jake, that I was going to be out of town that weekend, but I didn't open my mouth to confirm it. Hell, if he wanted me to kill for him, I wasn't giving this up. And if we never talked about it again, that was all right by me.

The name at the top of the file was Janet Stephens. She was a judge in the 5th Circuit Court, City of Boston. She was not married, but had an ongoing relationship with a female attorney named Mary Gibbons. She lived in a town house in the Back Bay, not far from Beacon Street, with a corgi named Dusty. The courthouse was downtown, a twenty-minute walk through the Common from her front gate.

The picture of Janet revealed a middle-aged woman with a broad forehead and cocoa skin. Her father was black and her mother was white, and she had that beautiful tone found in a lot of offspring of mixed parentage. Her eyes were a piercing shade of green, and her hair fell in tight dark curls down to her chin. Her nose was disproportionately big, however, and it marred what was otherwise a handsome face. She stayed in shape too, working out five days a week with a personal trainer . . . alternating upper and lower body workouts with cardio training each session. Her gym was equidistant between her town home and her courtroom.

Now, whether there was a hit on her because she sent the wrong guy up or because she was about to preside over an important trial, I didn't have the slightest idea. Maybe the contract on her life had nothing to do with her job. Again, I didn't know. My middleman made sure I stayed in the dark. It kept curiosity at bay, like a leash on an angry dog. The less we knew about the 'why's,' the less tempted we were to learn more about our clients. It was just an assignment, an impersonal killing, something I was expected to do by rote.

I was sleeping a dreamless sleep when Jim's voice cut through the darkness. He said something about the phone, and it took me a moment to realize he was standing in the doorway with a cordless receiver in his hand.

'I'm sorry . . . ?' I asked, still trying to shake out the cobwebs.

'There's a gentleman on the phone for you. He said it was urgent.'

Waking in this bed, in this room, at this time was so foreign, it didn't register to me what was happening as I sat up in the bed and Jim handed me the receiver. He backed out of the room to give me some privacy.

'Hello?' I said into the phone, my eyes still adjusting to the darkness.

Vespucci's voice reached through the receiver. 'It's a go.'

Vespucci. He had found me. He knew exactly what I was up to, had even obtained the home number to Jake's parents' house. The middleman, the fence, whose job it was to find out everything he could about a target, had also found out everything he could about me. These thoughts were ripping through my head in an instant, only to be broken when the dark Italian spoke again. 'Twenty-four hours.' And then the phone clicked off.

It's a go. Twenty-four hours. Six words packed with a meaning that stretched all the way from this bedroom to a town house off of Beacon Street. I stood up, suddenly awake, as though smelling salts had been twirled under my nose, and started to dress.

When I came out of the bedroom, carrying my pack, Jim was stooped over a pot of coffee, pouring it into two large mugs.

'I'm sorry the call woke you,' I offered.

He handed me a mug. 'I'm a hopeless insomniac,' he said, taking a sip of his coffee. 'I usually get up by four. It gives me time to think.'

'What time is it now?' The coffee tasted very good.

'Four,' he said, a twinkle to his eye. 'You need to split?'

'Yes, sir. Something came up at work. They need me to fill in.'

'No problem. Take the mug with you.'

'I couldn't—'

'Don't be silly.'

Just then, Jake's voice cut through the quiet of the room. 'What's going on?' she managed. She looked beautiful, standing in an over-sized nightshirt, rubbing the sleep out of her eyes. Looking at her there, it was all I could do to speak.

'I'm sorry . . . I got an emergency call. Everyone's calling in sick to work today and they need me to fill in. Must be the flu or something. But they said it would be double pay if I could get there by seven. I can't pass it up.'

She yawned and looked at her dad. 'Any more of that java?'

'Half a pot.'

'Well then, pour me a mug while I get dressed, old man.'

'You don't have to go. I'll just call a cab to take me to a rental car place. Company said they'd pay for it.'

She moved over and kissed me on the lips, sleepily, right in front of her dad. 'Don't be silly,' she said, sounding just like her father. 'I'll drive you. Pop . . . apologize to Mom for us.'

We rode most of the way talking about innocuous things . . . my impression of her parents, the neighborhood, the house, the bed, the dinner. I was glad not to have to concentrate on what we were saying; my thoughts were on the file in my backpack.

When we arrived at my front stoop, I kissed her on the cheek, mumbled a few words of thanks, and hurried up into my apartment without looking back. Already, my heart was beating as though it had been shocked with a charger. I made my way to my closet and selected a pair of brown slacks and a long-sleeved white shirt. Over this, I pulled down a navy blue blazer. The same clothes fifty thousand men in Boston were putting on at that very moment. Nothing memorable, nothing that stood out. There is a way of dressing, of walking, of casting your eyes, that people looking right at you don't even register your presence. This is a skill boys learn at Waxham, another reason I'm sure Hap recommended me to Vespucci.

I eased open the suitcase I kept under the bed. Inside, the tools of my trade, given to me by Vespucci when I stepped out of the Columbus Textile warehouse: a Glock 17 semi automatic pistol; a box of fifty 9-millimeter hollow point bullets; a serrated knife with a spiked handle; a cache of false ID's, credit cards, business cards. In case I was struck down doing my duty, my identity would be difficult to determine, giving Vespucci enough time to cover his tracks, probably by burning down this apartment.

I had not graduated yet to a sniper rifle, and though I am semi-proficient in its use now, it is not my preferred *modus operandi*. There is an adage that says the closer you can get to a mark, the more skilled you are as an assassin, but I think that adage is as porous as a sieve. Some of the dumbest killers in the world have stood two feet from their prey and pulled the trigger, and some of the most skilled riflemen have toppled their marks from distances greater than five city blocks. A close-contact killer may have to negotiate startled bystanders, while a marksman has to balance wind speed, sunlight, elements, obstructions, and the occasional spotter. Each takes expert skill. The trick, even as green as I was then, was to get in a position that would give me the most comfort . . . comfort in locating the target, comfort in killing the target, and comfort in escaping from the murder scene directly after the assassination.

I was standing near a bus stop on Beacon Street, reading the *Globe* like any other bored commuter, checking my watch occasionally, humming to myself a bland tune. The door to Janet Stephens's town house opened and she emerged, wearing a navy dress and white walking sneakers for her short hike to the courthouse.

As soon as she entered the Common, I folded my paper, tucked it under my arm, and followed from thirty yards away, adjusting my pace to match hers, so that we would remain the same distance apart. I felt certain that somewhere Vespucci was watching me like the eye of God to see how his newest charge would handle the pressure of his first assignment.

Janet passed a couple of tourists looking at the duck sculptures, then took a left down one of the paths dissecting the park. She walked at a pace somewhere between brisk and leisurely, not enough to break a sweat but quick enough to keep me on my toes. I could feel my pulse rising in my ears, like a phantom drumbeat, pounding, pounding. The middle of her back stayed tight as she swung her arms, and it seemed wider than the way it was described in the file, certainly wide enough to hit, to split open, to shatter the spine, even from thirty yards away.

She slowed as she left the park and came to a crosswalk. A blinking red hand on the light-box across the street forced her to a stop, and she used the chance to stoop down and tie a loose shoelace. I had no choice but to approach the same crosswalk; there were several other pedestrians also waiting for the light to change, so it wasn't as though I would be the only one joining her on the corner.

Still, it seemed like a giant spotlight was trained right on me. I looked past the businessman in front of me and concentrated on the middle of Janet Stephens's back, less than two feet away now, stooped over, the cloth on her dress fluttering slightly as she tightened the lace. Two feet away. The Glock felt heavy where it hugged my ribs, hidden behind the loose-fitting blazer. I scratched my belly with my right hand, a casual gesture, then reached further in my jacket, as though I were scratching a rib. The metal of the gun barrel felt cold on my fingertips. Right now. I could do it right here, at the corner of the park, pull the gun, and then . . .

The blinking red hand changed to the universal sign for 'walk'. Janet sprung up and quickly returned to her previous pace. I let the other commuters pass in front of me and held back until I had returned to a comfortable distance. I was still thirty yards behind when Janet Stephens disappeared up the steps of the courthouse.

Was Vespucci watching? Did he see me hesitate and make a mental note, maybe even write something down in a notebook? Was he judging me, right now, this instant? 'Columbus hesitated. A waste of an opportunity. Will need to cut him down first chance.'

Pushing these thoughts aside, I made my way down the street and stepped into a Korean grocery . . . a place as dark and dirty as a gopher's hole. The shelves had a caked-on layer of dust that hadn't felt the underside of a wet cloth in months. I picked up a box of Saran Wrap and then dropped the box on to the ground, like it had slipped from my fingers. As quick as lightning, I snatched the gun from its holster and slipped it into the crack between the lowest shelf and the floor. Same with the serrated knife. They might need a strong cleaning when I retrieved them later, but I wasn't worried that the Korean woman in the back was going to find them while sweeping. I don't think this floor had seen a broom in ages. With the knife and gun tucked out of sight, I picked up the box like nothing had happened, took it to the front, paid for it so as not to raise suspicion, and headed back into the sunlight.

The entrance to the courthouse funneled into a metal detector, marked by three security guards and a red rope cordon. I put my recently purchased Saran Wrap and keys into a tray and then walked through the detector, eyes cast low. I didn't look the security guard in the eye as he handed back my belongings, just took them perfunctorily and headed toward a cluster of elevators where a small crowd had congregated. From my file, I knew Judge Janet Stephens's courtroom was on the sixth floor. I also knew Judge Janet Stephens never took the elevator; she always climbed the stairs, part of her exercise regimen.

Just then, a curt voice from near the elevators shook the lobby: 'Jury duty, report to the sixth floor. End of the hall on the right. Jury duty, sixth floor, end of the hall on the right.'

I scanned the crowd, a varied group of vapid stares, people who looked like they'd rather be anywhere else. The kind of crowd you could sit with all day and no one would remember you.

The jury room was huge, and there were easily five hundred people inside. We were supposed to fill out cards and hand them in to the female administrator up near the front of the room, and then she would draw names for each pool. I took a seat in the back of the room without filling out a card. The only thing that concerned me was remaining anonymous and keeping an eye on the clock. Eleven-thirty. I knew from the file that on most days, Janet Stephens called recess at eleven-thirty.

The courtroom emptied at three minutes past the hour. I had been loitering for thirty minutes, trying not to look out of place, but it wasn't difficult to blend into the surroundings. There were three courtrooms on the sixth floor and people scurried to and from each like rodents trying to stay out of the light. Nobody wanted to be seen and nobody wanted to make eye contact with anyone else. The hall remained as quiet as a museum; the only sounds were the occasional clicking of a woman's heels, some defendant's wife or girlfriend trying to look her best for her man and the jury. Everyone spoke in whispers, like somehow, if they showed deference to this place, they might find themselves treated fairly.

The occupants of the courtroom – the jurors, attorneys, stenographers, bailiffs – all made their way to the elevator bank soon after the doors to the courtroom thrust open, heading out for their designated one-hour lunch. I moved over to the stairwell and disappeared inside.

Quickly, I moved to the fifth-floor landing and waited. I would need a little luck, just a little.

After a few minutes, I heard the stairwell door open above me. From Janet Stephens's file, I knew she liked to eat each day at the deli down on the northwest corner of the courthouse building. She always ordered steamed vegetables and brown rice, and ate quietly as she read over her morning paperwork. I also knew she never failed to avoid the elevators in favor of the stairs. It is routines like this – the mundane, the boring, the normal, people caught in a rut – that make it easy for an assassin to do his job.

I heard the door creak closed followed by the soft shuffle of white tennis shoes on the concrete stairs. My heart was pounding in my ears, loud percussive blasts like an Indian's tom-tom, TUM, TUM, TUM, TUM, TUM, as I blew out a deep breath, doing my best to regulate my breathing, then I headed up toward the sixth floor.

We both turned the corner on the short flight of twelve steps between the fifth and sixth floor. She directed a dismissive smile toward me, averting her eyes like she really didn't want to talk to a juror or some poor lost bloke in the stairwell while she was on her way to lunch. I didn't say anything, just looked past her, up at the next landing, my footsteps soft, my face friendly, nothing to alert her, nothing for her to worry about, just Joe Citizen pounding up the courthouse stairwell.

On the third step, she passed me, mumbling an insincere 'good day.' In the half-second when I moved past her field of vision, I had the Saran Wrap roll out of the box, pulling out a sheet in the same motion, and then with the speed of a lion, I pounced from behind, wrapping the plastic sheet around her face and pulling back with enough force to jerk her off her feet.

She was so surprised, so disoriented that she couldn't find her feet. In the next few seconds, I had wrapped the roll five times around her head as I continued to pull her backward, up the stairwell, where she would have a hard time gaining any sense of balance. Standing over her shoulder, I could see her eyes roll back, back, back, trying to find my face, trying desperately to make sense of this situation, but she couldn't see who was doing this to her. She flailed with her hands, trying to beat my shoulders, when she should have been trying to dislodge the plastic from her mouth and nose, but I couldn't blame her for putting up a fight, for trying to come to grips with the fact she was being suffocated by a stranger on the dingy steps of the courthouse stairwell, less than fifty feet from the courtroom over which she had presided these last eight years. When she finally stopped struggling and her eyes clouded over, I calmly left the stairwell and headed to the elevator bank. Not a soul stood in the hallway to mark my exit.

6

I am a fraud and a liar. I tell myself I am conditioned, I have discipline, my mind is my possession, an object over which I have control. I tell myself I have the ability to remain in the present, that what separates me from the civilians populating God's green earth is that I, and I alone, can shut off the past like turning off a faucet.

But the damn prostitute in the diner and then this woman who didn't even look like Jake, not really, maybe a little in the eyes, sitting at the table next to me at Augustine's had exposed me for the fraud I am. The faucet had sprung a leak and the leak had caused a flood of memories, but I'll be damned if I wasn't going to plug the miserable thing, right here, right now. I had too much else to worry about.

I am on the road again, heading south now, toward Indianapolis and then Lexington. I am heading out of the blue states toward the red ones, and I know presidential candidate Abe Mann will spend very little time on this part of his whistle-stop tour. He will want to head west quickly, for the key electoral votes represented by Iowa, New Mexico, Nevada, Washington, Oregon, and finally California. But he won't get votes from these states, not a single one from any state, because he will be dead.

I drive like I walk in crowds . . . drawing as little attention to myself as possible: beige rental car, cruise control one-mile-per-hour above the speed limit, blinker whenever I change lanes. I am starting to relax, to wind down, to let my mind drift into a pleasant nothingness, when I spy Pooley out of the corner of my eye, driving a black SUV, a Navigator.

He has the passenger window down and is easing alongside me. He signals with one finger, pointed toward the next exit. I immediately slow and allow him to pull in front of me, then follow him to a Shell station just off the Interstate.

'I've got strange news,' he says as we get out and stand next to our cars. He looks tired, like he hasn't slept in days, and his eyelids droop at half-mast.

'You tracked me down, it must be something big.'

'Archibald Grant . . . your middleman who went missing . . .'

'Yeah?'

'I caught up with him at a jailhouse outside of Providence.'

'Jail?'

'Yep. That's what took me so long to locate him. He got pinched on an aiding and abetting racket. Gonna have to serve a few in Federal . . . maybe Lompoc.'

'Shit.'

'Don't worry, he didn't roll on you.'

'You sure?'

'Positive. He knows beyond a shadow of a doubt you can get to him.'

'What about . . .'

'He wouldn't give up who hired him . . . but he said it was someone extremely close to the target.'

'Any hint he knew more than he was letting on? About my history with the mark?'

Pooley shakes his head. 'I don't think so. He's one of these guys who thinks he's a lot more clever than he is . . . you know what I mean? If he knew about your relation to the target, he'd want *me* to know that he knew . . . you see? It'd be a source of pride with him.'

I nod. 'So all we know is that someone close to Mann hired an assassin to kill him.'

'Well, here's where it gets strange, he didn't hire just *one* assassin.'

My eyes flash and Pooley sees it. 'I'm sorry. I didn't know and I know it's my job to know, so go ahead and be pissed . . . I'm sorry. I don't know how I could have missed it . . .'

'Who else is on this job?'

'He wouldn't say.'

'You couldn't coax it out of him.'

'If he hadn't been behind bars, maybe. But it was him and me and a sheet of bulletproof glass twelve inches thick. There was nothing I could do to be persuasive; I had no leverage. I don't think he believes you'll come for him over it.'

'Did you get any indication I might have a head start?'

'He didn't say. He just said the client wanted to make sure the target got clipped and despite your reputation, the client was willing to pay for three guys.'

'Three?' I try to keep my voice even, but I can feel the rising pitch of it in my throat.

Pooley nods. 'Yeah, he hired three guys to finish the job and he doesn't care which one of you completes it. He said the one who does will get the kill fee.'

'Christ.'

'I know.'

'That's two x-factors out there I can't be accountable for, and it only takes one to fuck everything up.'

'I know.'

'Did he tell them all it had to go down in California?'

'Sorry . . . I didn't ask. I'll go back . . .'

'No, fuck that. I need you to find out who the other gunners are . . . as soon as you can.'

Pooley squints in the sunlight, nodding steadily. He uses his hand as a visor to shield his eyes. 'Yeah, yeah . . . of course. Of course, Columbus.'

'How long will it take you?'

'I don't know. I'll do whatever it takes. A week, tops.'

'Okay. Meet me in Santa Fe in a week with those names. I don't want you to tell me on the phone. Only in person, you understand?'

'Yeah, Columbus. Of course.'

He wants to say more, but he can see in my eyes I'm not in the mood for apologies. So he hops back behind the wheel of the Navigator and pulls out without a backward glance in the mirror.

Bad luck. Bad fucking luck. I feel like ramming the palm of my hand through the steering wheel, but that would be rattling and I don't rattle. One thing I won't do is rattle.

I should turn around and head to the jailhouse outside of Providence, bribe my way in, stick a knife through Archibald Grant's ribs, tell him that's what he gets for hiring three men instead of entrusting the job to one. But he was just doing his client's bidding and if he left out a little information, what does he care? He figures one of us will probably take care of the other two, either before or immediately after the hit, so he'll only have one angry assassin to deal with when it's all said and done. And he figures once that assassin gets paid his kill fee, all apologies will be accepted.

I know I should quit the job, just pull a U-turn at the next exit and head back to Boston, tell Pooley to find me something else, something that doesn't hit quite so close to home. One too many obstacles are stacking up, one too many omens, but for some reason I'm powerless to resist, powerless to put on my blinker and steer this car around, like I'm being pulled by an invisible force, a magnet, something outside of me.

I want to kill my father. I want to be the one to do it, no matter what it takes. The assignment just sped up the inevitable; I was headed on this collision course long before someone paid me. Vespucci said fate causes paths to cross that we cannot understand, but that's not entirely correct. This path I understand perfectly. Abe Mann set me on it a long time ago, the moment he discarded Amanda B. like she was a dead animal he had run over in the street. I am his bastard, and I'll be damned if some other shooter is going to get to him before I do.

I check into the Omni Severin hotel in the middle of downtown Indianapolis. It is one of these large luxury jobs that tries to maintain its historic feel but comes across strangely anachronistic, like it hasn't quite made up its mind what it wants to be, and thus ends up being neither antiquated nor modern.

'I see we have you here for seven days, Mr. Smith.'

'Yes.'

'A non-smoking room? King-size bed.'

'Yes.'

The clerk, a pretty college student, I would guess, types at her computer. After a moment, she hands me a plastic key-card.

'Now, I should warn you, the final two days of your visit are when Abe Mann will be staying here, and things might get a little . . . you know . . . extra-security and what-not.'

'Really?' I ask, pretending to be pleasantly surprised.

'Yes, sir. Coming through on his "Connecting America" tour or whatever it is he calls it.'

'Are we on the same floor?'

'No . . . he's got the fifteenth floor all to himself. Him and his people, I should say. You won't have to worry about that.'

'Okay, great.' I give her a warm smile. 'That's something, being in Indianapolis at the same time.'

I think that's the reaction she's looking for, and she smiles at me cheerily as she points toward a bank of elevators and gives me directions to my floor.

When I get to my room, I turn on the television and there he is again, as ubiquitous as a celebrity. With twenty-four-hour news channels running at maximum capacity during an election year, I can expect to see candidate Abe Mann any time I flip around the dial. He's standing in front of thirty steel workers, every minority represented, each man dressed in full blue-collar uniform and donning a hard hat. Abe Mann has a hard hat on as well, and he's talking about something he calls a 'Bridge for Working Families,' shaking that palm preacher-style, like he genuinely believes what's coming out of his mouth.

The hotel has a pretty good-sized gym, and I decide to pound out my energy on a treadmill. I'm the only one running at this hour; there's a television in the corner showing sports highlights with the sound off, but I ignore it, just pounding my steps in place, settling into a comfortable rhythm, the only noise coming from my steady gait. I plan on running for an hour, and since I am running in place, the past has plenty of time to catch up to me.

I hadn't meant to change, and I was too myopic to understand what was happening to me. Yes, I had killed Mr. Cox with a sewing machine in the abandoned Columbus Textile warehouse, but I had loathed Mr. Cox, and I had killed him with passion, with emotion, with hatred. When Vespucci opened the door the following morning, I could walk away the same person I was, somehow cleaner, like emerging from a baptism.

But suffocating Judge Janet Stephens with Saran Wrap on the courthouse stairwell was markedly different. It was devoid of emotion, passionless, mechanical, and therefore flawed in a way I could not yet understand. I had done everything right; I had fulfilled my obligation, studied the file, found the weakness, exploited the routine, and my assignment was successful. So what was missing?

I had met Vespucci the next day at a coffee shop at his request.

'You have a bank?' he asked over a small glass cup holding an Americano.

'Yes.'

'Close your account.' He slid me a small sheet of paper. 'Go to this address when you need money. No more records, no more paperwork, no more checks. Everything will be kept in cash.'

'What will I find at this address?'

'A bank for those of us who don't like banks. You will find you already have an account there. And in that account is fifty thousand dollars that wasn't there yesterday.'

I leaned back, trying to mask that the sum staggered me. Vespucci knew it had, but he didn't say anything more. For a minute, we just sipped our espressos, leaving the air between us silent.

'When do I get my next assignment?' I finally managed.

'When you are ready.'

'I'm ready now.'

'No, Columbus. You need a month to get your . . . how should I say? . . . to get your *edge* back.'

I opened my mouth, but then closed it while his eyes measured me. He was right. I wasn't ready. Though I couldn't put my finger on what was holding me back.

'This business, this business you find yourself in, it pays well but it also exacts a fee, Columbus. Do I make sense? It exacts a fee up here . . .' He tapped his head with his index finger. 'The only currency by which you can pay this fee is time. You need some time so you can do what you do again.'

I nodded, but I knew he had more.

'I think it is not enough to do your job and walk away from it. I believe . . . this is hard to understand . . . I believe you must connect with your mark's mind . . . ahhh . . .' He waved off his words as though he were displeased with them, like they had failed to communicate what he was trying to say. I waited. After a moment, he spread his hands in front of him. 'Columbus, I did not give you enough lead time because it was a test to see how you would do. Typically, you will have eight weeks before an assignment must be complete. Use the time to not only know the routine of your mark, but to know what is going on inside your mark's head, to become your mark, to really understand his . . . or her . . . motivations. Once you have fully *realized* the connection, only then can you fully *sever* the connection. Do not ask me to explain why this is so. I only know it is.'

With that, he dropped a ten-spot on the table to cover our bill, excused himself, and shuffled out of the coffee house.

Jake could tell I had changed. She didn't know how to ask what was different about me, why I was acting morose, so she grew frustrated.

'What did I do?' We were sitting down to dinner.

'You didn't do anything.'

'Ever since we came back from New Hampshire you've been acting . . . I don't know . . . *bothered* by me.'

'I'm telling you this has nothing to do with you, Jake.'

'Bullshit.'

'What do you want me to say? You need to drop it.' I could feel my anger rising like boiled water.

This was our first row and I discovered she wasn't one to back down. 'Drop what? How can I drop something when you won't even tell me what I'm supposed to be dropping?'

I started to answer but she interrupted, 'I'd expect this from some people, but not you. Since the day I met you, we've been nothing but honest with each other. That's what having a relationship, a real relationship, is all about. You have to trust me and I have to trust you. There isn't any other way to do it – not a way that works, that really works.'

She was right, but my hands were tied. 'You're right, I'm sorry.'

I could see her eyes soften, but she held firm. 'You're apologizing but I don't even know what you're apologizing for. This isn't communicating. This is me talking to a brick wall.'

'I said I'm sorry, Jake. I'm trying to figure some things out, but you have to believe that the problems I'm having aren't about us. The *only* thing . . . the only thing I depend on each day *is* us. I know that's not a satisfying answer but I need you to accept it . . . I'll get down and beg you to accept it if that's what it takes. But I can't handle you going sour on me too. I just . . . can't. When the time is right, I'll tell you everything.'

Whatever defenses she had melted away. 'You promise?' she said, weakly.

'I promise.'

'You trust me? Completely?'

'You're the only one I do trust on this planet.'

'I love you.'

When I answered her with the same three words, I meant them fully.

7

My next assignment was a disaster. The name on the top of the page was Richard Levine, a numbers runner on the east side. Vespucci had done his homework, but even the homework had gaping holes in it, gaping holes due to a very specific reason: I was working a job where the target knew I was coming.

Levine was a five-foot-two slight figure with chronic headaches and a short fuse. He had made a fortune working the rackets among the union workers down by Boston Harbor, and as his bank account increased, so did the list of his enemies. A cautious man, he had a regular staff of five bodyguards . . . professional guys, former cops, men who hadn't had a chance to go soft. He lived in a large house near Beacon Hill and rarely went out any more, letting his minions work the books, deliver the payouts, and make the collections. A handful of guys were entrusted to enter his door, and all of these guys were known faces, fellas who had been on his payroll for ten-plus years. None of these men left the business either; the only way to get away from Levine was to die or disappear.

Vespucci didn't have schematics on the inside of his house; they had mysteriously vanished from the Department of Records downtown. My fence also knew better than to talk to any of Levine's men. I had eight weeks and very little information. But it was the last sentence in the file that got my attention: '*Mark knows he has a price tag on his head.*'

The son-of-a-bitch knew, knew someone had been hired to kill him, knew bullets were being loaded into cylinders at this very moment, intended to strike him dead.

What I had to do, what Vespucci inherently knew I must do, was to get inside the head of my mark, *realize* the connection so I could *sever* the connection, as he said. But how could I crack Levine if I couldn't get close to him?

I started by jogging down his street wearing a Boston College T-shirt and some athletic shorts I'd purchased from a bookstore close to the school. I'm sure I looked like every other out-of-breath runner, cutting through neighborhoods near the park to break a sweat and get the ol' heart rate up.

His street was common, lined with expensive homes, the stand-out feature being Levine's house at the end of the block. Gated, with an expansive lawn, it was a two-story Tudor mansion looking down on the rest of the homes like a pedantic schoolteacher in front of a classroom. I didn't stop to tie a shoelace and get more of a look; it was too early in the game to raise any eyebrows.

From the file Vespucci gave me, I pulled out a chart with the names and faces of Levine's pigeons, the low-level guys who handled the sports books around town. Vespucci had also included the name of a bar in Little Italy where a couple of the guys liked to whittle away time instead of going home to their wives. It wasn't much, but it was a start.

I eased into Antonio's on Stuart Street, just down from Maggiano's. It was a small place, dimly lit, with a long oak bar covering the length of the back wall. A couple of dartboards, a jukebox, three tables, a television tuned in to the Sox, and a fat Irishman pouring drinks for an eclectic crowd of locals, college kids, and tourists.

Two of Levine's bookies were at a table near the box, drinking beer and watching the game through jaded eyes. I tried to pick up snippets of conversation, but most of it revolved around the fuckin' Sox this and the fuckin' Sox that.

I watched the final out as the Boston cleanup hitter grounded weakly to the pitcher. 'Fuck!' I said loudly, and followed it with, 'that cost me a grand.' I didn't have to turn around to know my words had found their mark. As I downed the last of my beer, I heard chairs scraping over the wooden floor, then heavy footsteps, and finally two sets of eyeballs appeared on either side of me.

'You bet the Sox, kid?'

I turned around with a frown on my face, and made eye contact with the shorter of the two guys, the one I knew was named Ponts.

'Yeah. Shit. I know you should never bet your heart . . . but I had a *feeling* tonight.'

Ponts snorted. 'Happens to all of us.'

The taller of the two, a bookie who I knew was named Gorti, jumped in with . . . 'shit, don't it?'

'What you drinking, kid?' Ponts asked.

'Me?' I looked at the bottle like I didn't know. 'Budweiser.'

Ponts called out to the bartender. 'Three Buds, Seamus . . .'

'You don't have to—'

'Christ, you just lost a grand on the goddamn Sox. It's the least I could do.'

The beers appeared in front of us in a hurry. 'Thanks, then . . .' I said.

'Who you bet with, kid?'

I pulled down the bottle from my mouth and looked at Ponts suspiciously.

'Bet with?'

'Who's your bookmaker?'

'You guys cops?'

They looked at each other and started chuckling. 'Nah, kid. We ain't cops.'

'We are *far* from cops, I can guarantee you that,' added Gorti.

'Well, just the same . . . thanks for the beer. But I should—'

Ponts didn't let me finish the sentence, 'Kid, the reason I'm asking is because Ben Gorti here and me, Stu Ponts, Ben and me run book right out of this bar.'

'Oh, yeah?' I tried to look pleasantly surprised.

'That's right. And lemme guess, you're still using your daddy's bookie somewhere back wherever home is?'

I let out a smile like he was right on the money.

'Well, what d'ya say you let your old man run his own game and you start running one with us?'

'Really, I should—'

'Tell you what . . . what's your typical lay?'

'How much you bet, kid?' added Gorti, as if to clarify.

'I usually go five hundred. Unless I'm feeling it. Then, who knows . . .' I tried to sound like a fish who had just bitten on the worm and gotten the hook.

Ponts's grin widened. 'Well, I'll give you your first $500 bet on the house, and a five-thousand-dollar credit line. Does your dad's bookie give you that?'

'No, sir.'

'Call me Ponts.'

'Okay . . .'

He clasped me on the back with a beefy hand. 'Now, who you like this week in the Miami game?'

There is a common misconception following a successful assassination. Often, the people closest to the target will say they never got a look at the hired killer, they don't know how the assassin could have gotten close to their boss; the man came in like a ghost and put a bullet in their friend, husband, co-worker without disturbing the dust in the air. They'll say someone in their midst must have betrayed him, they'll look at each other with skeptical eyes, they'll check over their shoulders every time a shadow moves across a doorway, every time they cross in front of a dark alley.

But the truth is they've often known the face of the trigger man, they've probably shaken hands with him, probably done business with him, hell, probably bought him a beer in a small sports bar in Little Italy.

If I couldn't know Levine, if I couldn't make a connection with him, I could watch his pigeons, I could get to know his roots, where he came from before he lived in the big house on the hill at the end of the street. He got to where he was by being the best at what Ponts and Gorti did now. My guess is he was more ruthless, less forgiving then the typical runner. I didn't know if he demanded the same of his employees, but I intended to find out.

It didn't all go wrong on the day of the hit; it happened the night before I pulled the trigger. I was into the guys for most of my nut, the initial amount of credit they gave me to hook me. I played stupidly right off the bat; I didn't have time to make casual bets. I started with sucker plays, parlays, rolling any wins I stumbled upon, pushing the limits, and Ponts lapped it up like a stray cat with a fresh bottle of milk. In three weeks, I flopped on enough games to be into the fat man for forty-eight hundred.

I met up with him as he was coming out of Antonio's.

'Say, kid . . .'

'Hey, Ponts. Can I get on a parlay this weekend?'

'How much?'

'Double up, catch up.'

He let out a low whistle. 'Forty-eight?'

'Might as well make it an even five.'

'What say you give me the forty-eight you already owe, and we'll go from there?'

'Come on, Ponts . . . you said a five-grand credit line.'

'But, kid—'

'Forty-eight is not five.'

'Yeah, but you want to go in for ten—'

'Not if I win—'

'I don't know, kid.'

'Fine . . . I'll just put two hundred on a three-way parlay . . . B.C. getting three, the over, and Virginia Tech over Michigan.'

'You just want two hundred?'

'I want five dimes, but you said you'll only give me two potatoes.'

He looked at me sideways and pulled out a small notepad. 'The kid wants five dimes . . . I'll give the kid five dimes. Five to win fifteen on the parlay. Let's just hope your luck turns, buddy.'

'I got a feeling this time.'

He smiled and winked. 'I hope so.'

I hit the B.C. game but lost both Tech and the over. Now, I owed Ponts and Gorti ninety-eight hundred and I would get my first impression of how they ticked when wound up. I stayed away from Antonio's for two weeks, just to get their engines into the red. Maybe they thought I'd run out on them. Maybe they thought I wasn't coming back.

When I showed up at the bar, Ponts's mouth disappeared into a thin line. All hints of camaraderie and companionship were gone. I was not his friend; this was business.

'Where's the ninety-eight hundred?' he said as I sidled up to the bar. Gorti took a position on the other side of me.

'Let me finish my beer.' I was playing the spoiled college kid for all it was worth.

Ponts took the beer bottle out of my hand and downed it in front of me in two quick gulps. 'Now you're finished. Where's my money?'

I pulled out a roll of bills from my pocket. 'I got five large here. If you'll just let me place it on tonight's game . . .'

The fat man snatched it out of my hand, quickly handed it to Gorti, who began to thumb through it. After a quick count, he nodded back to Ponts.

'You got five days to come up with the other forty-eight.'

'Come on . . . why so hostile . . . ?'

'You think this is hostile? Hostile is Friday morning if you don't have my money.'

'Jesus. I went out of town for a few days. Here I am and I paid you.'

'You paid me half.'

'I don't see why . . .'

And then my voice trailed off, the words choking in my throat. The last thing I was expecting, and the very thing Vespucci had warned me about, rose up and stung me.

Jake walked into the bar with a friend of hers.

Now, my plan had been to show up on Friday and ask for an extension, to claim poor, to see how physical Ponts would get with me when I didn't have the money. I was beginning to understand why Vespucci preached making a connection with the target; it was my job to seek out the *evil* in people. Everyone has a dark side, and once I find that dark side, it is my job to home in on it, manipulate it, exploit it, enlarge it. I must see the evil in the target, taste it, put my finger in it the way Thomas did to the wound of Christ, so that the act of killing becomes diminished, becomes necessary. It is a trick of sorts, an illusion created by the mind to keep the horrors of the job at bay. I wanted to see what Ponts would do to me, so that when I killed Levine, I would understand what he had done to others. Then I could walk away from it like a vigilante instead of a hired gun, at peace with my decision to take someone's life.

But all that changed the moment Jake walked into the bar and saw me.

She immediately dove-tailed over to where I was standing and kissed my lips, saying my name . . . a different name than what I had given Ponts and Gorti.

I started to say something to get her to walk away, but Ponts read me like a book and interrupted before any words could come out of my mouth, addressing Jake directly.

'Hello, there! I'm Ponts and this is Gorti . . . we're friends of your boyfriend. What's your name, beautiful?'

She turned to them warmly. 'Jake. Jake Owens.'

Ponts grinned so large I thought he was going to swallow her. 'You go to school here, Jake Owens?'

She nodded. 'Almost finished at B.C. How do you boys know each other?'

'We're old friends from way back, aren't we?' and he said my name, the one Jake had handed to him.

'Yeah,' I mumbled. 'You know, Jake . . . let me finish up with these fellas and I'll come sit with you.'

'Okay,' she said, like she knew she had interrupted something she shouldn't have.

'It was nice meeting you, Jake Owens from B.C.' Ponts said, holding the words like he didn't want to let them go.

As soon as she was gone, his eyes hardened. 'I don't care you gave us a bum name, I don't care you think you're so fucking smart you can game us like a couple of fruits. What I do care about is the forty-eight big you owe us. Now you know that we know about Jake Owens from B.C. We get the money on Friday or somebody's day gets ruined. We understand each other?'

I nodded. 'Yeah . . . sure, Ponts.'

'Don't do anything dumb again, kid.' He patted the side of my face and turned back to the bar like the conversation was over.

I was sweating. I sat in my apartment, the window open, a nice breeze blowing in off the water, and yet I was sweating, like the room had nothing but stale air trapped inside.

I had ignored Vespucci's advice, I had kept up my relationship with a girl who loved me, and now she was involved. Two low-level bag men for my primary target knew her name and even worse . . . knew mine.

I was going to have to rectify the situation. Rectify it myself, without telling Vespucci what I planned. And I felt it had to be as soon as possible, money or no money. I didn't know what Ponts and Gorti would do to warn me, to send me a message even before Friday's deadline, so I had to compress my six weeks into that moment.

I sat in the shadows of a neighboring stoop, watching the front door of Antonio's. An intermittent rain was falling, and drops pooled on the lid of my black baseball cap before collecting into a puddle at my feet. My eyes were sharp, hard, focused. I waited, ignoring everything but the front door of the restaurant, not even stamping my feet to shake off the chill wind blowing in from the east.

At midnight, Ponts and Gorti shuffled out of the bar. They weren't stumbling; I'd noticed neither man ever drank more than a couple of beers the whole time they were at Antonio's. They wanted to look like they were there to have a good time, but Antonio's was a job to them, as mundane as any cubicle at any office in America. So when they left the bar, they were both sober.

From casing them over the last couple of weeks, I knew they both rode together in a four-door Olds mobile, the kind of car only the elderly and ex-cons purchase with any regularity. As soon as they both settled into the front seat, I flipped open the rear door and slid in behind them.

They both spun to get a look at me, surprised.

'What'ya doin', kid?' Gorti asked, a moment before I shot him through the passenger seat. He gasped for air – the bullet shattered his left lung – but I was no longer concerned with him, I just turned the gun on Ponts, who was hunched uncomfortably behind the steering wheel, breathing raspily.

'Jesus fuckin' Christ, kid, don't shoot me.'

'Just drive.'

'I got a wife at home—'

'I said drive.'

'Sure, kid. Sure.'

He turned on the ignition and put the car into gear, then slowly pulled it out onto the street. Little Italy was dark and empty at this time of night, the cold and the rain keeping the pedestrians at bay.

'Take the highway south. I'll tell you when to get off.'

Ponts tried to make small talk along the way. Told me it was only five grand and he could chalk that up to sour business. Told me his wife was talking about finally having a baby this year. Told me he didn't even remember my girlfriend's name if that was what this was about.

I let him talk as much as he wanted, until he finally gave up and drove the car in silence. I stayed out of his sight-line in the rearview mirror, allowing the danger to expand like noxious fumes in his mind. He didn't know where the gun was, where my eyes were, when the shot might come.

I gave him a few directions until we ended up outside the abandoned Columbus Textile Warehouse, where I had last taken Pete Cox's life and emerged, like a phoenix, with a new one of my own.

Inside, the warehouse was much as I had last seen it. No police tape, no evidence bags, no fingerprint dust. Cox's body and any sign of foul play had been meticulously erased by Vespucci's men.

I directed Ponts to a chair at an old sewing desk. His legs were shaky, but he managed to make it this far without passing out, even if his breathing grew progressively more labored, like a dog's pant after a hard run.

'What we doin' here, Columbus?'

So it was back to the name I had given him originally; that was a good sign. I pulled out some paper and a pencil I had tucked away in my pocket before I left my apartment.

'You're going to draw me a map.'

He started to say something but then just waited for me to continue. 'I want an exact layout of Richard Levine's house: bedrooms, living room, kitchen, shitters, laundry room, where he eats, where he sleeps, where he takes a dump. I want X's marking where his guards sit, where they head when they take their breaks, where they come in, where they go out. I want you to write down every detail you can think of about that house and all the people in it.'

'Fuck. You're the guy. The hired gun.' He looked up at me in awe, like I had just pulled the greatest magic trick of all time right in front of him.

I let my eyes go hard in answer. 'Start writing.'

It was about an hour to daylight when Ponts and I started walking up the front porch of Levine's house. I knew cameras were covering us, but I had a gun in his ribs and my ball cap pulled down tight over my head. Knowing where the cameras were positioned helped me keep my face off the security screens. And I knew we were coming about twenty minutes before the guards changed shifts. There is no man who isn't tired at 5:30 A.M., especially when he knows he's heading to a warm bed after a long, boring, rainy night.

We arrived at the front door, and Ponts rang the bell. An intercom affixed to a support column on the patio barked to life.

'What you doin' here, Ponts?'

'I got a favor to ask of Dick.'

'Come back after breakfast.'

'This can't wait, Ernie. This is my sister's kid I got with me. He works first shift on the docks, but he's looking for some fries on the side. I already told Dick about it; I know he's up reading the *Daily Racing Form* . . . come on, we'll be in and out.'

'Levine knows *you're* coming?'

'I mentioned it to him a couple weeks ago. He said he'd work it in 'cause it was me.'

Despite the fact that I had told him he would live through this if he just played his part to the end, the last sound Ponts ever heard was the door clicking open. He had served his purpose, and I didn't want to put off shooting him.

The whole thing took eight minutes. I pulled the trigger on Ponts and kicked the door back at the same time, smashing it into the first guard who was coming to frisk me. As he fell backwards, I shot him in the head, sending the back of his skull into a potted begonia in the foyer. The silencer attached to the pistol's muzzle kept the report from sounding like anything more than a small cough.

I didn't care about the dining room to the right, so I stepped left and shot the two guards seated around the kitchen table before they could even get their guns up. Two chest shots, and their blood poured into their blue starched shirts, a pair of purple ovals where their front pockets used to be.

Without breaking stride, I moved up the back stairwell, my legs like pistons as I attacked each step, moving quickly now, reloading my pistols as I went. First, I shot the guard sitting sleepy-eyed on a stool at the top of the staircase reading his *USA TODAY*, a face shot, so that all of his features became an indistinguishable red mask. Another guard emerged from a bathroom, a fat guy, an extra guy, the one Ponts hadn't told me about. I figured there would be some sort of play Ponts would try to make, a last piece of information he would hold for himself, so he could wait and use it when I would be surprised, vulnerable. But Ponts was dead and this poor player had the misfortune of taking his end-of-shift shit right as I was coming up the stairs. He didn't have time to exhale before I shot him in the heart.

The last guy left was Richard Levine, the one-time numbers runner and current bookmaking heavy of Boston, Massachusetts. And I hated him. Not because of his operation, or his business, or the evil I could imagine he must have harnessed to rise to the level he had.

No, I hated him because of what this assignment meant, what it uncovered, what it cost me. Vespucci was right all along. I couldn't go back to Jake, not now, not ever again. If I couldn't account for her whereabouts at all times, if I couldn't keep her behind locked doors, if I couldn't protect her from my world, then she would always be in play, always be a factor, always be involved in a race she didn't know she was running. And for all that, I loathed Richard Levine with every living cell in my body.

When I entered his bedroom, he was seated on a back patio, drinking orange juice and reading the *Racing Form*. He turned his head and his eyes met mine and he instantly knew my purpose, why I was there, what I was going to do with the weapon in my hand. For a moment, just a moment, his eyes dropped, like he was resigned this day would come, the race he was running had reached the finish line. And then as quickly as it was there, it was gone again, replaced by the steel and spit and resolve that had driven him the last twenty years. He leapt for the nearest chair cushion, knocking the table up and out of the way, sending his breakfast dishes flying in what he hoped was the distraction he needed to reach the gun tucked underneath the nearest wicker chair.

My first bullet caught him just below his arm, breaking his ribs and sapping the fight out of him the way a strong body blow can shut down even the toughest of heavyweights. It spun him, so that he wheeled into the overturned table and dropped into the mess of food and juice and shattered glass on the floor. The chair he was trying to reach spilled over in his fall, and the gun it harbored tumbled out just a few feet from where his body came to rest. He looked at the gun the way a covetous man looks at his neighbor's wife, so close, yet a mile away. I'm sure he was thinking, 'if only I'd been a little faster.'

My second bullet stopped him from thinking, permanently.

8

I am watching Abe Mann at a rally in downtown Indianapolis. He is standing on a podium, with a hundred fidgeting children on risers behind him, talking about building a foundation of learning in this country, talking about accountability and responsibility and private school credits and tax breaks for working families. Empty words told by rote with little feeling, like he's starting to sag under the weight of a hundred campaign speeches to a hundred sleepy-eyed crowds, with no end in sight.

I am one of those sleepy-eyed crowd members, though my half-closed lids are an act, a mask, a shield I can hide behind while my eyes seek out and record every detail of the event. There are four teachers on either side of the risers, wearing green and gold 'James A. Garfield Elementary School' T-shirts, two black women and two white males. The men are so obviously members of the Secret Service their presence is more warning than undercover work; they are dressed that way so the pictures in tomorrow's *Indianapolis Star* will not project a leader who needs constant protection.

A row of photographers stands at the front of the crowd in a small section marked by steel dividers. There are several goateed men, most with ponytails, and only a few women, snapping pictures between yawns, just doing their jobs. Any one of them could kill Abe Mann rather easily and at close range, but getting away would pose a problem. The kill is only half of the assignment; disappearing after the body drops is where an assassin earns his fee.

I would guess the crowd stands about five hundred strong, and I am dressed like most of the young men here: gray business suit, dark tie, black shoes, and black belt. Normally, I would have worn sunglasses, but the sky is overcast, and I do not want to draw any unnecessary attention my way. As I've said, there is a way of standing, of dressing, of combing your hair, of holding a blank expression on your face, of folding your hands, of yawning when someone looks your way that renders you all but invisible in a crowd, a room, even tight quarters, like a hallway.

I count eight Secret Service men mingling in the audience, conspicuous by the slight bulges under their arms that shoulder holsters make in clothing, and by the number of times they look around the crowd instead of keeping their eyes on the speaker. I can guess their ranks will swell as we move further west and closer to the convention. How many of them I will eventually have to negotiate is still to be discovered.

I wait until the speech is over and the audience disperses *en masse*. Although dozens of supporters trickled away before the event reached its conclusion, I find I can be more inconspicuous if I remain a sheep in the flock instead of a straggler. I catch one last glimpse of candidate Mann as he clasps hands with various attendees while leaving the podium. His face is fatigued, and although he is grinning, there is melancholy in his eyes.

From Indianapolis, the Mann tour heads to Little Rock, Oklahoma City, and Santa Fe. I follow, but I do not attend another rally, nor do I check into the same hotel as Mann and his entourage. But I do stand in front of the television and parrot the words of his speeches over and over until I have the lines memorized. I begin to understand how little of a political stump speech is improvised. He'll add a joke with local flavor to the beginning of each speech, something to let the crowd know he's interested in their city, their state, their problems. Then he'll transition into the same lines he's already used a thousand times. I understand his ennui. It is damn near impossible to bring passion to weightless words.

When I reach Santa Fe, I head for the La Fonda, a pueblo-style Spanish hotel on the plaza. A sign above the door indicates it is 'the Inn at the End of the Trail,' but that is a lie. The trail isn't anywhere near its end, not for me. I check in and wait for a knock on my door.

Pooley arrives three hours later. I have taken the opportunity to work in a light nap, and I feel refreshed when he steps into the room. He is holding a thick manila envelope. His expression is sober.

'What'd you find out?' I say once we ask after each other's health.

'One piece of the puzzle. They definitely hired two other assassins for this job besides you. Shooter number two is a Spanish contract killer named Miguel Cortega. He worked a little out of New York and Chicago before he made his way to D.C. Who knows what he did before crossing the Atlantic.'

'You familiar with him?'

Pooley shakes his head. 'I went through some back channels to pull the name, called in a chit I had with William Ryan out of Vegas. He made some calls and gave up Cortega.'

Ryan was a high-level West Coast fence who repped both sides: acquirers and killers. Pooley and I had worked with him once before and were both impressed with his professionalism.

'Had Ryan used him before?'

'Twice. Both long-range sniper shots and both confirmed kills.'

'A drop man.'

Pooley nods. 'Looks like it.'

'Does Cortega know he's been tripled, or is he in the dark like I was?'

'I told Ryan to tread lightly. He can't be sure, but he thinks he's running blind right now.'

'Does he know if Cortega has a kill date, or is he going to make a move upon opportunity?'

'The assignment is to drop the candidate the week of the convention, same as you.'

I let out a deep breath. 'Well, that's good at least. He's a pro, so he won't jump the gate early. Which means I still have some time to set the table.'

'Maybe. Maybe not.'

'Go on.'

'Shooter number three. I don't have a name, but I know who his fence is.'

'Who?'

'You're not going to like it.'

'Who is it, Pooley? Jesus.'

'Vespucci.'

I looked at my friend long and hard as that name engulfed me like a poisonous cloud. I hadn't heard it out loud in so long, I had sometimes wondered if that dark Italian was still in the game. I guess he is, and some strange part of me feels . . . what is it . . . pride? Pride that I have a chance to prove myself to that old bastard again? Pride that I will take out one of his men and complete the assignment out from under him? Pride that he will have to face the fact I am still alive? Or am I confused and the emotion I feel, for the first time in a long time, is fear?

Pooley coughs into his hand. 'I know his name brings yet another personal connection into this mission, but I think it's better you have all the cards in front of you.'

'Of course it is.' I snap out of my reverie and meet Pooley's eyes to let him know I'm back, focused. 'But you don't know who he put on the job?'

'I tried to get the information but I met a brick wall. I don't know what power that old Italian wields, but he has a lot of tongues afraid to wag.'

'Okay, good work, Pooley.'

He smiles. 'This assignment sure is stirring up some echoes.'

'Yeah.'

'There're plenty of other jobs out there. You can drop off and we wouldn't miss a beat.'

I shake my head. 'This one's mine, Pooley. And there's a reason it's mine, even if that reason is a little gray right now.'

'You're getting philosophical on me.'

'Maybe.'

'Well, I'll leave you to your ramblings then,' he says with a smirk.

'Can you do a couple of things for me before you head back to Boston?'

'Anything.'

'I want a new car, an SUV, something bigger.'

'Done.'

'And I want you to stop by Mann's local headquarters. Tell 'em you're a contractor, you handle special events all over the country. See what kind of process they have for securing bids on Mann events. See if they use a local or a national company. Someone puts up the risers, someone coordinates the kids and the construction workers and the cops and the soldiers to stand behind him. I want to know who and how they get the job.'

'You got it. It'll probably be late tomorrow, Friday at the latest.'

'Do what you got to do. Take the spare key on the dresser. I'll stay here until I see you again.'

He starts to leave, then stops, and turns to face me, holding up that envelope. 'I almost forgot. Here.'

'What's this?'

'Some more research I pulled. Don't ask me how. It's a . . . what's the word . . . addendum to the initial material. I think it'll help you focus.'

'Why do you say I need focus?'

'It's in your eyes, Columbus.'

I am sitting in a booth in McDonald's, the most American of fast-food restaurants. I read recently that Abe Mann likes to eat quarter-pounders here, a page he stole from Bill Clinton's playbook. By eating greasy burgers at a popular fast-food chain, he can give off the impression he is 'one of us,' a true 'man of the people,' not some stuffy aristocrat who sits for five-hundred-dollar haircuts and windsurfs on the waves outside his mansion in Nantucket. His handlers are playing their cards deftly; Mann's numbers continue to rise in the polls and his press has been favorable. He is on auto-pilot, careful not to make a mistake this close to the convention, not with his nomination at stake, and so his campaign is as lifeless as the burger on the tray in front of me. We are both on missions, headed for the same spot on the map.

A brown dog is loitering in the parking lot outside the window. He doesn't appear to belong to anyone, at least not any more, and he is skittish, like he's taken too many kicks to the ribs and isn't going to let it happen again. He is sniffing by the dumpsters across the lot, but whatever he's looking for, he doesn't find it.

I open the envelope Pooley handed me and slide out a stack of papers. It's another jigsaw puzzle, only this one is already put together, all the pieces lined up and fitted in place. Newspaper clippings and hotel receipts and bank statements and official testimony and diary entries, all presented succinctly and chronologically to tell a complete story. How Pooley put this together, or, more likely, who gave it to him, are questions for which I'm not sure I want the answers. It turns out my mother, LaWanda Dickerson, isn't the only woman Abe Mann removed permanently from his life.

Her name was Nichelle Spellman. She was a senior vice-president of regional planning for Captain-McGuire-Magness, a worldwide agriculture processor headquartered in Topeka, Kansas. She met Abe Mann for the first time when she spoke in front of a congressional committee formed to explore allegations of price-fixing amongst the farming conglomerates.

Over an eight-year period, they met frequently, and secretly, at various functions all over the world.

Nichelle Spellman had a husband of eleven years and a seven-year-old daughter. She was moderately pretty, a little plump, with dark eyes and dark hair. She was a bit Midwestern plain, but had an Ivy League education and a gift for making people feel comfortable. In her capacity as a senior VP for CMM, she also had a boatload of bribery money.

She had started off with small purchases, pushing the envelope on what congressmen could take as 'gifts:' tickets to Vegas shows, celebrity golf Pro-Ams, items that drew raised eyebrows from the ethics committee but no inquiries. Mann grew adept at hiding money, using middlemen, opening accounts all over the world. For years, the relationship grew until the amount of money exchanging hands became staggering. In return, Congress stayed out of CMM's affairs. Special committees dissolved. Allegations dropped. Price-fixing in agriculture didn't have the same sizzle as steroids in Major League baseball or obscenities in Hollywood, and so it wasn't difficult to turn a blind eye. A blind eye that came with a seven-figure price tag.

The relationship ended abruptly when the FBI snatched up Nichelle Spellman in a bribery sting. Mann was not aware of the Bureau's actions until after the fact. He tried to contact her on eleven separate occasions, but his calls went unanswered, unreturned. He needed her to remain silent. He needed to know she would take the fall, his name wouldn't come up, not when he had just been elected Speaker of the House. The FBI continued to build their case and there was talk of a Grand Jury, of testimony, of things being said 'on the record.'

On May 16 of that year, a week before the Grand Jury would hear Ms. Spellman's testimony, Nichelle's daughter Sadie was abducted directly out of her classroom. A man entered the school, telling the teacher he was from Nichelle's husband's office and Sadie needed to come with him right away. There was an emergency. The man seemed confident, articulate and unthreatening, and the teacher complied without hesitation. A week later, Nichelle pleaded the Fifth to every question the Grand Jury asked her. She was distraught but resolute; she was asked if she needed more time in light of her family's personal tragedy and she said no, this was her testimony, this was what she wanted on the record. The Grand Jury was stymied. Abe Mann's name never passed her lips.

One month later, an undercover Kansas police officer, along with Nichelle, her husband, and her daughter were all found dead in a snowy ditch near an abandoned airfield, shot at close range multiple times. The newspapers described it as a botched kidnapping hand-off, a sorry ending to a sad affair. The daughter's body had shown signs of assault. No suspect was ever arrested.

I put down the papers, turning the new information over in my mind.

It seems Abe Mann has grown comfortable ordering the deaths of people. Nichelle hadn't even talked, hadn't given him up, and he still wanted the loose ends tied, wanted the coffin lids closed so no one would have a change of heart or a wandering tongue at a later date.

How many times had he ordered executions besides the two I know of? How many bodies are buried deep in his congressional closet? Does he take pleasure from it, acting as God, acting as one who decides between life and death?

It seems I am more like my father than I thought.

At a table a few feet away, a man is eating by himself, obviously waiting on someone. His feet tap the floor nervously, and his eyes flit to the door every few seconds. Eventually, a harried woman comes in, two small boys in tow. I keep my head buried in the file, chewing methodically on my quarter-pounder, trying not to look up, even as the couple barks at each other.

'We said twelve-thirty. I've been here an hour.'

'You try packing up all their shit for a weekend with no help. None!'

'I tried calling your cell phone.'

'Well, maybe I was a little busy, did you ever think of that?'

'Well, maybe I'll bring them back an hour late on Monday.'

'Don't do me any favors.'

'Real nice, Amy. Real nice. Right in front of 'em.'

'Oh, don't you dare get self-righteous with me . . .'

After a few more exchanges, the woman storms out, leaving the father alone with the two boys. Each of them carries a backpack, and, on their faces, shame.

I finish my lunch and take the tray to the trashcan, dumping the contents and pushing the tray onto the shelf. The grease is still on my tongue, and even as I suck my large soda dry, it remains there, resistant and defiant.

When I step into the parking lot, it is impossible to avoid the small crowd gathered in a half-circle near my rental car. I don't want to meet any eyes, I just want to get to my car and drive away, but it is too late for that. They are looking at me, shaking their heads, wanting me to join in, wanting me to see what they see and feel the misery they feel.

The woman who dropped off her kids has stepped out of her minivan, but left the driver's door open, the engine idling.

'I didn't see it. It just darted in front of me.'

The brown dog lies on the ground in front of her van, his back legs broken, his eyes wild. He tries to get to his front feet but can't, and so lies back down, breathing rapidly, mustering the strength to try again, repeating the cycle over and over.

Try, fail, rest, try, fail, rest. Try. Fail.

I make my way past the courtyard of the La Fonda, past businessmen and women finishing their lunches, and head for the ground-floor hallway, the corridor to my room.

Then the world slows, the sound drops out, everything fades to a single image, like looking through a tunnel toward the light at the other end. A single image, as in-focus as anything I've ever seen in my life. A man is coming out of my room, a gun in his hand, backing out, fresh blood on his face, and his eyes meet mine. I recognize him, I *know* him. I haven't seen him in years, but I know him all right. I loaded his beer-truck, he introduced me to the dark Italian, he brought Cox into that textile mill. I always knew that he, Hap Blowenfeld, was a killer, that he had been recruited by Vespucci before me, that the beer-truck job must have been a cover for an assignment; and in that moment, that crystal clear moment in which we were seeing each other, I took in every detail about *this* Hap, the one in the present, the one carrying a brand new Beretta, the one who still weighs roughly a hundred and ninety pounds, the one who has a three-inch scar on his forehead that wasn't there before, the one who has Pooley's blood on his face.

And then, wham, everything speeds back to normal though it is all heightened, the colors somehow crisper, the smells stronger, and Hap doesn't hesitate. He levels his gun at me and fires a silenced bullet, but I am moving fast now like a leopard that has spotted a predator in the jungle bigger than he. I dart back toward the courtyard as the bullet slams into the wall just inches behind my head, and I know Hap won't follow me, he has been trained like me to blend in, but that isn't my concern, my concern is to walk as quickly and as normally as I can back through the lobby and out to my car, the Range Rover Pooley had waiting for me in the parking lot of the INN AT THE END OF THE TRAIL this morning, and maybe, just maybe I will not draw any stares, and maybe, just maybe I can spot that bastard driving off before he gets away clean.

I throw the car into gear and race around the building just in time to see a black Audi exiting onto San Francisco street, tires squealing as it passes from concrete to asphalt. Yes, finally, one fucking good thing in this terrible day, between that dog, that fucking dog with two broken legs trying to get to its feet after it careened off the front bumper of that haggard mother's mini-van and fucking Pooley, sticking around in Santa Fe when he should have been heading back East, but I told him to stay because I wanted more goddamn information, information I could have gotten myself, and I brought him into this life and because of me he's dead, poor fucking Pooley, dealt the worst fucking hands all his goddamn life.

I didn't have to see his body to know what had happened: Vespucci was a good fence and he had sniffed out the multiple assassins hired for this job and Hap had spotted me on Mann's trail because he would have been doing the same thing I was doing, trying to get inside the candidate's head, *make* the connection so he could *sever* the connection. And so he had seen me, and staked me, and he went into that room thinking it was me in there, but Pooley was waiting for me, and so got a bullet in his head when the door opened. If it wasn't that, then it was a version pretty damn close to that, and now Hap was widening the distance between us because he was in an Audi and I had cavalierly told Pooley to get me something bigger, an SUV, thinking I had all the time in the world to make my plans.

An hour passes before I realize the Audi is gone, and I am alone.

9

Darkness. Black darkness.

And pain.

I have checked into a nondescript hotel, and I am sitting on the bed in the darkness, listening to the occasional rumble of the big rigs as they make their way down Highway 84, and I am thinking.

Earlier, a local news channel mentioned the shooting at the La Fonda, and the dead man who had checked into the hotel as Jim Singleton, but they weren't sure of his identity. The police were investigating, but I knew the case would remain unsolved forever. The bullets in Pooley's body and in the corridor wall would be untraceable, the weapon had most likely been destroyed, and the man I knew as Hap Blowenfeld was probably far from Santa Fe, probably already on the road to Nevada, where Abe Mann was stopping next. They might have security camera footage of both Hap and me in the lobby of the building, but they will curse their luck that neither of our faces are recognizable, we both seem to be aware of the cameras and are always looking in the opposite direction.

Why had Hap tried to kill me? For the same reason I will put a bullet in both Miguel Cortega and him. Because the end game is the death of nominee Abe Mann at the convention, and we cannot afford to have anyone else fuck up our kill. Whoever hired us wanted three killers to make sure the assignment was done right, was done successfully, but it would be one man ultimately pulling the trigger. It is part of the job, a necessary hazard of the game we choose to play; when multiple killers are hired, multiple killings are assured.

But Hap hadn't killed me; he had killed a part of me, he had killed my only friend in this world, my brother, and for that he would pay with his life, Abe Mann or no Abe Mann.

Darkness. And pain. And Pooley.

After the Levine hit, after I killed the Boston bookie and all of his bodyguards, Vespucci asked for a meeting on the top of a parking garage near the water. The weather had taken a frigid turn, and snow collected on the ground in knee-high drifts, whitewashing all of Boston. On the exposed rooftop, the snow piled up unabated, and the wind was implacable as it whipped off the harbor's waters and slammed into us.

Vespucci was alone, bundled up in a thick parka, though he didn't wear a hat. He stood with hard eyes, glaring at me, treating the cold like it was just a nuisance, a fly to be swatted.

'What happened?' he spat at me as soon as I approached him.

'I severed the connection.'

'Severed!' His voice rose over the wind, the contempt unmistakable. 'It was a bloodbath! You killed seven of his men! You left a massacre behind you!'

'I completed my mission.'

'No, Columbus! No! You are mistaken. Your mission was to kill Richard Levine. Only Richard Levine!'

'I did what I had to do to assure the kill.'

He started to say something, then stopped, eyes boring into me. My face was red, but not from the wind stinging it. When he spoke again, his voice was heavy, dolorous.

'Columbus. You are not the right man for this line of work. It hurts me to say this. I believe this to be my fault. I did not . . . how do you say . . . counsel you as properly as I should have. I take responsibility.'

He stamped his feet, but he did not take his eyes off of me. I said nothing, waiting for him to finish what he came here to say.

'Your . . . rampage . . . has caused me some difficulty. The enormity of what you did forced the police to assign an entire task force to the investigation. And not only have the police increased their strength, but a few of the connected families in this city have also put out . . . um . . . what is it . . . feelers . . . to discover who it is that would do this to Levine and his men.'

His eyes softened. I think he saw in my face that I recognized the trouble I had caused him.

'I understand, now, Mr. Vespucci. I shouldn't have . . .'

'You shouldn't have continued to see Jacqueline Owens after I told you to stop.'

This caused my face to flush. I wasn't expecting him to bring Jake into this. How did he know?

'Ahh, yes. I know why you did what you did. I know these men discovered your girlfriend. And from there, could have discovered you. I warned you, Columbus. But you would not listen. Pah . . .' He spat on to the ground, like he was spitting my foolishness into the snow. 'So where does that bring us?'

'I'll make it right.'

He shook his head. 'I'm afraid it is too late for that. I wish you the best of luck.'

He started to reach inside his coat, and in an instant, I had a pistol up and pointed at his head. The speed of my draw startled him; I'm not sure what he was expecting, but I was ready. Even in my shame, I was ready.

He looked confused for a moment, then realized where his hand was, and what it must have looked like to me. Slowly, slowly, he pulled from his inside coat pocket a large manila envelope.

'Because of what you did, they will come looking for us. This is the last time we will see each other. I hope you understand.'

With that, he dropped the envelope into the snow and walked away toward the stairwell in the corner of the lot.

The envelope contained enough money for me to dump the apartment and move into an efficiency in Framingham, about thirty miles outside the city. The space was only about five hundred square feet; it had once been a cheap hotel, and the rooms had been converted by putting tiny refrigerators and a sink into the bathrooms. I had to buy a single burner to use as a stovetop, and it was furnished with a Murphy bed, a hard mattress that folded out of the wall.

Pooley moved in four days after I did. I spent a little money on a small car, a Honda, and picked him up at Waxham on the day he was released. He looked the same, gaunt and dishevelled, but somehow healthier. The last couple of years at Waxham had been good to him. He became something of a scrounger, partnered with a few guards, and created a large market for illicit goods inside the Juvey center. Subsequently, he bought himself a circle of protection from the bigger inmates, and was treated like a boss. He left the place with over five thousand dollars stored in a coffee can buried by a guard outside the walls of the place.

'I think my cell was bigger,' he said when I opened the door to my apartment.

'It probably was.'

'You have any beer?'

'Check the fridge.'

He found a bottle and popped it open, then took a long pull. My only piece of furniture was a lopsided couch I bought at a yard sale. Pooley plopped down on it while I sat on the floor, using one of the walls for a backrest.

'It's good to see you.'

'You look good. You look good.'

We sat for a minute, instantly comfortable, slipping back into our empathy for each other like putting on old jackets. I told him everything, everything I hadn't put into letters, starting with Jake mistaking me for her brother and ending with Vespucci's dismissal of me on the rooftop of the parking garage. He peppered me with questions as I went, asking for details, for clarifications, for specifics. He homed in on Vespucci's role in my life, and fired the inquiries like a machine gun. How much did he charge? How did he get his information? How did he meet his contacts? How many hit men worked for him? Did he do the background research on his own or did he have subordinates? How did he dress? How did he carry himself?

I tried to answer the ones I knew and guessed at the ones I didn't. Pooley was entirely nonjudgmental throughout; in fact, he was fascinated. He asked to see my weapons, and I showed him the pistols, how the racking chamber worked, how to load a clip, how to conceal it on my body.

'I could do it,' he finally said after we had fallen silent for a while, listening to the heavy motor of a snowplow rumbling down the street.

'I don't know, Pooley. Killing a target—'

'No, not the killing part. I don't have the stomach for it. But I could be your fence. Do what Vespucci did.'

My wheels were turning before he finished his sentence. 'How would you go about—?'

'I don't know. Start from scratch, I guess.'

'I'm not sure—'

'I was pretty damned resourceful at Waxham, Columbus.' He let the name out slowly, like his voice was thick with it, a smile on his face. In fact, from that point on, he never called me by my real name. Only the name Vespucci had given to me, my killing name. He continued, 'I'm serious. I am detailed, I blend in, I survive. I negotiated Juvey like a chameleon, all five-foot-nine of me; I was practically running the place before my release. I can get you the details you need to continue doing what you do. I'll pick up where Vespucci left off. I'll be better than him.'

'Where would you even begin to make contacts? It's not a field that invites newcomers. "Hey, you look trustworthy. Wanna kill someone for me?" '

'You let me worry about that.'

'I can't. I'll be worried too.'

'Whatever. Just give me six months. Between what you have and what I have, we don't have to earn another dime for at least a year. If it works, great. If it doesn't, we'll have plenty of time to call it off. Start flipping burgers or packing beer trucks or whatever else it is Waxham graduates do.'

I didn't say anything for a long time. Just pulled on my beer, my back against the wall, tossing it around in my mind. Finally, I looked over at him. He was grinning, his eyes shining.

'You sure you want to go down this road?'

'As sure as you were when you dropped that sewing machine on Cox's fucking head.'

I reached my hand over so we could clink our bottles together. 'Then let's do it.'

Three weeks later, they came for me.

'Three men just stepped out of a Mercedes.'

'What?'

Pooley was sitting on the sofa, his neck craned, shielding his eyes from the sunlight as he peeked out the small window. He just happened to be looking out at exactly the right time.

'They're splitting up, one out front, one heading to the steps, one moving toward the back. Black guys in suits.'

Black guys. Suits. Mercedes. Three things that didn't add up for this dilapidated efficiency in Framingham; three things that might as well have been a warning light on top of a lighthouse tower.

I didn't need any further information. In an instant, I was up and throwing open the case that held my weaponry. Five more seconds and I had two clips popped in place, Glocks double-fisted, racked and ready. Pooley scrambled off the sofa and I tossed him two empty clips. Like lightning, he had a shell-case open and was popping bullets into the clips as though he had been doing it all his life. I would have stopped to smile, appreciate the way his fingers maneuvered the bullets into place like a piano virtuoso working the keys, but I was all business now.

I crept up to the apartment door, and crouched beside it, then brought one of my guns to the center of the door, holding it out so the barrel pointed at the wood. Pooley lay down and put his head on the carpet so he could look through the small space separating the bottom of the door from the baseboard. A shadow crossed through the sliver of light in the hallway, and then he spotted two burgundy dress shoes approaching the door.

Pooley didn't hesitate, he nodded his head, giving me the signal to shoot, and I pulled the trigger seven times, blowing holes through the wood, the smell of gunpowder and smoke and blood immediately redolent in my nostrils.

I swung the door open and leaped into the hallway, over the bullet-riddled body of the black man who had come to kill me. He stared vacantly at the ceiling, a look on his face . . . Surprise? Confusion? I didn't stop to puzzle over it, but headed down the corridor for the stairwell that led to the alley behind the building.

A second black man was rushing up the steps just as I reached the landing, and he fired first, catching me in my right shoulder and spinning me backward, knocking me off my feet. He came up to finish me but made the mistake of pausing for a moment over my slumped body. Pooley shot him in the head, at close range, a fountain of red mist spraying the wall and splattering my face like I had showered in blood. He hadn't figured on me having company, hadn't bothered to scout me, to find out if I had any surprises waiting for him. In fact, the amateurish way these shooters had already botched this contract made me think Vespucci might not have sent them. Or if he had been forced to give me up, he maybe held out, did me a favor, gave me one last professional nod. If he had been forced to hire some guys to go after me – if the connected families in Boston had gotten to that olive-skinned Italian – well, at least he sent some minor-league hitters to the plate and gave me a fighting chance.

I kicked in the door on a first floor apartment where I knew the tenant, an electrician, worked on weekdays and wouldn't be home. His apartment had a window facing the front of the building, and Pooley and I squatted next to it to take a look at the third shooter, who was checking his watch, stamping his feet in the cold, and looking impatiently up to my window with increasing concern.

Pooley popped the clip from my Glock, reloaded it, racked it, and placed it in my good hand. Then he cracked the window half an inch, just enough for me to wedge in the barrel of my gun. The third shooter pulled out a piece of paper from the inside pocket of his jacket, checked the address, checked his watch, checked the address again, furrowed his brow, and then . . . wham . . . my first and only shot caught him in the center of his head, shattering his nose and caving in the front of his face. He stuttered backwards, and then dropped onto the snow-covered asphalt.

Pooley and I quickly gathered my gear, everything we could fit into one large trash bag, and headed into the parking lot for my car. The third shooter still lay dead in the snow, his blood congealed like a halo around his head. The building was tucked into a small street off the main highway, where traffic was nonexistent this time of day. Luck was with us, no one had driven into the lot in the five minutes it had taken us to get up to my apartment and gather our possessions.

I looked at the dead body, and then noticed the paper still clutched in his hand, the slip he had pulled from his inside jacket pocket.

'Let's go, Columbus. Now, before our luck changes.'

Pooley was right, I should have jumped behind the wheel of the Escort and gotten us out of there, but I wanted to know if that paper had something on it, some clue that would tell me who was trying to kill me and how I could stop it from happening again. I was only being cautious.

I grabbed the paper and sure enough, scrawled in pencil in a barely legible hand was my address here in Framingham, the target's residence, nothing more. At least I thought there was nothing more until I flipped it over.

Scribbled on the other side in that same masculine hand was another address.

Pooley must have seen the color drain from my face. 'What is it?'

'They have Jake's address.'

I didn't talk. I had the Escort's accelerator mashed to the floorboard, ripping up the highway toward Boston like a missile locked on its target. I was racing blindly, ignoring the increasing amount of pain in my shoulder, my mind focused on one thing, only one thing: getting to Jake. I wouldn't have slowed if God himself had tried to stop me.

'We don't know if they went to her first.'

I didn't answer, and Pooley gave up trying to talk to me. He just sagged back into his chair like the effort was too much.

I blitzed the car into Boston, and flew through intersection after intersection until finally I screeched to a stop outside of her apartment building. I left the car in the street double-parked, not bothering to look for a parking place.

'Columbus! Columbus! Take it easy, for Chrissakes. Do you know how you look? Like a maniac . . .' Pooley was shouting at me but the words weren't registering as I took the steps on her stoop two at a time. I didn't bother to buzz for entry; I just broke the glass door with my fist and twisted the latch from the inside, my hand sticky with blood. I flew up two flights of stairs before reaching her door.

I knocked with my bloody fist; I found I couldn't raise my good hand, the bullet in my shoulder had rendered it useless. Where was she? Oh, God, please tell me they didn't . . . I knocked again, pounded, bam, bam, bam, bam, bam, over and over and over. Please tell me they didn't touch her. Please tell me they didn't. Vespucci told me to stop seeing her and I did, I stopped, I left town without saying good-bye, I didn't phone her, I didn't send her a letter, I was willing to let it die, but not like this, bam, bam, bam, bam, not like this, bam, bam, bam . . .

And then the door opened. Jake's face filled the entryway, Jake's beautiful face, my god, she looked fine, healthy, unharmed, untouched, surprised to see me, about to be angry, but then she saw the blood on my shirt, on my hand . . .

'What happened to you?'

She pulled me inside the apartment, her face a picture of concern. I was overwhelmed with relief, couldn't open my mouth.

She spoke instead, 'I've been so worried. For weeks, not a word, not a call. I didn't know what I did to hurt you. I love you so much, I just couldn't understand it.'

She was unbuttoning my shirt, and she gasped when she saw the wound to my shoulder. She didn't think, just immediately darted to the kitchen and snatched up a rag, turned on the faucet and let the water run warm.

I knew then I would have to do the hardest thing I had ever done, harder than killing a man. To end this, to make sure this was finished, to make sure they would never come for her, I couldn't just run away and leave her behind.

She came back, holding the wet cloth, and began to clean my wound, but I grabbed her by the wrist and pushed her back.

'You have to move.'

'What?'

'You have to get out of here. Get your things, whatever you can carry with you in the next five minutes and get out of here. Go somewhere, anywhere, but get out of Boston and don't come back.'

'What are you talking about?'

'Just do it!'

My voice must have been like a slap to her face, tears sprung to her eyes.

'I don't understand!'

'I'm a bad man, Jake! I'm worse than bad. I'm a goddamn nightmare. You don't know a fucking thing about me.'

'What, what . . .' she sputtered.

'I never fucking loved you. I've been using you as a fuck rag. Something to sleep with to get my mind off of all the other shit in my life.'

'What are you talking about?' Her voice was barely a whisper, a squeak as the tears spilled out and soaked her mouth.

'You think I give a shit about you? You think I haven't been fucking twenty other girls just like you?'

'What are you talking about?' she said softer, her voice breaking.

'Now, I've gone and done it too. There are people out there who want to hurt you, Jake. People I'm involved with. I fucking gave them your address and now they want to see your ass for themselves. See if you're as ripe as I said you were.'

She took a step back, sobbing . . .

'I can't stop them from coming Jake. And they are coming. I don't know why I'm even telling you. I guess I just wanted to give you a sporting chance to get out of here.'

'I don't understand . . .'

'I don't give a shit if you understand or not. You don't leave today, then they come for you.'

'I love you,' she said weakly.

'You gotta leave right now.'

'But I love you!' she screamed, her voice finding a strength that surprised me. 'I don't know what you're talking about, but this isn't you. I don't know who this is, but this isn't you. If you'll tell me what happened, maybe I can—'

And right then I struck her, my bloody fist catching her in the jaw and cracking her cheek, knocking her down to the floor.

'Noooooooo . . .' she started to moan.

I kicked her then, hard, in the stomach. I heard my voice coming out of my throat, disconnected from my body. 'This is everything you need to know Jake. I'm not fucking around. The men I work with, this'll just be the warm-up session. If you're not out of Boston in the next ten minutes, they will be here themselves, do you understand?'

'Whyyyyyyyy . . .' she was whimpering now, the breath knocked out of her.

'Ten minutes. And you forget everything about me. You forget you even knew my name. And if I ever see you again, it'll be the last thing you see. I promise you that.'

I threw the wet rag at her face, spun, and marched out the door, leaving her crumpled frame sobbing on the floor.

Pooley and I watched silently from a nearby alley as Jake limped to her car, threw in a pillowcase filled with possessions, turned it around in the street, and drove away.

I never saw her again.

10

Violence defines all men. At some point in life's wheel, men are tested. A spanking from dad's belt, a slap across the face, trading blows outside a bar, a broken nose, a bloody mouth, a black eye, a gun pointed in the face, a knife jabbed underneath the ribs. A man's reaction to violence is imprinted upon him like words on a page. He might cower, or shy away, or watch unflinching. He might rise up, or be impassioned, or be aroused. Or he might become violent himself.

And what is the antithesis of violence? Love? Kindness? And can both of these opposites, kindness and violence, Cain and Abel, reside in equal parts in one man? Or does one side battle the other like opposing armies in a long-standing war? And if so, which is the strongest?

I make my way to Nevada, wounded, though not physically, and fatigued. I am no longer on the trail of the man at the top of the page, not yet at least. I am after a different quarry. I am hunting hunters now.

Congressman Abe Mann will not be speaking in Las Vegas, wary of its unseemliness to many voters, conscious of how being photographed in the American Mecca of gambling and money and prostitution will turn off the masses. Rather, he will be making only one stop in Nevada, in the capital, Carson City, before he moves north to Washington state. His press materials will only vaguely mention Nevada, and the dinner in the capital is private and barred from the press.

I do not know Miguel Cortega's modus operandi, but I am confident Hap Blowenfeld will be shadowing the congressman's movements. For that reason, though not that reason alone, Hap will be the first to die.

I drive into Vegas. A man I know lives here; I hesitate to call him a friend. Pooley's job is . . . was . . . to know other middlemen, men looking for contractors to hire for their missions. Often, I meet directly with these merchants, like with Archibald Grant in the warehouse when he handed me the briefcase that changed my life. The middlemen like to eyeball me, see me for themselves, measure me, the way old ladies pick up and shake cantaloupes in the produce section of the grocery. Pooley always said five minutes in a room with me would be enough to shatter any illusions of cheating me, of holding back anything but my promised fee. I hope that is still true.

I drive down Flamingo, heading west toward Summerlin, until I reach a neighborhood inappropriately named 'Wooded Acres.' Every house is built exactly the same way, a cookie-cutter paradise, a sea of beige stucco and rusty Spanish tile. Each house is adorned with a lawn the size of a postage stamp. The only 'woods' in the neighborhood are the scrawny palm trees inconsistently spotting the yards.

The nice thing about Vegas suburbs is that discretion is part of the milieu, built into the environment. Everyone seems to walk around with eyes downcast, avoiding direct contact with neighbors. It's like the heat and the barrenness of the landscape have infected the hearts of those who live in the desert. Or maybe too many people are involved in too many impolite occupations.

I park my car at the curb outside of a one-story house marked by the number 506. I've been here before, twice actually, under different circumstances. But this time is a first for me. This time, I'm looking for help.

The door opens before I knock, and a small Indian man fills the void. He is dark, balding, and has ears too big for his face. Although he is small, he is compact, muscular, like a pit bull. His name is Max, and his voice is raspy.

'Columbus . . .'

'Max.'

'Mr. Ryan is not expecting you.'

'I need his help.'

This causes Max to pause, blink a few times involuntarily. He waits for more.

'Can I come in?'

'Depends on the kind of help you're looking for, I s'pose.'

'My fence is dead.'

That's all Max needs to hear. He opens the door further and I step inside the foyer. Immediately, two large men frisk me, each with the same dark skin as Max. They could be his sons, or nephews, as they have the same balding pattern on top of their heads. I am directed to a chair next to the door, and I take a seat and wait. The two men stay on my right and left as Max heads away, bare feet shuffling silently over the marble floor. I keep my gaze steady on a spot on the wall five feet away. It is humbling asking a man for help, and I want the right measure of supplication on my face when I greet him.

He makes me wait, a signal he is the person in power in this situation. He wants me to know he recognizes the advantage. But I don't fidget, or cough, or straighten my legs. I just sit in the chair and stare steadily at that spot on the wall. My two bookends want to speak to me, are looking for an opening to chat me up, but I give them nothing. After half an hour, Max returns to the foyer. 'Mr. Ryan will see you in his office.'

A large window overlooking an immaculately landscaped back yard frames the office. A half-clothed woman reclines on a leather sofa pushed up against one wall; I cannot tell if she is awake, asleep, or bored. Ryan sits in a chair, watching a flat-screen television mounted on the wall above the girl. The volume is off, but the screen is alive with graphics showing what the markets are doing all over the world. He is wearing only a swimsuit, though he is not wet.

'How can I help you?' he says without taking his eyes off the screen.

'Pooley is dead.'

'So Max tells me.'

'I'm looking for one thing.'

'Yes?'

'Information.'

'What are you willing to exchange for this one thing?'

'I'll owe you a favor.'

For the first time, Ryan shifts his eyes to me and I feel the full weight of his stare. He measures me, considering. The girl on the sofa stirs, but I don't look, don't drop my eyes; rather I hold Ryan's eyes steadily, like they are connected to mine by a string. He is a man who deals in commodities, and I am dangling a big carrot.

'I take it the information is difficult to come by, considering the payment you're offering.'

'I don't offer it lightly.'

'I understand. What do you need to know?'

'In Carson City, a bag man is going to be looking to dispose of and replace a Beretta 92F nine-millimeter handgun. I need to know the supplier he will approach to make the exchange.'

He tosses these words over in his mind, calculating.

'You got a beef with this bag man?'

'Like I said, Pooley is dead.'

'I see.'

He moves over to the sofa and pats the girl on her exposed hip. Without speaking, she gets up, stretches, and heads out of the room, long legs cutting a swath in front of me until she is gone. He takes her forfeited spot on the couch and sits down heavily, facing me.

'Now I understand. It is not that the information is difficult. It is that the information would be imprudent for me to give.'

'I find that prudence is relative in our line of work.'

This forces a dry laugh from him. 'I agree with you. Here are my terms. Instead of owing me a favor, I wish you to work for me when your current assignment is finished. Permanently. I will be your new fence.'

'With what arrangement?'

'The same you had with Pooley. No more.'

'Why?'

'I've been looking to downsize, and you are what the Russians refer to in this business as a Silver Bear. Have you heard this term?'

I shake my head.

'You've never defaulted on a job. You take a full slate without resting, and you fetch top dollar on the open market. A Silver Bear. I can carry you as my only partner and I'll make more than I've ever made in my life. And I've made quite a bit.'

'You caught me off guard.'

'Well, to use your words, I don't offer it lightly.'

'Then I'll make you this promise. In exchange for the name of this supplier, I will agree to *consider* partnering with you. I don't think you can expect me to give you more than that.'

Ryan smiles broadly. 'It would be imprudent.'

I join him with a smile of my own as respect passes between us like we're exchanging currency.

'And you wouldn't be a Silver Bear if you answered me any other way.'

'You're probably right.'

He stands and folds his arms across his chest.

'Okay, Columbus. I agree to your revised terms. Go to a pay phone on the corner of Desert Inn Road and Paradise. There's a strip mall there with a phone on the north end of it, outside a 7-Eleven. I'll have the name for you by the time you get there.'

Carson City is an uninteresting capital located where Interstates 50 and 395 collide. It is a tiny town, its only purpose to serve its neighbors Reno and Lake Tahoe and the skiers who frequent Squaw Valley and Diamond Peak and Heavenly. It looks like an afterthought, like a little brother making do with the family's hand-me-down clothes. The buildings are old and pitiful.

I take the Interstate into town and head south, past a mall and a cemetery, until I find the exit for Colorado Street. I'm looking for an industrial park, a concrete slab with no windows, one of those blights on the landscape that looks like it was thrown into place with no more planning than a child scattering his blocks. This one isn't hard to find; the man on the other end of the pay phone in Vegas gave me impeccable directions.

I find a discreet parking lot and roll my beige sedan to a stop. Before I left Vegas, I jettisoned the SUV at McCarran and rented a new car, a Taurus. Through my windshield, I have a view of the only door on the outside of the industrial building, a steel door, solid, with an electronic keypad affixed to the adjacent wall. As an assassin, I have learned about strike moments, about vulnerability, about timing. A fortified target is the most difficult to take down, like Richard Levine holed up in his mansion. A supplier like the one I wish to speak to, like the one I am currently waiting to see, will work out of a bunker, well protected, well guarded, difficult to assault. Which is why I will not attempt to enter the industrial building, the outside of which is just a façade for a fortress. Rather, I'll lie in wait for as long as it takes.

A woman wearing a skullcap and wire-framed glasses emerges from behind the door several hours later. There is only one car in the parking lot, a vintage Mustang painted blue. She climbs inside, pulls the car out of the parking lot, and heads northwest, toward the mountains. She made a mistake choosing a flashy car; it's as easy to follow as if it had a red light on top. I don't know if she is going home, or meeting someone, or stopping at a grocery store, but it doesn't matter; at some point this evening she will be alone, and I will be ready.

It doesn't take long. The woman in the skullcap pulls into a Caribou Coffee parking lot, cuts her engine and steps out of the car to go inside. Her guard is down; my guess is she hasn't been in the supplier business long and has yet to understand the need for caution. When she exits the place holding a paper cup emitting steam, I am lying in wait.

'Tara?'

She jumps, startled, then searches my face, looking for recognition. 'Yes?'

'I need you to come with me.'

A thousand thoughts sweep like storm clouds across her face, all of them dark. I see her eyes dart to the coffee in her right hand, the car keys in her left, and then back to me, sizing me up.

'I suppose you'll be ready if I try to burn you or put these keys in your face?'

'Yes.'

'Is this about some business I did?'

'Do you want to have this conversation in a parking lot?'

She looks at me, processing the question, and then shakes her head. 'What about my car?'

'You should think about driving something less colorful.'

Hap is less than a mile away. He is planning on meeting Tara in thirty minutes to make the exchange, a new gun for old money. He doesn't realize I will be the one meeting him, but that doesn't make him any less of a threat. Assassins are wary by nature, distrustful by training. He might've picked up on something in her voice, a slight rise in inflection letting him know this call was being made under duress, that there was literally a gun to her head. She might have slipped him a code word in the conversation, something agreed upon at an earlier date, a word that is seemingly innocuous, but would signal the true nature of the night's exchange. I think she played it perfectly, innocently, but I'm not Hap on the other end of the line, and I'm not about to approach this confrontation lightly.

I have chosen the cemetery for the exchange, the place I passed on the way to Tara's office. It is after midnight and darker than I expected; the moon is only a fingernail scratching at the night sky. I have been here for hours, adjusting my eyes to the darkness. Not much of an advantage, but sometimes you only need the scales to tip the slightest in your favor to make your kill. I'm not worried about Tara trying to contact Hap and let him know about the trap; she won't be doing much talking for at least a month after what I did to her.

The cemetery is colder at night than I anticipated; the proximity to the mountains brings in a chill wind which seems to permeate right into my skin. The grave markers are small and spread out in neat rows, offering little protection from the breeze. I crouch on the cold earth, my back to a stone marker that reads: MICHAEL MATHESON, 1970–1979, as I watch the front entrance warily, two pistols cocked and loaded, folded into my lap. Hap has lived a few years longer than the boy on whose grave I sit, but I plan on having him join Michael Matheson tonight.

What I don't plan on, what I haven't foreseen, is that Hap is working this job as a tandem sweep. I know from Pooley that three shooters were hired to take out Abe Mann at his party's convention in a little less than a month. What I don't know, not for the next two minutes at least, is that two of them – Miguel Cortega and Hap Blowenfeld – are working this job together.

I am the odd man out, it seems.

II

I am bleeding in a cemetery, a fitting place, as though the land itself is beckoning to cover me up like it has so many others. I have two holes in me, one where the bullet entered my side and shattered my rib, and a second where it exited my back. Pools of gore are soaking my shirt and I'll admit I'm a little worried about the blood loss. I am not afraid I will die from this wound, not yet at least, but I am concerned about losing consciousness before I get a chance to take out the second shooter. I'm pretty sure I dropped one of them, at least I think I did. Fuck, I don't know for sure. I am suddenly very tired, like my eyes are filled with sand.

This isn't the first time I've been shot while working a job.

It was my seventh assignment with Pooley. We had settled into a comfortable rhythm; he proved intuitive at setting up a network of contacts and contracts, and resourceful at finding the information I needed to execute my job. He was right. He *was* a natural. He had quickly surpassed Vespucci in every aspect; he had a hunter's eye and a survivor's cleverness – Waxham had given him both – and he was much to credit for our early success.

One client was particularly impressed. I had killed for her recently – a New York job – a Wall Street trader who must've bought when he should've sold. The man had hired a private security firm for protection, but they were sloppy and unprofessional.

Pooley showed up a few weeks after the mark was found in pieces scattered across the George Washington Bridge.

'That job was a big one, Columbus. Our client . . . she's a whale amongst fishes . . . a leading player on the acquiring market.'

'Good . . . I don't want you to have to work so hard.'

He smiled. 'I was thinking I might take a trip. Get out and see the world.'

'You deserve a break.'

'I'm not going on vacation. This is a business trip.'

'Where to?'

'Italy.'

I looked at him skeptically.

'I told you . . . that last client was impressed. She wants to hire you again. Immediately.'

'The mark is overseas?'

'Yeah. I need a month to put the file together. Then you have six weeks to do what you do. She has a specific date she wants you to make the kill. June sixth. In the dead of night.'

'She'll pay for the specificity?'

'It's taken care of.'

I used the four weeks to get my mind right, as Vespucci had taught me. I fell into a routine; there was comfort in rigidity. I worked out hard, running five miles in the mornings, then several hours reading, flipping back and forth between contemporaries and classics: Wolfe and Mailer and Updike and Steinbeck and Maugham and Hemingway. Then a light meal followed by a sparring session at a boxing gym on the south side where everyone paid cash and nobody asked questions. Dinner was at home and I usually watched the news. Then bed. Every day the same. Comfort in rigidity. And I didn't have to think about Jake. I did not want to think about Jake.

Pooley handed me a brown manila envelope, our hellos and how-ya-beens out of the way.

'How was it?'

Pooley shrugged. 'They got a fucked-up way of doin' things over there. They don't like strangers unless they're throwing money around. And even then, they pretty much don't like 'em. But the food was good.'

'You get what you need?'

'It's all there. Our client had some pull.'

'You have any suspicions?'

Pooley shook his head. 'Naah . . . it's no walk in the park because of the specific time she wants it done, but it's nothing you can't handle.'

'I'm going to be in the visitor's dugout.'

'That's true. No home-field advantage.'

'All right, then. Thanks, Pooley. It's good to see you.'

'Good to see you, too, Columbus.'

The name at the top of the page was Gianni Cortino. He was fifty-two years old and currently splitting time between Rome and a coastal town named Positano. He was in the real estate business, but it appeared he had his thumb in a lot of pies: utilities, hotels, restaurants. He was a wealthy man; his net worth was counted in hundreds of millions.

Pooley had done his homework. Like many rich men, Cortino was tight-fisted with his wallet, like he had such a devilish time acquiring the money, it pained him to let any of it escape. His vice was cigars: Cuban Cohibas. He was devoted to his wife, his two sons, and his first grandchild, a boy, Bruno, born just eleven months previous. There had been whiffs of a scandal involving Cortino and a socialist politician in Florence, but the rumors turned out to be planted by an investment rival. As far as Pooley could tell, Cortino was free from graft. No whores, no gambling, no illicit goods, just a successful man in a country that is leery of success.

He also had a bodyguard.

The guard's name was Stephano Gorgio. Gorgio had spent thirteen years in the Italian special forces, mountain division, and had subsequently hired out as a mercenary in the Serbian war in Yugoslavia. His uncle was an early business partner to Cortino, and the two met after Gorgio returned to Italy. He made a proposal to Cortino to come on as his private bodyguard, and Cortino fired the security company he had been using and shook hands with Stephano. They had been together seven years.

Gorgio had two bullets in his shoulder, taken when the same investment rival who tried to smear Cortino also tried to kill him. Instead, the rival was choked to death bare-handed by Gorgio, bullets in the shoulder notwithstanding.

In the file were pages and pages of details, attempts at finding patterns in Cortino's life. Did he eat at the same restaurant every day? Did he use the same route to get to work? Did he travel from Rome to Positano at a certain time each month? Use the same roads? Take the same car? The train? There is comfort in rigidity. But there is also death in it.

I arrived in Rome at 3 P.M. and took a taxi to my hotel, a small one in the middle of the city, the Hotel Mascagni. It was owned by Cortino, one of the first he acquired after he came to Rome with a bit of an inheritance. While he had bought and sold and traded many properties in the twenty years he had been acquiring his fortune, he kept this one throughout. I wasn't sure what clue it would give me about the man, what it would do to help me realize the connection so I could sever the connection, but it was my first tangible piece of the man I came to kill.

The hotel contained only fourteen rooms on six floors and an old two-person elevator built into the tiny lobby. It had a bar and a restaurant – together the size of an American living room – and a small staff who nodded and bowed and gesticulated regularly. The building resonated warmth, the same warmth I got from reading Cortino's file, and I wondered if it was a mistake staying here. I was searching for evil to exploit in the man, and so far I found only charity and kindness.

I took the first two weeks to familiarize myself with the city, not as a tourist would, but as a rich businessman might. I avoided the ancients: the colosseum, the pantheon, the

Vatican, instead concentrating on the busy commercial streets named after months: Settembre, Novembre. I ate at restaurants I knew Cortino haunted, places specializing in seafood and pasta, but managed to avoid seeing him until I set my foundation, until I began to think like a local, establish my roots.

The third week I took a train from Rome to Naples and then hired a car to take me from Naples to Positano. I traveled the way Cortino did – although it was rare and inconvenient for such a wealthy man to travel by rail and car between the cities, Cortino lived as he did when he had no money. I imagine it was a way for him to remind himself of the struggle, that if he lost touch with his rise, he'd give way to his fall. It was a trait I admired.

The train was clean and comfortable and not at all unpleasant, a mixture of tourists and natives on their way to the coast. The station in Naples was the opposite, a dirty latrine in a bathroom town. Dark-faced con men looked for gullible tourists, but they only glanced my way before homing in on easier prey.

A driver took me to Positano in a white Mercedes van, following the winding, narrow road down the coastline. His English was limited and I was glad; I didn't feel like chatting. I knew Cortino lived high up on the hill overlooking the city, and with a population of less than 4,000, he would be a well-known figure in the town. I had read in the file that Positano was built into the side of a hill feeding down to the sea, but I wasn't prepared for the reality. Positano is a vertical city; the buildings seem to sit one on top of another as they move straight up a steep gradient, like a grocer's shelf that allows you to see the front of everything you're buying. Red and pink and yellow and white and peach and tan, the buildings cut into the green foliage like they are part of the mountain, only stopping when they reach the sky or the sea.

Tourists were everywhere. Fat Germans with fanny packs jostled each other as they cruised from shop to shop while Vespas plunged down the streets like a swarm of gnats, everyone and everything heading in one direction . . . down to the ocean. I loved the place. I loved the order of it and the simplicity of it and the singular logic of it; the church bells and the black sand and the quaint shops and the narrow alleys and the coffee makers and the gelato makers and the pasta makers and I was pleased I would kill Cortino here. Not in the bustle of Rome, where it would be infinitely easier to get away, not on the train or the station in Naples where the grime and the desperation were palpable. No, I was glad to be a part of this place, to create a new legend for a town that looked old and felt older. I don't know why I was happy, except to say for the first time, I had a strong feeling about a *place*, maybe my place in it. Like the job I did, the killing I did, the life I led up to this point were somehow reflected in this town, cut impossibly against the gradient, always on the precipice, always just a heavy rain from tumbling into the sea. There was something artistic about it, and infinitely sad. There was a warmth to it, not just a physical warmth but a psychological one, and if I couldn't have Jake, if I couldn't have someone who could cover me like a blanket, then maybe I could find security and understanding and promise and depth in this place, this impossible town.

I checked into a hotel positioned about halfway up the hill. My suite offered a deck overlooking the cliff and the sea and if I sat in the darkness inside my room, all I needed to do was lift my eyes to the top of the window to see Cortino's house, a salmon-colored mansion with high arched windows at the hill's summit. According to Pooley's file, he would be coming to town one week before I was to kill him.

I took the time to adjust to the place and have it adjust to me. I was just another *turista* in a town that fed itself on *turistas*, and I bled into the scene gradually, the way watercolors fade the longer the brush is applied to the canvas. I bought a straw fedora and wore it poorly; I lunched in the open-air cafés perched above the ocean; I milled through the souvenir shops and pressed my face to the glass of the pastry counters.

I took a boat to Capri – Newbury Street covering an island – and came back with a sunburn. I blended in, but never forgot why I was there.

'Would you like coffee, cappuccino, Coke?'

The waitress looked affable; she had pale blue eyes and tanned cheeks.

'Coffee . . . *grazie*.'

'*Prego*. Where are you from?'

'Los Angeles. United States.'

'It is my dream to go there. Very beautiful.'

'It is the dream of Americans to come here.'

'Ahh . . .' She looked down at the sea, a sight that had lost its magic for her long ago. 'I'll bring your coffee.'

I waited for her to return and greeted her with a smile. The place wasn't full. 'How many people live in Positano?'

'Four thousand, more or less.'

'Everyone knows each other?'

'Oh, yes.'

'Any Americans?'

'Yes . . . summer houses. An English couple too.'

'How much does a house cost here?'

'Depends on how high up you are . . . or how close to the beach.'

I sipped my coffee. She didn't look in a hurry to go anywhere else, so I pressed on. 'Like, say, that one up there.'

'The Cortinos. Wealthy family.'

'The house looks big.'

'It is. Five . . . how do you say . . . rooms for sleeping . . .'.

'Bedrooms?'

'Yes.' She smiled. 'My guess is . . . two million euros . . .'

I let out a low whistle.

'Yes, expensive. But they are nice family. They helped rebuild the church. Mrs Cortino . . . her legs . . . how is it . . . don't work. It is . . . much pity.'

'She uses a wheelchair?'

'Yes.'

'Must be difficult in this town.'

'Yes . . . but he takes care of her. Makes sure she still goes around.'

'That's very nice.'

'Yes.'

A couple of noisy Austrian tourists came in. She smiled, rolled her eyes, and went to help them find a table. I sipped my coffee, thinking.

His wife, crippled. In this town, it must be extremely difficult; the place wasn't exactly built wheelchair-friendly. None of this was in the file. Why did Pooley censor it? Did he think it would affect me? Was he concerned that after I had used my time to measure this man, I would find he was a good man, a man with no capacity for evil, with nothing to exploit?

I first saw Cortino and his bodyguard Gorgio a week later. He visited a church near my hotel, a stone edifice painted the same color as the cliff so it blended into the rock. The exterior was bleak, lacking the ornate iconography of most Catholic churches. I knew it was one of the first things he'd do when he returned to Positano; his file noted that he always walked to the church, lit two candles, and kneeled before the altar. For whom he lit the candles, I didn't know, maybe one for each of his deceased parents.

I sat at a nearby Mediterranean restaurant, eating prawns silently, careful not to attract attention. Cortino looked grave as he moved inside the church. Twenty minutes passed as I ate my seafood, waiting for him to emerge. When he exited, his face was transformed, beatific. This surprised me. Could a man's attitude really be improved so radically from the simple act of kneeling? What had he found in there? What words had his lips whispered? I discovered I was staring at his peaceful face, fascinated, and when my gaze flicked to the bodyguard, Stefano Gorgio, the man was eyeing me.

What a goddamn mistake. I looked past the bodyguard, through him, like I was just another daft tourist enjoying a taste of local scenery. This must've satisfied him, because Gorgio shuffled after his boss, helping him into a parked Mercedes two-seater. I didn't lift my eyes again; I just picked at my shrimp until I heard the car disappear around the corner, heading down the hill. Fuck. Gorgio was good, a real professional, he would certainly remember seeing me if I popped up near his boss's home.

I went back to my hotel room and turned off the lights, pissed . . . pissed at myself, pissed at the missing information from the file, pissed that everything I learned about Cortino made me . . . what? Envious? Of him? Of this life?

It hit me like a grease fire. Is that what I would exploit? My own jealousy? Not evil in him but evil in me? It spread out before me like a Polaroid coming into focus. How does an assassin bring down a good man? He summons up his own iniquity; he measures himself against the man and feeds on the distance he falls short. And where would that road lead, when there was no connection to sever? What price would I pay for focusing my hate on myself?

I holed up in the hotel and the few restaurants on my side of the hill until June 6 arrived, the day I was supposed to put a bullet in Gianni Cortino. That morning, I rented a scooter from a tourist trap near the main town center, entering when the place was most crowded. I was just one more American tourist in a sea of Anglo faces.

I headed down the single town road and then up the hill, black helmet obscuring my face. I wanted to take a peek at Cortino's house from the street, so I slowly motored by, using my peripheral vision to take measure of the place. Fortunately, there was no room for anything remotely resembling a yard. The house's roof was level with the street, stone steps led down from the street to the front door. There was no gate, no security cameras. Positano was too quiet and peaceful and small and remote to worry about crime, an illusion I would shatter by sunrise tomorrow. From Pooley's file I knew a side door was accessible from below; my partner believed the side door was most likely Stefano Gorgio's private room. I motored on, just one of a thousand scooters passing by that day.

At two in the morning, I checked out of the hotel, carrying only a small backpack. I explained that I had a car waiting for me at the bottom of the hill and the night clerk had me sign the requisite papers before settling back down to read the French newspaper *Le Monde*. Since I had dressed all in black the last few days, he didn't notice anything unusual about the way I wore it now. I set out on foot, my pace quick. While Positano has a lot of things, it doesn't have an active nightlife. The street was deserted, the only sound an occasional dog barking.

It took me an hour to descend the hill and then climb the road leading to Cortino's house. One car rolled up behind me, but I pressed into the nearby foliage and it passed without slowing. When I reached the bend that included Cortino's house, I ducked to his side of the street and disappeared over the hedge separating his house from the road. Instead of using the stone steps to head to the front door, I slid along the vines to approach the side door from above, a maneuver that kept me from having to cross the bay windows lining the oceanside of the house.

The side door was cracked open. Not wide, but cracked enough for me to see the gap. Why? Was this the way Gorgio aerated his room, letting in the ocean breezes? I didn't think it likely, not for a bodyguard. Warning bells rang in my ears.

I moved to the door, listening carefully for a full minute, but I didn't hear a sound inside, no snoring, no breathing, nothing. I armed myself and discarded the backpack in the brush, held my breath, and pushed the door open a crack. The hinges didn't make a sound, thank God for that. No response. I ducked my head in and out of the room in a split second, just enough time for me to scan the room or draw fire. My eyes had long since adjusted to the darkness outside, so the dark room held no secrets.

The room was empty; a single queen-sized bed sat in its center, undisturbed. I crept in quietly, barely breathing, my senses alert like a trapped animal, listening for anything. The hairs on my arms stood up as though maybe they could pick up on vibrations in the air and shoot me a warning. Why was that door open? Why on *this* night? For the first time, I realized how nonchalantly I had approached this job. I had found nothing to hate about my target, nothing to exploit, and so had granted him a free pass, had woefully underestimated the difficulty of killing this man, had failed before I began. I vowed not to make that mistake again.

Cortino's bedroom was on the same side of the house. I made my way out of the room, gun leading the way. I didn't hate him before, but I hated him now. Hated him for giving me nothing to hate. A few more feet down the hallway, and I was standing outside the master bedroom. There was something in the air now, something pungent, but I couldn't place the smell.

I tested the door and found it unlatched. I pushed into the room, slowly, carefully, soundlessly.

The odor of blood hit me flush in the face. There were two dead bodies in the bed, Cortino and his crippled wife propped up against the headrest, staring back at me with hollow eyes. Against the far wall slumped a third dead body, Stefano Gorgio; most of his face simply wasn't there.

I had come to kill a man who was already dead.

It took me a second to process this when I heard a noise behind me. I spun to see a woman standing in the hallway, smiling, a gun drawn.

Fuck. She had a date she wanted the job done. June sixth. In the dead of night. She even paid for the specificity. And now she had the perfect fall guy delivered to her doorstep, a stranger holding a gun, another corpse she could leave behind. The police would have a field day.

'Pooley told me you were good,' she said. 'And right on time.'

With that, she shot me in the chest.

12

Twenty minutes have passed and I realize I am alone in the cemetery in Carson City, Nevada. Whether Hap Blowenfeld or Miguel Cortega are wounded or whether they think they'd have trouble taking me, they failed to finish the job. They will regret this decision.

I struggle to my knees and the pain in my side is almost unbearable. Using the dead boy's headstone for support, I work myself to my feet and peer around. Empty. The sky is lightening in the east; clouds like pink fingers hang low on the horizon. I need to get out of here.

I hobble toward the gate where I left my car, hoping, willing it to still be there. The sun rises above the horizon and a tombstone to my left catches my attention. It is speckled with red droplets; they catch the sun like gemstones set into a ring. I crane my neck around the marker, not wanting to lose any time but I have to look goddammit, I have to see what made blood splatter like paint across the marble tombstone. First I see a hand, immobile, on the ground, and then a torso, and finally an unfamiliar face, still breathing.

I move closer, cautiously, until I see clearly he has dropped his pistol and is clutching a wound in his abdomen, a gut shot, the worst way to go. Somehow, he has made it through the night and is still alive.

'Miguel Cortega?'

His eyes shift to meet mine, but he makes no effort to talk. His breathing is raspy, like air whistling through a pinched pipe. Now I see he's been hit twice, a slug in the stomach and one through his lung.

'You were working this job with Hap. Together.'

He doesn't reply.

'Where's he going next? Where's he supposed to make the kill?'

Cortega just stares at me, blankly, his pupils dilating. A little pink stream curls from the side of his mouth and spills out into two tendrils down his cheek.

He's got another hour to live, maybe more. I could put a bullet in him to put him out of his misery, but I don't feel merciful. Fuck him and fuck Hap.

I hobble away, the pain like a hot iron pressed to my side, and am fortunate to find my car, untouched, in the parking lot.

Thankfully, roadside gas stations have evolved into full-fledged grocery stores, and I find enough bandages and anti-bacterial cream to clean my wound until I can get to a proper pharmacy. The clerk gives me the requisite once-over, but the blue ink of his jailhouse tattoos tells me he isn't going to ask any questions or raise any eyebrows. I drive on until I find a Motel Six. I check the wound, dress it as properly as I can, turn off the light, collapse on the bed, and sleep for eighteen hours.

The road between Lake Tahoe and Seattle is dry and barren. The eastern side of Washington is a desert, and the miles roll by plain and indistinguishable. I can only make it about two hundred miles before my side throbs so badly it threatens my consciousness, but I don't mind falling behind schedule. The convention is still over a week away, and Abe Mann is planning to dawdle in Seattle and Portland to rest up for the big event. He isn't scheduled to show up until the penultimate evening when he 'sneaks' on stage to give a kiss to his wife after her keynote speech. This is supposed to be a surprise but is as pre-planned, practiced, and scripted as a Broadway show. He isn't supposed to return to the stage until the final night, when he makes the most important speech of his political career. What *is* unscripted, what will be a real surprise, is he won't be returning to the stage at all.

I check into an Economy Inn in Walla Walla, Washington. It is on a strip with four other hotels just like it, way-stations for the tired and dispossessed. On the television, Mann stands with the Port of Seattle spread out behind him, thousands of containers stacked like a multicolored maze serving as his backdrop. He's talking about the need for tighter port security and stronger counter-terrorism measures and tougher restrictions on containers and more dollars invested to secure our borders. His preacher hand gesture punctuates every phrase, and his face looks properly stern, his eyes fierce and determined. He has found a topic he believes in, and it shows in his eyes. For a moment, I wonder what those eyes will look like when I kill him at close range. I wonder if I'll get him alone, so I can tell him his killer is also his son. I wonder if he'll even care.

A pharmacy sits on top of a hill on the opposite side of town. Without Pooley, without a middleman, I have no way to see a doctor or procure a prescription. As it is, I have to heal myself with over-the-counter medication, but I have done this long enough to know what to look for, how to up the dosages, how to dress my wound to stave off infection. I fill a basket with tubes of campho-phenique, rolls of gauze, bottles of extra-strength Tylenol gel-caps, boxes of Q-tips and spools of medical tape. I am fighting a fever now, and if the clerk looks at me strangely, I don't take notice. I pay in cash and leave quickly.

A tiny church shares the parking lot with the pharmacy. I didn't notice it on the way in, but as I toss the bags into the car, light reflects off the stained glass and catches my eye. My mind seizes on that look on Cortino's face as he came out of the church built into the hill in Positano. The look of peace he had somehow found inside that building and carried out with him. Improbably, I find my feet moving toward the church door.

The sanctuary is empty. No more than twenty pews divide into two columns and point toward a small riser holding a pulpit. A simple mahogany cross decorates the back wall. The afternoon light filters through the stained glass outside and bathes the room in soft ethereal light. I think about Pooley and suddenly my legs feel tired. I sit down and steady my breathing until a feeling of nausea passes. How long I rest, I can't be sure.

'Afternoon.'

A young man stands in the aisle, awash in the light from the windows. He is dressed conservatively, with a blue shirt tucked into grey slacks.

'Afternoon,' I manage.

'Are you okay?'

'Just resting.'

'You came to the right place.'

I am hoping if I stay very still he will go away. Instead, he sits in the pew in front of me and swivels his head to face my direction.

'Are you new to the church?'

'Just passing through.'

'A traveler?'

'Yes, sir. I'm sorry to slip in here . . .'

He waves his hand. 'A church with locked doors is like screen doors on a submarine. Purposeless. My name is Dr. Garrett.' He extends his hand and I shake it. For the life of me, I can't figure out why I haven't headed for daylight. Fuck, am I tired.

'You look young for a preacher.'

'That's kind of you to say. But I've been doing this for a long time. Twenty-somethin' years now.'

I smile weakly.

'Tell you what. I'll let you speak to the Lord all you want. If you need me, my office is just on the other side of that door.'

He stands up, and I'm not sure what I'm doing, but I hear myself say, 'Preacher?'

'Yes?'

He pauses standing over me.

'Aren't you worried about danger coming through the door?' I hear myself saying. But the voice isn't mine, not exactly. At least it doesn't sound like me.

The preacher looks at me thoughtfully. 'No. This place is about comfort, about sanctuary . . .'

But he stops suddenly as I stand up and grab him by the throat. His eyes change quickly, from confidence to surprise to terror. Well, that's not right. It's not I watching those eyes, not I pulling the pistol out of the small of my back, not I whose right hand explodes in a blur and smashes the pistol into the side of his face, smashes him again, pistol-whipping him furiously, bam, bam, bam, over and over and over . . .

'Why?' the preacher manages as he goes down between the pews.

And I don't know how to answer the question, I don't know why, I don't know who this person is beating a defenseless face on a defenseless preacher in a defenseless sanctuary until that face is a mask of blood and gore.

'Fuck, fuck, fuck,' the person who is not I mutters, and then spits on the moaning lump on the floor.

In five minutes, I am on the road again, heading west through the desert, the infinite white line of the highway sliding underneath my tires. It is not I who holds the wheel steadily, the pain in my side forgotten. It is not I with a grin on my face.

Clouds hang like a ceiling over downtown Seattle, low and grey and threatening. To the south, Mt. Rainier fills the horizon like a wart on the landscape. Something about it seems foreign here, wrong, like it broke away from a mountain chain and moved off to sulk on its own. This morning it is blindfolded, its peak lost above the clouds.

It is time to focus. I have yet to set up even the basics for my kill and subsequent escape. Since Positano, since I managed to crawl to the road with two bullets in me, since I somehow stole a Vespa and somehow fought off losing consciousness and somehow negotiated sixty miles to Naples in the dead of night without being stopped by the police and somehow holed up until Pooley could get to me, get a doctor to me, since that evening when I walked into a room to make a kill but instead walked into a trap where I was going to be the fall guy, since then I have put much greater thought into my assassinations. Vespucci placed importance on the psychology of the killing business, but in retrospect he paid short shrift to executing the executions. His job was to pull together a wealth of information, giving his assassins the best avenues to kill a target. But he left the actual task to his hired killers, left the method and the deed and the strategy to his men.

I had planned to get to Abe Mann at a speech he was to give in Los Angeles the day before the convention started. The only rule I had was that the kill had to be the week of the convention, but the exact time and place were left to my discretion. I knew he had plans to speak using a hundred local firefighters behind him, and I was angling Pooley to get the contact information about who arranged the 'staging' of these events. Once the information was obtained, I would manipulate either the person or the list or one of the firefighters so I would be included in the event, so there would be a spot for me on the dais behind him. I knew ten different fire stations would have to send men to fill those spots and there would be little overlap in the ranks. An unfamiliar face wouldn't be noticed, especially if I had set the table, so to speak, had the proper credentials and ID and documentation to pass myself off. I would use a Secret Serviceman's gun.

But that plan shattered like a broken mirror when Hap killed Pooley in Santa Fe.

Hap. Of course. Hap brought himself into the equation and Hap became the solution. By taking away my options, Hap *became* the option. I would find Hap Blowenfeld, I would locate him and instead of killing him, I would piggyback on his plan to kill the congressman. If I got lucky, I would leave him for dead, framed in the process, like the woman in Positano tried to do to me.

13

I am fortunate the bullet passed through my side without shattering a rib or puncturing an organ. I'm fortunate it is a clean wound and the bandages and medication have stanched the bleeding and diminished the pain. I feel better. Not whole, not onehundred percent, but better.

Now to find Hap. The supplier route to Hap failed spectacularly; that door was obviously shut, and I would have to open a new door. This time I didn't want to kill him, just find him and follow him.

I get up, shower, redress my bandages, dress casually – black jeans and black T-shirt – and take Interstate 5 into downtown.

I exit at Madison and head to the waterfront. I want to see the Pacific, to stare out at the horizon where the dark water meets the light sky. I find a metered parking space and make my way across a small patch of grass where businessmen and women lie in the sun, content to feel intermittent sunlight, if only for a few fleeting seconds.

I stand at the water's edge for an hour. Dark water meeting light sky. It is time to finish this. To forget connecting with Abe Mann. I realize I no longer need to connect with him, we were connected long before I saw his name at the top of the page. I only need to sever the connection, once and for all.

It hits me there, watching the light and the darkness disappear into each other. The connection I need to sever isn't the one between Mann and me. The connection I need to sever is the one holding me back.

I find a pay phone and dial a number from memory. After a brief exchange with Max, he puts me through to Mr. Ryan in Las Vegas.

'I agree to your offer.'

'You will let me represent you? Exclusively?'

'You have your Silver Bear.'

I hear an exhale through the line, like he is allowing himself a moment for this to sink in. It is a rare moment of emotion for a stoical man, and it pleases me.

'I am very happy. You will not regret this.'

'I'm sure I won't and I am happy as well, Mr. Ryan.'

'Call me William. We are partners.'

'William.'

'You are finishing a job now?'

'Yes. It will be finished by the end of the week.'

'And after, how soon would you like to work again?'

'Give me two months.'

'Where would you like to work?'

'The Northeast, preferably.'

'Is that your home?'

'Yes, Boston.'

'Ahhh. There is a lot of work in New York right now.'

'That would be fine.'

'I'll have a file for you in two months.'

'Great.'

He waits, knowing I have more to tell him.

'There is one other thing, William. One thing I need immediately on my current job. I don't have Pooley any more, and I will give you his commission for this assignment.'

'Yes, that will be fine. What can I get you?'

'I need you to arrange a meeting.'

'Yes?'

'There is an East Coast fence named Vespucci. I worked for him originally. He brought me in. We had a bit of bad blood when we went our separate ways.'

'Yes?'

'I need a meeting . . .'

'Okay . . .'

'In Seattle.'

'I believe this will be difficult.'

'That's why I'm joining you. Exclusively. Because your reputation is you handle difficulty very well.'

'Yes, I see. When?'

'As soon as possible.'

'Yes. How may I reach you?'

'I'll call you in twelve hours.'

'Yes. It will be done.'

I walk to the Pike Place Market, a short quarter-mile from the sea. As far as tourist traps go, this isn't a bad one, and I find it sparsely crowded at this time of day in the middle of the week. I buy a newspaper and eat some grilled salmon and stare at nothing and think of nothing. The fish tastes bland. Outside, it starts to rain.

The meeting is set for a bar at the Sea-Tac airport. This is a smart choice by Vespucci for obvious reasons. Shooters like to meet in airport terminals; security being what it is, it is damn near impossible to sneak in a weapon. I have yet to hear of a man killed in an airport bar; the locale is a safe-haven for dangerous men to meet and exchange pleasantries. And information.

I purchase a ticket to Toronto I don't intend to use and arrive an hour early to get my bearings. The bar is named C.J. Borg's, a small place with a single entrance and exit, dimly lit and half full, just off the Alaskan Airways terminal. I pick a booth in the back where I can watch the entrance. Even in a high security zone, I don't want to take any chances.

Vespucci is unmistakable as he waddles into the bar, squints as his eyes adjust to the absence of light, and then finds me in the corner. He hasn't changed, his hair is still dark, and his weight looks the same. The only difference is his eyes; there is a weariness there I didn't notice before, like whatever pleasure he once got out of life has long since evaporated.

'Hello, Columbus.'

'Hello.'

He keeps his expression, and his voice, even.

'You have been well?'

'No. Not very well, Mr. Vespucci.'

'Yes. I know as much. I am sorry about your fence.'

'Sorry doesn't quite cover it.'

'No. I understand.'

'Here's what I want. I want you to serve up Hap Blowenfeld or whatever his real name is. I know we got tripled up on this job and I know no one asked for it and I know we're spending more time trying to kill each other than trying to eliminate the target. I've already disposed of Miguel Cortega. I will do the same to Hap.'

'Why should I . . . how is it you say . . . serve up my own man?'

'Because I'm going to get to him one way or another. And I'm going to finish this job.' I level my eyes at him. 'And if you don't help me, I'm going to finish you.'

He starts to say something but I interrupt . . .

'Jurgenson in Amsterdam. Sharpe in D.C. Korrigan in Montreal. Reeves in Chicago. Cole in Atlanta. You know of these?'

He nods his head.

'I put them all down. They were supposed to be impossible and I got to them all. I've never targeted anyone off-job, but if you don't help me, you will be my first.'

He leans back, contemplating.

'You've changed,' he says at last.

'You changed me.'

His whole body sags a little in the chair, like I made the weight on top of his shoulders heavier. He leans forward, then pauses, like he wants to pick his words carefully.

'I know where she lives.'

For a moment, I say nothing. There is no need for him to explain whom *she* refers to; I know who she is without giving the name. It is a calculated move on his part, and if he is expecting me to blink, he played the wrong cards.

'I don't care.'

'Ahhh . . . I think you do care, Columbus. I think you would very much like to know what I know.'

'You don't think I could've gotten to her a thousand ways since that job eight years ago? I'm the one who sent her packing. Don't forget that.'

'You sent her packing because you care for her. You kicked her in the stomach because you care for her. You haven't tracked her down because you care for her. Maybe you haven't changed as much as I thought.'

I start to say something but it is his turn to interrupt.

'You threaten my life, Columbus, but I can say to you truly, I don't give a steaming pile of shit for my life. It is ending soon, and I am at peace. Whatever punishment I have coming, it will not be in this life, I can assure you. Whatever ways you can make me hurt, it will be a blessing. I have much . . . I have many regrets, I mean to say.'

His eyes are rheumy and his lids are heavy, but I am sure this is no ploy; he is searching for truth in a life filled with death and what he sees in the abyss makes him blink. He hasn't finished what he wants to tell me.

'You think pulling the trigger is difficult? You think executing the job is difficult? Think of what I do, what your fence did for you. We research these targets, these men, these women, we find out every intimate detail of their lives so another may end that life. We make the blueprints of their death. We take away their free will. We know the future. We know as we study them in the present, they have little time to live. We know it, but *they* don't know it, do you understand? It is a rare power, reserved for God.'

He moves his coffee cup from one side of the table to the other. 'Pah. Forgive me. I am old and tired. I cannot explain what this means. My words do not represent me well.'

I stare at him as though for the first time. This old man

who brought me into this life and now lives with regret. I had not thought of the toll it takes on the fence, the middleman, to compile those files I savor. I am able to make the connection and sever the connection, but he – and Pooley – only connected and then watched someone else do the severing. The fee exacted on them was both psychological and physical; I could see it now in Vespucci's bloodshot eyes.

I discover here, in this moment, I will fail. I let this assignment get the best of me, take the best *from* me. I let my rejected past overtake me and I ignored all the warning signs because of my own hubris. My threat to Vespucci has been rendered empty, and he knows it. Not because he manipulated me, but because he disarmed me by simply telling the truth.

I realize we haven't said a word to each other for several minutes. He is looking at me the way a scolded schoolchild looks at a teacher, waiting for me to dole out punishment, waiting for a blow that will never come.

Finally, I stand up, lost.

'Are we finished?'

'Yes.'

He lets out a breath and stands. 'Well. It was good seeing you Columbus. I mean that.'

I don't answer, and he shuffles away. It is dark outside when I leave the terminal. The rain is relentless.

I return to my hotel like a man walking in his sleep. I have no plan B, no backup, no contingency for getting to Abe Mann. I have every confidence I can get a bullet into him, but I have no way to escape, and I do not make suicide runs. I have nowhere to turn. I am out of ideas.

I will have to go south, to Los Angeles, and observe, and hope Hap doesn't sniff me out first, and look for an opening. If I have a chance for a clean shot, I'll have to take it and rely on my instincts to keep me alive and out of jail. I have no other options.

I begin packing my few things, when there is a knock on the door. I snatch up a pistol, crouch low next to the door-frame, and say, 'Yeah?'

Vespucci's voice comes through softly from the other side of the wall. 'Columbus. It is me. I am . . . unarmed.'

Something in his voice sounds dead and hollow, like he is damned, soulless. I lower my gun, stand up and open the door without hesitation. He must have followed me here from the airport, but the tone in his voice is not dangerous.

He is holding an envelope; his eyes appear lifeless, just dark circles in a dark face.

'I will not give you Hap.'

I don't say a word. He didn't come here to tell me what I already knew. He extends his hand and I take the proffered envelope.

'Candidate Abe Mann will be alone in this hotel room exactly twenty-four hours before he is to address the convention. Do not ask me how I know this or why I know this. It is information Hap has, and now it is information you have. The playing field is leveled, as they say.'

I am unsure how to respond, so I just nod.

'I do not do this for you because I owe it to you. I do it for me. Do you understand?'

'Yes.'

It is his turn to nod. He studies my face, like he is trying to commit it to memory, like this will be the last time he looks upon it.

'It is too late for me.' And with that, he moves away, into the shadows and darkness and implacable rain.

14

I stand in a field on the outskirts of Portland, Oregon, with a thousand citizens, watching Abe Mann talk on a raised platform. He is angry and it seems, for the first time since I've been stalking him, speaking off the cuff, without notes, without a script.

'. . . Politics in this country have descended into a two-party demigod where lines are drawn on every issue before anyone can manage a true original thought. It is a system built on discord. A system fostering sticks instead of carrots. We talk about extending olive branches and meeting in the middle and working with the other side of the aisle but it's all . . . well . . . horse-pucky.'

The crowd applauds nervously, like it senses something here is a little out of whack.

Mann continues like he didn't hear the clapping. 'I mean, come on, people. It's like two dogs tied to the same chain pulling in opposite directions. They can't get anywhere; they just stay in the same place, grunting and growling, impotent. Well, I tell you right now, someone needs to point those dogs in the same direction or put 'em both out of their misery.'

I am watching Mann's handlers on the side of the dais as they stew uncomfortably, trying and failing to get their candidate's attention. I notice him look their way, then his eyes go right back to the audience, ignoring their signals to cut it short. A fat guy standing to the side in an ill-fitting suit looks like he's about to go apoplectic, but Mann just keeps on talking.

'Here's the problem with that big capitol building on the hill. When the going gets tough, the weak ones cave. "The best lack all conviction while the worst are full of passionate intensity." No one finishes anything. Not how they meant to finish, I mean.'

His eyes scan the crowd, fall right on me like he's singling me out, and then pass on.

'They start out with the best intentions but there you go, two parties digging at each other every chance they get and with the pork, and the gravy on the pork, and the salt on the gravy on the pork, by the time you've been kicked in the teeth a couple hundred times, what you started out doing doesn't look a cock and bull close to what it ended up being. No one finishes anything. The center cannot hold. No one wants to . . .'

His microphone cuts out on him. It takes him a few sentences to realize what has happened, that he's been emasculated. He looks over at his handlers hotly, but then defeat spreads across his face like a virus. I am reminded of that skittish dog outside of McDonalds in Santa Fe trying to get to his feet, trying to force his legs to work again, trying to somehow shake off the brute force that had crippled him, and failing over and over and over.

Mann's own men have choked him, put the muzzle on him, and he shrugs and walks off the stage, his eyes cast down. He has been silenced, but his words still hang over the crowd, hang over me, until all of us shuffle away silently, like we're leaving a funeral.

I did walk off a job once without killing the target, without completing the mission. Just a year ago, last winter. I didn't want to work, had decided to take a break and recharge my batteries, but Pooley fielded an offer double our usual fee and I figured I could rest later, when the weather grew warmer.

I was suspicious about the fee, double wages could only mean this particular job would be unusually difficult. I had been wary since Positano, and I refused to make the same mistake twice.

The target's name was Jaquelle Val Saint, a French woman living in Dallas, Texas, a mistress according to the file Pooley cobbled together. She had changed her name to Monique Val Saint, though Pooley wasn't sure why or what the significance was. He made notes in the file indicating the fence he was dealing with on the other side of the table had been extremely reticent about giving information. Nevertheless, Pooley had done his job well, painstakingly accounting for all the details in Monique's life.

Her lover was Jacob J. Adams, a major real estate player in North Dallas. He had built a small fortune buying up factories, remodeling them, and then leasing the warehouses to manufacturers all over the Southwest. In the course of growing his business, he had greased enough connected palms to kindle small-time political aspirations of his own. It didn't take a lot of deduction to imagine how Monique ended up with a price on her head.

From the file Pooley put together, I knew Monique lived in a loft apartment with a view of downtown Dallas out her living room window and a swimming pool on the roof so she could keep her skin tanned golden brown. I saw she exercised five times a week at a local health club, but that number had dwindled to only once in Pooley's last week of surveillance. She had put on a little weight; maybe that had added to Mr. Adams's dissatisfaction.

According to the file, Adams's wife was unaware of the ongoing affair. Pooley was confident of it. This was important information; if the wife had plans of her own to confront Ms. Val Saint, it could cause me logistical problems. A heated exchange could conceivably complicate things at the wrong time, either bringing unwarranted outsiders – curious neighbors, or, worse, the police – into the equation, which would make my job all the more difficult. I wanted to move fast on this one: get in, get the job done, and get out.

I flew to Dallas, rented a car, and drove to an area called Deep Ellum. A brick factory had been converted to giant lofts on Canon Street, and I'm sure Adams had negotiated a good deal on the rent for his mistress. She was just leaving as I pulled on to her street, so I followed her discreetly as she turned and headed south toward the highway.

Eventually, her convertible Mercedes pulled into one of her favorite destinations according to Pooley's report, the Northpark Mall. I parked a few rows away and watched her as she crossed the lot.

Monique was beautiful, more than what I expected from the pictures Pooley had taken. She had natural beauty, high cheekbones on an unblemished face. Her hair was blond and stylish, not piled high like most of the Texas women heading across the parking lot. She wore baggy clothes over what must have been an athletic figure.

I followed her inside, trailing furtively. She crossed through the department store, Neiman Marcus, and headed into the mall proper. I waited while she window-shopped, using the glass of the storefronts across the corridor to watch her as she disappeared inside a Pottery Barn.

I waited for her to come out, but when she didn't, I made my way over to the store as casually as possible, face blank, hands deep in my pockets.

I could hear shouting from outside the store, but the voices grew clearer as I moved closer. Monique was standing at the sales counter, her face contorted in rage, screaming obscenities at two clerks on the other side of the table. Her face had transformed; where I had seen beauty before, now I saw raw ugliness. The dispute had something to do with a promised item not being in stock, and the poor clerks were cowering from this woman, this privileged woman, this mistress, who was lording over them, raging over them, simply because she could.

She would not be raging for long.

* * *

I watched her across the parking lot with narrowed eyes, allowing my hatred for this woman to build. Pooley had mentioned a 'difficult' personality in the file, but I had a special enmity for those who treat others like shit. The mark of character is how we treat people who can do nothing for us – the secretaries, the waitresses, the bank tellers, the check-out lady at the grocery store. She was making this job easier.

I followed her to a medical building and waited in the parking lot while she met with her doctor. Whatever illness she was attempting to cure would cease to matter as soon as she returned to her apartment.

She didn't have any other errands and so headed for home in Deep Ellum. I sat in my car for a good hour after she entered the building.

Most professional assassinations take place in the target's home. It is important for an assassin to let his prey settle into a routine, to get comfortable, to drop his or her guard in the familiar surroundings of where he or she lives.

I checked the clip on my Glock and headed inside, then took the elevator up to the fourth floor.

Her door had a standard Fleer lock. It took me less than ten seconds to pick it and quietly crack the door. Quickly, I entered the apartment, ready to strike if need be, but she wasn't in the living room or the kitchen off to the side. I heard the unmistakable sound of a shower faucet being turned in the master bedroom and moved in that direction.

Silently, I turned the bedroom door handle and pushed the door in at the same time. I took a step forward and only had a second to duck my head as a golf club swung my way. I managed to avoid a direct hit from the club head as she only grazed my skull with the graphite shaft. Still, I had to fight off the surprise of being discovered in the act, and I wasn't ready for the intensity of this woman.

She whipped the club back and prepared to strike a second time. She was only half dressed, and something about her bare legs caused me a moment's hesitation, which she took advantage of, swinging the club low and connecting with my left shin. I felt the bone crack and a flash of stars blurred my vision, but instincts took over and reminded me that whatever this woman was, she wasn't an experienced killer.

She tried to pass me, to get out of the bedroom to the more advantageous battlefield of the living room, and she almost made it, but I lunged for her and caught her arm, twisted her wrist back and jerked her body to the floor.

From there, it was a scrum. I had a hundred pound advantage, and although she had the desperation of a cornered rat, I used the pain in my shin to focus my intensity. I clawed at those bare legs until I was able to get on top of her. She tried to scratch me, to bite me, her jaws snapping like a turtle's, her eyes wild, rolling in their sockets. She pounded the heel of her foot into my shin, but I was focused, feeding on the pain, and I managed to pin her arms down, straddling her torso while I hooked my fingers around her throat.

I was getting ready to finish the job when I heard Monique's front door open behind me.

Fuck. I had to make a decision, had to time it right. While Monique struggled under my grip, I concentrated my hearing, listening for the telltale sound of footsteps approaching the door to the bedroom. Even with my bum leg, I could hoist myself backward off of her and use surprise and a solid forearm to get the new visitor down on the ground. From there, I would have to hope I had sapped the fight out of this woman so she wouldn't be able to help.

'Columbus!'

The last thing I was expecting was Pooley's voice coming from the living room.

'Columbus!'

Even as I processed this, I could feel my fingers loosening on Monique's throat. She coughed and made her body go as limp as a possum's.

Pooley appeared in the light of the living room, drawn by the coughing. He was sweating and breathing hard, and he peered in at me in the bedroom as I slid off the woman.

'She . . . uh . . .' he was trying to catch his breath. 'She's not the target.'

'What?'

As soon as I lifted my body off Monique's torso, she scrambled backward to the corner of the bedroom, leaving her back against the wall, hugging her knees and sobbing between coughing spasms.

'I fucked up. I . . . uh . . . the double fee . . . the two names . . . I thought it was . . .'

'This isn't . . .'

'She's pregnant. The hit is on the baby inside her.'

'Fuck.'

I stood up and Monique screamed, flinching back, her hands on her stomach.

I put my palms up in a calming motion, but I was staring hotly at Pooley. 'Fuck,' I repeated. 'How do you make that mistake?'

'I didn't catch it . . . I should have but I didn't. That's why I got here as soon as I could.'

I turned my eyes on Monique and she flinched.

'I'm leaving,' I said to her. 'I'm not going to kill you or your baby. But someone put a professional hit on that child and didn't care enough to explain it wasn't on you.'

She nodded, but her mouth was still pulled back in a snarl, like she was ready to fight again if I made a move in her direction.

I limped out of her apartment and Pooley helped me down the stairs all the way to his car.

What kind of person would put a hit on the child when hitting the mother would have served the same purpose? And what kind of psychological game was the person playing to sign off on the kill that way . . . name the unborn daughter but present it like it was the mother? Was it so the man or woman could rest easier knowing the assassination was little more than a forced abortion? So the person could blame the mother's death on the shooter, since it wasn't in the contract? The sin of omission easier to stomach than the sin of execution? Maybe I didn't want to know the answer. But I didn't finish the job that day, didn't go through with the assassination, because I didn't like being manipulated.

In Portland, the sky is cloudless for the first time in weeks and it feels as though someone has lifted a blanket. The horizon is clear, endless.

Abe Mann is heading to Sacramento, his last stop before heading to a convention in Los Angeles he will never reach. I am watching a news clip about Sacramento and Mann's impending arrival on the *Today Show* as I brush my teeth in the hotel mirror and a name starts to tickle the back of my mind like it is trying to get my attention.

Skyline Hall.

Skyline Hall in Sacramento.

When on a job, assassins sometimes pepper their conversations with nuggets from their real lives, their real backgrounds, to add sincerity, a touch of authenticity to whatever cover they're using to get in close to a target. This tactic has its strengths, usually gaining a mark's confidence to be exploited. But this tactic also has its shortcomings, like when it is employed on someone who isn't a target at the time, someone who remembers, someone who might become an enemy.

Skyline Hall in Sacramento.

Hap Blowenfeld told me a story the first time I met him as we loaded beer crates into the back of his truck, a story so I would bond with him, a story about how he had killed a kid with his bare hands over the theft of his father's wallet and had been sent to Skyline Hall in Sacramento, California, a Juvey center like Waxham.

If this story is true, if Hap had been at that Juvey center, then there might be some record of what his real name is, of where his father lives, of a living relative, of a way to get to him.

15

There are two ways to get information you aren't supposed to have. One is to sneak in and steal it. The other is to force someone to give it to you.

Skyline Hall for Boys is on the outskirts of Sacramento, on a deserted stretch of highway, away from any major roads. It looks like a high school with razor wire, a place built a long time ago with zero funding for repairs.

I case it for a day and mark the shift changes. Like with Richard Levine's security force, I know the best time to strike will be when the front desk is at its most chaotic, when tired government employees are handing the keys to the asylum over to bored government employees just getting started on another shitty day in juvenile hell.

I head up to the front doors and make my way to a chubby receptionist who is literally watching the clock.

'May I help you?' she asks without shifting her eyes to me.

'Yes. Hi. I'm with State Senator Vespucci's office. Can you point me to the records room?'

Now her eyes move from the clock to examine my face. She is pissed. I have arrived looking like work at the end of a long shift. Her face tightens until her mouth disappears into a thin line.

'What's this regarding?'

'It's pertaining research for funding grants.'

'No one told me.'

'Well, there was a fax sent a few days ago.'

She casts her eyes to an empty back office where an old fax machine sits on a shelf, then back at me, trying to decide if she wants to heave her considerable bulk out of her desk chair with only ten minutes left in her shift.

Finally, she sighs and gets up.

She moves inside the office and heads to the fax machine, looks around for some stray papers, but doesn't find any.

'Well, listen here. I don't know anything about no . . .'

She stops in the middle of her sentence, because I have come up behind her silently and now stand with a gun pressed against her rib cage. Outside that office, there is a little commotion as the new shift of workers enters, but inside, where we are, it is quiet.

Under her breath, she manages, 'Oh, lordy . . .'

'What's your name?'

She whispers, 'Roberta.'

'Roberta, you have a decision to make. We live in a world where we have choices and for good or bad, there are consequences to those choices. Now you're going to have to make one.'

'Don't Mister . . .'

'Choice one is you do exactly what I tell you to do and no one in this building dies. Not Lawrence the janitor, not Bill the counseling rep, not you, Roberta. And not those cute little grandkids whose pictures I saw taped to your desk.'

'Oh, lordy . . .'

'Choice two is you raise your voice, you cause a stink, you draw attention to me or yourself, and I go on a killing spree the likes of which Sacramento has never seen. Nod your head if you understand.'

She nods her head, her eyes never leaving mine, her face red, stinging, like someone slapped her across the cheeks.

'Good. Then no one is going to get shot today.'

I lower the gun so she'll know she's given the right answer, made progress.

'Okay, Roberta, now you're going to lead me to the records room. When we're in there, you're going to point me to the files covering the five-year period from 1984 to 1989. Can you do that for me, Roberta?'

She nods again, and then mechanically, robotically, she leads me out of the office and down a side corridor. No one looks at us, no one greets us, no one asks us what we're doing. It's just another Tuesday in a place where no one cares.

We spend just over an hour in the records room, undisturbed. Roberta has dropped her guard and is helping me dig through the materials, showing me booking photos of each child. Thankfully, they've been cataloged by offences, so I narrow the field to the most serious felonies, and I can skip over all the faces except the white ones, which makes the task even quicker. Still, there was an abundance of teenagers committing felonies back in the heyday of West Coast gang violence, so the job is still arduous.

Just when my patience is wearing thin and I think maybe Hap got the details right but changed the geography, I find the right picture staring back at me.

Younger, with more hair and less confidence, a teen-age Hap Blowenfeld glares out from a black and white photograph with an expression of faux defiance. The name on the file is Evan Feldman. It has an address for his father in Arcadia. It seems the only detail Hap changed was his name, and even that isn't too far of a stretch.

'That's it, then?' asks Roberta.

'That's it.'

'You gonna let me go, now?'

'How old are your grandkids, Roberta?'

Her eyes flash a little, like she has gotten comfortable with me and now regrets it. Softly, she whispers, 'The boy is five. The girl, three.'

'Well, if you want the boy to see six and the girl to see four, you forget you ever saw me and you don't mention this to anyone.'

'No, sir, I wouldn't.'

'If you do, some men might try to arrest me, but they won't. Some others might try to kill me, but they won't. And

I'll know it was you who told someone about today, Roberta. And then I'll come back to Sacramento. And let me tell you something as sure as I'm standing before you, I don't want to come back to Sacramento.'

'You won't have no reason to.' A tear spills down her cheek but her voice doesn't crack.

'I know I won't. I'm gonna take this.'

I pick up Hap's juvenile file and head out the door. I'm sure it will be a long time before Roberta gathers the strength to leave the room.

Arcadia is a town of urban sprawl gone wrong. It's buildings, buildings, buildings and concrete and asphalt and sewers and shit as far as the eye can see, all surrounding a horse track improperly named after a Saint, all within a stone's throw of the bad side of Los Angeles.

The address I have is on a residential street lined with squat one-story houses packed as close together as the city planners will allow. None of the houses seem too eager to do battle with an earthquake, should a fresh one arrive.

The address I have for Hap's father, Tom Feldman, is 416 N. Armstrong Rd., and as I scope out the unassuming house from down the street, I find myself praying there's an older white man still living in it. Just don't be a dead end. Not when I feel like I'm so fucking close.

There are times in life when Fate smiles on you, when you ask for a piece of luck and that piece arrives in a box with a bow on it. I asked for luck when I killed that prostitute back in Pennsylvania, what the fuck was her name, I can't even remember it now, just the smell of that grape bubble gum in the passenger seat of my rental car, and I was asking for luck here, luck I had done my homework, I had guessed right, Hap's old man hadn't died or moved or been kicked out for not making his mortgage payments. And here's the thing: luck has a way of shining on preparation, of rewarding those who put themselves in a position to take advantage of it when that gift box with the pretty bow plops into their laps.

Hap's father parks his car in his driveway, gets out and heads to his mailbox. His face unmistakably belongs to the sire of the man who killed my partner; father and son share the same features, the same small nose, the same eyes. I can feel anger and excitement building up inside me.

I slam my door shut and hurry down the street.

'Sir . . . ?'

He looks up innocently. 'Yes?'

'Are you Tom Feldman?'

'Yes . . .'

'Thank God . . . How you doing?'

'Fine . . . ?' It is more of a question than a statement.

'I'm so glad I found you. I'm friends with Evan . . .'

A broad smile crosses his face . . . 'Really? Well, nice to meet you . . .'

'Jack . . .'

'Nice to meet you, Jack. Evan should be here any minute.'

My heart leaps up into my throat. He's coming *here*? I haven't just found the father; I've got the son, right here, right now. The gift box just got shinier. The bow a little bigger.

But I need the element of surprise and if Hap or Evan or whatever the fuck his name is drives up now, the tables could turn in a matter of seconds. I manage to say, 'Excellent! He'll be so happy to see me.'

His dad pulls out a cell phone. 'He probably stopped off to load up on groceries. Let me call him and tell him you're here, Jack. Hurry him on his way.'

I keep my voice even, keep the smile on my face . . . 'That'd be great.' I pause, like I'm thinking more about it. 'You know what, though? He has no idea I'm coming to see him and I'd love to surprise him.'

His dad laughs. 'Sure. He hasn't kept up with any of his old friends, so this'll be a nice treat for him.'

I look down the street, my ears straining to pick up the sound of an approaching engine. I need to get out of the front yard, be inside the house when Hap comes through the door with grocery bags in his hands.

'Can I use your bathroom?'

'Of course.'

He leads the way up his front steps. 'How do you know Evan?'

'We used to run trucks together in Boston. Ten years ago.'

'You're kidding me. Well, I'll be.'

He approaches the front door, and my instincts fail me, I don't see it coming, I am so sure Fate is smiling on me that I don't notice the warning signs. The father asking to use his cell phone. The quick way he warmed to me.

We reach the front door and the old man opens it in a flourish and screams . . . 'Evan! There's a killer here . . .' and then I bash him in the side of the head before he can say any more but it's already too late.

I counted on a lot of things but one thing I never imagined is Hap telling his old man exactly what he did for a living. I didn't count on Hap being home and I didn't count on his father covering for him, and I didn't count on that old bastard bellowing out like a wailing siren.

I barely see a flash of feet bounding up a nearby staircase before I have a chance to get my bearings, have my eyes adjust to the light. If he had cared about his father before, enough to throttle a kid who had stolen his old man's wallet, he certainly doesn't care any more. The years of being a bag man have forced the survival instinct into him, and he is fleeing. If I kill his father, so be it.

I sprint into the house and dart for the stairwell when a volley of bullets cascade down at me like a dozen wasps defending the nest. As soon as the avalanche recedes and I hear his feet clomping away, I fire through the ceiling and then hurry up the steps two at a time.

I peek around the corner quickly, just enough to catch a glimpse, fully expecting another shot, but instead, I see Hap smash through a second-story window and I am moving to the end of the hallway and looking down and he is already rolling up off the grass like a cat and running away. I don't hesitate and fling myself out the window, bracing my knees to absorb the fall, and then roll with it and up at the same time.

He should have been waiting for me to jump and then shot me as soon as I hit the ground but he didn't and I'm up and running after him without missing a step. I'm faster than he is, and he's going to have to make a move as we sprint across lawn after lawn, but I can tell something is wrong with him, something's amiss. He hasn't tried to pop a shot off at me since the spray of bullets down the stairwell, hasn't tried to distract me or keep me at bay so he can duck between houses, and I realize I'm in luck after all; I caught Hap unprepared. He had to scramble off his father's couch when the old man signaled him and he only had time to sprint up the stairs and grab his gun but he had been lazy and hadn't scooped up a second clip and he's out of bullets now.

He makes his move, and just as a young couple down the street steps out of their front door, Hap lowers his shoulder and barrels into the house. I am twenty steps behind him and the husband just looks at me and yells 'hey!' but he sees my gun out and grabs his wife and backs away and I am past him and through the front door and I am hoping the layout of this house is different from Hap's father's house, different than the house he grew up in, but it looks familiar, and I hear a clinking coming from a nearby doorway, a drawer overturning in the kitchen and I scramble to the sound and smash through the swinging door but he is on me before I can get into the room and he buries a knife into my shoulder.

'Hiya, Columbus!' he says with eyes filled to the brim with fire.

I fall and my gun clatters across the tile floor in the kitchen and Hap scrambles for it, but I trip him up with my good arm and he topples and I am smashing him in the ribs with my fist as hard as I can.

Ten minutes is all we have to kill each other. Ten minutes from when that young husband whipped out his cell phone and dialled 9-1-1 as soon as we blitzed by him into his house, so if we're gonna do this, we need to do it now and get it finished and get the fuck out of here. Hap knows it and I know it and we're going to fight right here to the death in this middle-class suburban kitchen because there's no time and no other way to do it and it is and might as well be. He drives his fist into the kitchen knife handle buried in my shoulder, and fuck if I'm not blacking out but this is a goddamn hand-to-hand fight to the death and I cannot afford to go dark. Not now. Not after all I've done, not after I traveled from East to West, from Spring to Winter, from present to past to present and saw so much and gave up so much. Not now when the finish line is so close I can smell it like the salt in the air.

I open my jaws as wide as I can and bite into his side like a rabid dog and his arm that was reaching for my gun on the tile floor is forced back involuntarily by the pain and that's all I need. I get my knees under me and leap for the gun past his retreating arm and I snatch it up in my good hand, my left hand, and flip over and point it at Hap's head with my finger on the trigger, and I see it in his eyes. The life goes out of them like the electricity has been cut. He is defeated.

'Fuck.'

'Yeah.'

'Vespucci fingered me?'

'No. He stayed true blue.'

'Then how?'

'You told me a story once. The first time I loaded truck for you.'

'What?'

'You told me you killed a man who stole your father's wallet. You told me you did time at Skyline Hall in Sacramento.'

He nods now, resigned. 'I did?'

'Yeah.'

'I was still pretty new at this then.'

'Yeah.'

'Look, I'm sorry I killed your man. I was just doing what you would have done.'

'Yeah.'

He tries to sit up straighter, but the pain from my bite makes him wince a bit. 'Then I guess you gotta do what you gotta . . .'

I shoot Hap in the head at close range and his face disappears before he can finish the sentence.

Five minutes now. With a bloody arm, with a knife stuck in my shoulder, but with something else too: resolve. I climb to my feet, open the kitchen door that leads directly to the back yard and I am moving through it, into the sunlight, blinking my eyes.

16

I am the son.

The same side, the same shoulder, the same fucking arm. First a bullet, then a knife, and now my arm is virtually useless. It has turned an ugly shade of black – even against my skin it is prominent – and I'm not sure if it will ever function properly. I have it cleaned and bandaged and I hit myself with a cocktail of medications but I'm not a triage doctor and if I tried to seek professional help now I'd be out of the game.

There's a dead man named Evan Feldman in his neighbor's kitchen and there's my blood splashed on that floor and they'll be looking for a wounded man with blood type B positive trying to get stitched up at emergency rooms all over the city. I'm stuck with one worthless arm and the convention is now two days away and I have seventeen hours until Congressman Abe Mann will be alone on the twenty-second floor of the Standard Hotel in downtown Los Angeles.

I am the son.

Pooley is dead and the man who killed him is dead and Mr. Cox is dead and so many others are dead and Vespucci is alive and full of regrets. I am alive, but I'm not whole.

I have seventeen hours and I'll be damned if I am defeated now. Not after all this, not after I let the past back in and it forced me to my knees and goddammit, GOD DAMN IT, I'm losing my grip on the slippery ball of sanity floating somewhere in my head. There's a mirror in this cheap hotel room where the clerk didn't even look up when he took my cash and handed me a key, and my face is gaunt and pained and stretched as tight as a guitar string. I look into my own eyes and I force them to stare back at me, force them to fill up with that same resolve I've always relied upon, that same resolve that improbably got me out of that bedroom in Italy, that same resolve that kicked Jake Owens in the stomach in her apartment in Boston. I am Columbus, a Silver Bear, and whoever hired three assassins to kill Abe Mann the week of his nomination will not be disappointed because I am the son.

So how to get close to a man who has more security surrounding him than almost any man on Earth? How to get close to him even though I'm out of time and wounded and I have no resources at my fingertips?

And then it comes to me. The only solution, the only way to finish this. It was in front of me the whole time; it was in Vespucci's words and in my own mantra and it is as clear to me as the sky after a storm.

I fashion a sling out of a white T-shirt and shower and make myself as presentable as possible. In the dust-caked mirror, I shave my face and check my reflection and nod, pleased. I look plain and unassuming. The injury is unfortunate, a red flag, but nevertheless I no longer look like an escaped mental patient.

I drive from the decrepit hotel on the outskirts of East Los Angeles to Interstate 10 and then off a few side streets to Grant and the front of the Standard. The hotel is modern and angular and stark in that West Coast style that emphasizes design flair over comfort. A valet parker exchanges a ticket for my keys and I enter the white lobby and get my bearings.

It doesn't take me long to find what I'm seeking. A coterie of secret service agents huddle near a bank of elevators, stern expressions on their faces, eyes hidden behind dark sunglasses. A blonde female whom I recognize from standing on the sides of daises in Indianapolis and Seattle is dressed differently from the security officers but shares their grave expressions. She is holding a clipboard.

I approach her and feel every eye shift toward me, sizing up my arm in the makeshift sling.

'Excuse me.'

'Yes?' She studies me with a smile that looks as though it were forced on to her face under duress.

'How would I go about seeing Congressman Mann?'

She snorts and I see two of the Secret Service officers move their hands inside their jackets.

'I'm sorry. The congressman is unavailable at the moment.'

'He'll see me.'

She looks at the agents and they nod as if to tell her they are ready for any move I might make.

'And you are?'

'I'm his son . . .' and immediately they have me under the arm and are leading me forcefully away.

'Tell him LaWanda Dickerson's son! Tell him that!'

She looks at me queerly as I am jerked into an empty conference room off the lobby. Ten secret service officers materialize like magic and follow me into the room.

The senior officer is a man of forty or so with a bald head and hard eyes. He speaks with a higher voice than I would have guessed, like air blowing through an organ pipe, but he also speaks calmly, soothingly.

'Okay, friend. Let's start by seeing some identification. Can you hand me your wallet?'

I shake my head. 'I don't have one.'

'No identification?'

'No.'

'What's your name?'

'John Smith.'

He smiles, showing me I'm not going to get under his skin. 'Okay, John. I'm going to have the man behind you pat you down while I keep a gun pointed at your head. Is that okay?'

'Yes.'

This tells him two things. One, I'm not carrying a gun or a knife because he knows a man who is about to be patted down would gain nothing by lying about it. And two, I don't fear having a gun on me, which means I've undoubtedly had experience with it before. I can see this work itself out in his mind, but he keeps his face even. He pulls out his pistol and does as he said he'd do, points it a mere foot from my forehead.

'Are you carrying a bomb?'

All the eyes in the room are riveted on me.

'No.'

'What's wrong with your arm, John?'

'I was shot and then I was stabbed.'

'You sound like a busy man.'

'Yes.'

'Okay, John. Stand up and Larry will frisk you now.'

'Go easy on the arm.'

'Okay, John.'

I rise to my feet and the large man behind me pats me down as thoroughly as if he's taking my measurements. I wince as he searches up my bandaged arm and under it, not going easy at all. I regret saying anything; naturally that's where he'd search the hardest for anything untoward.

Larry nods at the senior officer and he lowers his gun. 'Okay, John. You are unarmed. You may sit.'

'Thank you.'

'What is your business with Congressman Mann?'

'That's between Congressman Mann and myself.'

'Okay, John. Would you mind if we took your fingerprints?'

'I don't mind.'

'Great.'

A pad of ink is produced and I get my fingers ready but before they are pressed onto the moist purple pad a door opens and a female voice speaks up to a room as silent as a graveyard. 'Abe wants to see him.'

The blonde with the clipboard. She chews the inside of her cheek, anxious.

The senior agent doesn't hesitate. 'That's a negative.'

'Abe insists.'

'Negative.'

'Would you like to speak to him, Steve? Because he certainly isn't listening to me.'

Steve nods and moves to a corner of the room, pulls out a cell phone and speaks softly. I can tell he's arguing with my father on the other end of the line, and I wait and it soon becomes clear he is losing the argument. His face falls but then he looks at me and his eyes harden again. I can make out that he says 'yes' into the phone before flipping the lid closed.

Twelve secret service officers lead me down a hallway with Larry on my left and Steve on my right and we are moving like a hangman's caravan toward two doors at the end of the corridor, the big suite on the top floor. We reach the doors and Steve gives me a curt 'wait here' and he enters into the room alone.

I wait for ten minutes, keeping my body neutral the way I've practiced for the last ten years until the doors open again and Steve emerges.

'Now, listen, John. There are going to be ground rules and if you deviate from those rules, we will not hesitate to kill you.'

I wait.

'You will enter the room and stand behind the line I've drawn for you on the floor. If you step over that line, Congressman Mann will ring a buzzer he's holding which will vibrate in my hand and I will enter the door and shoot you dead. Do you believe me?'

'I do.'

'You have ten minutes to walk out of that door. If you are still in the room after ten minutes I will enter and I will shoot you dead. Do you believe this to be true?'

'I do.'

'Okay, John. Then I'm going to let you in the room and start the clock. Please don't raise your voice. It might make all of us a little antsy and I don't want us to be antsy, okay?'

'Yes.'

'All right then.'

Steve opens the door and I step inside the suite.

A small foyer leads to a spacious living room. A red line of tape marks off the two rooms and I enter and put my toes on the line and there he is, after all this way, there he is sitting on a gray sofa thirty feet away, his eyes fixed on me like they are attached by a rope. He is bigger up close than he looked on all those stages and there isn't an ounce of apprehension on his face.

'Hello. I'm Abe.'

'My name is Columbus. And I am your son.'

I say this as calmly as if I were announcing the weather.

'How do you figure, Columbus?'

'I was the baby inside LaWanda Dickerson whom you knew as Amanda B. when you had her killed your freshman year in the Congress.'

He does not look down nor away. He is very good at holding his gaze steady, a conditioned skill that has served him well.

'It wasn't like that, son. I needed her to leave Washington and some men who were looking out for me took their job too seriously, too far.'

He stands up, keeping his hands in his pockets. 'But how do you know I'm the father?'

'I know.'

'She was a professional prostitute . . .'

'I know.' I'm answering his first question.

He looks at me the way an architect looks over his final blueprints, searching for flaws, mistakes. But he finds none.

'I do too. I can tell just by looking at you.' He exhales, heavily. 'But why come now? What do you want?'

'I was hired to kill you.'

He swallows once and removes his hand from his pocket. He's holding a silver box with a button on it. 'To kill me?'

'Yes, I'm a professional killer. I've killed men and women all over the world. I do this because I was born to do it. Do you understand?'

'Yes.' He looks at his hand and back at me. 'Let me ask you something. Do you think it was a coincidence you of all people were hired to kill me?'

'Someone told me fate has a way of making paths cross.'

'Yes. We just move through this world like so many puppets on strings.'

'No. Not me. I'm in control. Our paths crossed because I willed myself to get here.'

He studies me, like he's mulling this over.

'Do you think you were lucky? To get up into this room?'

'I think luck often favors the artful.'

'So how are you going to do it?'

'I'm going to improvise.'

'Before I press this button?'

'Yes.'

He nods matter-of-factly, then takes his thumb off the button and places the silver box on the glass coffee table.

'How are you going to escape?'

'I don't know.'

'That's not much of a plan.'

'No. But I got this far.'

'Yes, you did.'

'You have no idea what it took me to get here.'

'I presume your whole life, all your struggles, led to this moment.'

'Yes.'

'How much time do you have?'

'Six minutes.'

'Then listen to me. Here's how you're going to escape. You kill me and then you move through that door which leads to the master bedroom. The window is open and there are balconies going down. But there is also a balcony going up to the roof. You climb to the roof and you will find a window-washing cart on the opposite side of the building. Use the gearshift to drop at a rapid speed twenty floors to the alley below. You can be several blocks away before Officer Steve comes through that door.'

I've kept a poker face during this speech but I don't understand, can't comprehend what he's saying. 'Why are you telling me this?'

'Because I hired you.'

The truth rings out in the empty hotel room like a strong wind sweeping in and carrying out the fog.

'But why?'

'Like I said, I'm just a puppet on a string.'

'That's not good enough.'

'You only have four minutes, son. It's going to have to be good enough if you want to live.'

'But that's just it. *You* don't want to live.'

'You think I have a choice? I'm a bad person, son. I'm bad in a thousand ways. There is only one way out of this . . . I've tried everything else. I don't call the shots. I can't even scandal my way off the train. I'm not that man on television. I'm a monster.'

'Explain.'

He sits down heavily, like this confession has sapped his final bit of energy. 'Three minutes,' he says, weakly.

'Explain.' I repeat through gritted teeth.

'I didn't kill your mother. I didn't know they were going to do . . . *that*. Politics . . . politicians . . . we don't vote, we don't make decisions, hell, we don't even put on our own goddam shoes without someone telling us exactly what to do. Don't you see? Too many people rely on us to feed the machine, too many people own every little part of us to let vice tether us down. Power isn't in the big rooms in the Capitol, it's in the shadows and the corners and the dirty space under the rug.'

He's gaining momentum, picking up his natural cadence, speaking like he did in Portland, speaking like he did when he actually believed what he was saying.

'When I had my *problem* with your mother, some dark men made that problem disappear. You understand about dark men, I take it. I wouldn't have dreamed that . . .'

'And Nichelle Spellman in Kansas City? And how many others?'

He lowers his eyes. 'I can't stop it. It's like a black hole's been pulling me in all these years. There's no escape. Not for me. There are corrupt people who run this country. Really run it. Their interests are motivated by greed, by money. They'll do whatever they have to do to prop me up, keep me in power. They'll carve me in pieces till there's nothing left but scraps for the vultures.'

His speech is gravelly now, shaken, like the words themselves have been beaten down, pummeled, and his eyes are blank, as though he's talking to himself. 'And what do you think's going to happen after? When I win? What do you think's going to happen when I control policy, when I'm in charge of the NSA, when I'm Commander in Chief of the whole goddamn military? You think these dark men are going to vanish? You think they're going to let me be?

'Or do you think they're going to be emboldened, inspirited, galvanized to push the blackness further? I can't . . .' He shakes his head. 'I can't stop them. They won't let me stop them. My only choice is to . . . escape.'

I keep my voice filled with ice. 'You could cast them off. Force your own way.'

'No. You don't understand.'

'Buck them off your back, throw a chair through a window, escape . . .'

'No.'

'You could try. And if they hit you, rest and try again.'

'Maybe a long time ago. I'm tired now.'

'You could stay in the present, fight off the past, become a new man . . .'

'Impossible.'

'*You* can control your future. *You* can bend it to your will.'

'I can't.'

'You're a coward.'

'Yes.'

I look at the man before me, and he looks smaller than he did when I first entered the room. I have just one more question. 'Did you know? Did you know I'd be the one coming for you?'

He searches my face through half-closed lids. 'Would it help you if I said I did?'

I cross the room and am on him before he can take another breath. My fingers are on his throat and I squeeze with my left hand, my right hand useless, and our faces are inches apart but he has shut his eyes, letting this happen, and he doesn't resist, doesn't flinch as I close my fingers around his windpipe and then tear the skin and rip the throat out by sheer force, a grip more powerful than I can imagine, and Cox and Pooley and Dan Levine and Janet Stephens and Hap recede into the shadows, fade away, and blood is spraying that gray couch like a geyser emptying its crystal clear water and Abe Mann's eyes shoot open and roll back and he gags on his own blood, slumping off the couch and rolling on to the floor.

I am up and through the bedroom door and the window is open and I know he wasn't lying, maybe for the first time in a long time, he wasn't lying, and the words he said to me about my escape were honest and right and true.

I climb the balcony and scale the final eight feet to the roof and sprint across the gravel and tar to the other side like a man being granted his freedom and it's right there as he said it would be, an empty window-washer's cart like a boat across Styx, and I hit the button and it lowers quickly. My shoulder aches but I ignore it and the wind picks up and blows hard into my face and I can taste a bit of salt in the air from the endless ocean to the west.

EPILOGUE

I step out of the white Mercedes van and the driver opens my door and hands me my suitcase. The hotel is as I remember it, built into the side of the hill like a natural addition to the landscape. My room is large and comfortable and I walk to the patio overlooking the town and the sea far below and I cast my eyes up the hill and across until they settle on the Cortino house.

I wonder who lives in it now. It has been six years since the bodies of Cortino, his invalid wife, and his bodyguard were found murdered in their bedroom on an early June morning. The crime slapped the sleepy town awake, sent it reeling, but the passage of time and the endless lapping of the ocean on its doorstep gently nudged the town back to sleep. I imagine the doors of the houses high up on the hill are locked at night now.

The city of Los Angeles had a similar reaction the second time a nominee was assassinated while in its care. But there was no Sirhan Sirhan to exact revenge upon, just a John Smith with a nondescript face and a pleasant voice and an ability to vanish into thin air. Two years later, the case remains unsolved, despite every effort to gain some answers.

I am here in Positano getting my mind right. It is late summer and I informed Mr. Ryan I would need a few months between assignments this time. A few months without making connections, without severing connections, just a few months to breathe and live and remember.

I have worked exclusively in Europe since the Abe Mann killing, and Mr. Ryan moved to Paris to facilitate his role in my work. He has found the move from the desert to be agreeable, the law enforcement here more relaxed, the economy strong, the supply of contracts endless. I believe he is happy having a Silver Bear under his aegis, though we don't talk about personal things. Ours is a business relationship, and things are simple.

He traveled recently to Denver, Colorado upon my request. It is the first time he has made a file on a person who wasn't a target. I have the file in my hand now, but I haven't opened it. I was waiting until I arrived in this place, this town built into the side of a hill yearning to tumble into the sea. I sit heavily on a patio chair, breathe in the cool night air, and place my thumb under the seal.

The name at the top of the page is Jacqueline Grant, formerly Jake Owens of Boston, Massachusetts. The surveillance photo shows a profile of a woman stepping out of a car, hurrying across a parking lot to a grocery store. Her hair is longer than it was when I knew her and her face is a bit fuller. She looks content, or maybe I'm projecting this on to her image.

She has been married for three years. Her husband owns a restaurant. A clean, well-lighted place that serves hamburgers to locals. He is her age and treats her well. I wonder how they met. I wonder if she was unlucky with men after I kicked her in the stomach or if she swore them off until Alex Grant came into her life. I wonder if he was safe and she felt secure with him.

I wonder if she loves him.

HUNT FOR THE BEAR

Derek Haas

For Michael, who directed.
And for Molly, who produced.

I

If you're asking me to look back on my life and find answers to your questions, or if you're hoping for an explanation or an apology for my actions, you are going to be disappointed. I have not softened. I have not changed. Once I commit to killing a target, death follows.

I told you not to like me.

It is overcast in Rome. A wall of gray clouds have rolled in and settled over the city like a conquering army. Shop owners and businessmen cast upward glances, trying to gauge whether or not rain is inevitable. They think maybe the sky is just posturing, threatening, but they unpack their umbrellas just the same.

I am dressed in the dark slacks and long-sleeve sweaters commonly worn by locals this time of year. My Italian has steadily improved, though my accent will never be without flaw. I had hoped to master the inflections, to be able to pass myself off as a native, but my speech pattern lacks authenticity, and I am easily pegged as an English speaker within a few short sentences. This has hampered my ability to blend in, which I've always worn like a protective coat in the States. As such, I have learned to say as little as possible.

I make my way up a street named the *Largo Delle Sette Chiese*, and head for a small restaurant crammed to the breaking point with tables and customers and food and waiters too busy to give a damn about smiling. The menu is authentic Roman, as is the customer service; servers drop off plates and silverware and expect patrons to set the table for themselves. Most tourists aren't smart enough to frequent the place, the *Ar Grottino der Traslocatore*, preferring the homier pasta and fish shops around the Spanish Steps or near the Colosseum.

I drop into a wooden chair across from my fence, my middleman, an astute, stoic businessman named William Ryan. He has been my fence for a couple of years now, and though we relocated to Europe together following an assignment where my old fence was gunned down and I killed my father with my bare hands, our relationship remains strictly a business one.

'How was your flight?'

'Mercifully short.'

Ryan had bought a home in Paris in the expensive Eighth arrondissement, above an art gallery near the Bristol Hotel. We meet in Rome whenever he wants to hand me a new assignment. Files are only passed in person, never mailed. I have asked him to move to Italy, but he prefers the amenities of Parisian living.

'I trust you're ready to go back to work, Columbus?'

It has been two months since my last assignment, the execution of a corrupt Belgian police superintendent in Brussels. He had been a vain man who thought himself untouchable up until the moment I touched him.

A waiter breaks off to take our order and soon fills the table with *straccetti alla rucola* and *bistecca di lombo*.

'Yes. As soon as possible.'

I can only take off a couple of months before I get restless, itchy. Anything more and I feel my edge slipping. Once the edge dulls, it can take drastic measures to sharpen it.

Ryan extracts a thick manila envelope from a leather satchel. To anyone watching, we are simply businessmen conducting business in the bustle of a packed Italian restaurant. It is too noisy for other customers to hear our conversation, though we would never discuss anything suspicious in public.

I transfer the envelope to my lap, and it feels like a brick has been placed there, solid and heavy. An image pops into my head, a man being crushed to death under stones while groaning 'more weight' through clenched teeth. Where is that from? Something I read a long time ago, perhaps when I was incarcerated at a juvenile detention center named Waxham in western Massachusetts. I was sent there, along with my only friend, for killing one of our foster parents after suffering years of brutality. That place was responsible for my education in more ways than one, a rung on the ladder to where I stand now.

Ryan picks over his food. 'The client pays a premium.'

'Where do you gauge the level of difficulty?'

'Medium.'

I nod, absorbing this.

We finish our meal without talking, and when the waiter clears the table and takes Ryan's cash, we stand and shake hands.

'The job is in Prague. If you need anything additional from me, don't hesitate.'

'Thank you.'

'The logistics are covered in the file. Take care, Columbus.'

'You too.'

We head away in opposite directions.

The name at the top of the page is Jiri Dolezal. His file indicates he is a Czech banker, a man whose hands are buried up to the wrists in drug rings and prostitution rings and pornography rings and anything else illicit into which he can force his way. He is a bad egg, and it is obvious if he is suddenly discovered with his shell cracked, the Czech police will sniff around just long enough to look like they give a shit before labeling the case 'unsolved.'

Ryan's file on the subject is thick and thorough. My former fence, Pooley, excelled at putting these files together, documenting as many facts about the target as possible and compiling them into a dossier to give me a detailed glimpse into a mark's life. But Ryan is a true master craftsman, I have to admit; his work in this area – the depth of information he uncovers – is extraordinary, uncanny, far surpassing even Pooley's best efforts.

The pages inside the file serve two purposes. The first is practical: I need to look for the best place to strike the target and make my subsequent escape. Any piece of information might help. The route the target takes to work. The restaurants he frequents. The blueprints of his house, his office. Even personal information like the names of his children or his nieces and nephews or his dying father can feasibly come into play, can put the target at ease, can get me invited into his house or his office where I can shoot him without impediment. The more information Ryan provides, the less I have to rely on dangerous improvisation.

The second purpose the file serves is psychological. It is difficult to explain, but the job I do – the professional killing of men – exacts a mental toll. The only way to diminish this toll is to make a connection with the target, to find some evil in the mark and exploit that evil in my mind. An olive-skinned Italian man named Vespucci explained this to me a lifetime ago in a small apartment in Boston when I first walked this path. He said that I must *make* the connection so I can *sever* the connection. He said he could not explain why it was so, just that it was. I heard from Ryan that Vespucci had died recently, though I didn't hear how. I wonder if that old man went down swinging, or if he was finally crushed beneath the weight of his personal stones.

Still, there is one incongruous nugget in Dolezal's file. **Mark frequents a rare bookstore in Prague located on Valentinska. He collects Izaak Walton and Horace Walpole.**

The information seems odd to me, like a flower emerging through the crack of a sidewalk. Nothing else in the dossier suggests Dolezal is more than a humorless thug. His life seems regimented, colorless; and yet, here is something unconventional. A collection indicates a passion. So why rare books, and why these authors in particular? Make the connection. I need to make the connection, get inside the target's head, so I can sever the connection.

I enter a tiny shop in Rome on the Via Poli named Zodelli. The cramped room is lined with shelves, all holding leather-bound books behind glass enclosures. The bulbs are dim, and it takes my eyes a moment to adjust to the absence of light. A gray-haired woman sits behind a desk, marking a ledger with a pencil. I greet her in Italian and she looks up and smiles perfunctorily, then calls out 'Risina!'

I turn to better examine the nearest row of books and wait with my hands stuffed in my pockets. The shelf appears to hold several volumes of the same book, *The Life and Letters of Charles Dickens*, bound in red. From what I can see, the covers look as fresh and spotless as new pieces of furniture.

'These are first editions from 1872 . . .'

There are two facets to a woman's beauty. The first is internal, the beauty found in the kindness of eyes, in a simple gesture, in a soft voice. The second is physical, the kind that strikes you like a punch in the stomach and threatens to take your breath away, to suffocate you. The woman standing next to me is stunning. She's wearing a simple black dress, and her dark hair is tied up, but one strand has fallen away and passes over an eye to gently kiss her cheek.

And yet there is something else in her face. An undercurrent I've spotted on a few of my marks. What is it? Sadness? Loneliness? Whatever it is, it only serves to join the two facets together, like a peg bolting inside a lock.

'Here, take a look.' She unlocks the glass partition and withdraws one of the books from the shelf. I have to concentrate to pull my eyes from her in order to focus on the book. 'You see? It's a beautiful series. It has twelve Cosway-style portraits depicting Dickens over the course of his life.

Amazing. Octavo, see, with raised bands, green gilt inlays on the front panels, gilt doblures, watered silk endpapers . . . yes? Really magnificent. Perfect condition.'

I find my voice. 'Your English is quite good.'

She smiles. 'I went to university in America.'

'Which part?'

'Boston.'

'I know the city.'

'I loved it there. But Italy called. Italy always calls when you leave her. It is difficult not to answer.'

I hand her the book back and she looks at it one more time like she's studying the photograph of an old classmate before returning it to the shelf.

'Now, Mr. Walker, how can I help you?'

I had done some digging the last few days and, through a series of phone calls and references, made an appointment using a fake name at Zodelli with a Risina Lorenzana. My plan was to get inside my mark's head, understand his fascination with rare books, feel how he must feel as he tracks down and purchases an old manuscript. I don't speak Czech and didn't want to draw attention to myself by using the same bookstore as my mark, so I chose one near to me. I had been expecting a bookish elderly woman with a haughty manner like the one sitting behind the desk to wait on me. Not this. Not her.

'I'll confess I'm a dabbler. I have only a little experience in collecting rare books.'

'Do you like literature?'

'Very much.'

'Then you are no dabbler. You have already started collecting. Up here.' She smiles and taps her index finger to her temple.

'Are you familiar with Izaak Walton?'

'*The Compleat Angler*, yes? A wonderful book to collect . . . do you like to fish?'

'I like to catch things.'

Her smile widens, the kind that starts in her eyes before spreading to her mouth and cheeks. That underlying current fades a bit.

'I do too. I think it is innate, this feeling.' She touches my forearm as she says this, a chuckle in her voice. Even after she moves to the desk, pulls out a binder and flips through it, I can still feel her fingers on my skin.

She shakes her head, turning a page. 'I'm afraid I do not have any Walton on hand, but it is . . . um . . . not much effort to find one for you.'

'Is that how it works? Collectors come to you to find specific books for them?'

'Yes, that is part of the job, yes. Also, I hunt for books coming on the market . . . auctions, estate sales, through a . . . what's the American word . . . network? I have friends and contacts at other shops who let me know when something interesting is up for sale. A network, yes?'

'And rivals?'

'Yes . . . it can be competitive. But it is as you say, I like to catch things.'

Her whole face lights up when she says this, and there is something familiar about the expression. I think I've worn it myself a few times.

'How long would it take you to locate one for me?'

'First edition?'

'Yes.'

'I will have to call a few people, but I do not think long. As old as the book is, it was very popular in its time. There are quite a few on the market. I should be able to find it for a fair price. How may I contact you?'

I write down an e-mail address for her, and she hands me her card. 'You can reach me any time . . . that is my personal mobile number.'

'I look forward to hearing from you.'

'I'll start fishing,' she says with a laugh as I head for the door.

It will be a while before the image of her face leaves my head. And that undercurrent, that emotion she tries to bite down but can't quite pull off, is as intriguing to me as a wrapped box. I need to know more about Risina Lorenzana; I have to know more.

These are thoughts I should not be having.

Darkness descends on Prague quickly, like someone tossed a blanket over the sun. The city at night is quiet and expectant, the cold of winter chasing most tourists to warmer hemispheres. It is foot-stamping weather, and icicles hang like incisors from the buildings of Old Town. The moon hides, as though afraid of what's coming.

I am in my third week of tracking Jiri Dolezal, making the connection so I can sever the connection. It is easy to blend in here . . . thick, bulky coats, dark toboggans for the head, and full beards conspire to make all men look uniform. In the winter, it is simply too cold to pick out a stranger on the street, or to notice a professional killer as he stalks his prey.

I am in a basement restaurant near the St. Charles Bridge, an authentic Czech establishment serving duck, rabbit, lamb, and potatoes in a large pot brought right to the table. As beautiful as the city is – the bridge itself is a marvel of medieval craftsmanship – the insides of the traditional restaurants are mausoleums: dark, cramped, and smoky. I have my head buried in a book while my fork moves regularly from dish to mouth. I don't say much, don't move much, just blend into the wall like a piece of old furniture.

Two men sit in a dark corner, smoking Petras and drinking vodka. They run a nightclub for Dolezal, an ostentatious techno-dance hall that specializes in transporting women from the brothels outside of town to a less threatening location for tourists.

Ryan's file indicates that these men, Bedrich Novotny and Dusan Chalupnik, have been skimming money from the boss, bumping liquor prices on cash sales and ringing up only half the purchases while pocketing the rest. They also have deals with the working girls to pad their prices and split the profits, unbeknownst to their employer. It is a tightrope walk, this scamming of a scammer, and these men are either too reckless or too stupid to pull it off successfully.

They have been summoned to meet Dolezal tonight, and it is obvious from the way they pick at their food and tap their legs up and down continuously, they suspect the old man might have caught wind of their play. Though I can't speak their language, I gather they are comparing notes tonight, getting their stories straight before meeting the man they are defrauding.

It is one thing to read about a mark's misdeeds in a dossier, although Ryan does an amazing job of chronicling them explicitly. It is quite another to experience them first hand, to witness evil in a man up close, to see his face as he metes out punishment. I have learned over the years that perhaps the best way to get to know a mark is to watch his employees, to see how they carry themselves, witness for myself how they are treated. When looking for evil to exploit, watch the men right below the man. They are his representatives, a part of the mark himself.

After an hour, Novotny and Chalupnik don their coats and shuffle out into the night. I settle my bill and follow discreetly. Prague is a walking city for many of the residents, and these men are no exception. They certainly aren't worried about being tracked; they're both wearing bright red parkas and smoking cigarettes like they're determined to reach the bottom of the pack. They mumble to each other as they go, and though I don't understand the words, I can pick up the tightness of their speech, like their windpipes are constricting as they get closer to the meeting point.

They arrive at a corner where Partyzanska Street meets a set of railroad tracks and stand under a lamppost, their backs to me, waiting. My eyes have long since adjusted to the darkness, and it is easy for me to watch those red parkas from a stoop a block away. I am invisible here; even my frozen breath I've learned to trap in my black scarf by breathing slowly out of the side of my mouth.

Fifteen minutes pass and they check their watches. Their voices reach me over the wind, irritated, frustrated. If they were planning on coming here to make an angry stand, the delay has taken the wind from their sails. Just as a freight train approaches, rounding the corner, I see a large man approaching them from behind rapidly, pulling a handgun from the small of his back.

Gunfire erupts, two shots, the report of a low-caliber pistol, pop, pop, barely audible over the thunder of the train. The two men pitch forward, their foreheads opening, and crash to the sooty pavement, side by side, their limbs splayed out at absurd angles. The train passes and the shooter retreats down the adjacent alley to my right until I can no longer see him or hear his footsteps.

I wait twenty minutes, though I'm sure the killer is long gone, and then head back the way I came. I've seen all I need to see.

At Waxham Juvenile Hall, boys learned all the ways of dirty fighting, but nothing was held in more contempt and less respect than the sucker punch. Decking someone from behind with a fist to the temple, or shoving a pencil into someone's back was considered the lowest of the low, and any kid who pulled that shit soon found himself friendless, alone, vulnerable.

Jiri Dolezal took care of business by sucker-punching his men, gunning them down when they couldn't see it or hear it coming. I'm not sure if he pulled the trigger, or simply ordered it done, but I had little doubt it was his decision, his play, and it gave me all I needed to plan his death.

I return to Rome for one purpose, to pick up a first-edition copy of Izaak Walton's *The Compleat Angler*. There are a hundred ways I could have paid for the book and had it delivered to me without setting foot inside Zodelli's, but I find my feet moving through the door like they are operating on their own, no mind to guide them, enchanted.

'Mr. Walker!' Risina greets me warmly, and now it is my throat constricting.

'Good afternoon,' I manage.

'Just give me one moment. I have your book in the back.'

She heads through a swinging wooden door, leaving me alone in the shop. The truth is, I don't need to be here. I've done what I set out to do, to get inside the mind of my target, and the rare-book world is a dead end, a pointless triviality, with no evil to exploit. So why am I here? Why did I travel all the way back to Rome? Why am I waiting to look into a face flawlessly exhibiting both kinds of beauty? Because there's an undercurrent in her face I need to explore.

'Ahh, here it is. Have a look?'

I take the volume in my hand, and study the front . . . the author's name in white text above the black title of the book, and then an illustration of a pair of men nestled under a tree, casting lines into a river.

'Remarkable condition for a seventeenth-century novel, yes?'

I nod. 'It's amazing.'

'I will admit I read through it while I was waiting for you to pick it up. I studied literature in school, yes, but my seventeenth-century experience is limited. Milton, yes, some of the poets like Herbert, Donne . . . but Walton passed me by. You have inspired me.'

'I'll confess I know nothing about him. I told a friend I might start collecting books, and he suggested this one. But now I feel like I shouldn't touch it, just put it on a shelf . . .'

She makes a clucking sound with her mouth, like a schoolteacher correcting a student. 'No, no, no, Mr. Walker. Hang paintings on a wall, put photographs on a shelf, but books . . . no, they are alive. They are meant to be handled. Open the pages and read them. Only then are they worth collecting, once you know what's inside.'

I smile at her and Risina returns it, and there's that underlying hint of sadness there, like the bass note of a perfume. The corners of her mouth turn up, but only slightly. I feel a spot opening up in my stomach, like someone has hooked a line there and is towing me toward her. Goddamn, do I need to know more about her. But to what end? What can it possibly gain me but complications in a life where it remains essential I be alone?

After I pay for the book, she offers her hand. 'Please come back to see me, Mr. Walker. We can start to grow your collection.'

'I would like that,' I say, and since there is no other practical reason for me to remain, I head for the door. This will be the last time I see her, I lie to myself, and take one last look at her behind the desk as I head out into the street.

Jiri Dolezal will die tonight. He is in his office, working late, surrounded by a skeletal staff: an assistant, a bodyguard, and his cousin, who oversees his ledgers. Dolezal didn't luck into his fortune; he worked extremely hard at the business of evil. His work ethic would almost be admirable if he applied it toward say, fighting world poverty instead of exploiting teenage girls in the Eastern European sex trade.

Ninety-nine times out of a hundred, I do not know who hires me. Our fences are designed as a barrier between assassin and client, to protect us from each other. It is better this way. I don't need to know the motivation for why someone placed a hit on my mark. I only need to validate the inherent evil in my target so I can make my kill and walk away.

Occasionally, though, I discover the client in the course of the hunt. The file will hint at a possibility, and if beneficial, I can use that information to assist me. I just have to be right.

I break into the building using the oldest of techniques: a tension wrench and a steel lockpick. While Prague has made great strides toward joining the new century, security is surprisingly Old World. It is as though the new crop of organized criminals believes the fear and intimidation popularized by the old government regime is enough to keep danger at bay.

I march to the second-floor office and knock on the door, brazenly. I can hear everything go quiet in the room, like I've caught its occupants in some nefarious act, and then a man with a baritone voice barks an order to someone nearer to my position.

The door swings open and the secretary fills the space. She measures me with a dour expression. She says something in Czech, and I respond by holding up the book Risina tracked down for me. With my best British accent, I say, 'I understand Mr. Dolezal collects Izaak Walton.'

She frowns and clucks over her shoulder. After a brief argument from which I can guess the gist, the door opens further, and I step into the room.

Dolezal is behind his desk, ten feet away. He has a fat face and a nose that lists to the left, like it was broken and never reset. To my right is the cousin, who barely looks up from his laptop. The bodyguard, who is easily a head taller than me, stands next to him. I am confident he is the man who pulled the trigger on Novotny and Chalupnik, the one who shot them at close range from behind.

In my left hand, I hold the first edition *Compleat Angler*. It is like a magician's feint . . . it draws the eye to it and away from my free hand. The bodyguard steps in to frisk me, which is always a good time to strike. When the big man is stooped over, his hands on my waist instead of his weapon, he is vulnerable.

He starts to pat me down and my right hand finds that pistol he keeps in the small of his back. I have it out of his waistband and up in the blink of an eye. It's a double-action, nine millimeter Czech CZ-TT, a little small for me but it will do just fine in close quarters. Dolezal is still staring at the book in my left hand when the bullet shatters that misshapen nose of his for good. I hit him square, a sucker punch he never saw coming.

The loud report of the gun is like an electric shock to the bodyguard. He leaps backward, takes one look at his boss, and his face falls. I can see the calculations working out in his mind, can see his brain forming the wrong decision. The secretary starts to bellow like a siren but I'm not worried about her. The bodyguard sets his legs to pounce, lowers his head to charge me – if he's going down, he's going down a fighter even though the battle is already decided.

Just as I swing the gun around, the cousin rises up behind him, wielding that laptop like a mallet. He brings it down with everything he has on top of the bodyguard's head. The big man drops like someone kicked his legs out from under him as the laptop cracks across the back of his head, shattering into a hundred pieces.

The cousin gives me a satisfied look but I keep my face neutral, drop the pistol next to the capsized guard, and hurry toward the stairwell. I was hoping I wasn't going to have to kill the bodyguard. In my experience, killing anyone other than the target creates a mess. So I let the forgotten man in the room take care of him, the cousin, the one who hired me. Since I don't know where the secretary's loyalties lie, I am gone before she can make a decision. If she had planned it with the cousin, had been a part of hiring me, I'll never know.

I know exactly what I'm doing, goddammit. I'm clearing my mind, recharging my batteries, wiping my slate clean so I will be fresh for a new assignment. I am getting my mind right.

So why am I once again in Rome, sitting in a small *trattoria* near the Trevi fountain?

'I hate it, actually,' Risina is saying. 'My sister was six or seven when my mother was pregnant, carrying me. For some inexplicable reason, my mother asked her to name me. She was so young, and I suppose was playing off of the common name Rosina, which means "rose," and instead came up with Risina, which means nothing except that I have had to correct people all my life.'

'I would say "a rose by any other name" but I'm sure you've heard that before.'

She smiles genuinely. 'Only once or twice.'

The last fifteen years have taught me many things, but above all else is this: I cannot do what I do and maintain a relationship. There are no rules in the assassination world, no code, no honor amongst thieves. There are no civilians, no untouchable targets. If I continue to escalate this, if I continue to see Risina, then I have thrust her into this game despite the fact she will not know she's playing. I have pounded my head against this immovable wall twice before. With Pooley, who died, and with a girl I loved, Jake Owens, whom I had to forcibly remove from my life. I thought I could go back to her, but I was wrong.

So what am I doing here? Jiri Dolezal is dead; my connection to the rare-book world has been severed. So why do I keep returning to that bookstore on the Via Poli, why am I still pretending to be a collector, why did I hire Risina to track down another *Compleat Angler* for me? Why did I suggest dinner tonight?

Is it because I'm searching for some vestige of humanity in myself and I'm willing to put another life in danger, if only to satisfy my basest instincts?

I'll say it again. I told you not to like me.

2

The mark's name is Anton Noel. He is the fifty-two-year-old chief information officer of a French pharmaceutical company based in Paris named Ventus-Safori. He has worked there for over two decades, rising through the ranks since he was hired out of school as an assistant accountant in the late eighties. The attached surveillance photos reveal a man who has not passed on too many crepes since graduation.

Ryan and I met outside a cathedral in Turin to exchange the file.

'It's the same procurer as the Prague job.'

'That's the fourth time they've hired me.'

'They like your work.'

'I met the fence . . .'

'Doriot.'

'Yes. I met him in Brussels before the first job when he wanted to take a look at me. He was hard to read.'

Ryan looked at me with a level expression. 'Which means he's a professional.'

'Yeah. I get that. He's still the one handling affairs for this client, then?'

Ryan nodded.

'I don't want to get too tied to one contractor. I mean, I think we should—'

My fence held up one palm as though nothing further needed to be said on the subject. 'I understand. You still want this file then, or do you want me to beg off to Doriot?'

'No, I'll take it.'

He handed it to me, and I felt that weight again. Heavier this time. The stones piling up.

Ryan stared hard at me. 'You sure you're ready, Columbus?'

'Of course.'

He looked like he had something more to say, but I avoided his eyes. Finally, we shook hands and left.

Now, with the file in my hand, I pore over its contents, an uneasy feeling prickling my brain. *Am* I ready? What did Ryan see in me that made him ask that question?

Noel appears to be a typical rich European businessman. He keeps a mistress in a small apartment on the Left Bank. He employs a couple of Serbian bodyguards, veterans from a mostly forgotten war. He travels a few times a month by private jet to London or New York or Geneva. Peculiarly, he drives his own car, a Mercedes, and has his bodyguards sit behind him and in the passenger seat. This piques my interest, the way Dolezal's rare-book collection stood out on the page for me. If he's chauffeuring his bodyguards around, then he isn't particularly concerned with his own protection. Or he's arrogant, controlling, a trait I've seen in some of these business titans. They don't want to relinquish control of any part of their lives, even the mundane.

Possibilities emerge in front of me. Take him en route to work, while he's behind the wheel? Take him at the private airfield housing his jet? Strike when he's occupied with his mistress? Take that control he cherishes and turn it against him?

I should have left for Paris already. I am four weeks into an eight-week assignment and I should be following my mark, forming strike plans, identifying his weaknesses, searching for evil.

But I am with Risina, in her small apartment in Rome, keeping that weight off me, even if the relief is only temporary.

Her cooking is awful. The pasta is chewy, the sauce is bland, the cheese on top is strong enough to melt my nose, and I love every bite of it. A home-cooked anything is enticing for someone who barely knows the meaning of the word 'home,' and if the wine has to flow to wash it down, so be it.

She looks at me across the table, her fork poised in midair.

'I seem to talk a great bit about myself, and when I leave you, I realize I've learned nothing new about you.'

'I find you interesting.'

She points the fork at me. 'I know what you're doing and it won't work.'

'What am I doing?'

'I am going to ask you a direct question and you are going to turn it around back to me.'

'Ask.'

'Okay. I will ask this. What do you do for a living that brings you to Italia so often?'

'That's an easy one. Why did you start working with book collectors?'

She laughs and wags her finger. 'I told you.'

There are two parts to lying, and both require practice. One is to hold your eyes steady and to speak with only a hint of inflection. The second is to make the lie so plain and uninteresting as to rule out any follow-up questions.

I set my face. 'My work is boring. I work for an airline company. I buy and sell parts for airplane wings. I line up contracts all over the world.'

'You see. That is not boring. You are an international businessman.'

'A boring international businessman.'

'But as you say, you travel all over the world.'

'Doing a job any man can do.'

'I think you are modest.'

'Just telling the truth.'

And the corners of her mouth turn up into a smile, this one stretching farther, because she is with a man who tells the truth, who is safe, who is humble about his life. The sadness below the surface has dissipated, at least a bit.

She takes a bite of her pasta and makes a face.

'My cooking is terrible.'

'No,' I say and keep my gaze locked. 'I mean, I can't feel my tongue any more, but it's really wonderful.'

She erupts in laughter, the infectious kind, color coming to her cheeks.

'Okay, we're going to try something only one time,' she says as she pushes her plate to the center of the table, dismissing it.

'What?'

'We're going to ask each other one question and no topic is how-do-you-say . . .'

'Off limits?'

'Yes, taboo. Off limits. And the other has to answer truthfully, no matter what is asked. Maybe we'll learn something and want to learn more, or maybe after hearing the answer, we'll decide we just aren't . . . we just don't want to keep seeing each other.'

'Sounds dangerous.'

'Possibly.'

'Okay, I'm in.'

'Okay?'

I nod and she smiles.

'Can I ask first?'

I nod again.

'Why do you want to see me, Jack?'

I don't have to set my face, don't have to lie, not this time. 'I want to know who put that sadness in your eyes, in your cheeks.'

She leans back, the answer catching her off guard, and folds her arms across her chest. For a long moment, she doesn't say anything, and even the air in the room seems to still.

'Is that your question to me?'

'That's my answer to your question. I haven't asked one yet.'

She nods, forces a smile. Her voice stays low. 'Okay, then, what is your question?'

'We don't have to—'

'Don't be silly. This was my idea.'

'Okay. Are you ready?'

She lowers her eyes like she's bracing herself, and her nod is barely perceptible.

I wait until she looks up, then arrest her eyes with mine. 'My question is this. What is the recipe for this pasta?'

She blinks, and then starts laughing again. It is a sound that will stay with me for the next few weeks, holding me afloat like a life preserver.

The signs are there, if you pay attention. Little things: you bang your shin into the coffee table in the morning, or you step off a curb into a puddle of sewer water, or you can't find your wallet, your keys, your jacket, no matter how hard you look. Bad luck has a way of building momentum, of summoning its strength like an ocean wave before crashing down over you, knocking you off your feet. If you can spot the signs, you might be fortunate enough not to drown.

Paris is chilly and gray in February, though it is desperately trying to maintain its charm. There is something sad about it, like a hostess doing her best to keep a party together after the first guests start trickling away. Stores and restaurants are open, but outside tables are empty and silent. People shuffle by without talking, hurrying to get where they're going, lighting cigarettes without breaking stride.

I have seen Anton Noel four times. Once, at a charity auction where I monitored him from a crowd inside an art gallery. Once, at a business conference where he droned on in French about the necessity of product diversification in emerging global markets. And twice, I have watched him driving his Mercedes, heading out of the gate where the Rue du St. Paul meets the Rue St. Antoine.

The gate is well guarded, with two dark-suited men perking up whenever the boss is about to roll outside, and a bevy of cameras pointing out at the street. I can watch the gate from the front window of a café a block away without drawing attention to myself . . . just order a coffee and a pastry while I pretend to read an American newspaper. The guards are a signal; they sit relaxed throughout most of the day, slumped in stiff chairs, even when a delivery truck or visitor crosses through the gates. However, when a white phone near the gate rings, they both rise to attention and stand erect, eyes sweeping the area, always five minutes before the black Mercedes drives out, Noel at the wheel, his bodyguards in the passenger seat and behind him.

Most often, it is this type of security I find myself up against: lax, poorly conceived, untrained. These guards – and the ones riding in the Mercedes – are simply window-dressing, as empty and impotent as a scarecrow in a field. They work as a deterrent against amateur thieves and muggers and kidnappers, but are worthless against a professional contract killer.

And herein lies the rub: it is my duty, my obligation, to keep my concentration at the highest level, to eliminate my prey flawlessly, even when faced with unworthy opposition. This is how I became what the Russians call a Silver Bear, an assassin who commands top fees because he never defaults on a job. I became one by never underestimating my mark, by treating every job as if it were my last.

'Your espresso.'

'*Merci*.'

The shop owner has shuffled over carrying a saucer and a small cup and I keep my face pleasant and unmemorable.

'This weather . . . pfff,' he says and I just want him to hand me my drink and move back to the counter. I've learned not to start up conversations, not to engage with Europeans who spot an English-speaker and want to practice the language. There is a way of holding my face still, of acting like I am deep in thought, concentrating on the paper, that makes waiters or shop owners leave the food behind and walk away without thinking further of it, without thinking 'I should remember this asshole. I better keep an eye on him.'

My behavior is working, the man is already whispering *pardon*s as he sets down the saucer, is already taking one step backward, but he didn't place the saucer carefully on the railing and the plate and cup topple over, spilling espresso all over my pants before crashing to the floor.

He starts cursing himself in French, all apologies and wishes for forgiveness and how could he be such an oaf, and I just tell him not to worry about it, it's cool, don't worry at all, but now others are looking at me in the shop and my anonymity is slightly compromised.

Bad luck. You can remain focused, hone your concentration, but you are powerless against luck when it sours and turns against you. I cannot allow it to build, so I am up and moving out the door, leaving five euros behind which should be enough to make him happy his error didn't cost him my business.

I am going to kill Noel today. I am going to kill him on this street, when I see the guards receive the phone call and the black Mercedes pull out of the gate and turn in this direction, toward the end of the narrow lane. I am going to be seated on an old Honda motorcycle, idling on the left side of the road. When he drives past me I am going to shoot him in the face through his driver's side window. The car will be moving when I shoot him, which will cause the vehicle to continue forward into a row of parked cars, so that by the time his bodyguards and any on-lookers realize what is happening, I will be ten blocks away.

I was planning on having five minutes after I hear the white phone ring to quietly pay for my drink and head out, still reading my newspaper, and then I would sit on top of the motorcycle, folding the paper back, appearing like I'm finishing an article while my right hand slips inside my jacket and finds my Glock. But now that plan has to be modified.

I can't loiter at the end of the street, can't draw any suspicion to myself. The time Noel leaves varies each afternoon; the only clue is the white phone ringing.

I should abort, should do this job tomorrow, but I hesitated too long in Rome, didn't get started on my surveillance until the sixth week on this job and the contractor is expecting a dead body by the time the sun sets tonight. I have put all my eggs in the white phone basket. My two previous scouts proved it would be an effective strategy, a way to exploit his flawed sense of security.

I can't go back to square one anyway; the café owner would remember me now. If I entered his shop tomorrow at the same time, he would have another reason to recognize my face and make contact and continue to apologize and my anonymity would be surrendered completely. It has to be today.

I deserve this bad luck because I am mentally unprepared. Risina. Even now my thoughts are drifting to the last conversation we had, seated in the train station in Rome, her hair pulled back in a tight ponytail.

'There is something about you, Jack, between the words that you say.'

'You're making me sound more interesting than I am . . .' I had a hard time looking away from her. I am a man who is always checking angles, noting the body language of strangers in my periphery. And yet my eyes continued to lock on hers like she was the only one in the station.

'For someone who loves books as much as I do, I'm terrible at reading people. But with you, I feel like there's a missing chapter. Someone maybe ripped it free and you're reluctant to put it back.'

'Who told you you were bad at reading people?'

'I know I am, Jack. I've had very few . . . I've gotten to know very few people.'

'Well, I'm glad you want to get to know me.'

'I do. I want to know—'

The white phone is ringing, snapping me back to the present. My luck isn't so bad after all, I am halfway to the small Honda motorcycle and I no longer have to come up with a plan to loiter and watch the street. Anton Noel has unwittingly sealed his fate by simply leaving his office early. It didn't take me long after I landed in Paris to find evil in the man to exploit. I learned through Ryan that his company, Ventus-Safori, is famous for rushing experimental drugs to market, for paying off France's government drug administration to ensure their pills are first on pharmacy shelves. This has resulted in three recalls since Noel rose to power, twice after the deaths of more than a dozen adults due to heart complications from hastily manufactured cholesterol blockers. And once, following the deaths of three infants from a cold medicine that should never have been allowed on the market. Internal memos revealed all three were known to be risky, but bribes in the right places assured millions of Euros were made before the company's troubled medications could be removed from store counters. All lawsuits were fought vigorously, and the company's stock price withstood the bad press. I had little doubt Anton Noel had carefully factored in the risks and was more concerned with profits than with his customers' health. Or lack thereof.

The black Mercedes is emerging from the gate as the two guards stand sentinel on either side, providing their hapless guise of security.

I am seated on the motorcycle as planned, my right hand gripping the handle of the automatic pistol. In the rectangle of my sideview mirror, I can see the car turning my way and heading up the street. Just a few more seconds and Noel will be dead and the spilled coffee on my pants will just be a nuisance instead of a premonition of more bad luck to come and I can head back to Rome to see that smile on Risina's face and that one strand of hair kissing her cheek and the car pulls up alongside me, about to pass. My gun is out and up and only then do I realize Noel is not behind the wheel but riding in the passenger seat.

The file said he always drove. Always. My two previous visits to the Rue St. Antoine confirmed the veracity of this statement, and my strategy was conceived to exploit it. So why this fucking day? Why right now of all times in the year for him to let his bodyguard drive and he is hunched over a BlackBerry in the passenger seat, punching in God knows what and his bodyguard's eyes go wide as he spots my pistol just a foot from his window and the wave of bad luck rolls over my head and my second of hesitation is enough.

The guard jams on the accelerator like he's trying to kick his heel through the floorboard and the Mercedes jumps like a whipped horse just as I register what is happening and fire my pistol. I only catch the bodyguard's shoulder through the window, but it might be enough. On any other day, it would probably be enough.

Instead of crashing, the Mercedes is tearing down the Rue St. Antoine, clipping the sides of parked vehicles as my thumb hits the ignition and I straddle the Honda while one hand holds my Glock and I gun the motorcycle after the fleeing sedan.

I allowed this to happen, hell I *caused* this to happen because I took this job lightly. I blinked, I stayed in Rome when I should have been here dissecting an infinite number of preferable ways to kill this target instead of cavalierly choosing *this* way, this ridiculously flawed, inept way.

No more. I set my jaw and drop my eyes into slits and pin down the throttle while the heel of my boot hovers over the back brake like a wild ram steeling itself for an attack. I am Columbus, I am a Silver Bear, and when Anton Noel leaves that Mercedes it will be at the hands of a coroner.

Ahead, the sedan whips into a hard right down a one-way commercial street in the middle of the Jewish quarter and I unleash the ram, slam hard on the rear brake as I lower my center of gravity so the motorcycle almost lays on its side and then springs up again, closing ground like a shark after a wounded swimmer.

Bad luck can be trumped by an experienced killer and the driver must be bleeding with little way to staunch the flow from his gunshot wound and his arm must be useless now. I can spot the second bodyguard swiveling in the back seat, trying to keep tabs on me while over his shoulder Noel's face has blanched and his eyes are open and filled with fear.

I have to force the driver into a mistake.

Traffic ahead causes the Mercedes to make another clipped right turn down a narrow street and I realize the driver can *only* make right turns, it is too difficult for him to mount a left with just his good arm to spin the wheel. Maybe with a little practice, but he's had none, and I don't think he's used to driving the boss's car anyway.

The frigid weather has kept most pedestrians off the sidewalk, but a few are crossing the street ahead and it is time to make my move. I throttle the motorcycle forward and to the left of the Mercedes, aligning myself with the back bumper, so close to the rear windshield that I can practically smell the breath of the second bodyguard. He has a pistol up, a snub-nosed .38, a show weapon, a gun he has probably never fired and he is afraid, afraid to even take a potshot at me, afraid the gun might kick back and hit him in the face.

As I suspected, the driver is unable to steer into me. I can hear Noel shouting in French in the front seat, but the second bodyguard ignores his pleas, won't take aim, is swiveling in his seat trying to keep an eye on me, and I brake quickly and sweep the bike around the backside of the Mercedes so I am now on the right bumper and the intersection is practically on us and the driver thinks I have made a mistake and now he can bump me off my perch.

He jerks the wheel to the right, oversteering as I believed he would and the front of the car smashes into a parked Peugeot van just shy of the intersection and its inertia keeps it going so it flips wildly and starts tumbling like a pair of dice, smashing into a couple of unfortunate pedestrians, killing them instantly, before sliding belly up to a stop.

In the next moment, I am off the motorcycle and walking calmly, purposefully to the passenger door of the car. It only takes me an instant to crouch down and look at the bleeding, helpless visage of Anton Noel.

'*Aide*—' he mutters a moment before I shoot him in the face.

Men and women race into the street from nearby buildings, bewildered by the sudden eruption of the accident, and somewhere in the distance, the bleating two-note shriek of a French police siren fills the air.

3

I stand at a pay phone outside the train station in Naples, waiting for it to ring. I am angry. The emotion has been brewing inside me for three days, unabated.

I failed. I was sloppy, I was unprepared, and two pedestrians died in Paris because they chose to brave the cold and cross an avenue at the most unfortunate of times. They are dead and here I stand, alive and empty.

Le Monde reported their names as Jerome Coulfret, a forty-five-year-old jeweler, and Jason Baseden, a twenty-eight-year-old fitness instructor. They did not know each other. Further information about them is scant. They are merely a footnote to the professional execution of Anton Noel, the pharmaceutical CIO shot down as he left work in the middle of the afternoon in Paris.

Though I am waiting for it, the phone's ring manages to startle me.

'You are safe?'

Ryan's voice is unemotional, impassive.

'Yes.'

'The city is on edge. Investigations are under way.'

'I understand.'

He pauses, and I wait. There is more he wants to say.

'I have been doing what I do for a quarter of a century. I have no regrets. So tell me why I'm having misgivings about our relationship now.'

'I fucked up. What do you want me to say?'

'I want you to say you are committed to your work.'

I press the receiver against my forehead and close my eyes. I'd like to tell him I don't need a goddamn lecture – that I'm more angry with myself than he could ever be – but maybe I *do* need to hear it from him. Maybe I do need a good tongue-lashing, a slap in the face. Something, anything to push me back to the surface where I can breathe fresh air again.

'I underestimated the time necessary to complete this job. It won't happen again.'

'I'm not assuaged.'

'Well, there's nothing I can—'

'You can stop seeing the bookshop owner.'

I feel a dull pulse in my ear where the cool plastic of the phone receiver presses against it. I don't know why I'm surprised; a good fence finds out everything about his targets, and similarly knows everything about his assassins. I won't insult him by asking how or why he was tailing me. I know he was right to do so. And I know he was right to tell me to stop seeing Risina.

'I'll take care of it.'

He wants to say more, but it is his turn to be circumspect. After a moment, his voice comes through the phone again, softer.

'We should meet. Discuss our strategy for the remainder of the year where we can talk freely. I think it might be time to evaluate a return to work in America.'

'Okay.'

'A week from today.'

'Okay.'

There is no need for us to discuss over a telephone where this encounter will take place. We have planned our meetings sequentially. The last one was in Turin. The next one will be here, at the train station in Naples. We always meet at noon.

I'm about to say 'goodbye,' but the line has gone dead in my hand.

The Piazza Navona is a giant oval surrounding an Egyptian obelisk and a large fountain in the heart of Rome. The emperor Maxentius built the oval in the fourth century as a stadium for chariot races, where losing competitors were often executed before they left the competing ground. I wonder how much blood has been spilled here over the centuries, what forgotten man once stood where I stand, defeated, waiting for a sword to run him through.

Risina is eating lunch alone.

The day is unseasonably warm, and the cafés and shops are crowded. She is waiting for me to join her, but I can't seem to get my feet to move.

This life asks so goddamn much of me and in return, I get what? Solitude. Anonymity. A name hung on me without meaning. Money in an account I rarely touch. Fleeting human connections severed violently, dispassionately. I have become faceless, a living ghost, a walking embodiment of a vengeful god, meting out punishment with remorseless certitude. I have to trick myself into thinking the punishment is deserved, but that's just a minor inconvenience, right?

And the secret – the truth I keep tucked away like a stolen painting – is I *like* it. I like the power, I like the excitement, I like the hunt. My first fence, Vespucci, once said we held a power reserved for God, that we know our target's future long before he or she does. This power wore him down like those heavy stones on the old man's chest, but it is the opposite for me: a lift, a tonic.

The question is: at what cost? At what point does the necessity for some kind of lasting human connection tip the scales away from the thrill, the allure, the power of the hunt? At what point does it tip to an empty nothingness? I'm not sure I know the answer.

An elderly man stands near me, his hand on the back of a bench, watching people as they pass. He wears a simple smile, and his clothes, though old, are pressed and clean. He is humming a tune to himself, something old and classical, a short, happy melody I vaguely recognize. A young woman in her twenties approaches, kisses him warmly on both cheeks, and I only catch a concerned question from her in Italian . . .

'You are warm, Grandfather?'

. . . before they shuffle away. I swallow hard, can feel my hand balling into a fist, can feel the weight in the scales tipping off its median. I sneak one last look at Risina, and, before I make a decision I might regret, I leave the Piazza Navona alone.

In Naples, a week later, I am thumbing through my first-edition copy of *The Compleat Angler*, biding my time while I wait for Ryan to step off the train from Rome.

I have had time to think, to get my mind right, and there is only one solution. There has always been only one solution. I have decided I will tell her. I have to tell her.

I won't need to hear the reproof from Ryan, the judgmental tone in his voice. I know what I have to do. I know the only way the scales can tip.

I will never have grandchildren to comfort me when I'm old, to ask me if I'm warm enough as I stand contentedly in the middle of a crowded square humming a tune. I can't have things that can be taken from me, that can be used as leverage against me. I chose this life, and the cost is mine to bear. I will have to jettison Risina before the sinking ship drowns us both.

I am standing with my back to a corner made by a newspaper stand adjoining the rail-station wall. The terminal is always bustling as passengers try to dodge the thieves, liars, and beggars aiming to separate them from their money. It is easy to fade into the backdrop here.

The train from Rome arrives and I spot Ryan climbing down from one of the middle cars. He is dressed conservatively, as always, but there is something odd about his gait as he heads my way. He's favoring his left leg, limping a bit, and, as he strides closer, I can see one side of his face is swollen and purple.

I head toward him, but he is deliberately looking past me, over my shoulder, at some imaginary person thirty feet behind me, avoiding eye contact completely, and everything about this encounter is wrong.

'Turner!' he says loudly as he approaches, like he's calling out to the phantom behind me. 'Jeff!'

Turner. Turner. What's in a name? A pre-planned warning. A signal decided upon when we first went into business together. Ryan has been set up, compromised, and he's letting me know to ignore him, to keep walking, to get the hell out of there as quickly as I can.

I lock eyes on a woman stepping off the train and wave to her like *she's* the one I've been hurrying to see and as I move past Ryan, I hear the unmistakable sound of a bullet whizzing past my ear before it slams squarely into Ryan's back. From the angle of the shot, I know the shooter is ahead of me and as Ryan crumples to the dirty cement, as the crowd on the landing starts to scatter in all directions like shrapnel, I catch just a glimpse of a dark-suited, bearded man holding a pistol two platforms over.

His eyes find mine and it's enough. It was a smart play to take out Ryan as soon as the fence opened his mouth. By shooting him, this professional killer flushes the true target. He drops Ryan and watches the crowd's reaction, focusing in on anyone who looks up at the bullet's flight path instead of scrambling away in a panic. He looks for a professional, a man who doesn't jump at the sound of a gun firing in a crowd. It's what I would have done.

Goddammit, the jig is up; he knows I'm the quarry, the one Ryan was coming to meet. Without thinking, I draw my Glock and unload back at the bearded man, off-balance, knowing instinctively my shots will miss the mark yet give me enough time to duck for cover.

A train is backing away from the station on the tenth platform, and I bolt for it, trying to make myself as small as possible, careful not to run in a straight line. I know enough about putting bullets into people to hopefully avoid the shooter putting one into me.

Anton Noel. The sloppiness of the kill came home to roost. Of course he had friends in high places, friends who wouldn't be encumbered by police procedure or official leads, friends who would hire dark men like me to hunt down and execute the executioner. The man's company counted life and death as numbers on an accountant's ledger, so why should I be surprised someone close to Noel hired a professional to exact revenge? This hired gun got to Ryan and worked him over and Ryan led the bagman to me, but not before he called out for 'Jeff Turner,' giving me one last professional, undeserved nod, before he died with a bullet in his spine.

I hear a gunshot ricochet off the pavement somewhere near my right foot but I don't break stride, just zero in on the door to the debarking train. A quick glance over my shoulder reveals the bearded man sprinting my way, out in front of a host of light-blue uniformed Italian Railway Police officers.

'Interpol! Interpol!' he is shouting, but he is no more a part of the international criminal police organization than I am. Interpol agents aren't the swashbuckling lawmen seen in countless films or read about in mystery novels. They don't carry guns, can't make arrests, and rarely leave their offices. His shouting is creating the intended effect amongst the Railway officers, however: confusion.

A few more steps and I bang on the last train door, the pressure causing it to swish open. I leap through it, and immediately crouch next to the luggage rack, pointing my gun up at the doorway, waiting, hoping the bearded man will make a mistake, try to chase me inside, but all I spy through the sliver of the doorway is the last bit of the tenth platform moving away as the train rolls out of the station.

When Risina opens the bookshop, I am already inside.

'My God—'

'I'm sorry. I didn't mean to startle you.'

'How did you—?'

'The door was open.'

'It was?'

I nod. 'I was going to stand outside and wait for you, but when I saw the door, I thought you were already here. I just walked in and you came up behind me.'

She looks puzzled, worried. 'The alarm—'

'I don't know what to tell you.'

She hurries over to the cases of old texts, but no glass has been broken, no volumes appear to be missing.

'I remember—' She stops to curse in Italian. 'I thought I locked up like usual.'

She shakes her head, her hand flitting to her temples, brushing her long black hair away from her forehead. She looks at me in the middle of the room, like she has just remembered something. 'You stood me up. We had a date for lunch.'

'I had some unexpected business.' I am watching her eyes. 'I meant to call, but things happened quickly.'

She nods stiffly, and I'm not sure she believes me, as though she's heard that excuse before. That underlying sadness is fluttering just below the surface of her skin again. It doesn't matter; I have cards left to play and despite my own misgivings, I plan on playing them. I don't fully understand why, but I *have* to play them.

'I need to ask you something.'

'Yes?'

She moves over to the ornate desk in the back of the room, checking the drawers to see if any have been forced.

'I have to go away for a while. I have to do some things that are important to me, which may require me to leave Italy for some time.'

I watch as her shoulders sag a bit, as her head lowers. 'I see.'

'No, I—' I stop, choosing my words carefully.

She looks up from the desk to meet my eyes, sensing that the words I choose will carry weight.

'It's that . . . my question is this . . .' I can feel my throat tighten. 'Will you wait for me?'

4

How much is a name worth?

In the killing business, names have value. The names of targets can command staggering sums, depending on the difficulty of the assassination. The name of a U.S. cabinet member might be worth more than say, a Wall Street trader or a low-level crime boss. The name of a CEO guarded by a host of expensive and professional bodyguards might be more valuable than a police officer who is about to testify and is too smug or pig-headed to bother with protection. But these aren't the only names in the business of death that hold worth.

Fences, middlemen, go-betweens are hired to keep us from knowing whom we're working for and to keep clients from knowing whom they're hiring. They are windowless walls erected to protect us from ourselves, to keep ends from becoming loose. But there was a breakdown of the wall protecting me; someone used William Ryan's head as a battering ram and knocked right through it. I don't know who that someone is yet, but I plan to find out.

I know a name too.

Doriot is the fence who hired me to kill Anton Noel, the same fence who hired me four times in the past. He's on the acquiring side, meaning he works with clients directly and then selects assassins to fill his jobs.

Before the first assignment, acquiring fences often meet with gunmen so they can kick the tires on the showroom car. They want to get a look and feel for the killer they will be contracting; they want to be able to assure their client they are on top of things, all will go smoothly, they have a relationship with the killer and they trust the job will be cleanly and professionally executed. Clients tend to get jumpy as the contract inches closer to fulfillment; an experienced acquiring fence placates the nervous party by extolling the achievements of the assassin hired to do the job. It always helps to say he knows the gunman personally, even better if he's used the same assassin in the past.

Whether or not Doriot sold out Ryan is immaterial, though he seems the most likely candidate. He's the only direct connection between Noel and me. I don't care about revenge; I'm going to dispassionately put a bullet in whoever hired someone to kill me. It is the only way to take down the contract on my life, to pull the scent away from the hound's nose.

I have two guesses as to the identity of the man who put a price on my head. Either he's someone close to Anton Noel, as I speculated before, or he's the same man who hired me to kill Noel and after the sloppiness of the job, he wants all ties to the assassination severed. Since I'm not sure yet how to tackle the first hypothesis, I'll start with the second.

Brussels is a cold city in the middle of Europe. It is a mixture of old and new, of modern skyscrapers and shopping pavilions and art-deco houses standing shoulder to shoulder with Gothic cathedrals and pristine fifteenth-century town halls. Currently the seat of the European Union's Council and Commission, the city and its people are aloof, taciturn. The entire place feels like a museum that allows you to enter, but asks you to speak softly and not touch anything. It is somewhat telling that Brussels's most popular attraction is a statue of a little boy pissing into a basin.

Doriot lives here. I met him once, in a secure building near the river, about two years ago, before my first assignment for him. Like I said, acquiring fences like to kick the tires, and Doriot wanted to kick mine.

I remember it was cold that day, and I entered the address from a secluded street near the Zenne river. The front door opened and locked behind me, leaving me in a ten-foot-by-ten-foot 'holding' room. An intercom in the wall barked at me. The killing business flourishes all over the world, but, conveniently, its agreed-upon universal language is English.

'May I help you?' A baritone voice with a slightly German accent that sounded like it was coming from the bottom of a well filled the room.

'I'm Columbus. I have an appointment with Doriot.'

'Step back from the door, empty your chambers, and place your clips on the floor in front of you. Then clasp your fingers behind your head.'

Most acquiring fences surround themselves with a small army of protection, at least the prominent ones do if they want to stay prominent. I was used to this. I didn't get defensive, I didn't protest, I just did as commanded without revealing an ounce of emotion on my face.

After a moment, a giant of a man entered through the opaque door in front of me, holding a leather bag. Quietly, he collected the three clips I had placed on the floor, along with the two bullets I had ejected from the chambers of my Glocks. Finished, he turned and faced me.

'Hello, Columbus.'

'Hello.' I kept my fingers interlocked behind my head.

'I will have to frisk you now. Yes?'

I nodded and he ran his hands over my body, patting me down. I kicked off my shoes and he checked my ankles, then the seams of my pants. His hands were massive, the size of melons. He gave me a thorough examination, then, satisfied, stepped back.

'My name is Brueggemann. I work for Monsieur Doriot. You have heard of me?'

I shook my head and he watched my eyes, checking to see if I was withholding anything. Then he made a 'tsk' sound, sucking air between his teeth. 'I used to do what you do. Yes? For many years. Over twenty. Yet I am still here.'

'Not many can say that.' I thought this was what he wanted to hear. Challenging strangers at this stage of the game is foolish, a good way to get yourself in a bad way.

He nodded. 'No, not many. Now I work safety for the boss. And the boss is always safe, you understand?'

I shrugged, keeping my expression a well-practiced neutral. 'I'm just here to pick up my assignment. I have no interest in tearing down fences.'

He smiled, revealing a gap in his front teeth I could've driven a rig through. His eyes didn't smile, though; they stayed chained to mine. 'You may see Monsieur Doriot now. Make sure you do not approach him. Yes?'

I lowered my arms and straightened out my jacket. 'Not a problem.'

I was ushered in to see the boss, a small man with awkward frameless glasses perched on his nose. He was sitting behind an oversized desk. Brueggemann never left my side. I answered the usual questions impassively, while Doriot studied me the way a rancher examines a prize bull. He had heard about the jobs I'd pulled in the States, had heard about my reputation, and a few pointed answers to his questions let him know I had done the work Ryan claimed. I had the feeling he wanted to ask more, to try to open me up, but he knew the futility in that, and so gave me my assignment and had Brueggemann show me to the door.

The next day, I cased the building, invisible in the shadows of a nearby alley. Names hold value and Brueggemann had given me his, ostensibly to advertise his reputation. But if he had once been a contract killer like me, he had lost a step, gone soft in his retirement, the way a moonlighting cop lets his defenses down when he's sitting on a security guard's stool. It was a mistake giving me his name. The cons outweighed the pros; the scales tipped away from his favor. I knew his boss Doriot would be careful to avoid detection or pursuit when he entered or exited the building in Brussels where he did business . . . he was a deliberate and methodical professional. He would vary his routine, have multiple entrance and exit points, take illogical routes to wherever he laid his head. Ours is a business where reputation is prized but anonymity is essential. We have to be able to float into this world, this game, and then shut the door behind us when we leave. A private, personal life can never be fully realized, I have learned this all too well, but we can do things to make the likelihood of clashes between the two worlds, if not impossible, at least improbable. Still, I hoped Brueggemann's lack of foresight in revealing his name would mean he was lax when covering his own tracks.

I didn't have to wait long to find out. He exited the building through the same door I had entered the day before and headed north up the street, toward the city center, walking with his hands in his pockets, not even checking over his shoulder or scanning shop windows for reflections. Being as big as he was, he was as easy to follow as if he'd been painted red. I hung back and stayed with him until he retreated into a three-story apartment building only a quarter of a mile from the office. A minute later, a light came on in a corner window on the top floor. Brueggemann had led me right to his doorstep.

So why did I follow him?

Because names hold value, and you never know when you'll need to collect a trinket from your safe.

Two years later, and I am waiting in his hallway when he lumbers to his door. He has his hands in his pockets and is humming a song I don't recognize.

'Hello, Brueggemann.'

He turns his head at the sound, slowly. Being so large, every movement he makes takes an eternity. His eyes find the gun in my hand and then flit back to my face. The only flicker of emotion he gives is a slight pursing of his lips.

'I remember you.'

'Good.'

'Columbus, yes?'

'Yes.'

He pulls his hands out of his pockets and takes a small step toward his apartment. In his left hand, he's holding a set of keys.

He looks ahead, like he's speaking to the door. He is trying to keep his voice even, relaxed. 'The boss told me many things about the work you've done. He said you were particularly good with . . .'

And then he swings away from the door and towards my face, lunging with his left, the keys leading the way.

I wanted this to happen, and I don't blame him for trying. If I had come on strong, kept my distance and then ordered him away with my gun in his back, he would have made an attempt to challenge me at some point. It's better to get it done early, break the man's spirit, so the remainder of our time together can be spent usefully.

One of the things I learned at the Waxham detention center was to fight dirty against older and bigger opponents. Many believe the best way to take down a big man is to drive your heel into his kneecap, buckling it, chopping his legs out from under him so he'll fall like a redwood. This always sounds good in theory, but the reality is it takes a precise, well-balanced kick, and if you miss above or below, then you're either striking thick thigh muscle or the rock-hard bones of the shin. It's not easy to do in a juvey yard, much less in the tight confines of a Brussels apartment corridor.

No, the preferable strike points are one of two places. The groin is excellent, on both men and women, and with enough impact, a single strike can sap the fight out of even the roughest of giants. But Brueggemann is swinging wildly, and the hallway isn't all that well lit and I don't want to miss his crotch, so I go for the second option.

The little light available in the hall reflects off the fleshy white skin of his neck and I quickly duck his arm and pop him with everything I have square in the throat.

The results are immediate, the keys go flying and he collapses to both knees, clutching his gullet while he sucks desperately for air. His face turns crimson, his eyes roll back and fill with tears, his breath sounds like a cat mewing.

I just wait.

Finally, he's able to get some air back into his lungs and he looks over at me, defeat sweeping across his face like a bitter wind. He shrugs, still on his knees.

'What . . . do you want?'

'I want you to take me to Doriot. I want you to lead me to your boss where I can get to him and I don't want him to know I'm coming. Do you understand?'

'Yes.' And inexplicably, a small grin creases his face, revealing that big gap between his front teeth.

We stand in Lantin, about 60 miles west of Brussels, outside of the jailhouse. It is a blocky building, one of those holdovers from the sixties that were made with little imagination.

Brueggemann has his arms folded across his chest.

'When?'

'Three weeks ago. The police stormed a restaurant he was dining in . . .'

'Where were you?'

'He said he needed to be alone.'

'Convenient.'

'Yes.'

I look over at the bodyguard, who keeps a smug expression on his face. 'You think he wanted to be caught?'

'He didn't pay me enough to think.'

I shake my head. It is frigid outside, but my face feels warm, flush with blood.

'You speak to him since?'

'Not a word.'

'Goddammit.' I look at the prison, shaking my head.

Brueggemann speaks up. 'You will let me go now, yes?'

I nod, and he doesn't wait for more. He spins and marches back in the direction of the town without a backward glance.

Carrots or sticks.

I stand against a wall in the prison yard in Lantin, waiting for Doriot to come out. I am dressed in the yellow jumpers assigned to all Belgian prisoners, my hands in my pockets, my toes numb from the cold. Mostly, the night is as black as coal, but occasionally the moon makes a brief appearance before ducking back to safety.

Often in doing what I do, there is information I need, or travel arrangements I must have, or access to a building I must be granted. I can't do it alone; I rely upon strangers to get me the things I require. And so I have to decide in each instance which avenue is the best to get me where I want to go: the carrot, or the stick? A bribe, or a threat?

I didn't want to take too long to get to Doriot. That bearded man is still hunting me, and the way he worked over Ryan suggests he got ample information before he shot him in the back. I own a home in Positano along the Amalfi coast of Italy, and I imagine the man who flushed me in Naples surely went there next.

An official visitation with Doriot would've been insufficient. Three feet of bulletproof glass separating us would render any threat moot. I had to get inside where I could work him close.

It didn't take me long to find out which bar the Lantin guards frequented. A place known simply as 'The Pub' featured television screens showing rugby, soccer, and cricket, with taps that served Stella, Jupiler, Hoegaarden and Leffe. I stood at the bar and mumbled to a waitress in English and watched the shifts change and the prison guards mope in for three straight days. I didn't know Dutch and only minimal French, but I've found reading faces is as important as speaking. I wanted a sap, a guy with the most hang-down expression stamped on his mug like an advertisement for desperation. And I wanted a guy with a family.

On the third day, I clocked the same man coming off the night shift, a sad-sack, overweight guy with a moony face expressing a permanent look of bewilderment. On my way out, I asked him for a lighter in English without making any hand gestures and he produced one from his two-pocket shirt. He spoke English, or at least understood it, and that would help.

He rode a Vespa and I followed him from a casual distance until he reached a tiny apartment resembling a college dormitory. His wife barked at him from a window before he even cut the engine of his bike. She was holding an infant. He would do.

I stood in his living room when he came out of his bathroom, wiping his hands on his pants. His eyes had trouble conveying to his brain what he was seeing, a stranger in his living room, holding a pistol in one hand and a stack of cash in the other. His wife was in the bedroom, breast-feeding the baby.

'I need a favor from you.'

His eyes wouldn't leave my hands, as though his neurons had stopped firing, his mind had shut down. Finally, he searched my face for some sort of sign he wasn't hallucinating.

'I'm going to need you to get me inside the jail and bring a prisoner to me in the north yard, alone.'

He blinked, but nothing came out of his mouth.

'If you do this for me, you'll have the ten thousand euros in my right hand and you'll never see me again. If you fail, or you fuck me in any way, then your wife and your baby are going to get what's in my left. Nod your head if you understand.'

Carrots or sticks. Sometimes, if you want to be sure, you choose both.

I can hear Doriot coming before he rounds the corner. He is spitting curses in French, propelled against his will by the moon-faced guard I threatened. He had probably just racked out for the night in his cot and was surprised to be awoken, singled out, and shuffled outside to the yard.

He turns the corner and his eyes peel open, all signs of sleep vanishing. His adam's apple bobs as he swallows dryly. He reels back against the guard, but the man holds him there, firm.

'Hello, Doriot.'

Doriot tries to swivel his head to meet the guard's eyes. 'He's a killer! He's here to kill me.' But the guard just shuffles away.

'That's debatable. Why'd you sell Ryan down the river?'

It doesn't matter what his response is, I'm watching his eyes. His French accent is thick; it seems to pull his whole face down when he speaks, but his eyes don't waver or blink. 'I didn't . . . you have no right accusing me of this thing, Columbus.'

'Your client wants me dead.'

His eyes slide back and forth, like he's puzzled, searching for an answer. 'What is this you're telling me?'

'The man who hired me to put a bullet in Anton Noel.'

'Yes?'

'He's upset.'

'Why should he be upset? You fulfilled the contract.'

'It was sloppy.'

There is a glint of hope in Doriot's eyes now, like he can sense we aren't on the same page and his life might be spared because of it. 'Sloppy? What is this *sloppy*? My client would have cared nothing if you'd blown up a rail platform with five hundred people on it just to kill that bastard Noel.'

I chew on this, turning it over in my mind so I can see it from all angles. The little man in front of me isn't faking his response. I believe him. Or at least I believe he isn't involved. But that's a far cry from his client not being involved. His client might have been equally upset with Doriot and not used his services for this particular bit of cleaning up.

'Why'd you let yourself get thrown in here?'

'Reasons that have nothing to do with you.'

'You see how easily I got to you?'

He lowers his eyes. 'Yes. That does concern me. Yes.'

'What is your client's name?'

'You know that I cannot—'

'If he's happy as you say he is, then he'll never know I was barking up his tree. If he's not happy and hasn't included you, then it'd be in your best interest for me to get to him. Before he gets to you.'

I can see the wheels turning behind his eyes as he maps the various moves in his head like a chess player trying to envision the board ten plays ahead. Finally, he nods.

'His name is Thomas Saxon. He's an American. I have worked for him more than once. He is a hard man.'

'I know all about hard men. What city?'

'Atlanta.'

'All right then.' I nod at the guard, who comes back over, looking relieved. He starts to whirl Doriot back the way he came.

'Wait,' the little man says, and the guard stops for a moment. Doriot looks over his shoulder at me. 'What happened to Ryan?'

'Shot in the spine in the Naples train station.'

He gnaws on his lip for a second, then nods at the guard. As their footsteps recede and the prison yard falls silent, I turn my eyes up to the nameless moon right before it disappears behind a cloud.

5

He's toying with me.

I've seen the bearded man twice since leaving Belgium. First, I thought I'd lucked into spotting him at Gatwick airport. I was walking through the terminal, heading to catch a cab to Heathrow, airport-hopping so I could fly directly to Atlanta. I took a turn at the last moment, realizing the taxi stand was to the left, and I caught his reflection behind me in the glass window of a coffee klatch.

I have trained myself not to flinch. Ever. Not to hesitate, not to give a moment's pause. He had scented my trail faster than I thought possible, but now he'd made a mistake. I lined up in the taxi queue, checked my wrist like I was looking at my watch, and then ducked into the baggage claim so I could stand behind the carousel and watch the only two entranceways into the room. He never came through the doors.

I waited patiently, then quickly bought a tan coat from an Austin Reed store and pitched my gray one in a trashcan. It wasn't much, but maybe it would steal me a moment, and sometimes a moment is all I need.

I didn't see him again that day. I switched flights and holed up at the Savoy on the Strand, spending two days in the lobby reading, watching the door. He never showed and I started to doubt whether I had actually seen him in Gatwick. It had only been a moment, a split second, just his face some forty feet behind me, and how could I be sure, really sure it was him?

Because my life had always relied on these moments of perspicacity. If I started to doubt them now, I might as well quit, really quit. I might as well head back to Rome, scoop up Risina Lorenzana and try to disappear where no one would ever find us. But I couldn't do that, not now. Someone with a gun was looking for me and in my experience, hiding would only delay the inevitable. Instead of trying to outrun him, never knowing when he'd catch me, I needed to turn my boat and steer into him with everything I had. Let the crash determine which of us swims away free.

I saw him the second time in Atlanta at the Lenox mall. I pitched my tent at the Sheraton in Buckhead and headed to the shops to give my wardrobe an overhaul. It was teeth-chattering cold in Georgia, and the tickling at the back of my neck told me to ditch everything I'd worn in Europe and start over, buy casual clothes and blend into the background, especially if I was going to be spending time in the South.

I was riding up an escalator, exposed, vulnerable, when I saw him on the first-floor landing, looking directly at me. Smiling. If he wanted to pop me there, he could have. Hell, he *should* have. Which begged the question, how many times had he gotten this close since Naples and not finished the kill? I instinctually ducked down to tie my shoe, riding out the rest of the escalation below the shooter's sight line. I kept low, acting like I was tugging my socks up and practically crawled into Macy's like a crab darting across the sand. I didn't want to get cornered in a store with only one entrance and exit. I needed options, quickly.

The department store had its own escalators in the center of the clothing area, but standing exposed and upright on a moving staircase is a dangerous game, as I had just been reminded. Instead, I ducked to the back of the store and zeroed in on a pair of elevators, usually reserved for women with strollers. Doors were just closing as I hustled aboard and pressed the button for the bottom floor of underground parking.

I waited there for over an hour, in an obscure corner with no traffic, freezing my ass off. I didn't see him again.

* * *

In my hand, I'm holding a Nokia pre-paid cell phone I picked up at a mini-mart near the Holiday Inn in Decatur where I'm now staying. I employed every anti-surveillance technique I know in driving away from Buckhead, veering on and off the highway, racing red lights, making unexpected turns, and I'm pretty sure I haven't been followed, but I'm not positive, goddammit, and this fucker has me doubting myself in ways I have not doubted in a long time.

And yet, if he wanted to kill me, if that was his end game, then he made a colossal mistake in not doing so when he had the chance. If he's so fucking smug that he's choosing to play games, choosing to reveal himself so that I know *he* knows where I am, then I'm going to pluck whatever weapon he comes at me with right out of his hands and ram it down his fucking throat. Toying with your target is a novice's play, a cocksure move intended to intimidate your mark into making a mistake. But there are flaws to this play, and chief amongst them is that he has given away information about himself.

My pursuer carries a knife in his left sleeve, I'm sure of it. In the two instances where I spotted him, I took in the folds of his jacket, and both times, the left sleeve bunched up near the wrist opening, then smoothed out toward the elbow. It wasn't much, and I'd only had a second to look, but it was there.

Maybe he has been paid not just to kill me, but to stick me up close, to disfigure me, a vendetta killing. I've heard of bagmen taking this kind of work, not just ending a mark's life, but disgracing him in death, pissing on his grave. Come to think of it, it would require the killer to work in close, and maybe that's why he'd been aiming low in the train station in Naples, when the bullet skipped off the pavement by my feet. Maybe he had been aiming for my knees, hoping to wing me so he could carve me up like beef at the slaughterhouse. Or maybe I don't know what the fuck I'm talking about.

I dial a number from memory, look at the digital clock next to my bed, and wait for her to answer.

'*Ciao*?'

'Risina. It's Jack Walker.'

Her voice warms immediately. I can feel the smile through the phone line.

'*Buongiorno*, Jack. I was just opening the store.'

'I thought you might be. Do you have a moment?'

'Yes. Yes. How are you?'

'I'm . . . fine.'

'You don't sound fine.'

'I don't? I'm tired, I guess.'

'Where are you?'

'The States. East Coast.'

'It is late there.'

'Yes.'

'Well, I'm very pleased you called. I was thinking about you.'

'I'm glad you were. I think about you too much.'

She laughs. It is a sound low in her throat, as soothing as a touch. 'You can never think about me too much, Jack.'

I wait for a moment, and there is an odd comfort in the silence, like the distance between us has been erased. I don't know why I feel the compulsion to say what I'm about to say, but the words come out of me before I can decide against them.

'I was just remembering a story I read once. Something from when I was a kid.'

'Yes?'

'Maybe you can figure out for me who wrote it.'

'I can try. It is a children's story?'

'Well, I read it when I was a kid, but I'm not sure where or how I came across it. I'm not sure how old I was when I read it. A lot of those years are blurry for me.'

'It's a famous story?'

'I'm not sure. I don't think so. I haven't come across it in a long time. But some things in my life made me think of this story, and I thought maybe I'd tell it to you and see if you'd heard of it. I'm not even sure if it's very good or particularly profound.'

'Well, now I'm definitely intrigued. Let's hear it.' I hear the sound of her leaning back in the desk chair, and I picture her with her knees pulled to her chest and one arm around them, holding them tight, those venerable leather-bound books surrounding her like a theater audience. 'I haven't unlocked the shop door yet and Alda is not coming in until after lunch. My ear is yours.'

'Okay. Well, here goes. I don't remember the name of the story. And the main character doesn't have a name. In fact, that's the point of the story . . . I think . . . anyway . . .'

'I'm listening . . .'

'Well, this guy, just a normal guy, he kisses his wife goodbye, leaves his house, dressed like he's going out for a jog, but he's not, he's actually got his kid in his arms, a little boy, a two-and-a-half-year-old toddler who looks just like him.

'And every day they do this . . . he and his kid take a walk together, all over the city. Or rather, he walks, pulling a silver wagon with his kid buckled safely inside. And they walk everywhere, I mean everywhere, looking at the fire trucks and the police cars and the ambulances and the construction trucks; and all the time, the dad's pointing out this thing and that thing and the kid's taking it all in like a sponge.

'The dad'll pull him for hours, for miles, end up in neighborhoods nowhere near his own, and everyone that passes them on the sidewalk or in the street looks at the two of them longingly and thinks that this father and this son who resemble each other are just a little part of the world that is right. That all the death and mayhem and war and assassinations and everything else wrong in this world is pulling them into the blackest of abysses, but this thing, these two walking by, father and son, these two are what's honest and true and hopeful. And maybe they're the *only* two, you know? Maybe everybody else has a little blackness in his life, but it all fades away to white, because when people spot this guy and his son walking down the street, they just can't help but smile.'

I can hear her breathing, but she doesn't cough or sigh or interrupt. I can't remember the last time I've talked this much, but the words continue to tumble out of my mouth like an avalanche.

'And they're on this block a good mile from their house and the dad is in the middle of telling his son about this big cedar tree on the end of the street he likes to visit, that the tree probably looks to the boy like it's taller than a skyscraper, and right there, right in the middle of his sentence, the man's left arm seizes up on him, his breath catches in his throat, and he falls down dead. Heart attack, no warning, right there on the sidewalk. He topples over like someone shot him and lies face down on the concrete.

'The kid doesn't know what's going on, he's only two and a half. Is the father playing some sort of game with him? That's all this kid knows. So he calls out to his dad, "Da-ad. Da-ad." You know, like it's a song, like it's a game. But his father doesn't, his father *can't* get up.

' "Something is wrong" registers in the kid's brain . . . even caught in the middle between two and three, this message comes through loud and clear, but he can't get out of the silver wagon, he's stuck there, buckled in tight. He starts blinking tears, crying in that way toddlers cry, his lips curved in an "o," his wail silent then strong then silent again as he can't catch his breath to pound it out.

'And then a man comes up, this homeless guy, this guy who reeks of alcohol and cigarettes and the kid thinks at first maybe this man will help him, help his dad, who is still lying face down on the sidewalk, but the raggedy man descends like a vulture, his eyes darting, he barks at the kid to "shut the hell up" as he's rifling through the father's pockets and there's not a damn thing the kid can do about it.

'The guy takes what he can and hurries away, leaving the kid, the boy who isn't much more than a baby sitting there in the silver wagon, stuck there, a mile from home, where he can't see anything but his father lying there dead on the sidewalk and still no one has noticed. No one has come for him. The mother is oblivious in a house a mile away and the father and son are gone for hours sometimes and she's still forty-five minutes away from even thinking something's wrong.

'The kid starts to cry again, because he's scared now even if he doesn't know why, but he's scared in that part of him where deep, deep down through centuries and centuries of ingrained behavior we know we're in danger even before we are.

'And right then, just as he's getting worked up to really wail, a woman comes rushing out of her house. She'd just been looking out the window and saw that kid and that wagon stuck on the sidewalk and the man fallen over and he hasn't gotten up and she rushes over to check on the man, and she feels for a pulse, but she knows he's dead, and so quickly she has that seatbelt unbuckled and has the kid up and in her arms and she's saying "it's okay, it's okay. What's your name, child? What's your name? Can you tell me your name?"

'And the kid knows his name, he does, it's on the tip of his tongue, his parents have called him it a thousand times and he's said it himself a few times too, but it won't come out, he can't make it come out and so he just shakes in her arms, sobbing.'

I sit there for a moment, listening for her on the other end of the phone.

'That's it. That's what I remember.'

Her breathing has stopped, like she's afraid to exhale. After a long moment, she breaks the silence. 'I wish I could tell you I knew this story. But I don't.'

'Yeah. I haven't been able to track it down.'

'Well I like it. I like it very much. I need to think about it some more. Consult some other sources.'

'If it's not too much trouble.'

'No trouble at all.'

'Well, thank you. I really appreciate that, Risina.'

'Are you certain you're okay?'

'Yes, I'm certain.'

'I'm very glad you called me, Jack. I'm still thinking of this story. I can see why it stuck with you.'

'Yes.'

We talk for another ten minutes about nothing before we say our goodbyes. I head into the bathroom, wrap the phone inside a towel, and then smash it with the heel of my shoe until it shatters into pieces. Slowly, methodically, I flush each piece down the toilet.

Thomas Saxon isn't quite a billionaire, but he doesn't mind when people make that mistake. He's a vulture investor, a corporate raider, a man who never found a shortcut he wouldn't take. He was a frequent attendee of the Predator's Ball in Los Angeles in the eighties, when a few men created enormous wealth by building an entire financial market around junk bonds. Information was key – whether it could be gained legally or illegally didn't matter. The SEC caught up with a few, others escaped scot-free, entire companies were carved up, chewed up, and spit out, but everyone involved made the kind of money that has strings of zeroes at the end of the number. The suckers were the ones who worked within the system, and the suckers never came out on top. Tommy Gun, as his friends called him, was nobody's sucker.

He is living in an enormous house in East Atlanta, out past the airport. It was originally built for Evander Holyfield's mother, but after she died, the champ didn't want to set foot in it again. Saxon paid cash and moved in within a week of the funeral.

Like a lot of financial guys, Saxon thinks he is invincible, immune to the dangers that felled some of his friends and rivals. He narrowly dodged charges from the SEC in 1987 while he watched his associates drop like flies. He thought he was untouchable, special, lucky. This feeling of grandeur ultimately manifested in the hiring of dark men like me. How many men Tommy Gun has sentenced to death, I have no idea. Does he do it because of petty rivalries? Out of hubris? Or is it all just about money? I don't have a fence to put files together for me, so the information I have is only what I can cobble together over the Internet or through an assortment of shadow guys I've come into contact with over the years. I am beginning to suspect Anton Noel meant nothing more to Saxon than numbers across a ticker, that his death was engineered to affect the price of Ventus-Safori's stock. Yet, I feel a nagging at the back of my brain, like something doesn't want to add up so easily, like the square peg is just a little too unwieldy to fit inside the round hole.

Often, an assassin will get to a mark through his vices. A guy might have a mistress, or visit a regular whore, and since he has to be sneaky about meeting the woman, he compromises himself, makes himself as easy to pick off as a duck at a broken-down shooting gallery. He might enjoy a specific type of cigar, or a certain bottle of wine, or participate in an illicit card game, and a contract killer can get to him by posing as a delivery guy or a rival gambler. Everyone has vulnerabilities; it is an assassin's job to exploit them.

Saxon doesn't keep a mistress, smoke cigars, or play poker. He doesn't visit whores or collect French wines or smoke a little weed on the side. No, what Saxon likes to do is fish.

Every weekend, he drives an hour north of Atlanta, into the mountains, alone, and fly-fishes the Soque River. Fishing is a solitary endeavor, a chance for him to commune with nature. Maybe he does it because it brings back memories of him and his old man casting their lines. Maybe he does it to get out of the rat race and clear his mind. Or maybe he thinks stepping into the water will somehow wash his sins down the river.

I tail him for three straight weekends before determining the Soque River as the place our lives will intersect.

I am standing in the men's room of a tiny store named Ramsey's Bait and Tackle off of Highway 197 in the town of

Jackson Bridge. A biting wind has kept most anglers near a warm fire this weekend, but not Saxon. Every Saturday, he makes the trek north, no matter the icy temperature or thick frost on the ground.

Saxon hasn't yet come to the store, but he'll be here soon. I take a quick look in the mirror and set my jaw, steeling myself, getting ready. The bell over the door in the front of the shop jingles.

I turn on the water of the sink and position myself behind the bathroom door so I'll be hidden when he enters. I take one last breath as the handle starts to bend downward. If I were waiting for Saxon, this would be over in moments. But I'm not waiting for Saxon.

It is common to use a shiny lure to catch trout, letting the sun filter down through the murky water until the bait catches the fish's eye and suckers him toward the hook.

For the last two weeks, I made a show of stalking Saxon. I watched him out in the open, paced the perimeter of his office, followed him out to his favorite fishing spot in a red SUV. I was letting the sun reflect off me, hoping to reel in my catch.

The door to the restroom pushes open and the bearded man is coming through cautiously but not cautiously enough. I grab his head and the back of his pants and drive him head-first into the bathroom mirror, shattering it, cutting a red streak across his forehead. He's a professional – up until two seconds ago a pretty god-damn *smug* professional – and he immediately tries to counter, wailing backward with his left elbow, but I move with the blow and use his own inertia against him, whipping him around for a second meeting with what's left of the mirror.

He's got heart, I'll give him that. He drops like a rock, plunging to the linoleum floor as he tries to whip my feet out from under me but I sidestep his scissoring legs and stomp with everything I have on top of his kneecap until the bones crunch like gravel. He wails in pain, instinctively, and reaches into his sleeve for his knife but it's not there. He looks puzzled for a moment until his eyes settle on my hand.

'You stupid fuck.' I am holding his knife in one hand and my pistol in the other.

'Let's work something out, Columbus,' he says from the ground, his hands raised, his right leg snapped at an angle like a wishbone. He's got a thick Irish accent that lends a strange softness to his words. His voice doesn't match his face in the least.

'What part of me were you supposed to take back to your client?'

He measures me, trying to determine if he should lie. He also wants to keep me talking; as long as I'm talking, he's alive. I would have tried the same thing.

'Your trigger finger.'

'Kill me first and then the finger?'

'Aye, cut it off while you're alive, but yes, that's it.'

He lowers one elbow to the ground, leaning back, breathing hard, blinking blood out of his eyes. It is seeping down the contours of his face and collecting in his beard so the whiskers turn a blacker shade, creating an odd aura around his face, like he's getting younger before my eyes. His hand creeps toward his side like an inchworm, but I don't shift my eyes to it.

'You the only one Saxon hired, or are there more?'

'Who's Saxon?' The inchworm keeps inching.

'The guy who's going to call all this off.'

'If you say so, brother.' Inching. Inching.

'I say so.'

And the worm reaches his belt, and in a blur the bearded man has a gun in his hand but my first silenced bullet takes off the top part of his hand, sending the gun skittering across the linoleum until it comes to a rest next to the toilet.

He looks at me with true shock in his eyes just a moment before my second bullet closes them forever.

6

The spot on the Soque river where Saxon likes to fish is private, part of a fishermen's lodge that has been standing for generations. Security is laughable, reliant on a few 'no trespassing / private property' signs and two guards with snowy hair and bulging bellies, as threatening as field mice.

I step out of a small copse and stand directly behind Saxon. He looks like he wandered out of an L.L.Bean catalogue, standing on the bank of the river, wearing navy waders and a plaid hunter's shirt underneath a thick multi-pocketed vest. He is tying a spinner on his line, pulling the knot tight with his teeth as I approach.

'Catch anything?'

He gives me a once-over, like I've just befouled his sanctuary.

'No.'

Then he turns his back on me, as if I might disappear. When I don't, he sighs dramatically before looking at me again.

'You staying at the lodge?'

'No.'

'Well, this is private property, buddy. And I like fishing alone.'

'I caught something this morning.'

'Good for you.'

'You might want to take a look at it.'

He waits, and I can see the thoughts warring behind his eyes: do I humor this asshole and maybe he'll go away, or do I tell him to get the fuck out of here and possibly incite him?

The first choice must win out. Resigned, he offers, 'Okay. Show me your catch.'

I toss something at his chest and he fumbles his pole as he tries to get his hands on it. When he looks down at his palm, he realizes he is holding a man's finger.

He drops it like it's toxic and stammers, 'What is this?'

'The trigger finger of one of your hired killers.'

Fear sweeps across his face and his cheeks burn as though they've been slapped.

'Call them off.'

'What?'

'The fence you're currently using. Tell him to call off the contract.'

'I . . . I don't . . .'

'Don't insult me, Tommy. I've already gotten to Doriot in Belgium. I know you're behind this.'

I can see terror in his eyes, true fright. This is not at all uncommon in clients who hire killers. More often than not, they are feckless men, men who like to give orders from a safe distance without ever entering the battlefield. They imagine they have courage – ordering the deaths of others through multiple chains of command – but that courage evaporates like boiled water as soon as they come face to face with a man who pulls the trigger. So much for being a hard man. Saxon is as hard as a minnow.

I lower my hands into my pockets conspicuously. His eyes widen as he imagines what I hold there.

'No checking out, no going to the lodge. Just walk out of here slowly, and I'll follow you to my car. You arrange a meeting with the fence on the way. We go together and we end this. Nod if you understand.'

'Yes, sir. I understand.' He looks like he has something more he wants to add, but he's afraid to open his mouth. I nod to him. 'My lawyer is the one who arranges everything with the . . . um . . . other guys.'

'Fine. Your lawyer, then. Let's move.'

* * *

The drive back is silent. Most men in his situation try to chat me up, to make themselves appear likable, misunderstood, human. But not Tommy Gun. No, he steers the wheel with a scowl on his face, like an unrepentant sinner forced to sit in a Sunday morning service.

He's afraid of me, yes, so he turns that fear to anger. The miles roll beneath the tires and he simmers, a pot of water about to boil over. If he's waiting for me to say something, to break the silence, he's misjudged me. Keeping men like him uncomfortable is a skill, and one I'll admit I enjoy using.

His lawyer's name is Colin Goldman and he lives in Buckhead, not far from the mall where the bearded man watched me on the escalator, smiling when he should have been shooting. Colin is a small man with a big house.

We stand in the grass of the back yard, a good distance from the rear porch. The lawyer is shivering, wearing a robe over a T-shirt and boxer shorts, his feet in slippers. I didn't give him an opportunity to change after he answered the door.

'How many gunmen did you hire?'

Goldman coughs into his fist, nervous. He searches Saxon's face. 'I would advise you not to—'

'Tell him.'

'He could be a Fed.'

'He's not a Fed. Look at his eyes. He's a goddamn killer. Tell him.' Saxon's confidence is back, now that he has someone smaller than him to lord over.

Goldman blows out a measured breath. 'Ummm . . . just one.'

'Well, your one is dead. I shot him in the bathroom of a fishing store in Jackson Bridge.'

'Jackson Bridge?' The lawyer looks confused.

'He wanted to get in close, so I let him get in close. Then I shot him in the face.'

'I . . . I don't understand.'

'I don't give a shit. You hired one and you failed. You should've known better than to send a cut-up man after me. Now, I don't give a fuck if you didn't like the way I worked the Noel job. I finished it, and it's done. You want payback, you poked the wrong animal.'

'Wait, what're you talking about?'

It is my turn to feel uncomfortable. An uneasy feeling is starting to settle in my stomach. Square peg, round hole. Men in their positions usually look shamed, crestfallen, like they got caught in the act and are on their way to the guillotine. But these two are genuinely surprised, genuinely bewildered.

'You sent a man after me.'

Goldman stammers as he stamps his feet. 'We . . . we only have one open job, I swear it. We're taking out an SEC officer. In New York.'

Saxon speaks up. 'We understand the Noel job was successful. Why would we—?'

In an instant, I have a pair of Glocks up in either hand and am pointing them point-blank at both of their foreheads. A well-positioned gun held in a steady hand makes a hell of a lie detector.

They draw back instinctively. 'Ho! I swear it. Whoever you are, we have no beef with you. You have to believe us.'

I backhand the lawyer with the barrel of my pistol, so he goes down in a heap, and then I point both barrels at Saxon. The fear in his eyes is pellucid, tangible. He cringes, and there is anger in his voice.

'Goddammit, listen to me. I don't know who you are or what you believe I did, but if you think I put a price on your head, you've never been more wrong. I know my targets, all of them. Y-you got this one wrong.' He breathes hard, like he just ran a marathon. 'Noel is dead and that case is closed. No reprisals. You got this one wrong.'

Here comes that wave again, that bad-luck wave that has dogged me since Paris. Bad luck because this isn't ending in Atlanta, not in the back yard of a little man's big house in

Buckhead. And certainly not ending in the bathroom of the Ramsey Bait and Tackle Shop off of Highway 197. Bad luck because where one killer fails, others will surely follow until I find out who has done the hiring. Bad luck because now I know Saxon and the bearded man were telling the truth.

The silver wagon has stopped, the handle has dropped, and I have a name but I don't know it. It has to be in front of me, somewhere. But where, goddammit?

I know the Noel job triggered this. The heat that assignment brought led someone to Ryan, and Ryan led that someone to me. So it had to be a man who knew Ryan fenced for me on that job, and the only link in that chain is Doriot.

Replaying my conversation with the Belgian fence, I remember he was quick to go where I led him, to finger his client, Saxon. In retrospect, it was too easy. Someone had gotten to Doriot first, before me, which is why he got himself tossed in jail. He was just buying time, as much as possible, till this whole thing washed over. He's going to regret having misled me.

The bearded man made a solid play initially, taking out Ryan to get to me. Even though he lost the war, he dealt me a crippling blow. Losing my fence, my middleman, is like missing a limb. I need information, someone to bang an idea off of, someone who can root around in the dirt for a bit and get back to me with a truffle.

The last time I saw a fence named Archibald Grant, he was in the process of hiring me to kill the Speaker of the House of Representatives. But Grant withheld some information at the time of the assignment, namely, that he was asked to hire three assassins instead of just me. My friend and fence Pooley died because of this omission, gunned down in my hotel room in Santa Fe, New Mexico, in the middle of my assignment. I would say Archibald owes me a pretty damn big chit.

Archibald served sixteen months in Lompoc on an aiding-and-abetting collar, but within eight hours of his release, he was back in the game, contacting his old associates, setting up new contracts. Boston must've been too hot for him; he relocated to Chicago, where he has had little difficulty pitching a new tent. It is just as well; I have too many memories floating around Boston.

When he steps out of his bathroom wearing only a towel and shuffles into his kitchen, I am sitting at his breakfast table.

'Fuck me!' Archibald jumps like he's seen a ghost, then covers his heart with his hand, trying to calm himself. He takes a long look at me, recognition in his eyes. 'Well, I'll be goddamned. Columbus.'

'How you doing, Cotton?'

That takes him by surprise. He hasn't heard his given name, Cotton, in a long time.

'You know that one, huh?'

'I know a lot of things.'

'You pop my bodyguards downstairs? The doorman too?' He makes the trigger-pulling gesture with his fingers when he says the word *pop*.

'Nah. They don't even know I'm here.'

'Motherfucking Columbus. I heard you lit out of here after the Abe Mann blam-blam. Went to Europe or some shit. I would've put you to work, man, but . . . .' He reaches into his refrigerator and pulls out a jug of milk before moving over to the kitchen table to sit across from me, never finishing the sentence.

'Yeah? I'm splitting time.'

He takes a pull straight from the jug, then wipes his mouth with the back of his hand.

'Well, I'm sure you were sore 'bout the way the business was the business. But I was only following orders. And I paid your new boy Ryan triple fee. That may not make it all the way square but it puts some shape on the edges, I would say.'

'I need some information.'

Archibald smiles. 'That's what I do.'

'That's why I came to you. Someone put a hit on me.'

I let him absorb this. I can see his eyes widen a bit as he calculates the ever-shifting leverage between us.

'What's Ryan thinking?'

'Ryan's dead.'

'Shiiiiiit.' He lets this out low in his throat, like a growl. 'So you want to know . . .'

'I want to know who put the paper on me.'

'Right. Right.' He rubs his chin theatrically, like he's really stewing over the issue here, trying to figure out how he can help me. Archibald is the type who made gains all his life by convincing people he's stupid.

Finally, he nods. 'Well, this is gonna take me a few days.'

I stand. 'Then I'll see you in a few days.'

'You come to my office on Friday. I'll shake the trees and see what falls.'

'Okay.'

'You want the address?'

'I'll find you.'

I can feel his eyes on me as I exit the room.

I lie low until Friday. My mind keeps turning back to Risina, and that story I told her, the one about the boy in the silver wagon, the kid looking down at his dead father, the kid who didn't know his name. When the walls start to close in on me I venture out from my hotel room to visit the Art Institute. I find myself standing in front of Magritte's painting of a locomotive racing out of a fireplace, smoke billowing out of its smokestack as a clock on the mantle above it points to nine. I can feel that wave rising over me as I stare at it, transfixed. The juxtaposition of those disparate images hits close to home to a hired killer standing amongst tourists and students and art lovers in the quiet starkness of the museum.

They think I'm just another patron, no different than them, in their world. They better hope their own clocks never strike nine.

* * *

I arrive at Archibald's office on Harrison, a former factory that must have manufactured an array of piping, based on the uncut aluminum lying around and the smell of stale air.

Six dead-eyed security guards stand sentinel, eyeing me as I approach. I don't have to say who I am, they know, they've been told, and they step aside as one shows me in to see the boss.

His demeanor has changed. I was afraid of this, was resigned to it, but I guess I had hoped he still had a residual fear of me and was eager to stay in my good graces. But Archibald Grant, above all else, is an opportunist.

'Here's the what-for . . .' he says as soon as I sit down. 'You ever see that movie *The Replacement Killers?*'

I shake my head.

'Jet Li? Directed by a black guy?'

I shake my head a second time.

'Well, you should check it out, Columbus. Rent it on Netflix. You know, when the shit settles. Anyway, I got ears all over, including all the way over on the other side of the Atlantic. Here's what you got staring at you down the other end of the barrel.

'Three killers. An Irish Setter named Leary what's got a beard and carries a blade.'

'He's dead.'

'Yeah, that's what I heard. Took two pops down in Georgia.'

'You heard right.'

'I told you I got ears. Here's where the replacement killers come in . . . one didn't do the job so your enemy hired two more.'

'Hydra-style.'

'Yeah, hydra-style, that's good. Anyway, you got a man out of Czech Republic goes by the name of Svoboda . . . which I heard half the country goes by the name of. He's supposed to be a silver bear like you. Top, top, top shelf and then the shelf above that. I tried to get him in for a job once, but his fence just scoffed at me. So he must be collecting a pretty penny on you.

'And if that weren't enough ketchup on your hot dog, the other killer is an Argentine woman named Llanos. Don't ask me what that name means, cuz I don't know shit. I do know this woman executed some serious blood contracts down in South America. Her rep is that she's like morning frost . . . cold as ice and disappears when the sun comes up.'

'Maybe I'll get lucky and they can pick off each other before they get to me.'

'It's been known to happen.'

'Yeah, well . . . I'll have to plan for the opposite.'

'Yeah.'

He leans back in his chair and laces his fingers behind his head. 'Now we get down to the flop, turn and river and get all the cards out on the table.'

'Lay 'em down for me then.'

'You kill these two, four more coming. You know it and I know it. This big Papi wants you dead and he's got the bank account to make it happen, no matter how long you run. What you need to do is get to the source.'

No, Archibald Grant may be a lot of things, but he isn't stupid. He's setting up a new proposition; his body language is as easy to read as a map. He's got all the pieces out on his chessboard, and he's preparing to mount an attack.

'I know who it is. I know the owner of the purse strings. I know who put the paper on you.'

His fingers stay laced, and a grin spreads out on his face. I can barely look at all those teeth. I'm not going to help him along any further, so I hold my tongue.

'I'll give you the name too. I owe you that. For what happened to you and your fence on that Abe Mann job. It's just that I need you to do a little something for me first.'

'Oh, yeah?'

'Yeah . . . nothing you can't handle straightaway.'

'What is it?'

'A local job.'

I shake my head. 'Out of the question.'

'Now look here. I need this. It's personal. I moved into Chi-town and there's a pair of pests I haven't quite scattered out of the kitchen. I worked up a file on 'em, but I don't want to use any of my guys. Best to look like these bucks made enemies elsewhere. That's where you come in. You can make it happen, cap'n.'

'How about I *make* you tell me the name and then we never see each other again?'

He hasn't knocked that smile off his face. I imagine he has some hole card he wants to play; I might as well get it out on the table too so we both can see it.

'Well, see, let's not get hasty here. We're businessmen doing business. I went the extra mile for you, getting information you need to survive, and now I want something *from* you. And here's the kicker, Columbus . . . I'm the only one in the entire world who knows you took out Abe Mann right before the Democratic National Convention. You think that case file ain't still drawing teams of Feds and half the local departments in this country? You a smart guy . . . hell, maybe the best gun in the world. Fuck if I know. But I gotta take care of mine, and if I put a file in a safety box somewhere that outlines what I know, only to be released to the Federal authorities in the event of my untimely death, can you blame me?'

I start to say something, but he interrupts, still smiling. 'And before you start talking about my family or my wives or my nieces and nephews or my grandpappy back in Georgia, just know that I don't give a South Side fuck about none of 'em. Knock yourself out. The only person on the Earth I care about is the one talking to you right now, and I'd say it's in your best interest to keep me alive.'

He's got me and he knows it. There's nothing I can do but play along.

'I eighty-six your rivals, you give me the name?'

'We'll be all square.'

'Then give me the goddamn file.'

He leans forward in his chair, and I didn't think it was possible, but his smile grows even wider.

7

The names at the top of the page are Dalan and Darius Webb. The attached pictures reveal a set of identical twins, black men in their late thirties. Sharp blue eyes contrast with dark skin and malevolent expressions. At first blush, they look like mirror images, but a closer inspection reveals Darius's nose as slightly longer, his jaw slightly sharper. Archibald's work in the file is meticulous and exact, like he relished the chance of putting this one together.

The Webb brothers like to keep to themselves, only venturing out of the condo they share near Lake Michigan when they have a meeting, either with one of their hit men or with a prospective client. Their unit sits on top of a well-guarded building, a place where people with a lot of money pay a hefty mortgage to keep those without a lot of money at bay. The dearth of firsthand information about their condo leads me to believe Archibald never penetrated it.

I've often struck people at their residences. The advantage the target holds in terms of knowing the location is countered by the simple fact that most people relax at home, let their guard down once the front door is locked. But the Webb brothers' choice of living quarters suggests their defenses are always engaged. Deliveries are halted at the door. Strangers are turned away. The only people allowed to enter the elevator have to be accompanied by a resident. No exceptions. Inconvenience has been traded for safety, with no regrets.

Archibald's file moves on to describe the brothers' operation. They have a roster of eight to ten gunmen whom they employ regularly, small-time guys who mostly work right here in Chicago. The Webb brothers are characteristic of the seedier side of the killing business, the cheap alternative to what I do, the 2-for-1 coupon in the back of the Shopper's Guide. They don't charge much, they take any job that comes their way, and they send as many guys as necessary to get the work done, no matter how sloppy. There's a market for low-rent killing, and these guys fill it.

My first fence taught me that to kill as I do, to execute a contract on someone's life and then walk away from it cleanly, I needed to *realize* a connection with the target so I could *sever* that connection. I needed to find aspects of my target's life I could hate, not just tangentially, but physically, viscerally *hate*, not just the noun 'hate,' but the verb 'to hate,' actively *hate*, with passion and concentration and emotion behind it. Only then could I kill, could I snap that connection, before moving on to the next target.

The Webb brothers are easy men to loathe. They take the art of my business and make it base and common. They have no respect for the profession. I can see it in the somnolent eyes staring out at me from the picture attached to the file.

They work out of the Union Stock Yards, what used to be the capital of the butchering industry in America, where Upton Sinclair famously focused his unblinking prose. Now heavily industrial, the only butchering ordered here appears to be of the human variety.

Their base is a renovated warehouse on Pershing Road. It is well armed and well guarded. Archibald has been inside, must have been when he first came to town and the brothers failed to realize they were meeting with a rival. His sketches of the layout are detailed, precise. They have three rooms, dimly lit, windowless. An office for each brother adjoins a conference room where they hand out assignments, meet with clients, put their files together. They have one permanent employee, a secretary named Craig Juda, a former Israeli soldier who files more than paperwork. Archibald spends a great deal of ink on Juda: his schedule, his history. He poses the biggest threat to making a clean hit. I'll avoid him if possible, kill him if necessary.

The trick to working a double, like this assignment, is to kill both marks within moments of each other. If I manage to kill one but not the other, I risk the target turning into a serious threat, fueled by anger and revenge and adrenaline. Or worse, the target goes underground, into deep hiding, off the page from whatever information my fence is able to put together ahead of time.

The best bet is to drop Dalan and Darius before either twin can process what befell the other.

Archibald Grant and I sit in the Golden Bull restaurant, a Chinese food dive near the Lakeside Hospital. After dropping off our food, the waitress moves over to a corner to take a nap. It's my kind of place.

'I hear what-tell the South American chick? Llanos? She's here in Chicago. Right now.'

'How do you know?'

'That's my business.'

'You running a play on me?'

'I'm *telling* you, man. I'm trying to help you.' He doesn't meet my eyes, just digs his fork into his rice bowl. This is worrisome, though not entirely out of Archibald Grant's character. He's as shifty as desert sand, and I have a nagging feeling I made an error seeking him out.

'You got a leak in your office then. No one knows I'm here.'

'Someone do. If that leak came from my office, there's gonna be blood on the floor by the end of the day, I guarantee you that.'

I don't respond, and he keeps shoveling chicken and rice into his mouth, his fork scraping the side of the bowl.

Finally, he looks up, clearing his gums with his tongue. 'How's the other thing shaking?'

'It's going to go down in a matter of days, maybe sooner in light of what you just told me. Make yourself available immediately after with the name I want on the tip of your tongue.'

He leans back and flashes me that smile. 'After all I do for you, you still don't trust me?'

'Thanks for lunch,' I say, pushing my chair back.

'You gonna get 'em through the mother?'

I don't answer as I leave the restaurant.

I need to do this now, today. If someone leaked to Llanos my location in the windy city, then Svoboda can't be far behind. Who knows if they've already spotted me? Who knows if Archibald called that lunch meeting so they could start tracking me? Maybe they negotiated a deal with him. He points me out like Judas in the garden by sitting with me in the restaurant, and they pledge to descend upon me once I've taken out his rivals. It would be a dumb play on Archibald's part: either assassin will kill me as soon as he or she can, regardless of the promises they proffer to a small-time Chicago fence. Like I said before, Archibald is no imbecile. No, my gut says he was telling me the truth in order to warn me, that he wants my work finished and his rivals in body bags. After I complete the mission, well, that's another story. After I kill the Webb brothers, all bets are off.

He's right, of course. I'm going to get to them through their mother.

Her name is Laverne Contessa Webb and she lives alone in a home north of the city, in Evanston, near the Northwestern campus. She is the secret the Webb brothers have kept hidden since the moment they entered this line of work. They invented a biography for themselves, concocting an origin story out of the Western district of Baltimore: orphaned twins, victims of the drug wars of the early eighties.

They can talk a good game. They know the names of streets and row houses and corner boys and dealers from

Baltimore in case someone has a cousin or a nephew from that part of the country and checks up on them. They know intimate details of major drug events from the past, when and where they were standing when Big Randy bought two to the head on Fayette Street, where and when they were standing when Tej Junior took over the corners on West Lombard. And yet, none of this history is true.

Dalan and Darius Webb grew up in Vancouver, Canada, the sons of a Methodist preacher. The preacher had a small congregation, a decent salary, a modest home, and a doting wife who loved him unconditionally. The preacher's wife, however, was not their mother.

Laverne Contessa Webb managed the office of the small church, serving at once as its accountant, secretary, social planner, fund-raiser, and any of hundreds of other functions including, on occasion, sermon author. She worked closely with the preacher and fell for him when his mild flirtations gave way to serious advances. Once she became pregnant, she was chased from the church by a congregation who liked to listen to ancient stories about forgiveness while avoiding any themselves. The preacher rebuked her mercilessly as sin incarnate.

She fled to her childhood home, a small farmhouse in Iowa, where she and her elderly parents raised the twin boys. They were home-schooled, they worked on the farm, and they grew up with innate distrust. And when they chose this life, the killing life, they held on to only one thing from their sordid past: the love of their mother.

Damn, Archibald is full of surprises. That kind of backstory can take months, maybe years, to cobble together, especially since the marks worked very hard to concoct their own version of the past. But Archibald had discovered it all, laid it out in the pages of his report like a true crime novelist. And as much as I want to put a slug in the man's head for the aggravation he's causing me, I keep finding things to admire about him.

* * *

Laverne answers the door wearing a shawl around her thin shoulders. She is slender and frail; she's lost weight since Archibald managed to capture a few photos of her, like she's been fighting an illness and a strong gust of wind might blow her away.

'Ms. Webb?'

'Yes?'

'You . . . uh . . . you don't know me, but I've driven a long way to find you.'

She raises her eyebrows and sticks out her lower lip, taking me in. 'Oh?'

'I'm from Vancouver, ma'am.'

She stiffens at the name of the city, and I press forward. 'My father recently passed away.'

'I don't understand what . . .'

'Before he went, he asked that I find you, get in touch with you. It took me a long time, but I put the pieces together. Do you mind if I come in?'

I can tell she is thinking about it. 'Would you mind telling me what this is about?'

'I'd rather do it inside.'

She folds her arms.

I force an embarrassed smile on my face. 'My father was a deacon at the King's Cross Methodist Church there in Vancouver, and he wrote a letter he wanted me to share with you. He said it was very important I give it to you. I think he's looking for some kind of absolution.'

Her eyes move from my face to some point in the distance, like she's trying to see through to the past. Slowly, she nods. 'All right, then.'

'Thank you.'

She steps aside and allows me to pass into the house, a mistake she will soon regret.

She is doing fine. Scared, yes, but doing as I ask as best she can under the circumstances. The cordless phone is up to her ear, and she watches me fearfully. Her eyes flit to the Glock resting comfortably in my right hand.

After a moment, one of her sons answers the line.

'Yo.'

'Darius?'

His voice warms immediately. I guess I'm a little surprised she's able to distinguish between her two sons after hearing one syllable, but never underestimate a mother, I suppose. 'Hey, Mom. How you doing?'

'Not so well.'

'What is it?'

Before she can answer, I snatch the phone out of her hand and affect a gangland accent. 'Bring me some money, yo.' And then I hang up. And wait.

Juda, the bodyguard, is the first one through the door. Darius is right behind him, gathering steam as he barrels into the foyer. Both men have guns out and up in broad daylight, dismissing any worries of nosy neighbors watching them.

Dalan, the younger of the two twins by exactly seven minutes, hangs back by the car, double-fisting a pair of chrome .45 automatic Colts, high-caliber, knock-out punch guns. I'm sure he's there to ambush anybody foolish enough to try to escape out the front door.

My first shot hits him flush in the forehead while my second catches him under the chin as he drops. I didn't use a silencer, purposefully making as much noise as I can. The sound of the gunfire initiates the intended effect, Darius screams a guttural, maniacal wail as he bursts back out of the front door and races to the body of his twin brother, slumped backward against the rear tire of their Navigator, a lure too shiny to resist.

My third shot rips through the back of Darius's head, sending half of his skull into his dead brother's face.

Juda, standing halfway between the front door and the car, spins and looks at me where I lie on top of Laverne's roof. My gun points directly at him, a sure shot, a clean kill if I pull my index finger toward me an inch. I don't want to kill Juda, though. Not unless he does something stupid. As I mentioned before, I've found trouble can grow exponentially if I leave more of a mess than necessary, and bodyguards are always more interested in a paycheck than revenge.

He doesn't take his eyes off me. He's a true professional, a man who has seen his share of bodies, and he knows he's dealing with a killer who has the advantage. Slowly, he drops his guns and backs away, backs away, backs away, until he reaches the sidewalk. Then he turns and starts running, a sprinter, a man with nothing but monetary ties to the brothers and a will to live.

In a few moments, I am off the roof, leaping into the back yard and sprinting in the opposite direction, to my rental car parked on a neighboring street. I tied Laverne Webb to a chair in her kitchen, and I don't want to be within five miles of her house when she frees herself and comes looking for me. What I won't do is underestimate the mother.

8

I am sitting next to Archibald Grant's bed when he turns on his light. He doesn't flinch, just sits up and props himself against the headboard. He is growing accustomed to having me in his life.

'I might've been with a lady.'

'You aren't.'

'But I might've been. And you would've scared the insides out of her, creeping up in here like that.'

I shrug. 'The job is done.'

'The brothers are planted?'

'Head shots. Both of them.'

Archibald smiles, all teeth. 'Well, all right. You can wake me up for that kind of news any day of the week.'

'Give me my name, and I'm on my way.'

'Yeah, yeah. We had a deal and you came through true blue. Open up that drawer in the bedside table there.'

Inside is a black notepad, the kind with a wire coil on top. I pass it to him.

'Hand me my glasses there.'

I do, and he sets an old pair of bifocals on his nose, then starts flipping through the notebook, muttering to himself. 'All right. Uh huh.' He makes nodding motions with his head as he continues to flip. Finally, he stops on one page. 'Here it is. The name you're looking for. Les'see, it's: Alexander Cole-Frett. Not sure how to pronounce that. Here, take the page.'

He rips it out and I look at the name. *Alexander Coulfret* in block capital letters. The name looks familiar, but I can't peg it.

'That's all I have, Columbus. But he's the guy putting his signature across the contract on your life. I know *that*.'

'You have any idea why?'

'Can't say I do.' He shrugs, feigning ignorance, his porcupine quills, his tortoise shell, his built-in defense.

I fold the paper away and stand.

Archibald takes off his glasses and folds his hands behind his head. 'Say, this been a pleasure for me, working with you. I mean that. We should do it more often.'

'Good luck, Archibald.' I'm already moving toward the bedroom door.

'Columbus?' He waits for me to turn. 'Don't tell no one about my glasses.'

I can't help but smile. He scoots back down, rests his head against the pillow, and closes his eyes.

Coulfret. Coulfret. Where have I heard that name? It's French; I'm on the right track, but I've studied Noel's business dealings and his family tree going back generations and that name isn't there. And yet I know I've seen it. I know it.

I am sitting in the Hall public library on South Michigan, just about to type Coulfret's name into a Google window when the first bullet rips through my side. It's a low-caliber round but goddamn does it hurt, like someone swung a hammer into my rib cage.

A civilian's natural reaction is to drop to the ground when struck by a bullet no matter where it hits the body. It is ingrained from watching thousands of cop shows, thousands of movies, countless hours playing good guys and bad guys: when a gun goes off, the victim clutches his or her heart and falls to the earth like a punch-drunk prize fighter. But a professional killer knows better, knows you can live a long time with a .22 bullet inside you, knows that instead of dropping to the ground, you should be moving away from the direction the bullet hit your body.

I wasn't expecting this, had no warning other than the small cracking sound to my right followed by the blow to my side, but my instincts take over and people are starting to scream and flee and I act like I'm going to fall, only to leap onto the computer table, just as another crack and a bullet rips into the ground where the person holding the weapon thought I would drop, but I'm up and off the table and diving for a row between two bookshelves.

I catch a glimpse of some dark hair, and I know it's Llanos, the one from Argentina, and she managed to get one bullet in me but I'll be damned if she's going to manage two.

I chose poorly on the row; there are nothing but bookshelves and a concrete wall in front of me, so I swing low and dive through the 'H's in the biography section, scattering hard-covers like buckshot, until I burst out on the other side of the shelf, hitting the ground hard.

My ribs now feel like someone is trying to rip them out of my skin and I'm fighting to breathe, holding my shirt tight over the wound, but I'm pretty sure the bullet caught bone and stayed there, didn't ricochet, because I'm not throwing up blood, not yet, and my wits are still about me. I may not have anything else, but I've got that.

My eyes sweep my new position, homing in on the exits, because one thing is sure, a woman shooting a man in the middle of a Chicago public library is going to draw a hell of a lot of police. She knows it too and that may be my only advantage. She simply doesn't have time to try and finish the job, not if she wants to escape.

Across the aisle, I spot a door marked 'Employees Only' and it's my best shot, my only shot, a break room or a snack room or something leading down or up or outside.

I grab a large book with the hand not pressed to my side, Lincoln's face on the cover, and fling it across the open aisle, no-man's-land, and I am moving while the book is still in the air. Lincoln draws the bullet instead of me and before a second shot is fired, I cross the ten steps to the employees' door, and I'm through it, startling a corpulent woman in a small hallway who smells like cigarettes.

'Smoking section!' I shout, a little louder than I would have liked, making the universal sign for cigarettes with the first two fingers of my good hand pressed to my lips and she's too surprised to do anything but point a chubby finger at a door at the end of the hallway.

Twenty yards and I'm slamming through the opening into sunshine and fresh air and freedom. My side feels like someone is jamming a spear into it; my right hand looks like I dipped it in paint.

The alley behind the library opens to the street and I spot a cab idling at the curb with a skinny white kid behind the wheel.

'Out now!' I scream as I fling open his driver's door, and in my periphery I see Llanos streaking around the corner, gun out and up. The woman has sand, I'll give her that.

The driver unbuckles his belt as he puts his hands up but he isn't moving fast enough. I yank him the rest of the way out of his seat, on to the sidewalk, and just as another volley of bullets pelts the side of the cab, I slide behind the wheel, throw the car in drive, and jam the pedal through the floorboard, not bothering to close the door. I couldn't if I wanted to, my left arm is pinned to my side; my right guides the wheel. It slams shut from the momentum as the car races forward.

I don't have much time. My vision is already going hazy at the edges, like I've stumbled into a tunnel. I need to think of something. Anything.

A quick glance in the rearview mirror, and goddammit, this Llanos woman is tenacious. I see her commandeer a second cab much as I took the first, and it roars away from the curb like a lion tracking wounded prey. She knows she landed a blow, and like a prizefighter crowding an opponent into the ropes, she'll be damned if she'll give up that advantage.

I throw the car around a corner, blinking doublevision out of my eyes, and if I'm going to do something, I'm going to have to do it now. My hold on consciousness is slippery at best, and the pain in my side is burning, like half my body has been lit on fire.

Before she can take the corner, I slam on my brakes, smoking the tires and just as quickly, I throw the stick into reverse and mash the pedal.

When killing a mark, there is only one sure way to put the target down permanently: a headshot. With a car, the principle holds, and any time you can sacrifice your trunk for your opponent's engine, you should launch at the chance.

I can't turn around, so I utilize the rear view mirror and grit my teeth and hope, hope, hope I'm timing this right and just as she blitzes around the corner, I thunder into her in reverse with a full head of steam.

Her hood crumples like an accordion, bucking the yellow cab up so the back tires threaten to flip over the front. Then the rear tires slam back to the pavement before her entire cab spins to the side.

I spin too, but am still facing away from her, thank God, and my engine is humming softly, so I shift back into drive and plow forward. My left rear tire is airless but the axle feels like it has kept its alignment and this poor cab may not get me far, but it should be enough. I eye the sideview mirror; Llanos's car remains in the middle of the street, smoke rising from its hood like a funeral pyre and if she makes it out before the whole thing goes up, at least it'll be with her confidence rattled. At least I gained that.

Now that my adrenaline is in full retreat, I feel tired, so damn tired, like I'm trying to walk along the bottom of the ocean. I need to make a move, a decision. I can't get much further limping in this cab. I have to find help. Goddamn, I need a fence. I have to . . .

Squash. Butternut squash soup, to be more specific, drips on my tongue and hits the back of my throat. I can smell it full in my nostrils, warm and salty. It might as well be a bone-in rib-eye. It tastes like the most delicious morsel I've ever put in my mouth.

I open my eyes and am staring at a young black woman, pretty, unthreatening. She is ladling the soup into my mouth with one hand under the spoon to keep it from dripping on to my chest.

'Hello.' Her voice is warm, barely hiding a southern accent.

'Hello.'

'How you feeling?'

'Stiff.'

'You had a twenty-two slug in you, lodged into your rib. You want to see it?'

'No, thank you.' She spoons another bite into my mouth and I can feel the heat moving down the length of my chest after I swallow.

'Just a second.' She sets the bowl down and bounces over to a nearby door so she can stick her head into the hallway. She isn't dressed like a nurse or a caregiver; she's wearing a tight skirt and a half-shirt that shows off a belly ring.

'Archie! He's up!'

So I made it here after all. I remember throwing that Lincoln book – thanks for drawing another bullet, Mr. President – and I have images of a fat finger pointing me toward daylight and a cab barreling in reverse – but everything else bleeds together like Polaroids shuffled in a deck. I wanted to make it to a pharmacy and get the things I needed but I was slipping in and out of consciousness and didn't have a choice. I thought about Archibald and I must've made that decision but I don't remember doing so. I have no idea if I drove, walked, or crawled here. I'm vulnerable now, and I'm indebted to a man who knows how to exploit vulnerability, but I'm not sure I had another choice.

My side is throbbing, but what really bothers me, what my mind keeps turning over and over as it blocks out the pain is the play Llanos made. Archibald had warned me she had picked up my scent in Chicago, and so I went to a public library with a perfect view of my surroundings. Yet, she still took her shot there, even though her chances of finishing the job were limited. Then she kept after me, long past time when she should've retreated. The only reason she would do that, I imagine, is the third assassin, the Czech named Svoboda, is also here. She wanted to collect the kill fee before him, or she was worried he'd come after her first. Either way, she tried to force a low-percentage play. I'm going to make that decision come back to haunt her.

Archibald pokes his head in the room and I have to squint from the glare off all those teeth.

'Back from the abyss.' His voice is as bouncy as the girl's step. 'I must say I thought it'd be a while before you knocked on my door again. I guess something up in the universe got us tied together on the same string.'

'Thanks for the patch-work.'

'I got a surgeon who likes cash money and doesn't like paying malpractice. We got what the Nature Channel calls a symbiotic relationship.'

'You got a mirror?'

'This face? I got a house full of 'em.'

He moves off and the girl smiles at me. 'Archie tells me you're the best he ever worked with.'

'Archibald talks too much.'

'Been that way since we were five. He had half our school working for him. The teachers too. Only one he couldn't keep up with was our mother.'

'I'd like to have met her . . . just to complete the picture.'

Archibald steps back into the room, holding a hand mirror. 'That old lady taught me everything I know.'

'She'd roll over in the grave to hear that.'

So Archibald – Archie – has a sister and he thinks we're square enough to let me in on that secret, even after I got to the Webb brothers through their mother. It's a calculated move on his part. I showed up at his place completely helpless, exposed and dying; in return, he exposes himself, personally, to me, tying us even tighter together. Maybe the universe really does have us dangling on the same string.

I take the mirror and hold it at an angle to get a look at the wound in my side. Peeling the gauze and bandage back, I'm impressed with Archibald's surgeon. The wound is clean and the stitches are tight and even.

'I told you,' Archibald says from the door.

'Yeah, pretty good.' The pain is awful now, throbbing in time with my heartbeat. I don't want to know what it's going to feel like if I cough.

'You need some Tylenol or something?' the sister asks.

'I'll take some if you got 'em.'

'Not a problem.' She turns to go, then stops. 'I'm Ruby, by the way.'

'Columbus.'

'I know who you are.'

I've got a laptop in bed with me, and I'm chasing down the name Alexander Coulfret. Nothing on Google except an article from 2003 listing the victims of a Paris bus crash. An Alex Coulfret is among the dead, the tragedy taking place when a train leaving the city sideswiped a stranded bus. Nothing else. One mention of a dead guy and that's it. Whoever he is, he's kept his name blank in a world where most names are a keyboard click away. Maybe Archibald misspelled it.

I try typing in just the name 'Coulfret' and I'll be damned. Fourteen articles from various European papers pop up, all focused on one particular incident, the murder of capitalist Anton Noel in the middle of Paris. I swallow, knowing I've found the right set of keys. Now, which one fits into the lock?

I click on the first article, the one I read in *Le Monde* while waiting in the train station in Naples before Ryan died giving me his warning. I scan it quickly, searching, searching . . . nothing leaps out at me and then I see it: Jerome Coulfret. A forty-five-year-old jeweler. One of two unfortunate civilians struck down when Noel's car flipped in a Paris intersection just as they were crossing it on foot. An innocent guy, cursed with black luck, caught in the wrong place at the wrong time. The confrontation in the bait-and-tackle store, the shot in the library, the bullet removed from my side, they had very little to do with Anton Noel after all. It was my sloppiness, my improvisation, my botched job that led to Jerome Coulfret's accidental death. Like I said, trouble grows exponentially when you leave more of a mess than necessary.

I'm guessing Jerome has a brother who might be a bit unhappy with the way my assignment to kill Noel went down.

I'm getting dressed when Archibald comes in and leans against the doorframe.

'Three weeks here. I was just about to ask you to get the fuck out.'

I smile. How the hell this guy grew on me, I have no idea, but he has. I can't laugh, though, not with my ribs feeling the way they do.

'I gotta get back before the noose gets any tighter. End this thing.'

'You don't have to tell me. You think I want two top-shelf killers figuring out I'm the one played Florence Nightingale with you? Or get on this Cole-Frett's shit list? They might start thinking I'd know how to find you and want a word with me. I'll pass on that, thank you very much.'

I finish and reach for my pair of Glocks. 'You cleaned these for me. You thoughtful bastard.'

'Not me,' Archibald says, raising his palms as he backs out the door. 'I'd say goodbye, but something tells me I'm going to see you again.' He's down the hall by the time I emerge from the room.

Well, I have to give him a tip of the cap. I thought he'd try to lord this over me, ask me to pay off my new debt to him by shouldering some other difficult assignment. At the very least I thought he'd ask me to join him, partner with him, the same way William Ryan did after my first fence, Pooley, died.

But if he wants something from me, he's saving it for later. I wonder how long it'll be before I hear the front doorbell jingling on that one.

When I get to the door, Ruby is there, blowing on a warm cup of coffee.

'Back to the shooting business . . .' she offers, her eyes merry.

'I'm just trying to keep the shooting business off me right now.'

'So I heard.'

'Archibald tells you a lot.'

'Who do you think handles most of his contracts?'

I'll admit, I didn't see that coming. Family members often work together on the business side of the game. But this is the first time I've encountered a brother and sister who are also fence and assassin. The Grants grow more interesting by the minute.

'You're a bagman?'

'I know a little about a little.'

'Well, now I know who cleaned my guns.'

'You noticed.'

'Yes. And thank you.'

'Don't mention it, Columbus. If I'm ever shot in the ribs in Europe, I'll know who to come find.'

'You'll have to find me first.'

'That's the idea.'

'See you around.'

'I hope so.'

She takes another sip of coffee and heads back toward the kitchen.

9

I have two stops to make before I begin to hunt Alexander Coulfret in France.

First, I need to visit my home in Positano. I realize this is pregnant with danger – the worst mistake a man with a price on his head can make is to walk through his own front door. But I'm growing weary of looking over my shoulder, and I need to load up on supplies and check to see if my residence has, in fact, been compromised.

The second stop involves Rome and a woman with a meaningless name who I can't get off my mind.

Positano is built into the side of a cliff, and I fell in love with it the moment I arrived here to kill a man named Cortino many years ago. When I needed a place to live abroad, it called to me just as Risina described Italy calling to her. I too found it difficult not to answer.

I bought a modest house about halfway up the hill and used it sparingly, so the locals would think of it as my second home. The long-time residents of Positano are as insular as the city itself, and I utilize their natural distrust of 'summer people' to avoid forging relationships.

The sky and the sea are almost the exact same shade of color as I drive into the city on a motorcycle. I have spent my adult life blending into the background of every environment: dressing myself, carrying myself and expressing myself in ways that are the opposite of eye-catching. The motorcycle I drive is old and rusty and unmemorable, the same as a hundred bikes swarming the Italian countryside at the moment.

I park the bike near the beach, a twenty-minute walk from my front door, and start the climb. From my vantage point below, I can see the outside of my house, a beige two-story manor, perched on the side of the cliff. It looks undisturbed, and I'm not sure if that is a relief or a cause to be nervous. At least if I could pinpoint something unusual – a window shade up, broken glass – I could proceed with a plan. I have no choice but to be acutely cautious.

As a killer, I train myself to map out escape routes, no matter where I am or what I am doing. I do it without thinking, as natural and involuntary as exhaling. When I bought this house – Ryan actually did the buying, through a third party – I immediately set about renovating it, alone. The killing profession teaches you many useful disciplines; a basic knowledge of carpentry can be indispensable in a number of ways. I didn't upgrade the fixtures in the kitchen or expand the closets in the master bedroom. The upgrades I managed were for one purpose: getting into and out of the house without being seen.

I ascend stone steps laid out for homeowners and adventurous tourists, climb half of the hill, and then break from the main path when I am assuredly alone.The pain from the wound in my side has diminished, but not completely. It throbs now, marking each step with a pinprick to my ribs. I have heard about people's ability to compartmentalize pain, to suppress it, put it down in a hole below the line of consciousness, but fuck if I've ever been able to do it. My ribs hurt, and the only thing that will get me back to feeling a hundred percent normal is time.

Along a smaller trail, I can approach my house from the side, and if I squeeze in next to the wall and a dense row of evergreen hedges, I remain invisible. Near the base of the wall is a crawlspace entry. Its only distinguishing mark is a thin beige rope. I can tell from its position that the rope is undisturbed, just as I left it. I use it to pull the cover free. Before I enter, I reach my hand inside, and from memory, punch a sequence into a small alarm I installed just above the opening. A tiny beep indicates the space has been uncompromised since I last left. I take a breath and push through into the darkness.

From here, I only have to crawl a few feet to an area where I can stand, and from there, I open a hidden entrance into a laundry room next to my kitchen. The room is silent and musty, like the air has been trapped in here for months, a good sign.

After twenty minutes and a thorough inspection of each room, I am convinced the house is clear and remains undiscovered. If Leary, the Irish assassin I dispatched in Georgia, had beaten the information out of Ryan, he didn't have a chance to follow up on it. If he has passed the knowledge of my residence to anyone else, they haven't come calling. Yet.

I own only a few pieces of furniture, a bed, and a closet full of dark T-shirts, dark jeans and shoes. I undress, take a shower with the water turned up just below scalding, redress my wound, and then wedge as many clothes into a duffel bag as I comfortably can. A false front in the closet gives way to my weapons stash, and I load a black backpack with pistols and ammunition and extra clips. Finished, I take a look around the house, and allow myself two minutes at the back window looking down the cliff face at the black sand and the gray sea. In my head, I'm already using the word 'the' instead of 'my.' It's 'the' house, not 'my' house.

Twenty minutes later, I am straddling the motorcycle, my duffel in the storage compartment under the seat, my backpack secure on my back. This will be the last time I see Positano, and I feel a melancholy pang in my chest. It looks as it always has: quiet and proud. I turn my head, kick-start the engine, and motor away.

An assassin's life is marked by movement. Loiter too long in one place and you won't be pleased with what catches up to you.

* * *

I can guess what happened. Risina's co-worker handed her a cryptic message when she arrived at work. 'Anonymous man called. Has first edition Lewis and Clark, 1814. Must sell. Meet in St. George lobby. 9:00 P.M.'

Risina must've smiled, curious, intrigued. She must've asked Alda to describe the man's voice, but Alda probably shrugged dismissively. The man had requested Risina specifically, that's all Alda knew. He was just a man on the phone, and he kept everything succinct.

Risina might have called around to see if other contacts in the rare-book world had caught wind of a first edition Lewis and Clark entering the market. The lack of confirmation probably piqued her curiosity.

She must've gone home and chosen a black suit to wear. Conservative, but feminine. A suit conveying that her occupation dealt on the intersection where business and creativity collide.

She must have then walked to the hotel, pleased her anonymous caller chose a place just a few blocks from her home. She had her financial ledger tucked in tight at her elbow, a check and a pen ready if the seller needed to make this deal happen immediately.

She had no idea a man was watching her from the moment she left her apartment. She had no idea the man was scouring the area like a hawk, looking for any hint of abnormality, any hint of a pursuer, any threat to himself. She had no idea that the man was heavily armed, that the man was a professional, that the man was dangerous.

She probably sat in the lobby of the St. George Hotel, growing anxious and annoyed with each passing minute. She probably wondered if she was the victim of a hoax or if Alda was losing her mind. At some point, she wandered into the library, just off the lobby.

Her beauty was electric, powerful. It drew eyes to her like a beacon cutting through fog. She was the opposite of the man. It almost hurt him to approach her.

'Hello, Risina.'

She turns and her smile is broad and warm.

'Jack!'

'You're not going to be too upset if it's just me instead of Lewis and Clark?'

She crosses to me instantly and embraces me with her whole body. I can't remember the last time I held someone in my arms like that, without reservation.

'You are a bad man.'

'I've told myself that many times.'

'You could have just called me and told me you were in town.'

'What would've been the fun in that?'

She hits me playfully and pulls back, smiling. Goddamn, she is beautiful.

'Did you get a room here?'

'Yes, but that's not what I—'

'Take me to it.'

An hour later, we lie exposed on the sheets, her head on my chest, her fingers intertwined with mine.

'I can honestly say I thought about you each day you were gone.'

Her voice is low in her throat, like a cat's purr.

'I'm sorry I couldn't get back here sooner.'

'How was business?'

'Ongoing.'

Her lips form a moue. 'Does that mean you'll be leaving soon?'

'Yes.'

'This is how it's going to be, isn't it?'

'Just for now.'

'Don't tell lies for my sake.'

'I'm not. I've been thinking quite a bit about changing jobs.'

'Oh?'

I stroke her hair, tracing her eyebrows with my thumb.

'Yes, finding something where I wouldn't have to move around so much.'

'And you would settle in Rome?'

'Would you like that?'

'I like you, Jack. Very much. There is something inside me that tenses every time I see you. I don't know how to describe it, but it happens. It is something I look forward to . . . this feeling . . . and not knowing when I'm going to experience it again has been . . . difficult for me.'

She takes her hand out of mine and sits up on her elbow so she can look at me. 'I'm sorry. I'm not expressing myself well. The way I mean to.'

'You're very pretty.'

She frowns. If I can change the subject abruptly, so can she. 'Tell me about your scars.'

She looks down when she says this, like she's afraid of my response.

I knew it was coming . . . her fingers had traced my wounds earlier, and I winced once when we shifted places. But I'm not sure, even now, I'm not sure I'm ready to let her in. Once that door swings open, it is impossible to close.

She senses my hesitation and lies back down, resuming her position with her head on my chest. For a minute, I think she isn't going to speak again, that she may fall asleep right there. But I am wrong.

'A man paid for my education. In America.'

I know she has more to say, so I wait.

'I was seventeen and worked in a small grocery store on the other side of Rome, near Vatican City. I worked there from the time I was thirteen, making a few lira after school so I could help my parents. The man who owned the store . . . his name was Giuseppe Rono. My parents and others in the neighborhood didn't like him, didn't trust him. He had moved into the neighborhood from a farming village near Siena. He was unmarried and had an ugly face.

'He would come to the gymnasium at the school and watch the girls play soccer, even though he had no daughter on the team. There were whispers – I heard them from my friends' parents, from neighbors – of how his eyes would linger too long on the girls running and jumping and playing. It was a time when people didn't talk about such things, and still, there was talk. My parents wanted me to quit working in his shop, but I refused. I was a strong-willed girl, and I was at an age when I would choose to do whatever my parents forbade. As the weeks progressed, Giuseppe Rono and I became friendly. I would stay after work to talk to him about the latest gossip from school and he would listen to it all, passing on advice and taking an interest in all my activities, always ready to lend his ear.

'One afternoon, he called me into the small office he owned behind the store. He was seated behind a wooden desk, and his hand was down in his lap where I couldn't see it. His arm was moving slightly, and I could see he was sweating, even though it was cool that day. His face was smiling, but it was . . . I don't know how you say it in English . . . ?'

'Lopsided?'

'Yes, that's it. A lopsided smile. I remember thinking I was a fool, I had failed to heed everyone's warnings and they were right about Giuseppi Rono. I cursed him, though the words wouldn't come out. I hated him, though my face couldn't move. If I'd had a gun in my hand, I would've shot him right there. I know it.

'He wanted to show me something, he told me. I was paralyzed . . . I knew I should turn and run away but my legs wouldn't work, I couldn't make them work.'

She takes a breath, gathering herself.

'Goddamn him, I thought. Damn him for betraying me like this. He started to stand up and I wanted to tear my eyes away but I couldn't avert them. I couldn't move, no matter how much my mind screamed at me to go, just go! Run away from that place screaming . . .

'I looked down at his lap, and in his hands, he was holding a sheet of paper, folding it and refolding it nervously. "Risina," he told me, his face expectant, hopeful. "Risina, I had a wife and child who died many years ago in an auto crash in Siena. My daughter, her name was Christiana, she would have been your age." His voice was shaking, and he continued to turn that paper over and over. "I have contacted the University in America, the one you told me you could not afford. I have set up an account for you, Risina. To pay for your schooling. It was money set aside for Christiana, but you have been the daughter she was to me. You must accept this, Risina. You must let me do this for you while I can. It would mean everything to a brokenhearted and lonely man."

'I don't remember what happened after that ... I remember hugging him so hard I thought he might break. I remember my parents coming into the office ... he had already contacted them and explained his situation. They were ashamed, but proud. Proud of me and my chance for an education. I remember my father's hand pumping Mr. Rono's, and I remember the smile on Rono's face so large I thought it would light up the sun. And all I could think about as I hugged him, all I could think about was that I had rushed to hate him just ten minutes before. That I would have shot him with a gun if I'd had the chance. That I had cursed him.

'He died of cancer the month after I graduated. He was too sick to attend the ceremony, but he wrote me a letter which I carry with me always.'

Her voice stops but the story remains between us like a tangible object.

I run my hand through her hair again, splay it out against my chest, unsure what to say. After a moment, she takes my fingers back in hers.

'I've learned there can be a great distance between perception and the truth. And I know there are things about you you wish to keep a mystery from me. Just know that I won't rush to judge you, Jack. The one thing I will never do is judge you.'

* * *

The shower is therapeutic, and the pain in my side from the bullet wound has diminished to nothing more than a twinge. I feel better than I've felt in a long time, for as long as I can remember, actually.

I can see it now, like a map unfolded in front of me. There is an end to this, to this life. I can shed it like a snake's skin. Throughout adulthood, I've felt like this job defined me, was a part of me, was inside me. But I see it now, I can *see* it, goddammit, maybe for the first time.

I haven't left it, haven't escaped it, because I didn't *want* to leave this way of life. I never cared about the money; it was the challenge and the skill and the craft and the power I devoured like an addict. And after years of doing the job, of sharpening my abilities, of mastering my prowess, of forgetting Jake, the only woman who knew me as something other than a killer, I'd lost any measure of what my life could be without it.

But Risina changes that. Is she an ideal? Is my desperation for human contact coloring how I view the woman asleep in the bed outside this bathroom? Am I purposely turning a blind eye to her faults, creating in my mind a Madonna void of blemishes, when the truth must fall far short?

The answer is: I don't give a damn.

I am out of the shower, dried and dressed, tying my shoes when she stirs.

'You are leaving?'

'Yes. Take your time. Order breakfast to the room.'

She sits up, unselfconsciously. I can't help but look at her, drinking her in. Like her laughter before, it is an image I know will sustain me over the next few weeks, as I finish this and free myself.

'Do you think you will be long this time?'

'I don't know. I don't think so. But I don't know.'

'Is there danger you will not come back at all?'

'Why do you ask?'

'I know what those scars are, Jack. There's a bullet wound in your side. Old bullet wounds in your shoulder and on your chest. I can only imagine what made the other marks.'

She says it matter-of-factly, with no malice in her eyes.

'I will be back. I promise.'

'I believe you.'

'I will tell you everything when I return.'

'I believe that too.'

I head for the door and reach for the handle.

'Jack . . .'

'Yes?'

'Be sure and bring that first edition Lewis and Clark with you when you come back to me.'

She is grinning and her eyes are merry.

'I will.'

I pull the door behind me and walk away from the room, down the corridor, alone. My smile disappears by the time I reach the street.

10

Alexander Coulfret is going to be a difficult man to kill.

Without a fence, a middleman, to put a file together, I am learning the craft on my own. I have a new respect for the job Vespucci, Pooley, and Ryan did, the job Grant and Doriot still do. I suppose I could have phoned Archibald Grant in Chicago and seen what blanks he could fill in regarding Coulfret, but I just don't want that particular string tied any tighter. I already owe the man enough.

When I've needed information in the past, I've either stolen it from the shadows, or I've compelled someone to give it to me against his or her will. In those instances, the information I seek is specific – the location of a particular mark on that given day, say – and I don't have to worry about returning to the source again.

But compiling a background file on a man, a large dossier so I have myriad choices of how and where and when to strike, requires a much different approach.

I start in the offices of *Le Monde*, posing as an American film writer. My former fence Pooley once explained people will do anything to help you if they think there is an outside chance of being immortalized. People from all walks of life – waitresses to senators – would open up to him and spill their secrets as he appealed to their vanity, claiming to be a screenwriter, a reporter, a novelist, a film producer. I intimate I am researching a script centering on Parisian crime, a *French Connection* for the new millennium, and I need background information on a man named Alexander Coulfret.

A public relations woman escorts me to their catalog room, where every article, every scrap of paper, including reporter's notes in some instances, has been added to an enormous database. The woman, BeBe, is genial and coquettish. She sets me up in a cubicle, asks if I need anything to drink, hands me her card, and then leaves me alone with the computer.

Hours later, I emerge from the building with the following information.

A young man named Alex Coulfret was arrested twice in the nineties, once for robbery and once for stabbing a man with a knife, though the victim made a full recovery. Both articles mention jail time, but there is no followup reporting to indicate whether or not Alex was found guilty or whether he served. Both arrests occurred on the east side of the city, in the Eleventh arrondissement, near the Bastille. Information about the perpetrator is scant, a 'white male in his twenties' the full extent of the description.

Only one other occurrence of the name appears in the newspaper, a mention in the bottom of that article from 2003, the one I found when I first punched the name Alexander Coulfret into Google back in Archibald's apartment. I barely glanced at it before, but now I study the details a bit more closely. A train leaving Paris crashed into a stranded bus just outside the city, killing twelve people. Listed alphabetically among the dead: Alex Coulfret. The article is maddeningly short – no other details emerge about the victims – like it was written just before the evening deadline. I check the next day's edition and find no mention of the crash; the story was swept away by the bombings of the U.S. embassies in Tanzania and Kenya.

These buried facts are tiny seeds, just specks of information, but they start to grow into a portrait of the man who paid the contract on my life. First, I'm guessing he was born in or near the Bastille district; the connection between the two arrests indicates proximity, familiarity. Second, the types of offenses certainly keep in line with a low-level member of a criminal organization. Not every arrest makes the paper. I wonder how many more crimes Alex committed or was arrested for in his early adulthood. Third, a man who has the resources to hire a trio of professional killers also has the resources to fake his own death, to land his name on a list of the deceased following a fatal public accident. The short time – ten years between *Le Monde* mentions – gives me pause.

I've been in a position to observe the inner workings of organized crime many times. Most mafias operate similarly: loyalty is rewarded; men rise through the ranks by some combination of battle-tested fealty and unfettered nepotism. Usually, this process can take an entire lifetime, and even then, a man's stupidity or nerve can hinder him from rising past a low-level position within the enterprise. That Alex Coulfret ascended from armed stick-up man to a position powerful enough to fake his own death in such a relatively short time means my enemy is most likely intelligent, artful, and ruthless.

If I'm wrong, and the three mentions aren't as colorful as I'm suggesting, then it does me no harm to assume the man is formidable. But I don't think I'm wrong.

The next avenues I plan to investigate are the local police files on Coulfret. Perhaps they have more details tucked away in the back of a detective's cabinet than in the database of the newspaper. Maybe the police know all about the man and are actively hunting him now, as I am.

I call BeBe at *Le Monde* from a pay phone near the Bastille and enlist her help in introducing me to a friendly police detective in the eleventh district. She is more than happy to do so; she knows just the man with whom I should speak, a detective named Gerard. How soon would I like to get started?

I hang up after agreeing on a meeting point and walk toward that creperie. I notice a young boy who can't be more than six or seven, holding on to his father's hand, coming toward me on the sidewalk ahead. The boy has to take two steps just to match his father's pace, and the man never looks down at his child, lost in his own world. My mind turns to that silver wagon with the dropped handle. Why is that image so damned important to me? Why is it always on the edge of my mind, waiting like a stranger in the shadows, prepared to leap out and suffocate me at a moment's notice?

I think I know the answer, though I don't want to face it. Years ago, my father hired me to kill him, though I didn't know all the details until the end. I thought I had mentally closed that door, put it behind me, walled it off, but maybe it can never fully be closed. At one time I thought I had control over the past, could shut it off from my mind like turning off a faucet, but I was wrong. Maybe it will always be with me, breaking its valve and pouring out whenever I'm vulnerable. Maybe . . .

I catch a flash of silver ducking into a fabric shop across the street.

Something was off about it, something a little conspicuous, like a signal, and I cross the Rue Sedaine quickly, without thinking, reliant on years of heightened instinct. I know it'll be a problem ducking into an unfamiliar store and there will be a delay as my eyes adjust from light to dark, but my feet carry me on, almost involuntarily.

What did I see? A piece of clothing? The flash of sunlight reflecting off of a gun barrel? I was too entranced in watching that kid and his father and that silver handle in my head and now I'll have to grit my teeth and enter the place and if the Argentine woman wants to shoot me again then she should've pulled the trigger while my mind was on that boy who couldn't remember his name.

She didn't, though, and I'll rely on my intuition as I pop through the door and scan the room. The fabric shop is small; there's no one inside except an elderly Persian woman behind the cash register, but a carpeted stairwell with a sign pointing up reading 'shawls' in English looms next to her.

I have my Glock in my hand as I head up the stairwell, trying to keep my footfalls silent, but the noise is deafening in the oppressive quiet of the store.

An uneasy feeling tightens my throat and I can feel the short hairs on the back of my neck rising. I've made many mistakes since taking that file from Ryan outside the cathedral in Turin, but this takes the fucking cake, plodding up a narrow stairwell toward a dimly lit second floor with a possible assassin at the top. If I get shot, I'll go down pulling the trigger. If I get jumped, I'll go down swinging. I'm ascending the final step, and there is an armed woman up here, but not the one I thought.

'She's here.'

Ruby Grant, Archibald's sister, stands next to a tiny window, peering down at the street. She nods for me to join her, and when I do, I catch a glimpse of another woman, this one with inky hair, stalking quickly down the sidewalk, searching, confused. I've seen her before, in a library in Chicago. The last time we met, I was ramming the back end of a yellow cab into the front end of hers.

Below, the woman breaks from our sight line and is gone.

Ruby appears amused, like she's in the middle of telling a brilliant joke.

'That's Llanos.'

'Yeah . . .'

'She got to Archie.'

'Got to him?'

'Well, got to talk to him, I should say. Archie's good at talking. Always has been. He put her on your trail, then put me on hers.'

'He's starting to rack up too many favors.'

'He likes you.'

I'm not sure how to respond to that, and Ruby sees it on my face. Her grin grows as effortlessly as an exhale, what must be a family trait.

'So you flew all the way here to warn me?'

'Don't go gettin' ideas. Professional preservation. At this point in the game, you being dead doesn't do my brother much good.'

'What do you think me being alive does for him?'

Ruby shrugs. 'Something I guess Archie will figure out at a later date.'

She nods out the window. 'So how you want to handle this?'

'I'm going to drop her. Quietly.'

'I *know* that. I'm just asking if you want me to tag-team with you.'

'No. I'm afraid I already owe your family too much for my own good.'

'Suit yourself.'

I turn to head back down, hurrying so I don't lose the trail of the woman who came here to kill me.

'Columbus . . .'

I stop.

'See you soon.'

I nod and clomp heavily down the stairs, afraid she's probably right.

Llanos is half a block in front of me, addled. She was good enough to pick up my trail without alerting me, but not good enough to keep from losing the scent when I zigged when she thought I would zag. One mistake. As is the case so often in what we do, one mistake is the difference between Llanos living through the day and never seeing tomorrow's sunrise.

She checks the street signs, watches the shadows, and I can see resignation manifest on her face. She lost me, even though she's not sure how. She retraces her steps, bewildered, and then hurries in a trot toward the Rue de Lappe and the crepe shop where my meeting with the police detective is supposed to take place. So she must've been listening in on my call or wrenched the information from the PR woman at the newspaper, BeBe. I hope it is the former.

If I am going to ambush her, it is best to do it now, before she reaches the creperie a few blocks away, before the officer I'm supposed to be meeting witnesses the shooting.

An ambush is all about information and timing. I know where she's headed, which allows me to dart over a block to the south, then up the street at a sprint, then over again to arrive in front of her. The timing centers on waiting until the final possible moment to take the first shot, to remove her defenses before she has a chance to engage them.

I stop at the corner, waiting for Llanos to materialize in front of me. She's as oblivious as a rat sniffing cheese attached to a metal spring. I estimate I have thirty seconds before she emerges. The street is mostly deserted, so I'm not concerned about witnesses; perhaps the driver of a passing car will see something, but usually the shock of violence, the cacophony of a gunshot, gives me the freedom to hustle away unnoticed from the scene.

A door opens next to me and a crowd starts to spill out on to the sidewalk, children and parents and grandparents, and it is some sort of celebration complete with balloons and streamers and laughing and singing and they are passing me, heading for the corner directly in front of me, the intersection of the Rue de la Roquette and the Passage Thieré where I plan to take Llanos's life.

She should be approaching any second now and she'll be surrounded by the crowd, but she won't be protected, and as I instantaneously form a new plan, my hand moves from the Glock inside my shoulder holster to the blade I keep near my waist.

The seconds slow and the world stops spinning and the children freeze in mid-smile as my senses warp like they've been jolted with electricity and Llanos steps out from the street into my view, and she's ignoring the festive families, looking straight ahead when she should be checking around every corner instead of hurrying to make the next block.

I cut through the crowd like a scythe and her periphery vision kicks in as I approach with the blade in my hand and she's a moment too late as I swing my arm in a fluid arc and the stiletto smashes into her throat at the precise point above where her windpipe disappears below her sternum.

I don't break stride, keep moving, cross the street and duck a right, heading for the little bastion that started a revolution. When she falls to her knees, clutching her throat, trying to keep the blood from spilling out through her fingers, when the first child screams and when the parents pull all the boys and girls and grandparents away, hoping they haven't seen too much, I will be gone.

11

The officer smiles warmly when I greet him, half standing behind a wedge of a table in the middle of the crepe shop at the end of the Rue de Lappe.

He has ordered a croque monsieur, devoured the first triangle and is two bites into the second when I shake his hand.

'You are Mr. Walker, yes?'

'I am. Thanks so much for meeting me.'

'It is my pleasure, my pleasure. Ms. Lerner tells me you are a writer?'

'Yes . . .'

'Very pleased to meet you. My name is Gerard. I too write a little fiction. Nothing published as yet, but I am delighted to say a little printing press from Lyon has been in contact with me recently and has expressed interest in reading my next submission.'

He is a round man, with wide shoulders and only a hint of a neck, constructed like a snowman. Somehow, he takes bites of his sandwich while maintaining the cadence of his speech, and words tumble out of him at the same time as his food disappears from his plate. It's fascinating to watch, like a magician with a rabbit, and I have a hard time paying attention to what he's saying.

'But they say writing is to write what you know and my occupation as an officer in Paris has led to many, many interesting stories, I can assure you, so let me, may I ask, what type of writing is it you do?'

'Well, a little bit of everything but mostly film writing.'

He pats his heart affectionately, a theatrical swoon. 'Ahh, it is my dream, yes? Hollywood, movies, your words on the silver screen, yes? And what is it you have written that I might know?'

'Well, nothing that's been produced as yet, but that's why I'm here. Hoping to collect more information about organized crime in Paris.'

He winks, as happy as a child opening a present. 'A *French Connection*, yes? That is what Ms. Lerner intimated to me, and I immediately said "ah, yes" because you see I have been working on a crime story as well as I'm sure you can imagine. I hope you do not steal my story, no, ha, ha, I'm certain that there is plenty of crime to go around, certainly in Paris, yes?'

His radio squelches and I hear a burst of information in colloquial French about a stabbing but he moves his fat fingers down to his waist and quickly twists the knob to cut off the sound.

'Pssh, interruptions, interruptions, now let me tell you the story I am working on, yes, and then you can tell me how I may help you and maybe when I'm finished with my new manuscript you can sell the rights to Martin Scorcese for me, ha, ha, ha, yes?'

Without waiting for me to respond, he plunges into his tale of a put-upon French policeman in the Bastille district who is misunderstood because of his weight problem. He is the hero, you see, and much smarter than even his superiors care to admit. Twenty minutes later and Officer Gerard is finally concluding the narrative and somehow a croque madame has joined her husband in his stomach without the detective missing a single plot twist or stultifying morsel of dialogue.

When he finally reaches the end, breathless, I force on my most engaging smile and tell him I am certain my agent in Hollywood will want to read the novel as soon as it is finished. He laughs like I've told a hilarious joke, emits a greasy burp, and then shakes my hand without bothering to brush the crumbs from his shirt. 'Maybe we will both be walking down the red carpet next year, yes, yes, ha ha.'

Thirty minutes later, we are inside the conference room dedicated to Organized Crime within his department's headquarters, flipping through detailed files covering the last two decades.

It only takes a few more seconds of flattery before I am alone.

The first time Alex Coulfret officially came to the attention of the specialized branch of the French police was eight years ago. A new lieutenant named Chautier had been promoted within the Organized Crime department and was challenged with tightening a rope around the professional criminals moored in his district. He had been educated in New York and Washington and had returned to his native city with a different approach to tackling the problem, one that promoted sending a mix of uniformed and plainclothes police officers out onto the streets, not to make arrests or threaten incarceration, but simply to listen. A neighborhood is a living entity, Chautier preached: it sleeps, it eats, it breathes, and quite often, if you allow it a slight bit of freedom, it talks.

One name popped up on the lips of citizens again and again: Alexander Coulfret. From what the police officers could surmise after sifting through rumors and eyewitness accounts and exaggerations and embellishments, Coulfret had started as muscle for an aging boss named Dupris. He was used for everything from shakedowns to collections to enforcement, and his brutality earned trust and loyalty from his boss. This was at a time in the late nineties when French professional crime was changing from a family affair to an every-man-for-himself dogfight, and Coulfret was Dupris's pit bull, a sure bet in a shaky world.

More of Alex Coulfret's life comes into focus as I continue to read. The police reports include organizational charts, and Coulfret's name ascends the pyramid rapidly, almost month by month. Names and faces above his keep dropping off the chart, an indication a principal player died or went missing. It isn't difficult to hypothesize how. By the time I finish flipping through the files, Coulfret's name has replaced Dupris's at the top.

There are three pictures of Coulfret in the file. Two are from his previous arrests, when he was still a young man. He appears stocky, muscled, sinewy. He has a razor-thin mustache and an angular face, but his eyes crackle with intelligence. His expression – photographed while being arraigned – appears bemused, unperturbed, like the thought of going to jail is a minor inconvenience, a mosquito to be swatted. His nose is large and hooked and looks misplaced below those eyes.

The third picture is from a surveillance photo, taken just before his name appears on the list of deceased following the train derailment. The man has aged, and his mustache has grown into a full beard, but his expression is the same. He is standing in front of a restaurant, pointing to someone outside the frame. His physique remains athletic; he doesn't appear to have gone soft after he found himself at the top of the ladder. His nose is the same, a toucan's beak.

I snatch the photo from the file and hide it in my sock. The police won't have much use for it when they construct their new pyramid.

I'm able to glean a few more bits of information – he's never been married; he's childless; he speaks English, German, and Italian, as well as French.

I spot an interesting nugget in one officer's report. '**Plant listening device through Coulfret's nose? Avid wine collector. CI describes him as having an advanced sense of smell, proud of wine sniffing. Wire bottle with mic?**'

They must not have attempted this . . . at least I can't find a report or transcript centered upon a bugged wine bottle. Yet, it is nuggets like this that I file away. Hints to his personality.

The man likes his grapes and fancies himself as a bit of a connoisseur. Perhaps I can build a strategy around this idea as I get closer to my quarry.

The rest of the reports offer nothing of consequence, and are perhaps most intriguing by what is absent from them. No one is sure where Alex Coulfret is currently living. Most of the reports don't buy his death, theorizing he moved to Switzerland or London or Rome. Others place him in a different section of Paris, the First or Second arrondissements, thinking maybe he changed his face, had some work done. Only a few think maybe the train crash death is real, that Occam's razor explains why their trail has gone dry, that the easiest explanation is usually the correct one. Coulfret died on that train and his body was cremated before proper identification could be done. End of story.

I'm looking for a different explanation. I don't believe a man like Coulfret ever leaves his neighborhood after exerting so much energy to rule it. It's a power source for him, a fuel, and moving away would wither that power as surely as starving a man would waste him down to skin and bones. The answer must be, as is so often the case, rooted in the past. The missing piece of information, the piece absent in the reams and reams of police records, the piece no officer cared to chronicle is this: what compelled Alex Coulfret to fake his death? And with so few people fooled, especially the police, it means he only needed someone to believe the ruse for a short time. So who is that someone, and was he fooled?

If I can discover the answer to that, then maybe I can discover where Alexander Coulfret is holed up now.

Officer Gerard is all smiles as I leave the police building.

'You will e-mail me when you get home, yes? Please call if you need anything or want some background information or need some spicy dialogue delivered the way a true French police officer talks, ha, ha. Maybe you'll have a part for this handsome face in your movie, yes? But I don't come cheap, ha, ha, ha, yes?'

I shake his hand, and he pumps it warmly, like he doesn't want to give it back, afraid his connection to Hollywood will evaporate like a mirage. I assure him I will shoot him an e-mail as soon as I return to my computer, and he finally nods and steps back into the station, mollified.

In my hotel room on the Rue de Balzac, I sit on the end of the bed and withdraw two photographs from my sock. One of Coulfret, the other of a low-level enforcer named Roger Mallery I managed to also nick right before I closed the file.

From what I am able to discern, Mallery is an up-and-comer within Coulfret's network, low-grade muscle who makes sure narcotics deals go down smoothly. He lives with his brother on Rue Stendhal in the Twentieth arrondissement in a one-bedroom flat and serves as a part-time butcher in a pork and chicken shop up the road. He has been picked up by French police for questioning on several occasions, most notably when three West African men tried to set up a rival supply chain in the Bastille district and ended up with their throats slashed by a serrated carver's knife. He didn't back down from the interrogation – 'gave as good as he got,' stated one detective's report – and was never arrested.

But one item stood out in their files, and I focused on it like it was written in red. Mallery has a side business with his brother, and he doesn't think the cops are aware of it. The French police are currently gathering information about this business, building a solid case to bring it down, aware that a bust here could serve as a key to opening a bigger box but so far they have yet to make a move on the two men.

So I'm going to move first.

When I walk into the butcher's shop, he is behind the counter, thinly slicing ham from a roasted pig.

'Hello.'

'English?' he asks, just looking up for a moment before returning to his work.

'American.'

'Pshhh . . .' like the mere act of thinking about my country has given him a migraine.

In person, he is larger than I guessed from his picture, though he's not overweight. In fact, he seems skinny, fit, and yet somehow, well, *big*, like a blown-up photograph where the scale changes but the proportions remain the same. His face is dark and rough.

I wait for him to ask me what I want, but realize after a minute this is futile. He ignores me while continuing to slice razor-thin pieces of meat, his fingers working the blade hypnotically.

'Can I have a half-pound of bacon?'

Mallery looks up, grunts, and moves over to a small refrigerator from which he withdraws a paper package of meat. A minute later, and he's moving to the cash register.

'Eight-fifty.'

I exchange euros for the package, and he considers me with sleepy eyes before returning to his cutting board.

When I don't leave the shop, he lifts his eyes again, waiting.

'I'm looking for a passport.'

He stops cutting the pig and hammers the blade down in the butcher's board, then moves to a sink, washes and wipes his hands, drawing it all out in a puerile attempt at intimidation.

'You lose one?'

'No.'

I keep my eyes level so he knows I mean business.

'What makes you tell me this?'

'I'm sorry. I might have been misinformed. Is your name Mallery?'

He just stares at me, non-committal.

'I was told you're the man to see about papers.'

'Papers? What is this, papers?'

I nod like I've made a mistake. 'I apologize. Thank you for the bacon.'

I reach the door to the shop, and his voice stops me. 'What kind of passport?'

I turn around, and though he is not grinning, his expression has shifted to agreeable.

'Italian.'

'Five thousand euros.'

'I paid three in Naples.'

'Then go back to Naples.'

I consider, then reach down to my wallet, but he clucks his tongue.

'Not here. The shop closes in two hours. Come back when you see me locking the door.'

'I'll be here.'

He resumes slicing the ham, the conversation over.

I follow Mallery through a maze of alleyways and side streets. His apron is off, hanging from a hook in the butcher's shop, I'm sure, but the smell of his work clings to him like a cloud: fresh-cut meat and viscera and blood. He's riding a ten-speed, and with his huge bulk, he looks ridiculous on top of the bicycle, like a clown riding a miniature.

When we reach a wide sidewalk, he slows to match my gait, side by side. Perched on the bike, he's at least a foot taller than me, maybe more.

'Who told you about me?'

I have anticipated this question. I know it'll be risky, but I don't believe he'll breach etiquette to check my story.

'Coulfret.'

This doesn't elicit more from him than a raise of the eyebrows.

We stroll and roll along again in silence for a moment. I feel him wanting to say more, but he's fighting the urge. Finally, he loses the battle to stay cool. 'You do work for him?'

'Yes.'

'What kind of work?'

I point my finger like a gun and bend my thumb like a hammer cocking.

He raises his eyebrows again. 'He didn't hire you to kill me, did he?'

I shake my head when I see he was trying to make a joke.

'How many jobs have you done for him?' he asks.

'You want to talk about this inside somewhere?'

He appraises me, then nods, appreciating my caution. We move along again in silence until the street takes a few more turns. Finally, we arrive at a courtyard. He dismounts, and swings the bike up on to his shoulder with no more strain than if he were lifting a sack of feathers. He presses a few buttons into a keypad, a security gate opens, and we move inside.

His apartment is more spacious than I would've thought: two bedrooms and a comfortable living room filled wall to wall with computer equipment. A log fire in the fireplace casts odd shadows over the room while it beats away the cold. A small kitchenette with a large refrigerator stands at the far end, behind a counter that separates the two rooms.

A man who can only be Mallery's brother looks up from a monitor as we enter. Roger swings the bicycle up on to a set of hooks attached to the ceiling and then gestures in the direction of his sibling.

'This is Luis.'

'Hello.'

The man nods, cautious.

'You mind if I pat you down?'

'Yes.'

'You are carrying a weapon?'

'Several.'

Mallery grimaces. He's not used to men like me, and it shows. I could've lied, could've told him I am unarmed and then wait to see how thoroughly he wanted to frisk me before

I have to react, but he is testing me, testing to see if I'll let him be the alpha dog in his own home. My refusal lets him know what level of professional I am. He chews his lower lip, then foregoes the frisking.

He moves over to his brother, and they converse briefly in French.

Luis addresses me, his voice more resonant than his brother's, but deferential. 'You need Italian passport, correct?'

'Yes.'

'The Netherlands would be easier for you.'

'I already have one for the Netherlands.'

Luis smiles. 'Okay . . . Italian it is. You have money, correct?'

'Five thousand euros. You'll get it after I've had a chance to inspect your work.'

'Of course. You have a preference for a name?'

'Something common.'

'Yes, okay. I will take a photograph first.'

He directs me to a red line he has taped to the floor, facing his computer. After he clicks his mouse, he spins the monitor so I can take a look. I nod, and Mallery appears beside me, holding a bottle of wine.

'Let's move to the kitchen and have a drink while we wait.'

He's had eight glasses and is laughing hard at my story, having lost track of my intake after I matched him the first three times he refreshed our drinks.

'So it comes down to this, I'm down to my last day to do this job, I've been fighting a goddamn fever for the better part of two weeks, I haven't really had time to formulate a secondary plan, so it's now or never and more and more it's looking like never.'

'What time of year?'

'Middle of July and hot as hell. And you've never experienced heat until you've been in Houston in July. You can park your car right outside the door to your air-conditioned building, and by the time you take the ten steps and get behind the wheel, you're soaked through. Hundred percent humidity. Believe me, the last thing a gunman needs to battle is sweaty hands. Throw a fever on top of that and it's like I was walking around on fire.'

Mallery laughs. 'Please continue.'

'So the mark is visiting this construction site across the street and the amount of time I have to pop him is predicated on an elevator ride—'

'Why did someone want your target dead, by the way?'

'I have no idea. I don't ask questions, I don't seek answers, I just kill the mark at the top of the page.'

'Incredible.'

'Yeah, so I know the bottom of that elevator disappears into a subterranean chamber, a bunker, and if he got down there, who knew when this bastard would ever emerge again, so if I was going to do it, I'd have to do it right then. I was completely out of time.'

'Would I know this man?'

'You've seen his face in the business section of the *Wall Street Journal* if you follow stocks at all . . .'

Mallery waves like it's not important. He just wants me to keep going.

'So I'm in the high-rise across the street and he's in this elevator surrounded by muscle, and the wind kicks up, a scorching hot wind from the west, but I don't mind, the entire shot's maybe five hundred meters and I slow my breathing to a standstill and sight the target and this guy better have prayed his affairs are in order as the elevator car moves halfway down the building and I pull the trigger and . . . nothing.'

'What?!'

'The gun jammed. Nothing and no time to check it and I am on my feet and scrambling down the five flights of stairs as fast as my legs can carry me.'

Mallery is laughing so hard, tears have sprung to his eyes. He pours himself another glass.

'Down, down, two at a time and all I have on me is my Glock which is a damn fine gun but only at a range of thirty meters or less and I've never missed a target and I'll be damned if this asshole's gonna be my first.'

'What did you do?'

'So I bust out of the door and look up and see that the target's elevator has about four floors to go and I am a city block away and since that building is under construction there is a barbed-wire fence surrounding it which is another good forty meters from the mark. I am taking all this in at once, and I'm not even thinking about traffic or pedestrians or civilians or police, I have to shut everything down and concentrate only on the moment, *this* moment, killing *this* target on *this* day, right then. It's hard to describe but the world becomes like a tunnel, everything else is blocked out, the only thing remaining in your vision is the strike point on your mark, where you have to shoot him to make sure he stays down forever.

'Even fighting this fever, I'm moving at a full sprint, plowing across the street and if a car slams on its brakes to keep from mowing me down, I don't hear it. An assassin isn't supposed to get his heart rate up, is trained to stay cool and collected, but my ticker is revving like a Lamborghini and my eyes are damned near blurry from the extra adrenaline accompanying my blinding headache and the gun in my hand feels like it's made out of cement.'

'My God . . .'

'The elevator car is almost to the ground, is just starting to slip below the surface and the mark and his half dozen bodyguards begin to disappear, first their feet, then their knees, and at that moment, all of them at once look at me, this wild man, red-faced, fisting a gun, sprinting across the street toward them like a guided missile and I can see their faces react, the two closest to their boss try to shove him down while stepping in front of him and then their torsos are disappearing and I have one shot, one chance in a million to thread the needle, an incredibly difficult shot even if all conditions are in my favor and I'm not half-dizzy with sickness . . .'

'Yes? Yes?'

'And so I hit the ground, belly up, focus everything I have on my mark so that I can tell you how many freckles he has on his forehead, point the gun and pull the trigger just as the elevator dips below street level, gone.'

Mallery is half-on, half-off his seat. His eyes are bulging, wide with anticipation, like a fish approaching a worm.

'What happened?'

'I missed.'

'Ha ha ha ha! You missed? What do you mean, you missed?'

'I missed.'

'Oh my God, you are too much. You and this story. This is the proverb, eh? The one who got away, ha ha ha ha?'

'I didn't say that.'

Mallery looks back up at me, delighted there is a coda. 'But you just said you missed!'

'I missed *then*. But he went home and I took some aspirin and killed him in his bed that night.'

'Ha ha ha! Ha ha! Oh, you are destroying me here . . .'

Luis speaks up from the door, holding an Italian passport in his hand.

'Roberto Rossi.'

'You should hear this story, Luis! This guy—'

Luis is smiling but his eyes are suspicious.

I stand up and take the passport from him, stumbling a bit so they'll think I'm inebriated. Roberto Rossi is the name Luis chose for me, a good one, as common in central Italy as John Smith. His work is professional, astute.

'You know what you're doing,' I say to Luis. It never hurts to get a compliment in when someone is eyeing you warily.

'I've forged a few.'

'I can tell.'

Mallery stands, looking over my shoulder. 'I may be the athletic one in the family, but Luis got all the brains. His work is perfect. That passport will not be questioned.'

I pay Luis the five thousand euros and fend off Mallery's protests to stay for one glass more. Passport in hand, I leave the way I came.

Like I said, the key components in an ambush are information and timing. I've set the hook in Roger Mallery, and although I believe I could have persuaded him to talk about his principal employer Coulfret, Luis remains a wildcard, the smart brother, the one who does the work and keeps to the shadows.

Information and timing. And if I do my work properly, I'll continue to remove Mallery's defenses before he has a chance to engage them.

12

If I were Svoboda, as soon as I received word Llanos went down with a knife to her windpipe in France, I'd hop the next flight to Paris. I'd immediately head to a bank near the Charles de Gaulle airport where I keep a safety deposit box loaded with weapons. Assassins store pistols, bullets, clips, knives all over the world, always near the airports. Airport security being what it is has made traveling by air the most vulnerable time for a professional hit man, which is why I would get myself armed as quickly as possible. And if I didn't personally have a stash of weapons in Paris, I would arrange one through a capable fence.

Next, I'd use contacts in Paris, either with the morgue or the police or the underworld, to arrange a viewing of Llanos's body. I'd want fifteen minutes alone with the corpse. I'd examine the fatal wound and try to reconstruct in my mind the way it had gone down. Since I'm a Silver Bear, the 'shelf above the shelf' as Archibald put it, I've been on the dispensing end of enough wounds to grasp a good idea of how this death unfolded.

If I were Svoboda, I'd now have a bit more knowledge about my mark, the man named Columbus I've been paid to kill. I'd know that for whatever reason, my target switched from his normal weapon of choice, a Glock handgun, to an inferior weapon, a stiletto blade. I'd know he used a neck shot, a straight puncture to the throat instead of a risky slashing motion. I'd know that he got the jump on the woman who was assigned to kill him. I'd know that he's better than I might have been told.

Then I'd look at Llanos's face – milky, empty – and I'd think about my quarry doing that to her, punching out her ticket when just the day before she had been young and lithe and alive. I'd think she was doing the same job I was hired to do, the same job I'm doing now, and my target discarded her like she was waste. I'd let my hatred build like a kindling fire, stoking it, fanning it, until it consumed every cell in my body.

And then, if I were Svoboda, I'd leave the stale trapped air of the morgue to walk back into the mottled throng of Paris. I'd close my eyes, breathing in the night, focusing my mind, feeding off my hate.

Then I'd open my eyes again, set my jaw, and begin to hunt.

Mallery is digging into a roasted duck at a sidewalk restaurant named the Café de la Comedie near the Louvre. The hand that holds his carving knife is blemished with the brick hue of bloody knuckles. Earlier, I watched him pound that hand into a gray-haired man's face in a warehouse next to a chocolate shop. I didn't quite catch why the gray-haired man deserved his beating, but as soon as he saw Mallery step through his door, the look of resignation on his face told me he knew it was coming. The old man took it pretty well, all in all.

I'm standing by the bar, drinking an Italian beer, watching him.

His phone buzzes, and he picks it up, reads something on the screen, then tries to work his thumbs over the little buttons, sending a text back. I wait, and eventually he gets up.

Sure enough, he spots me as he's heading to the bathroom.

'Roberto!'

I shoot him a cold look and he immediately clams up, his eyes as round as bicycle tires. 'What?'

The best thing to do in this type of situation is to keep him off balance, defensive.

'What were you doing with your phone?'

'Texting . . .'

'Does Coulfret know you do that?'

He puzzles over that one. 'I just text with my brother. I don't ever put anything on here that—'

'You ever see Coulfret use a mobile phone?'

'No, but—'

'That's because mobile phones lead to arrests.'

'But I—'

'Never mind. I need your help.'

It helps to shift directions like this, keep him back pedaling.

'What do you mean?'

'Come if you're going to come.'

'What about my bicycle?'

'Leave it, goddammit.'

And with that, I head out of the restaurant and into the street.

I can smell him before he reaches me. He must've slapped cash onto the table to cover his bill, made sure his bicycle was properly locked, and then hurried to catch up to me.

I don't look over my shoulder, don't acknowledge him, just keep walking forward. He whispers from behind me. 'What are we doing?' Then catches up so we are walking side by side.

'A job.'

He makes his fingers into a gun just like I did the day before, wiggles his thumb, and repeats, 'A job?'

'Yes.'

'Holy mother of Mary. What's the job?'

'To take down a target. Stay in the shadows.'

He steps out of the sunlight closer to the wall, but can't manage to fit his whole body into the shade, as big as he is.

'Who is the target?'

'A woman. A hundred times out of a hundred I'd do this job alone, but Coulfret wants to see how you'll do.'

Mallery swallows like he's trying to force down an egg. 'Coulfret wants you to use me?'

'What'd I just say?'

'This woman. Who is she?'

'The wife of a man who shouldn't have tried to extort Alexander Coulfret.'

'My God.'

'Two of us working together is known in the game as a tandem sweep. That's what we'll be doing . . .'

'I don't have a gun. I have a knife, and I have these . . .' he says, rubbing the scabbed knuckles of his fist.

'You won't need either of them.'

'But—'

'Just use your head and do exactly as I tell you, when I tell you, okay?'

'Yes, of course. What do you think? I do not listen? I will listen.'

We round a corner, and fifty yards away stands a farmer's market selling fresh produce and meat and spices.

I hold up a Polaroid, a picture of a woman at a distance. 'This is our target. She's in that market now. She won't leave it alive.'

Mallery looks back and forth from the photograph to my face to the photograph, trying to commit it to memory like he's studying for exams but it's all happening too fast.

'Now here's your role in this . . . are you ready?'

Without hesitation, he nods.

'Shooting the target is easy, I could do it in my sleep, it's never a problem, listen!'

He's still riveted by the Polaroid in my hand and when I bark at him his eyes jump back to my face.

'The getting away is the problem, it's always the problem, it's the difference between more jobs or a life in prison or worse, so the escape has to be planned and precise and if you fuck this up in any way, I'll kill you myself.'

He shakes his head; he won't fuck this up, he swears.

'Okay, good. Now you're the pigeon, the possum, the flop, okay? The misdirection, the diversion. You're where everyone casts his eyes so he doesn't see what's going on up the magician's sleeve.

'I want you to walk into that farmer's market and find the woman. When you see her, I want you to turn to the nearest produce stand and start in with a coughing fit. Can you cough?'

Immediately, he produces a cough so loud I think he's going to rattle a window.

'Not now, goddammit!' I say through gritted teeth and he stops like someone jerked a needle off a record.'Okay, while you're coughing, you won't hear anything except maybe the soft report of a silenced bullet, but out of the corner of your eye, you will see this woman drop. Do not look at her, don't you dare fucking look at her.'

He shakes his head again; he won't look at her, don't worry about that.

'When you see the woman hit the ground . . .' I wait for a few pedestrians to pass, acting casual, and Mallery follows my lead. As soon as they're out of earshot . . . 'When you see the woman hit the ground, I want you to stop coughing and walk away as calmly and as quickly as you can in that direction. Can you do that?'

He nods; he can do that.

'Now listen to me and listen to me like you've never listened to anything in your life. Do you know the story of Lot's wife? From the Bible?'

He shakes his head and I act like I'm even more frustrated with him.

'Well, you're going to want to look back, see if anyone's following you, see if a crowd has started to gather around the body, see if someone is fingering you or me or calling for the police, but you don't look back, don't do it, don't do it if the Madonna herself appears in front of you and screams at you to look back, do you understand me? You don't give any person at all a reason to remember your face. You just walk the fuck out of there, return to the café we just left, order yourself a glass of wine, and you fucking sit there until I come and get you, do you understand?'

'Yes. I walk away.'

'You walk away.'

'Yes.'

'Good, now let's see what you're made of.'

I clap him on the back and we set off for the market. He swallows hard, like he thought he'd have more time to prepare himself but here we are. It's sparsely crowded with local housewives picking up their daily bread and whatever vegetables and meat they plan to cook in the next couple of days. Few tourists are in this neighborhood this time of year, but the late sunset has brought in quite a few afternoon shoppers.

Our target is near a fruit stand, picking up and squeezing oranges. From where I hover over Mallery's shoulder, I can see him stutter-step as he recognizes her from the photo, a big clumsy signal a trained target would pick up on as easily as someone yanking an alarm. But we're in luck, the mark keeps picking up those oranges, in her own world when she should be paying attention to the wolf on her doorstep.

Mallery spins in place, wheels on a cheese seller's stand, and starts coughing like his lungs are exploding. It's a pretty damn good distraction, and most of the heads in the market spin in his direction, including the one belonging to our mark.

I come up beside her, my hand inside my coat pocket, and when she drops suddenly, Mallery does as instructed, he stops coughing and books it out of there, heading left out of the stand.

Usually, I would keep moving to put as much distance between the scene of the crime and myself before witnesses start tripping over themselves to see what happened. But I wait, following Mallery's ample gait with my eyes, watching to make sure he fights that urge and doesn't look back. Don't look back, don't look back, I'm willing him with my eyes and he doesn't turn, he does as he's instructed, and he rounds the corner at full stride.

When he disappears, I reach down and help the lady to her feet.

'You all right there, missy?'

'That's Ruby to you,' she says with a smile.

When I reach the Café de la Comedie, Mallery is sweating. There is an empty glass in front of him, and I'm guessing he's drunk at least half of a bottle of wine. He almost upsets the table in his hurry to greet me, eager for my approval.

'It's done, correct?'

'Yes,' I smile. 'You did well.'

'Just as instructed.'

He's like a dog. Unsatisfied with just a pat to the head, he needs a scratch behind the ears.

'Yes.'

'I did not look back.'

'Good. Then no one will have followed you.'

'I heard sirens. Sitting here. Waiting for you. I was worried.'

I had seen police blowing past on the way to a motorcycle accident up the road. I didn't think about it at the time, but I'm glad Mallery believes the sirens belong to our affair.

'Never worry about me. Only yourself.'

'We will do this again?'

I shrug. 'We'll see what Coulfret says.'

'You will tell him about today? How I composed myself?'

'Of course. Have another drink.' I grab the waiter as he passes and order a fresh bottle of wine.

'I can't believe it,' he says, true wonder in his eyes. 'He usually uses me for . . .' and he makes a couple of punching motions, a jab, an uppercut. Then pops one of his big fists into the other hand. 'But this . . .' He shakes his head. 'How much, do you mind my asking?'

'How much what?'

'How much do you collect for a kill?'

I've got him now, though he doesn't know it.

'A hundred thousand Euros.'

His eyes light up, filled with dollar signs. 'Maybe I can . . . maybe he'll use me more for . . .'

'Maybe. We'll see what Coulfret says.'

A couple of glasses more and he's relaxed, giddy, speaking maniacally, the adrenaline getting the best of him.

It only takes a nudge from me. Information and timing.

'Let me ask you a question. I heard Coulfret faked his death a few years back.'

'Oh, yes. Brilliant.'

'Why would he need to do that?'

'You don't know this story? A story-teller like you?'

'Please.'

'How much time do you have?'

'At least another bottle of wine's worth.'

'Done!'

And he pounds the table as a third bottle arrives.

Alex Coulfret's first love wasn't a woman, but a building. He grew up in the Eleventh arrondissement, a block away from the Bastille, in a Haussmann-era residential edifice on the Rue Saint Maur. The building had twenty-two apartments, the smallest of which belonged to his father and mother. The apartment was in the basement, and they'd never have been able to afford it if it hadn't been for his father's position as resident supervisor, a nice way the French have for saying 'custodian.'

The older of two brothers, Alex often accompanied his father on the daily tasks involved in keeping twenty-one tenants of a nineteenth-century building satisfied. Leaky pipes, peeling wallpaper, backed-up sewer lines, cracked windows, chipped floor tiles, faulty wiring, elevator repairs . . . Alex and his old man took care of all of them, working odd hours, always at the beck and call of the residents. In a building where everyone was of the same social stratum, the lower class consisted solely of this one family in this one apartment.

Alex spent his childhood learning every inch of that building. The crawl spaces, the roof, the rest of the basement with its clattering laundry machines, the copper pipes running behind the walls, the tiny balconies facing the courtyard, the floor drains leading down to the sewers. The residents looked on him and his brother with genuine affection, always ready with a pat to the head or an offered piece of peppermint candy. There were few children in the building, and the ones who were around Alex's age went to private schools and had their own sets of friends.

Alex's father died while carrying a bag of cement across the roof. His heart gave out: he dropped the bag, sat down, and died. Alex was fifteen, and it was like someone had cut out the best part of him. When the owner of the building, Mr. Hubbert, came round to pay his respects and tell his mother they would have two months to find a new apartment, Alex was ready. He showed the owner how to repair the washing machine, how to refill the split plaster on the second-floor corridor, how to keep birds from settling on the roof. He proposed that he would drop out of school and take over the duties of his father, that he knew the building better than anyone, that the free place to live for the three of them was all he needed . . . he'd find other ways to supplement his income. Mr. Hubbert was sympathetic and agreed to Alex's terms on a trial basis. If tenants complained, he would have to make changes. But no tenants complained.

A genial man on the second floor, a retired professor named Mr. Condrey, gave Alex books to read to whittle away his evenings: Hugo and Dumas and Maupassant and Maugham. He taught him to dig deeper, behind the hero's journey and into the themes buried just below the surface: loss of innocence, jealousy, revenge as well as hope, patriotism, love. He found Alex to have a rapier mind and a thirst for intellectual stimulation. Alex, in turn, taught his brother, Jerome. If Alex couldn't go to school, he'd be damned if Jerome was going to miss a single day. Maybe he wasn't Jerome's father, but he damn sure acted like it.

The family still needed to put bread on the table, and Alex's mother took a job at a local bakery, selling croissants to tourists. Even bringing home the unsold pastries wasn't enough to keep the lights on, to keep wood in the fire. They needed more income, something, anything.

Alex had heard of Augustus Dupris from a pair of gossips who frequented the meat market. Dupris ruled the neighborhood (and several others), working and living out of a building two blocks away from Alex's. He had set up narcotics lines directly into Afghanistan and had profited greatly importing opium and heroin into the capital. In turn, he parlayed that business into providing protection, gambling, and prostitution in a city where most citizens turned a blind eye toward individual hedonism.

Still age fifteen, Alex presented himself to Dupris, explaining who his father had been, where he lived, what had happened to the family, what they were subsisting on, and how he could be of use to the professional criminal. He did his best to speak deferentially and intelligently, to make his case, explain how he could be an asset. He said he'd do any work the boss demanded.

Dupris slapped Alex across his face and told him to go back to school, go back to his family, to leave, and never to return. His men escorted him out of the building and Alex walked the two blocks home with his tail between his legs, but with a strong sense that he was being tested. Determination rose within him.

For weeks, Dupris couldn't leave the building without seeing Alexander Coulfret. The teen followed the middle-aged boss like a dog looking for scraps. When Dupris asked one of his men for a newspaper, Alex was already there, holding the latest edition. When he cut the tip off a cigar, he'd find Alex before him, holding out a struck match.

'You aren't going away?' the man finally asked the kid outside a hotel. 'You aren't going to do as I tell you and leave?'

Alex shook his head.

Dupris smiled, like he couldn't quite figure out what made Alex's clock tick. 'Then come to my building tomorrow at ten. And bring me some coffee.'

Alex ran all the way home. That night, he cooked a ham for his mother and brother, the first meat they'd had in a week.

In the beginning, he delivered things for Dupris, sometimes to people who didn't want to be reached. He grew a reputation for being extremely clever, an intellectual cut above most of the mutts who worked for the boss. Where this might foster resentment, Alex had a way of recognizing trouble before it emerged, like a firefighter watering down fields to control the path of the flames. His cohorts couldn't help but like him, and he pulled their strings like a master.

He was a man who could talk at any level depending on to whom he was speaking, who knew the language, the idioms, the dialect of the streets, who could hold his own with the lowest pigeon on up to the boss himself. Guys he worked for found themselves working for him without quite understanding how the reversal had transpired.

By the time he was twenty, he had been arrested a couple of times but slipped any sentence harsher than a slap on the wrist. He taught Dupris how to maximize his gains by being merciless, by squeezing the suckers for every dime. In turn, his bank account grew.

His mother suspected something evil behind the income, but was so pleased to have food on the table, so pleased to see her younger son attending a private school for gifted students, that she instinctively knew better than to ask questions. She just wanted to put her feet up after a long day at the bakery and have wood to burn in the fireplace. Alex thought about telling her to quit her job – he was making more than enough to cover their expenses – but he resisted. The work kept her going, kept her vigorous, and somehow he knew it helped her to cope with the illicit money coming into the apartment.

When he turned twenty-three, he was Dupris's right-hand man, mostly working from the shadows. Dupris was starting to fear him as much as admire him, but the kid was like watching an avalanche cascade toward you and only being able to appreciate it. Alex was as devious as he was cunning, and he wasn't afraid to get his own hands dirty to prove a point.

All the while, he, his brother, and his mother stayed in that little apartment in the building on the Rue St. Maur. The residents still looked down their noses at the family in the supervisor's flat, and Alex never strayed from fixing the faucets and the leaky pipes and the faulty heaters.

When Alex turned twenty-four, a real estate mogul named Saulter made a bid to buy the building. The original owner, Mr. Hubbert, was growing old and his only heir lived in the United States. The son wanted whatever price his father could get for the building. He had never set foot inside it and had no plans of moving back to Paris. Saulter made his offer. Paris was growing more expensive and the mogul felt if he could renovate the apartments, he could make a sizable profit. His plans for renovation also included getting rid of the current occupants.

Alex had by this time amassed enough wealth to buy the building himself for a fair price, and made an offer to Mr. Hubbert, but Saulter didn't give a damn about fairness. He was a capitalist in the true sense of the word; the biggest stack of dollars determined the winning bid, and he was prepared to outbid the son of the janitor.

Alex met with Mr. Hubbert for the second time in his life. The man was close to dying, was exhausted, and he spoke in a whining whisper.

'What do you want me to do, Alexander? What would you do? Ask yourself. I am doing this for my son in America. If you had come to me first, if there was no other choice, I would happily sell the building to you. I know you would take care of her like she was your mother or your wife. But Mr.

Saulter came first and he will outbid you until you cannot match his offer. What would you have me do?'

Alex told him he was responsible for his own decisions.

'I know how you acquired your wealth,' the old man said. 'The things you've done for Augustus Dupris. If you say I *must* sell to you, then I will do so. I do not want trouble.'

Alex repeated to the old man he was responsible for his own decisions, but assured him since he had shown Alex's family trust and kindness, no harm would befall him.

Mr. Hubbert told him he intended to sell the building to the mogul, Saulter.

Alex made two stops on his way home. First, he asked Dupris for an advance of two million francs so he might match Saulter's offer. But Dupris was drunk and with a woman and chose an inopportune moment to put Alex Coulfret in his place. He denied his request and called his prodigy a homesick fool. He offered Alex some wine and when he declined, protesting how important the building was to him, Dupris told him to lighten up and enjoy himself and to quit being so goddamned serious. Alex left enraged.

His next stop was Saulter's private residence in the heart of the Seventh arrondissement. When he went to bed that night, Saulter had three German shepherds and a German wife. When he awakened from a fitful sleep, he had none. Alex was waiting for him on a chair in the corner of the room. He told Saulter to move away from Paris and never look back, but not before Saulter phoned Mr. Hubbert to withdraw his offer for the building.

Augustus Dupris felt two emotions upon learning the next day that Alex Coulfret was the new owner of the building he had grow up in on the Rue de Maur. Anger and fear. He did not like the way those two emotions made him feel, like a weight had settled in his stomach. He did not like the way his second-in-command had circumvented his decision-making.

He did not like the way his other foot soldiers looked at Coulfret – the same way they used to look at him.

He decided to hire some dark men. He might have been successful except that a low-level hood named Martin Feller saw the future and made the decision of his life, rolling the dice and putting his hat in the ring with Alex. He had overheard Dupris bragging about the contract he had taken out on his right-hand man's life. And so Feller tipped off Coulfret.

Alex could've brought it to a head the moment he found out about the hit, could've walked the two blocks to Dupris's house, forced his way in, and shot the man and everyone who stood with him. God knows he wanted to. But the chess player inside him won out; instinctively, he knew that if the last rung of the ladder on the rise to the top is stepped on with brute power instead of *earned* through cunning, through artful intelligence, then his reign would always be contested, would always be marked with bloodshed.

So he faked his death. He waited for the right opportunity, then put money in the palms of a trusted few, and convinced Dupris and his hired killer that they had lucked out, that nature and a fickle god and two vehicles colliding had done their dirty work for them, that sometimes things have a way of working themselves out.

A week went by, two. Dupris inquired about buying the building himself, but Jerome Coulfret, the brother, resisted. His education had instilled in him a keen business sense, a sense that would serve him well in the jewelry trade years later. The ownership of the building suddenly became important to Dupris, like having a tangible trophy to put in his case, a symbol for the rest of his men to see what happened if they chose to tangle with the boss. He became obsessed with owning it, refusing to let Alex's pissant brother keep this prize from him.

Recognizing the volatility of the situation, Jerome told Augustus Dupris he feared for his and his mother's safety, and he wanted assurances that if Dupris bought the building, no harm would befall them. Dupris agreed but Jerome wanted a commitment in person; he insisted that Dupris come to his small janitor's apartment in the basement of the building and he would sign over the papers in front of witnesses.

Dupris brought three of his most trusted bodyguards, men whom he used for intimidation and enforcement. They entered the building on the Rue de Maur, suspecting nothing. They paraded down the hallway, suspecting nothing. They piled into the cramped elevator and pressed the appropriate button, suspecting nothing.

The cable snapped and the elevator car plummeted, dropping thirty feet in three seconds and slamming like a thunderclap into the concrete foundation. It bounced, crumpling like a crushed soda can, and came to rest at an eighty-degree angle at the bottom of the shaft, like a domino about to topple. Dupris and his men were injured, sure, but nothing life-threatening. That part would come in a moment. They were more shocked and confused, still trying to figure out what happened.

The doors just above their heads pried open from the outside, and light spilled into the car. They looked up expectantly, eager for aid, for someone to help them out of the collapsed car.

A ghost stared down at them: Alexander Coulfret, back from the grave, resurrected in a building he knew better than anyone. His face was sinister; there was triumph in his eyes. He glared at the men, as helpless as sardines packed in a tin, and started firing.

Maybe Mallery didn't tell the story quite so fully, but he laid out the broad strokes, and it didn't take much digging to fill in the details. I've found that once you possess a few nuggets, it's much easier to pry the whole story out of people. If you listen, a neighborhood will talk.

13

He's in the building on the Rue de Maur, of that I'm certain. And either he's a complete recluse, holed up in a tiny apartment, running his kingdom from the shadows, or he had his face changed, happy with the way the police or perhaps his rivals were fooled by his accidental death ruse. My guess is the latter. The men in his organization are way too deferential for Coulfret to be a shut-in. That kind of power comes only from a firsthand, iron-fisted rule. The fact that the police never quite bought the ruse tells me he didn't need to use it for long.

To get to him, to end this, I have two choices. Try to infiltrate his building, or try to flush him toward a place of my choosing.

I mentioned a few ways I go about gathering information: I can steal it. Or I can force someone to give it to me under duress. Or, like with Mallery, I can feign friendship in order to extract what I need. But there is another way, one I've employed on occasion. It's tricky, but it can be effective.

I buy a cheap camera from a souvenir shop near the Rue St. Denis and start scouring the sidewalk for prostitutes. The ladies populate this street at all hours of the day, dressed in their dystopian view of evening wear, ready to approach a john for business as soon as his gaze lingers for more than a fleeting moment. There is no cream of the crop here, no high-priced whores, no beautiful young women lost under a layer of makeup. The women on the Rue St. Denis are well past the age and weight when they should be parading their wares.

My eyes settle on a particularly homely sample and I speak to her as best I can in French.

'How much?'

'Thirty.'

'How would you like to make three hundred?'

Her eyes reflect the age-old battle between fear and avarice. I can read her thoughts as easy as if she spoke them aloud: *Whatever he wants me to do can't be good for my health, but three hundred euros is more than I've made in a month.*

'What for?'

'To ride in a taxi and take some photos.'

'With you?'

'By yourself.'

'Psssh.' She waves at me like I'm insane.

'I have a taxi waiting.'

'I don't know what cheat this is . . .'

'No cheat. Here's thirty just for listening to me. Here's two hundred and seventy, which I'll give you if you take this camera in that taxi and fill the camera with photos of the second block of the Rue de Maur. You'll be back here in thirty minutes.'

Her brain is trying to calculate the percentages of risk versus reward but the entire effort is simply too much and her eyes refocus on the money in her hand and the rest of it within grabbing distance.

'You do this right and there'll be more jobs like it, all over town, paying even more.'

'Just take photos?'

'When you approach the block, hold the camera like this, here, not up to your eye, but down at the bottom of the taxi's window. Click, wind here, click, wind . . . do it on both sides of the street. I've instructed the taxi to drive slowly, but not too slowly. Take as many as the camera will allow. The taxi will then return you here.'

'Fifty more now,' she croaks. Two of her teeth are missing and the remaining ones are stained with lipstick.

'Not a euro more until I have a full camera.'

She grimaces and then shrugs, takes the camera, and waddles over to the taxi.

I keep my word when she returns. She'll try to remember me, the man wearing a hat and dark glasses, should I come back to the Rue St. Denis, but by that evening, I have no doubt alcohol will have wiped her memory clean. Besides, I have no plans to return to that particular street.

I develop the pictures at a one-hour photo on the opposite side of town, far away from the Bastille district Alexander Coulfret calls home. Nothing from the photo-shop worker indicates that he gave my pictures anything more than a cursory look. And why would he have noticed anything more than typical tourist photos of a sleepy Parisian block?

Back in my hotel room, the photographs are laid out across an ottoman I'm using for a desk. The whore wasn't exactly Ansel Adams, but she did an adequate job, all things considered. She took thirty-six photos, covering the entire block, and only had her thumb in one frame.

Here's what I learned that I didn't already know by way of the internet. The block has five buildings on either side, with a series of shops fronting most of them. The adjacent buildings to the one owned by Coulfret contain apartments above a pastry shop and a dressmaker's boutique. The location where a shop would be at the bottom of Coulfret's particular building is a mystery; paper blinds fill the windows.

Across the street stands a trio of similar buildings, containing two clothing stores and a pharmacy. All six shops – including the empty one – have cameras facing the street, sophisticated equipment for disparate places, all made by the same manufacturer. It seems Coulfret's real estate ambitions have grown to include most of his block. I wonder if all six buildings are connected, and, if so, how. Paris has an extensive underground sewer system, and perhaps he's taken advantage of it.

The whore's photographs also reveal men sitting with a certain lassitude on three benches positioned on both sides and across the street from Coulfret's front door. Six hard-looking men, three benches. My guess is they rotate out regularly, and who knows how many more are waiting inside that shop with the papered-over windows?

Storming the building is starting to look like an ugly proposition, a long-odds loser.

Ruby Grant smiles over her cup of coffee. We're on the Left Bank, in the back of a café once frequented by Hemingway and Fitzgerald and Joyce.

'I'm worried about you, Columbus. For a loner, you're starting to ask me to hook up with you quite a bit.'

'Who says I'm a loner?'

'Every file ever written about you.'

'What do the files say about you?'

'If I see any, I'll let you know.'

'You're a blank slate . . .'

'With this face, I'm sure a few people have noticed me. Right before I shot 'em.'

'You ever think about checking out?'

She looks at me sideways. 'Of the game? Nah, I'd just waste away. You?'

'Just thoughts.'

Goddamn, I have no idea why I'm telling her this. It's like I'm floating a balloon. Maybe if I can practice here with Ruby Grant, I can persuade myself to put this life behind me the next time I see Risina. Jesus, is that it?

I discover a tiny bit of disappointment in Ruby's eyes.

'Well, I'd stop thinking those thoughts if it were me. You start going down that road, you don't realize you can't turn around until you hit a dead end.'

I nod. 'Ahhh, I'm just blowing air. This life is all I got.'

She knows I'm snowing her now, but she's happy to get off the subject.

'Archie really has a file on me?'

'He's got a file on everyone he ever met. Says you shot a cigarette out of his mouth once in Boston.'

'Well, that's true.'

She laughs, an effortless, warm sound.

'All right . . . you know so much about me, time for you to 'fess up.'

She spreads her hands out like she's ready for me to ask anything.

'Tell me how you started pulling trigger for your brother. I've never seen that before, a brother–sister, fence and assassin.'

'Ahh, it's nothing. I worked for him for a while . . . helped him put files together . . . got into places he probably wouldn't be able to get into. A couple of years at that, and I told him I was itchy to try it.'

'And he just said "okay"?'

She looks at me out of the tops of her eyes. 'Oh, I get it. I see what you're doing here. You wanna hear about my first time?'

It's my turn to shrug.

'Fine, fine. You can be the first to hear it, then, other than Archie who knew the story anyway. Just go get me one of them macaroons they got up in the window there and then settle back, 'cause I got a tale to tell.'

I do. And she does.

'The first time – you never forget the first time, you know what I'm saying? Well, Archie was worried about me, even though I was born for this, truth be told. So he just kept putting it off and putting it off until I told him, "Archie, if you don't hurry up and give me an assignment, I'm liable to just go ahead and make you my first target." At this point, I'd been following marks for at least a couple of years, and Archie knew I could handle my business, but he was reluctant to let me out of the starting gates.

'Finally, he relents, looks at me sideways, and hands me this file.'

'A creampuff,' I offer.

Ruby laughs. 'Oh, yeah. A cakewalk. An easy-greasy, "stroll down Broadway and collect two hundred dollars as you pass Go" kind of hit. Archie'd just been waiting for a tasty peach like this so I could pop my soda.'

'I don't blame him.'

'Shit, I don't either. I didn't. Not then, at least. So I look over the file, and it's exactly what you'd expect. Some mid-level guy works in a paper mill, up for a union position and I guess someone didn't think too favorably of that. This guy, shit, I don't even remember his name, Black or Brown or something like that, we'll just call him Brown, well, Brown's got a routine he's been following every work day for twenty years. Gets up—'

'Family guy?'

'No, never been married, lives alone, all by his lonesome . . .'

It's my turn to laugh, 'Jesus.'

'I know! Anyway, gets up, goes to this little diner slash coffee shop, eats two eggs, two pieces of toast, two strips of bacon . . .'

'Two cups of coffee.'

'You got it. Then he drives in to work, punches the clock, works his eight, punches out, hits a bar named George's along with half his co-workers, and heads home. Wash, rinse, repeat.'

'A creampuff.'

'Ain't that the truth. A guy stuck in a rut. A thousand ways to drop this guy and all of 'em as clean as a whistle, as my mom would say.'

She stops to take a bite of the macaroon, then swallows quickly so she doesn't lose momentum.

'So here's the kicker. Archie tag-teams it—'

'Shit.'

'Yeah. Wants me to double up with a long-time shooter he's got in the stable, name of Tuesday – Tuesday Schmidt or something like that. Ever heard of him?'

I shake my head, and she waves like it doesn't matter.

'Why would ya? Anyway, this guy's pulled jobs for Archie for as long as I've known him and I've read his file and he only works once in a blue moon, but he seems good to go, so whatever. I mean, I'm annoyed, but whatever.

'Archie assures me this bagman is going to just show me the ropes, but I'll get the kill shot, and I guess that's what matters, because the truth of it is . . . how will I react? It's one thing to follow a mark and make notes in a file, another to actually – ah, hell, you know what I'm talking about. Jesus, how long is this story? You sick of it yet?'

'No, believe me, I'm entertained.'

'I'll try to pick up the pace just the same. So Archie puts us together and I meet Tuesday for the first time, and he's not at all what I was expecting. Maybe his file needed updating or something, but this guy is a biscuit away from three hundred fifty pounds and he's gotta be at least sixty years old.'

'Christ.'

'Tell me about it. I start thinking maybe Archie's doing the favor for *this* guy, not me. So we ride around together and we stake Brown for at least a week to make sure the file's up to snuff, though I know it's going to be. Say what you want about my brother, but Archie can put a file together, that's for sure.

'Anyway, we sneak into this mark's house when he's at work to get the lay of the land, we eat breakfast at the diner, we even get into his mill and scout it out, all the homework, you know. Tuesday's pretty entertaining, actually, got a million stories he's spooling out like fairy tales – the moral of this story is "don't leave your safety on," the moral of this story is "carry an extra clip in your bag" – that type of thing. He's got me in stitches half the time we're working this job.

'Finally, seven days of sitting in the car with him and he leans over and asks, "how you wanna handle this?" I don't even think two seconds and I say, "hit him when he gets home after the bar." The fat man shrugs and says suits him fine, see ya tomorrow night, and that's that.

'Of course, I don't sleep that night, I don't eat the next day, I'm all geeked up like it's Christmas morning, you know. Now I got to wait around all day since I'm the one who said let's hit him at night, so I end up getting in my car and following the mark to make sure he's still sticking to his pattern—'

'Don't tell me you jumped the gun.'

'No, not at all. I just wanted to watch this guy and see what's what. And let me tell you, it was a hell of a feeling, knowing he was gonna die and him not knowing it . . . does that make sense?'

'More than you know.'

'I got a confession to make. I like the way it felt.'

'Yeah. It's the nature of the beast.'

'You got that right. Anyway, I make sure the target goes to the bar after work like normal, and then I head over to meet Tuesday at the meeting point where we decided to hook up. He's there when I get there, and I climb in his sedan, take a look at him, and let me tell you, he's not looking so hot. His face is red and he's sort of sweating all over.

' "What's up?" I say, and he just shrugs and says, "nothing."

' "You all right?" I say, and he mutters something like "why wouldn't I be?" and we take off for Brown's pad.

'I'm thinking, "oh man, tell me this old veteran don't have cold feet or isn't shaky or something . . ." not on my first pull, you know? "Please tell me Archie didn't tag-team me with a guy who's suddenly having second thoughts about the shooting game."

'So I got one eye on Tuesday and one eye on the prize and we wait and wait and eventually Sweet Georgia Brown comes home and I'm out the car door three seconds after he heads inside.

'Tuesday climbs out of the front seat and blocks my way and I'm like, "listen, old buck, if you lost your nerve . . ." and he stares bullets at me and sort of growls like a junkyard dog and says, "wait, goddammit. You gotta let the mark settle in and catch him with his head on the pillow. Patience, lady, patience."

'I give him my best stink eye but he's having none of it, and he's right after all, but I swear something's off about him. His face is splotchy, bright red in the cheeks, white on the forehead, and he's dripping sweat, and I don't know what to think.

'So we wait and wait and wait some more, and I'm listening to Tuesday's heavy breathing like he's on some phone sex line for what seems like a week, and finally the clock hits the hour and I nod at him and he shrugs and opens his door.

'We check the street and there ain't a soul in sight at two in the morning, so we head up to the house. I pull out a pick but check this out, the motherfucking mark doesn't even lock his front door.'

I chuckle and she leans forward, eyes dancing.

'Tell me about it. This ain't just a cakewalk, it's a trip around the whole goddamn dessert bar. So we move into the living room and I can hear Brown snoring in the back so I make a hand signal like I'm gonna go take care of business, and I look over at Tuesday and the man's face is stark white, all color gone, like I'm looking at Casper the fat fucking ghost. He's holding his arm like this and I swear I have no idea what the hell's happening and right then he topples over, all three hundred fifty pounds of him falls sideways like a building coming down, right on a glass coffee table, I shit you not.'

'Heart attack?' I can't keep the chuckle out of my voice.

'You got it. And this coffee table doesn't just break, it explodes. I mean it sounds like someone set a bomb off in the room. KABOOOM!'

She smacks the table for emphasis.

'Before I know what's happening, I mean I'm just processing this shit, I turn my head to see Brown, buck naked, standing in the doorway to his bedroom, holding a sawed-off shotgun.

'My heart's beating like a drum and I remember the thought going through my head . . . I'm wondering what we must look like, a dead fat guy collapsed on his coffee table and me looking like I do, holding a gun in my hand.

'I don't know if he thinks we're burglars or what, but I guess he figures it out pretty damn fast, because he points both barrels at me and pulls the trigger.'

I raise my eyebrows and Ruby grins, anticipating my surprise.

'Click. That's all he gets. You think I didn't notice that gun under his bed when I staked his house? I know I'm not supposed to touch anything but I wasn't going to take any chances. So I took the shells out of the barrels and left it right where it was.

'Good thing.'

'Damn straight.'

'And Brown?'

'I knocked the surprise right off his face.'

'And Tuesday?'

'Never saw Wednesday again.'

I give her the slow clap and she pantomimes a curtsy as we both laugh.

'I'm impressed. You tell a good story.'

'Now you know more about me than anyone in the game.'

'I know I better check to make sure my gun's loaded if you're coming for me.'

'You're right about that.' She stands. 'I'll be right back,' and with that, she heads to the sign marked 'WC.'

Like her brother, Ruby Grant has grown on me quickly. We are opposites – we approach this job from radically different directions – and yet maybe that's not such a bad thing. Maybe I can learn from her as much as she learns from me. Like getting inside a mark's head, maybe getting inside Ruby's head will show me a different angle, a different way to navigate this business.

She drops two fresh macaroons on the table as she takes her seat. 'Pistachio and vanilla,' she says. 'You gotta try both.'

'No, thanks.'

'More for me,' she shrugs as she bites into the green one.

Swallowing, she starts in with 'All right, then. Enough about my humble beginnings. Let's focus on the matter at hand. What's going on and where do I fit in?'

'I'm going to take out the man who put the hit on me.'

'He dies, no one to pay out the contract, the hit goes away?'

'That's the idea.'

'So where is he?'

'Holed up in one of six buildings on the Rue de Maur. Heavily defended. He's known the neighborhood and the buildings his entire life. Oh, and I don't know what he looks like . . . I'm pretty sure he had his face changed.'

She waits, her expression unreadable. Then she manages, 'Shiiiit.' Just like her brother.

'I know.'

'What d'you need me for? Sounds like the same type of cream-puff as my Mr. Brown.'

'Uh-huh.'

'You got blueprints of the six buildings?'

I shake my head.

'Any of 'em?'

I shake it again.

'You know how many guys he's got?'

I just keep shaking.

'Fuck you, Columbus. I mean seriously, fuck you.'

'I'm not going to go *in* there . . .'

'No shit you're not.'

'I'm going to bring him out to me.'

She nods now, regaining interest. 'Okay, okay. Now we're talking. How do you plan to draw him out?'

She leans back and waits for me to paint the picture. I give her the basics while she finishes her macaroons. The table we occupy in the back corner has allowed us both to speak freely, as opposed to the States where we might have had to worry about hovering waiters. Here, the staff usually gives you all the room you need.

After I finish, she leans forward. 'Okay. Okay. I dig where this is going.'

'Good. You're in, then?'

'Depends.'

'On?'

'I talked to Archie today. He wants to be your fence when this is over. That's why I've been hanging around. I'm supposed to seal the deal.'

Well, there it is. I knew it was coming; I just didn't know when.

'I'm not sure there's going to be much more for me when this is over.'

'Uh-huh.'

'I've put in quite a few years now, and I'm still young. I lied when I said it was just a thought. I've been thinking about it more in the last month than in the previous thirteen years. There might be a way out for me.'

'How long you been giving yourself that speech?'

'Not too long.'

'No, I didn't think so.' She shifts so she can look me straight in the eyes. 'Listen, if you think there's an escape hatch for you, I'll tell Archie not to stand in your way.'

I nod, and she leans forward again. 'But if you can't get out – if you try it and things go sour – then he's gonna want you in the fold.'

I sit back and rub my hands on the top of my head and think of Risina and then of a dropped silver handle on a stopped silver wagon and think of giving everything to her by giving everything away. And then my eyes fall on Ruby sitting in front of me, in this world, my world, and something in me keeps seeking her out, again, a few times during this hunt, a game in which I'm more hunted than hunter, and my instincts are out in front of my intellect. Do I want Archibald Grant to be my fence? Have I been angling for that without even realizing it? And what does that say about my plans to give this life up? Maybe I'm deceiving myself.

'Okay.'

She doesn't ask for confirmation, doesn't want to prolong my internal conflict. She's the kind of woman who knows what an 'okay' means without having to dig it out and analyze it.

We settle the bill, head to the front of the café to make plans for our next rendezvous and maybe we're being cavalier and maybe we're too comfortable and maybe there were signs, the way there were signs in that coffee shop on the day all this began.

I look up to see Roger Mallery riding down the street atop that goddamn bicycle and his eyes find us, and the look of confusion on his face lasts for what seems an eternity as his mind works out the mechanics . . . that I told him I was working for his boss Coulfret, that I needed his help on an assassination, that our mark was the very much alive girl standing next to me, that the whole thing was a lie . . . I can see it all come together for him, one plus one can only equal fucking two, and he must spot my eyes narrowing, hardening, because he swallows, lowers his chin, and starts pumping his pedals desperately, like a sprinter. His bike responds by hurtling down the street as though it has been fired out of a cannon.

Ruby recognizes Mallery just moments behind me and I think she says something to me, but my legs are already moving, and I dart across the street and barrel as fast as I can down the sidewalk.

As large as Mallery is, he sure knows how to work that fucking bike, and his lead grows as he cranes his neck practically under his right armpit to make sure I'm not gaining on him.

Three workers are unloading boxes out of a black delivery truck with the engine idling, and if luck wants to spin around on a dime then I'm sure as hell going to take advantage of it.

I'm in the driver's seat and throwing the truck into gear and ignoring the shouts of the angry workers and if there are any police loitering around for the next couple of blocks then I'm just going to have to deal with them later because I cannot let this man warn Coulfret.

He looks back for me on the sidewalk and then spots me behind the wheel of the truck and I discover a moment of panic in his eyes. Often, panic in your enemy can provoke a mistake, a stutter, an opening to his defeat. But it can also lead to a surge of adrenaline, a dip into the reservoir of energy he has buried inside him.

Mallery turns back, grits his teeth, and recognizes an advantage. There is traffic in the one-way street up ahead, and he doesn't have to stop. He zips up a lane of his own creation, between idling cars and the rigid curb. I slam on my brakes and just catch a blur as a Vespa whips past me, Ruby atop it hunched over the handlebars like a jockey on a thoroughbred, and then she rounds the corner moments behind Mallery. At least one of us chose the right vehicle.

Fuck this. I hop the delivery truck over the curb and ride up the sidewalk, scattering pedestrians, bouncing on faulty hydraulics like I'm inside a washing machine. I spin the wheel and the truck responds, swinging to the right, somehow keeping on all four tires, and my fears are realized, no sign of Mallery on his bicycle or Ruby on the Vespa and a cluster of additional traffic ahead. I roll up a block, my head on a swivel, eyes scanning everywhere, and I catch just a glimpse of an overturned moped lying like a felled beast in the middle of the street of the adjacent block.

I jump out of the truck without bothering to throw it into park, ignore the foot traffic on the sidewalk, and as I get closer, I can see Mallery's bicycle also lying flat on its side, looking alien in that way bicycles do when they're not upright, half on and half off the curb, front tire spinning.

Again, I'm stymied, no sign of the big man or Ruby Grant, and then I hear the distinctive crack of a pistol firing. It came from somewhere up and to my left, and I duck my head and sprint inside the residential building in front of me. Something is troubling about that crack; Ruby prefers a high-caliber weapon, a .44, and the crack sounded sharp, quick, more like the pop of a kernel of corn, and I'm not sure about any of it, what exactly I heard, what was an echo, what was amplified, but that damn butcher better not have a gun. I've been with him twice before and never known him to carry a firearm.

I fly up a flight of stairs, mounting them two at a time, and almost shoot Ruby in the head. She's crouched against a wall, looking amused, like she is expecting me, and what took me so goddamn long, and isn't this whole affair a lot of goddamn fun. I don't know how she does it – I'd like to think it's all a façade – but I've been around her enough now to think maybe she's found some way to swallow the strains of our chosen profession and fuel it into something else. What? Passion? Maybe she's wired differently. Maybe she just enjoys it. Maybe I'm more like Ruby than I'd care to admit.

She smiles as I lower my gun and ease my index finger off the trigger.

'He's carrying a pea-shooter. Got a shot off at me and ducked around the corner.'

I look above her head. A fresh bullet hole is plugged into the wall.

'He have a way out?'

'I don't think so. Just got a quick scan of the building when I headed inside, but I think those stairs behind you are the only way down.'

She taps a ceramic 'Fire Emergency Exit Plan' sign next to her head. The writing's in French but the map is clear: it displays the floor plan with a broken line showing a route to the stairs behind us in case the building goes up in flames.

I see something else on the map and point to it. 'It's not the only way up.'

Her face falls, now inspecting the sign while wrinkling her nose. 'How much time you think we have?'

She's talking about police response time – someone reported the delivery van stolen, someone witnessed the chase, someone spotted the overturned Vespa and bicycle, someone heard the gunshot.

Still, it's a lot to add up for even the most opportune French police officer. So before enforcement becomes a nuisance, I'd give us . . .

'Fifteen minutes. Maybe more if we're lucky.'

'Dammit.' She pushes away from the wall and we stalk toward the corner, instinctively deciding that I go high and Ruby take low. We swing around the bend in perfect synchronicity, prepared to duck and fire at the same time, but Mallery isn't waiting for us.

I kick open the door to the roof, catch just a glimpse of the sun reflecting off of metal, and pull Ruby back as a tempest of bullets pounds into the open door frame. A second late, and we would've both caught taps to the head.

'Well, that was your one chance,' I call out.

'Go to hell, you lying son of a whore.'

I can see him through a wedge in the doorway. He has his gun hand up but keeps throwing glances over his shoulder, at the roof's ledge.

'Don't do it, Mallery. You're too big of an oaf to think you can jump across that alley.'

His face loses color as he realizes I can see him, and he sprays the doorway with another volley of bullets.

'Can he make it?' Ruby whispers.

I shrug and then peer through the slit where the door is hinged to the wall, where I can see it on his face. I was hoping for resignation but instead he has resolve, and he's measuring out the steps it'll take him for an adequate runway before he launches.

Ten steps. It's not going to be enough. He's just too big and I doubt he has much experience in long-jumping and he keeps the gun pointed at the doorway, but he's going to have to lower it and turn his back on me to make the leap. He breathes once, twice, filling his lungs with oxygen, psyching himself up. Now or never.

I shoot him square in the back, toppling him before he takes his fourth step. He spills forward, headfirst like he's trying to dive into a swimming pool, five feet short of the ledge.

Ruby and I approach cautiously, but I know from the way he dropped, the bullet took his life immediately. The leak on this faucet is plugged. Or so I think.

'Let's skedaddle,' Ruby says, but there are two objects out in front of Mallery's body. He must've been clutching both of them when he fell. One I knew would be there: his weapon, a little Browning automatic.

The other is his phone.

I stoop, pick it up, and look at the face. It only takes a moment to realize what Mallery had time to do while he held us off at the stairwell door.

'What is it?'

'He texted his brother.'

The text reads: ROBERTO ROSSI'S A FRAUD. TELL COULFRET.

I look down at Mallery's body. Somehow, his chin is up and his corpse is looking at me. I'm not certain, but I think he is smiling.

An ambush is information and timing, but a footrace boils down to improvisation and speed. I have Mallery's phone in my hand and there has been no return text, so I'm hoping his brother Luis hasn't yet received the message. Surely he would've tried to call or text back. Maybe I'm lucky and he doesn't have his phone with him.

Ruby and I scamper out of the building without hearing any sirens and finally something is going right for us and maybe good luck can build up like bad luck or at least keep the hounds at bay.

We arrive at an empty cab stand with two idling taxis and time moves no slower than when you're reliant on someone else to drive you somewhere.

'Nothing on the phone?'

'Not yet.'

'Then we jump this bastard before he gets the message. Easy as pie.'

'I haven't had a good pie in a long time.'

'Well, don't look at me,' Ruby says. 'I wouldn't know where to begin to bake a motherfucker. But I'm sure it's easy.'

'Maybe yes, maybe no.'

'Look, even if this boy gets the text . . . he calls your mark and . . .'

'He can't call. Coulfret doesn't use phones. Mallery told me that when I first saw him texting his brother.'

'Even better. But let's say he gets to your mark, and warns him you're on to him, that doesn't give the big boss a whole hell of a lot more than he already had.'

'He'll have my face.'

'What?'

'Passport photo. The brother is a forger . . . phony passports.'

'That was your in?'

'That was my in.'

'Goddamn.'

The cab pulls over near the Bastille and I throw a wad of euros over the seat and we're out the door. The plan, if you can call it that, is to move backwards from the Rue de Maur to Mallery's apartment. If Luis is coming to warn Coulfret, maybe we can intercept him along the way.

It's a ten-minute walk, even at a hurried pace, but there's no sign of him and the phone in my hand remains silent. I plug in the code to the security gate I saw over Roger Mallery's shoulder the first time I came here, and Ruby and I step into the courtyard. Luis has two ways to exit his building, twin stairwells at either end of the entrance. I choose east and Ruby takes west, and we enter the stairwells simultaneously.

The corridor is darker than I remember, but that may be a mind's trick; I was in control the last time I was here, and I am on the defensive now . . . ever since Roger Mallery rode by at the most inopportune time in this city of millions and sometimes coincidence is just coincidence but it's unlikely, I realize now in this lightless stairwell, damn unlikely. Occam's razor would be slicing the shit out of this one – the most reasonable explanation is that Mallery was tailing me, and I don't know where my head was but I didn't spot him and that may be the most worrying development of this entire fucking affair.

I turn up the second flight of stairs when the hallway lights up in a bluish glow and my hand vibrates, indicating an incoming text on Mallery's phone.

Three words: GOING FOR HELP. And right then I hear a gunshot, definitely Ruby's gun, and a scream of pain, definitely Ruby's scream.

'Oh, Jesus,' I think and maybe say aloud, but I'm already breaking out of the stairwell and sprinting the length of the hall, passing dozens of apartment doors, one of which is opening to investigate the commotion but I cannot hesitate, just plow through the west stairwell door and Ruby is on her back on the landing with a butcher's knife buried in her arm, just below the shoulder.

She's not shrieking, just angry, steeling herself to yank out the knife.

'No!'

'What the fuck do you mean, "no!?" '

Well, if she's healthy enough to snap back at me, then she's going to be okay.

I pull my shirt off. 'Use this to stanch the bleeding,' and before she can bark at me again, I toss her my hotel key . . . 'Room 202. Bag under the bed.'

I'm already flying down the stairs when she yells, 'Drop his ass, Columbus!' after me.

A footrace may be improvisation and speed, but now it's just speed and he's got a block and a half on me as I blast out of the building and sprint after him.

Unfortunately for Luis, his brother was the athlete in the family.

The street is mostly deserted this time of day, and I have my gun out and up and am running with it like it's a relay-race baton. Sprinting like this, the trick is to never put my finger inside the trigger guard, not until I mean to shoot. And I'm not going to take a wild shot, not unless I have to, not unless he gets close enough to the Rue de Maur that I have no other choice.

I close on him now like a wolf after a rabbit, and he takes a mad right around a corner, leaping in front of a pair of Vespas, causing their drivers to brake, lose control, and slide out on the pavement.

I follow behind, hurdling the lead bike like a goddamn Olympic athlete while maintaining my speed. I don't know these streets that well, certainly not as well as Luis, but I'm pretty sure he's going to have to take a left to cut into the Rue De Maur if he's going to have a chance at reaching Coulfret's building. I duck to the lefthand side of the street like a sheepdog guiding his charges into a pen, and Luis makes a mistake, the biggest mistake a man can make when he's being pursued by someone who wants to kill him.

He looks over his shoulder.

There are two reasons this is a bad idea.The most obvious is that he is no longer watching where he is going, no longer looking at the sidewalk in front of him, and any slight crack in the pavement could send him sprawling.

The second and equally devastating reason is the man being chased gains a glimpse of how much ground his pursuer has made up, spots the look of conquest on his enemy's face, realizes the hopelessness of his goal. It's enough to sap the energy out of even the fittest of men.

Luis takes one quick look over his shoulder and I see his eyes go wide, his adam's apple bob, and a look of panic spread across his face. Like I mentioned with his brother, panic can cause two things.

He stutter-steps, giving up precious ground, stumbles a bit, throws his arms out to gain his balance, and is successful enough to keep moving forward.

But the panic gave me all I need. I overtake him in a dead run, and raise the gun when I'm a foot away. One step, two steps more, and I fire close, right into the back of his head.

He drops like a stone, and I only stop long enough to snatch up one thing from where it fell on the pavement before I'm up and running again. I don't know if anyone is following me.

I'm not going to look over my shoulder.

14

Ruby lies on my bed with her eyes shut.

'Don't say it.'

'Say what?'

'Just don't.'

'I wasn't going to say a word.'

'You get him?'

'Yeah. And his phone. I tossed both his and his brother's into the Seine.'

Ruby nods, expressionless.

'But I'm uneasy about the computers in his apartment. I couldn't risk going back there, and once the police look into the dead bodies, they're going to find—'

'Don't worry about it.' She hasn't opened her eyes. And now that I move around the bed, I see she's dressed the knife wound with the kit from my bag.

'Why shouldn't I worry?'

'I took care of it.'

'How?'

'I threw all their computer shit into the fireplace and lit it up.'

'With a knife sticking out of your arm?'

'Nah, I yanked it out before you got out of the building. Used your shirt to tie it off, like you said.'

She opens one eye to take me in, see if I remain shirtless. I'm wearing an oversized hoodie I found in a souvenir shop three blocks from where I overtook Luis. Even at close range, I avoided getting his blood on me, and raised no eyebrows in the store.

Ruby closes that eye again. I move to the bathroom sink and splash water on my face. It hits me at once, the weight of it, the near miss of having my face out there, the near miss of Coulfret knowing exactly who is gunning for him, and another pair of dead brothers who dipped their toes in a dangerous world, got caught in the maelstrom, and drowned. I don't know how long I stand at the sink with the water running. Seconds could be minutes could be hours.

'You know how you told me you were thinking about quitting the business?'

'Yeah.'

'Well, I got something to admit to you.'

'Oh-kay . . .'

'Fuck it if you don't want to hear it.'

'I'm listening.'

That eye opens again to gauge my face, to see if I'm mocking her. Satisfied, she resumes. 'When I banged through the door on his floor, all of a sudden, he was in the doorway, looking at that gun in my hand. And I don't know what to say but I flinched.'

'Well, hell, that's nothing. It happens to all of us.' Not true, but it felt like the right thing to say.

'Jesus, it's not that. I don't give a shit about that. I mean, I would've liked *not* to have flinched, because that's what allowed the frog to bury his knife in my arm, and caused me to miss, so yeah, I'm not happy, but no, that's not what I'm spilling my guts about.'

She waits to see if I'm going to interrupt, but I keep my mouth tight. Her voice falls quiet, like the words are coming from a place deep inside her.

'When he got the knife in me and I dropped my gun and went down . . . well . . . I was scared. Not a little bit scared, mind you. I was *terrified.* It was probably only a few seconds, but it seemed like the clock stopped and the only thing I was thinking was "please don't let him go for my gun." My mind was telling my body to fight, claw, scratch, but it was like there was a complete and total disconnect and I couldn't move.

'I've never felt that before. I thought I was going to die here in Paris in some crappy apartment building and no one would ever know why or who I was or what I was doing. I'd just be a Jane Doe or whatever the hell they call it here. I was really, bone-deep scared. "Please don't go for that gun, please don't do it . . ." That's all I could think.'

Her eyes are wide now, searching my face. I open my mouth, but she interrupts before I can speak. 'Goddammit, Columbus . . . lie to me. That's what I need to hear right now. Just lie to me.'

I start to speak again, but decide against arguing. Instead, I give her what she wants.

'Everyone gets scared,' I say without a hint of conviction.

She turns her eyes to the ceiling and looks at nothing, her face tightening. The lie stays in the air a long time.

The train is cramped and crowded and smells like life. It is a good way to hide in plain sight or to lose oneself in the dark recesses of the mind. People shuffle on and off like ocean waves, constant, unaware of the sameness in their differences. I can ride for an hour without looking up, without moving from my seat.

Fear like the fear Ruby experienced is a costly motivator. It causes one to make ill-conceived choices, give in to irrational decisions. It can cause a person to overplay his advantage, like Noel's wounded driver trying to steer into me, or it can cause paralysis, a complete abdication of thought and function, like Ruby on the Mallery stairwell. And once fear takes hold of a person, it nests, laying eggs and defending its territory with sharpened claws. It becomes a drug, a fix, something the host thinks is necessary in order to perform. It's the opposite, though . . . hollow, a false high, a placebo.

I was going to use Ruby to lure him out, play off of that one nugget I found in the police reports. Get to him through his nose. Use what I'd learned from Risina regarding the rare-book world and apply it to the rare-wine world. Get her to pretend to be a highend merchant, offer him a wine he couldn't refuse, a taste of a 1921 Petrus, and be there when he accepted the invitation.

But Ruby Grant's career will end soon. She'll slip or she'll panic or she'll step back when she should be moving forward. Fear is nesting inside her now, whether she knows it or not. The bluster, the swagger . . . that was the act. Maybe she'll have the foresight to walk away, to get out of the game early, before her ticket gets punched. But more likely, someone will take advantage of a simple mistake and put her down.

I won't be around to see it.

I need to move quickly. The dead Mallery brothers are probably on slabs at the morgue, and it won't take long for someone in Coulfret's organization to tip him. Once he learns one of his killers, Llanos, died in the city, immediately followed by the slaying of one of his henchmen, he'll understand I've come looking for him. I have yet to draw a bead on the third assassin, Svoboda, but there's no doubt in my mind he's somewhere close by, circling.

I need to lure Coulfret out of that apartment building on the Rue de Maur tomorrow, before he has a chance to bury in like a tick and wait out my demise.

I'm still going to get to him through his nose. And as much as I'd like to do this on my own, I'm going to need help.

'You want to be my fence, we start now.'

Archibald's voice comes through the pay-phone line. 'I thought you might come around, Columbus. We tied to that string like I said.'

'Yeah, yeah . . . we'll discuss structuring our deal and parameters and all of that as soon as I get back to the States. But right now, I need some assistance in Paris. I need a scrounger who can work on the fly . . .'

'Say no more. I got a fella works outta London . . . I'll have him there on the first train in the morning—'

'It's gotta be tonight, and he's gonna have to pull some serious strings.'

'Where you gonna be?'

'Hotel Balzac. Room 202.'

'He'll be there in two hours. Name's Olmstead. Bald, glasses.'

'Thanks.'

'My pleasure, Columbus. See you when you see me.'

Olmstead enters in the dead of night. He's as Archibald described: shaved head, thick square-framed glasses, but he's big for a scrounger, over six feet tall. For someone whose job it is to acquire things, often illegally, I was expecting a slight figure, a man who doesn't stand out on surveillance-camera footage.

As is so often the case in this world, there are no greetings between us as he moves to the small desk in the room, sits down, and opens a tiny notebook.

'Now what is it I can get for you, Columbus?'

'A water and power truck. A jumpsuit, the kind a city worker would wear.'

He looks up. 'You're in luck. The water service in Paris is moving from a private company back to a city-run municipality. It's in complete and total flux. This year is the transition and it's running as smoothly as cobblestone. Won't be a problem.'

He's got a blue-collar accent, and scars on his knuckles speak to his resourcefulness.

'What else?'

'Doctor's masks.'

'Okay.'

'Mentholatum.'

'Okay.'

'And I need the truck filled with bags of manure.'

He doesn't miss a beat. 'Bovine? Horse? Organic compost?'

'The kind that smells the worst.'

Ruby watches us from the bed, lugubriously. I don't have to tell her she's out.

'Okay, what else?'

'I'm going to need two nameless guys . . .'

'Shooters?'

'No, wallpaper. Two men dressed in the same uniform as me, directing traffic, nodding at pedestrians, and running like hell as soon as I pull the trigger.'

'That's gonna be expensive.'

'I'll pay 'em whatever you think they're worth.'

'What else?'

'That's it.'

'I understand you need this in the morning.'

'I want to be rolling by eleven.'

'Then I'll meet you two blocks to the east, in front of the Parc de Monceau, at 11 a.m. tomorrow.'

'I'll be there.'

He closes his notebook, coughs into his fist, and leaves without saying goodbye.

When I look at Ruby, she simply rolls over and faces the wall.

Coulfret's men pay us no attention as we park a block north of his building. Our truck has the blue-and-white insignia of the city printed on its side, and it only takes a moment for me to pop out of the back and open the adjacent manhole cover.

As I mentioned, Paris has an extensive sewer system, historic enough to generate its own tourism business. It would provide a somewhat easy path to enter Coulfret's building from underground if that were my aim, but I'm wary of attacking there. Like the Webb brothers, his home turf is well guarded, he knows it better than anyone, and I have no intention of ending up in the bottom of an elevator shaft.

The two men Olmstead found are impassionate and more or less featureless. They toss me bag after bag of compost as soon as I descend into the cavern beneath the street. The size of the chamber is commodious; I barely have to stoop. It takes me a dozen trips back and forth, but soon I have all of my materials in the right location underneath the Rue de Maur. Directly above my head is the main sewer line running into Coulfret's apartment building.

We move the truck to the middle of his block, directly across from his front door, and the first of Coulfret's bodyguards approaches, a young man with an out-of-style bowler cap. My two hired pigeons and I have doctor's masks covering our noses and mouths, and we are in the middle of prying up another manhole cover.

Bowler Hat speaks in colloquial French with a thick nasal accent.

'Keep moving. You have no business here.'

I try my best to respond in a passable Parisian accent. 'We're having trouble with the sewer conversion.'

'I don't give a whore's fuck if you are prying out golden piping beneath the street, you don't do it here. Pack up your truck and—'

'You'll have to take it up with the city—'

'I'm taking it up with you, you son of a—'

And then I see him instantly recoil as the stench hits him, his forearm flying up to cover his nose.

'My God . . .'

Two of his fellow bodyguards spring up as their cohort flinches backward. The nearest one, a bald mustachioed thug I recognize from the whore's pictorial spread, clamps his hand inside his jacket and raises his voice. 'What is it, Anton?'

'Shit!'

'What?'

'It's shit. These sons of whores smell worse than a monkey cage.'

The two approaching bodyguards now catch a whiff and reel backward. 'Gadddd . . .' I hear one of them grunt.

'I told you we were having problems. You didn't want to listen.'

'Yes, yes, Jesus. For the love of the virgin, please, just cover that goddamn hole and drive away.'

In a ruse like this – what is essentially a short con – if you play it right, the mark will believe it is his idea to give you what you want.

I nod at Bowler Hat, then turn to my men. 'Okay, cover it, boys. They don't want our help, they don't want our help. I'm sure they'll have an easy time rescheduling with the city.'

My pigeons start to recover the manhole when the first of Coulfret's inner circle steps out of the apartment building, waving his hands in the air, gagging.

'What the fuck?' he chokes out in our general direction.

'What is it, Philippe?' Bowler Hat shouts back at him.

'The toilets are flowing backward with shit!'

'Inside?'

'Yes, inside, goddamn. Where do you think I just came from?' A couple more of Coulfret's inside dwellers emerge like bomb victims from the house, sucking in huge gulps of air as soon as they make it to the sidewalk. Their disgust is coming out in angry cries directed at Bowler Hat, just for his proximity to us. He yells back defensively in a high-pitched voice that sounds like it is pouring directly from his nose. 'I didn't do a fucking thing. I'm trying to get to the understanding of this!' He turns back to me, eyes red and teary.

'Fix it, you stinking whore. Fix it or so help me, I'll rip off your face and flush you down the sewer myself.'

He then rips the doctor's mask off my face, snapping the elastic band, and holds it up over his own mouth and nose, daring me to complain.

'Okay, okay, no problem.' I whistle at my guys to get back to work. 'I'm really sorry.'

'You should be sorry, you enormous shit bag.'

He's taken a few steps back, and I pretend to watch my men work on the manhole cover, but my eyes are locked on the front door of Coulfret's building as more of his men emerge.

I'm scanning for anyone who looks like he's had plastic surgery on his face. I know Coulfret's height and weight and build and I've seen three pictures of him from before he faked his death, and I'm certain I'll spot him when he clears that front door. If he fancies himself a wine connoisseur, then there's no way he had any work done on his bird-like beak. I'm willing to bet he changed his eyes and his hair and his chin and his jawline but not that aquiline nose with the bridge that looks like an architect sculpted a flying buttress. I'll know it when I see it, and I'll put a bullet right through it and jump in the truck and get the hell out of here.

Two new men emerge from the front door, though neither can be Coulfret. One is too young and the other a foot short, and the din they raise as each comes out of the house hurling curses at the sky sounds like a demonic choir. One more thug trickles out, but he's far too skinny, and then I hear Bowler Hat yell at someone over my shoulder.

'Gerard! Is this the kind of shit we can expect from the city taking over? Shit, shit everywhere?'

I don't have to look over my shoulder to know who he's summoning; I understand from the first 'ha ha' I hear bellowed back. The obsequious detective from the Bastille district who happens to be writing a novel about French crime approaches behind me, the same one who left me alone with the files on Coulfret.

Not now. Not right now.

Another two heavies lumber out of the building, but neither is Coulfret and he's gotta come out any second and I don't need much but I need that now. The way to him is through his nose, and there just isn't any conceivable way he can hold out much . . .

'Ha ha! Anton, it seems the stench of your sinful life is finally catching up to you, yes? Ha ha!'

The fat detective sweeps past me, biting into an apple, and I turn just enough to give him my profile, and for some reason he seems immune to the smell and he's happy to set up shop two feet from me, chomping on that apple like he's about to sit down for a picnic.

Three more men flood out of the door, one holding a handkerchief over his face, covering his mouth and nose. Is he Coulfret? He's the right size, the right body shape. But I can't tell with half his face obscured.

'Is this really bothering you, Anton? I would think a pig like you would be right at home in a den of filth.'

I inch closer to the front door, toward the man holding the kerchief, waiting for him to lower it, please lower it, and there's something familiar about his eyes, but I can't be sure. Lower the kerchief, just give me half of a second to look . . .

'Why don't you do something about it, you miserable goat?'

'I am doing something, Anton. I am out enjoying a nice walk in the neighborhood I love to serve, keeping an eye out for any unusual business, and do you know what I've been wondering?'

'I don't give a damn what—'

'I've been wondering why Roger Mallery and his brother were murdered in separate places last night.'

Another two goons step out into the sun and join the man with the kerchief, and they are both too large to be Coulfret, but their body language indicates a deference to the man they've joined. If he'll just lower that fucking handkerchief and let me catch a glimpse of his nose . . .

'What is this you say to me? What of Roger Mallery?'

'Dead on the roof of a building on the Left Bank, and the same night his brother is murdered on a street two blocks from here. But you know nothing of course, ha ha. You are just a know-nothing imbecile . . .'

I'm riveted by the man holding the kerchief to his face and I can tell the exact pattern on it, a yellow and white floral stitch, and I can tell exactly how it folds back at the top into a little triangle, and I am imploring him, willing him with my eyes to lower it. Detective Gerard and the goon with the bowler hat pay me no attention, an arm's length away, as my pigeons stoop over the manhole cover like they're actually working, trying to find a leak in some subsurface piping. I have to hand it to Archibald's scrounger, he found unflappable men and whatever he's charging for them, I'm going to double it as soon as we get out of here.

'I'm up to my ears in shit here and you want to question me like I'm down at your stinking police station?'

'Why is your face turning red, Anton? Is it because the story I heard is true about you having an incident with Roger Mallery concerning some thuggery you did together near the river Seine?'

'Do you think, you cow, maybe my face is red because the street smells like a toilet and now the building behind me is stinking to heaven and this miserable ass is gawking when he should be working.'

The man with the kerchief is just lowering it as I realize Bowler Hat is talking about me. And there it is, that unmistakable hook nose, and yes, the shape of his face has changed, and yes his eyes have changed, but that nose remains the exact bulging mar to his face I first examined in his mug-shots. The man is Alexander Coulfret, the one who put the price tag on my head for accidentally causing his brother's death, I'm sure of it.

I can feel Detective Gerard turning in my direction. I block him out, keep my eyes on my target as I drop one hand behind my back and return it fisting my Glock.

'Mr. Walker?' I hear Gerard say, confused.

I turn my eyes just enough to see Bowler Hat hesitate, his brain working out that I am raising a gun and he is going to be too slow to stop me.

The manhole cover clanks down hard on the ground as my two pigeons recognize the moment is at hand and sprint away like track stars.

Surprise is slipping quickly, and a professional killer knows the wise move is to close the distance to the mark as efficiently as possible. I abandon all pretense, break character, and charge Coulfret, arm raised stiff.

He spots me coming and is smarter than his men, puts it all together in an instant, how I flushed him out and am now moving in to finish the job.

A threatened animal's instinct is to break for home, shelter, security, the place he feels safest, and Coulfret does the same, spinning on a dime and darting back for his front door.

Gunshots break out around me as the bald mustachioed heavy or maybe Bowler Hat or any of a half-dozen thugs I'm ignoring try to squeeze a shot off at me, but I remain focused on the prize and pull the trigger and a puff of red mist explodes as I wing Coulfret just as he bursts through his door.

There is nothing I can do but follow.

15

The stench is a being, all-encompassing, a physical presence, as powerful as a kick to the stomach. Despite my precautions – I rubbed mentholatum under each nostril, the way coroners do when dealing with corpses – the manure trapped in the building has successfully battered my defenses. All I can do is push it to the side of my brain, treat it like a wound, like pain, and ignore it as best I can.

I thought Coulfret might have mounted an assault as soon as I barreled through the door, but only a blood trail leads down the corridor to my left. Instinctively, I spin around and double-bolt the door. He turned this building into a fortress, which I can use to my advantage to keep his men at bay. If there are other ways inside, I hope this at least buys me enough time to finish my work and somehow escape.

The blood streaks on the concrete floor are more splashes than drops, and though I didn't see exactly where I hit him, it had to have been more than a glancing blow. He's not going to last long without medical attention, and maybe not even then. My first thought is to take my chances and concentrate on getting the hell out of here, but I have to know this is over, know Coulfret is dead, know the contract has been lifted. If I don't see it with my own eyes, if I don't finish him, I'll always be looking over my shoulder. This has to end now.

I hear pounding on the door behind me, big angry blows like someone is trying to put his foot right through the steel, but the locks are holding as I continue to stalk down the hall. It'll take them some time to break it down, but I don't know how much. I don't know if it'll be enough. The red streaks become even more prominent on the tile, more defined as I follow them, picking up my pace.

The blood trail ends at the closed doors of the elevator.

Stairs. There has to be a stairwell nearby. I know he went down to the basement, the place he's most comfortable, and if he thinks I'm going to walk into the elevator car and wait for the drop, then the blood loss is affecting his head.

I fumble with a door nearby, nothing, then a second gives way, and I'm in the stairwell. I slow my breathing and deaden my footfalls as I soft-step down the stairs. I may be exactly where I don't want to be – in the mouth of the monster – but his wounds even the playing field and I am going to see this through now or die in his basement like all the others.

He wanted to send me a message, but I have a message to send back, one that reaches beyond these walls to the world within a world where I have my flag planted. My message is this: if you put paper on me, if yours is the signature on the contract, if you pay a hit man to hunt and kill the assassin known as Columbus, then you're signing your own death certificate.

I kick open the basement door, hoping the explosion of sound will draw a shot, but no volleys come my way. The blood trail is thicker now, large splashes of crimson leading from the elevator to the end of the hallway. The smell of shit pervades every pore in my skin. My eyes fog up, and I do my best to blink away tears.

The blood streaks end in a foot-wide puddle and lying next to the mess is the body of Alexander Coulfret. He has stopped just outside a door marked simply '24,' and I know it is the room he grew up in, the one he lived in for so many years.

And this is how you die in our business. Not gloriously, not surrounded by your loved ones, not in a peaceful bed with a priest giving you your final communion. No, you die on the street with your throat punctured by a stiletto blade. You die humiliated in the bathroom of a fishing-supply store. You die on a rooftop flopping forward, caught in mid-stride.

You die on the stinking floor of a stinking basement just a few feet from where you first learned to walk.

Coulfret's body shudders. He is not dead, not yet. A cough starts from somewhere deep inside his chest and comes out as a gasp. He rolls over as slow as a glacier and turns so I can see his face. Blood covers his lips and I'm reminded of the whore who took the pictures, the one with the lipstick smeared across her teeth. His complexion is the same as hers, and any color he once had is in full retreat. It turns out my bullet found the side of his neck, and he can no longer raise his hand to cover the wound; he's too weak to even try to keep the blood inside.

I'm shocked he made it this far, lived this long with a wound that severe. It's a testament to Coulfret's strength, an additional volume chronicling his force of will. And yet it's also cause for alarm. When the mortally wounded live this long, it's usually because they have something left they want to say, some unfinished business they wish to complete. Coulfret still breathes because he has a message to send me.

'You're Columbus,' he croaks out, spraying blood when he hits the last syllable.

I don't answer, and his eyes are only focused in my general direction.

Another coughing fit racks his body, and it takes me a moment to realize he's not coughing. The bastard is laughing. It's an unnerving sound, a devil's chortle.

With every bit of his strength, he pounds out his last words. 'You think killing me frees you?'

His eyes shift again, this time to the door to his father's apartment. For a second, I think he is finished, but he has three words left to say.

'The contract pays.'

Footsteps pound the stairwell at the same time as the elevator dings. Coulfret's men have finally knocked down the front door and infiltrated the building and, despite the smell, seem determined to check on the boss's health and then hunt me down.

Before the men fill the basement like roaches, I kick open the door marked '24' and disappear inside the janitor's apartment, Coulfret's childhood home.

The contract pays. The fucking contract pays. The goddamn fucking contract pays and all this was for naught. I am under it now, choking on it, swimming through shit of my own creation, and it will be impossible for me not to drown.

He must have set up some sort of trust where the contract pays out to the first man who returns with my scalp. That's what he wanted to tell me, what he wanted me to know before his eyes glazed over. I am Sisyphus with his rock, Tantalus with his grapes, and despite the fact I took the stairs, the elevator still collapsed thirty feet with me inside. I thought there was a chance out of this life with Risina, but that image is a mirage, a cruel trick of the mind. I am never going to break the water's surface, never going to breathe clean air. Even in death, Alexander Coulfret has made sure of that.

A contract killer has a bullet with my name on it, but not these men and not today. Their footsteps are a stampede outside the door as they congregate around Coulfret's dead body. In a moment, they'll be coming through this door and every door in the building, trying to find me.

Inside Coulfret's kitchen, covered by a throw rug, I find what I'm looking for: an old-style floor drain. I pull the manhole cover tool from my pocket and pop the metal grate, then ready the heel of my boot to knock the copper pipe away. One, two, three kicks and it falls back, hanging limply like a broken arm. I drop through the floor into the sewer, just as the door to Coulfret's apartment flies open.

I have half of a minute head start. I hope it'll be enough.

The sewers are pitch-dark, but there is a pinpoint of light five hundred meters away and I realize it's from the manhole cover on the neighboring block, the place the pigeons and I first unloaded the manure. We must not have put it back all the way, a mistake I don't usually make, but occasionally a mistake can be a savior.

Since I'd spent a great portion of the morning in these sewers, I'm slightly familiar with them, another advantage I should have over my pursuers. I know to run at a crouch to avoid overhead piping, and I know the walkway near the walls is relatively flat and so I set out as quickly as I can toward that sliver of light.

It grows sharper, more pronounced as I approach and grip the steel ladder leading up to freedom. I hear voices, amplified off the stone but still far away, screaming about grabbing a flashlight, screaming about the smell, screaming about my escape.

'So this is Italy? Kinda what I thought. Old buildings and old people.'

We're in Siena, a small town an hour outside Florence. It's quiet and confined and a bit isolated, and we sit in the tiny dugout basement of a traditional restaurant. There's only one stairwell descending to this level, and I sit facing it.

Archibald Grant has flown in for the occasion, namely to mollify his newest partner. He looks up from where he's picking at a bowl of pasta, wipes his mouth with his napkin, then clears his throat.

'So this french fry put paper on you and told you after you popped him that it pays no matter what?'

'That's it.'

'Yeah . . . I've heard about something like this before. It's rare and it's tricky, but there's a way around it.'

'I'm listening.'

'This Cole-Frett . . . he got family?'

'All dead.'

'Wife, spouse, nieces, nephews?'

'No.'

'Loyalists in the organization?'

'I don't know. I know of one I heard about. A guy who helped him with his original coup. Martin Feller.'

Archibald writes the name down in another one of those coil-wire notebooks.

A shuffle by the stairs draws our attention and Ruby descends into the room, smiling. Even with her arm in a sling, she has her bounce back. As she takes a seat at the table, Archibald flashes her his grin.

'What's shakin', baby girl?'

'Ready to eat a goddamn burger at Blackie's.'

'I hear that. I been out of the country for all of twenty-four hours, and already I feel a bit wobbly. Why the fuck can't they cook up a regular burger and fries here, man?'

I just shrug.

'Goddamn. Okay, anyway, what'd you hear about fallout from Paris, Ruby?'

'The organization's in complete disarray. That whole neighborhood's locked down tighter than Leavenworth. Not only did you kill the boss . . . a French cop was killed there too. Shot down in the street just outside the building.'

This is news to me. I wonder if Detective Gerard tried to interfere or, just as likely, caught a stray bullet intended for me. I liked that fat man; listening to him on the street talking to Bowler Hat, I realized the chatty, dim personality was an act, a weapon to uncover whatever he was trying to dig up. Underestimating him was my mistake, but I guess it doesn't matter now. If he suspected I was anything more than the writer I pretended to be – the more I think about it, the more likely it must be – well, I guess that suspicion died with him.

Archibald breaks my reverie, still addressing his sister. 'You know who filled the power vacuum?'

Ruby shakes her head. 'No, but I get the strong sense Coulfret wasn't all that well liked by his men.'

Archibald turns to me. 'Okay, you see? This might not be as desperate as it seems. He may have extended the contract even after he's down in a box, but he still has to have someone physically pay out the transaction. Could be his lawyer, could be a fence . . . or could be this Feller you mentioned. Whoever it is . . . that's the person we need to negotiate with. Not the way you do it, with that Glock of yours. The way I do it . . .'

Ruby finishes his sentence. '. . . with that silver tongue.'

'You know it.'

'I'm not much on sitting and waiting. I've been running around with paper on me for too long and I have to admit, I don't like the feeling.'

'Give me three days. I'll hit Paris and shake the bushes.'

'And me?' Ruby asks.

'Bite into a burger at Blackie's.'

'Say no more. I'm out of here.' She stands, smiling again. Any residual effects of what she told me about her fear of dying seem to be forgotten. She is her old cavalier self, and if it's an act, like Detective Gerard's dummy bit, it's a good one. Maybe I was wrong. Maybe she'll come through this after all. She certainly doesn't seem bitter that I excluded her from storming Coulfret's building on the Rue de Maur. She wouldn't have been much help with that bum arm anyway.

I stand, and she looks disappointed when I offer her only my hand.

'I'll see you back in the forty-eight, Columbus.'

'Yeah. Thanks for everything.'

'Don't mention it.'

She heads across the room and ascends the stairs.

As soon as she's out of earshot, Archibald whispers conspiratorially. 'What d'ya think?'

'Of Ruby?'

'Yeah, of Ruby. Who the fuck else would I be talking about?'

'I like her.'

'You think she's gonna make it as a professional?'

I keep my voice even, walking the line between telling him what he wants to hear and what he doesn't. 'How the hell should I know? She worked through some tight spots—'

Archibald holds up his palms and stands. 'Say no more.'

Maybe I should try to placate him, reassure him about his sister. Maybe I should voice my concerns, let him know about the fear I saw gripping her back in Paris. Maybe I should say a lot of things, but I can't seem to muster the energy.

'All right, then, three days.'

'I'll be here.'

The circle in Siena contains a single tower that sticks up from its center like a middle finger. I stand at the top of it, staring out over the town and the neighboring Tuscan countryside. I feel at once both exposed and safe, a paradox that is somehow comforting. This is the place I reside, straddling the line between vulnerability and security. It is the world I have lived in for as long as I can remember. If my fate is to spend the rest of my life hunted, I won't do it in the shadows: I'll stand at the top of the tower and dare the bastards to come.

And I'll do it alone.

The wind picks up and chases gray clouds across a gray sky. The horizon seems close and blurred at the edges, claustrophobic. Only a smattering of pedestrians are on the sidewalks below, grouped in twos and threes. The wind provides the only sound, a low whistle like a dirge.

More than anything, the aftermath of this mission has made one truth clear: the next time I see Risina will have to be the last. She deserves better than me, better than what I can give her.

A knock at the door and Archibald enters, flashing his broadest smile, though this one's not part of his act. He's genuinely happy with himself.

'What'd I tell you, Columbus?'

'What'd you tell me?'

'I said to let me take care of it. So I took care of it.'

'Come on. Get to it.'

'All right, all right. Here's the straight word. The killer I told ya 'bout what calls himself Svoboda? He's still after you, and he's not gonna stop till he's dead or you're dead.'

That sounds like nothing to smile about, but before I can say anything, Archibald keeps going. 'Something to do with the kill fee being promised already and no one wanting to deal with the ramifications of canceling on the motherfucker. But . . . and here's the big but . . . come to find out a lot of people are glad Cole-Frett is ten toes up and six feet under.

'Power vacuums don't take long to fill, no matter what language you speak. The name you gave me, the one who was loyal to him? Feller?'

Archibald draws his finger across his throat. 'Dead. Found bobbing up and down in the river they got there with his wrists cut and bled out. Authorities called it a suicide, but you and I know better than that. These boys want to wipe their hands clean of all things Cole-Frett. They sure don't want to pay no more kill fees. As far as they're concerned, you did them a favor. What's done is done and bygones be bygones and let's sweep it all under the rug. They got enough to deal with concerning the dead cop. If Svoboda winds up plugged, more power to ya is the message they gave me.'

I nod, digesting the information. 'So then Svoboda and that's it?'

'You get him before he gets you, slate's clean.'

'So let's get him.'

'How you want to handle it?'

'Turn the boat around and meet him head-on.'

Archibald smirks and points his finger at me. 'I like the way you think.'

'You gotta dig deep, Archibald. I want the file to end all files on this guy. I want to know anything and everything about him.'

'Ain't gonna be a walk in the park. I'm pretty good in the States, but over here's like walkin' around with my hands tied behind my back.'

'Do whatever you can, and do it quickly.'

'All right, Columbus. Where you want me to be?'

I say it without thinking. 'Rome. Piazza Navona. One week.'

He looks at me long and hard, but I keep my face unreadable. If he knows I have a girl there, he's keeping the information to himself.

Finally, he nods. 'I'll be there.'

When I approach my motorcycle, Ruby is waiting for me. 'I haven't left yet.'

'I noticed.'

She looks like she has something she wants to get off her chest. She rubs her fingers over her knuckles, then takes a long breath.

'I got about twenty minutes before I head to Florence. Listen, I just thought I'd—'

'You don't have to say anything.'

'I do, though. I do. So let me do this.' She looks down at her feet and toes the pavement rubble. There's no hint of pretense in her voice, only earnestness. 'It's that . . . when you told me before that you were thinking about getting out of the game, I know you meant it.'

'Nahhh. Like I said, I was just yammering. Forget I brought it up.'

'No, you weren't. You saw something in me that told you it was okay to drop all the barricades we build around ourselves. You showed me your real face.'

'Maybe. I don't know . . .'

'It's why I trusted you enough to tell you about me, my first time. I like the bond we share, Columbus. It's a hell of a lonely job.'

I nod, knowing she has more.

'So, who is she?'

My throat starts to constrict and I cough into my fist, just . . . what? Attempting to hide from the truth? Am I that conspicuous? That easy to read?

'What d'you mean?'

'There's a girl out there who has you thinking of ditching this life, checking out of this world.'

Something inside me that I thought was further from the surface rears its head.'Yeah, there's someone . . .'

'Well, then, here's what I'm trying to say, so I'll just say it. This girl wherever she is, whoever she is . . .'

'I know. I know. You don't have to tell me. I need to . . .'

'You need to go to her and leave this game and never look back.'

I guess surprise registers on my face, because Ruby pounces on it like a cat.

'I told you I read your file. I've read a lot of files on a lot of hired killers. And the one thing they all have in common is that they have nothing and nobody and no reason to leave this gig. Every one of them is alone. They're all like condemned prisoners waiting for the executioner to lead them to the noose. I'm included in that. I thought that made me better, somehow above it, like I was a wolf standing on a mountain looking down at the sheep. But you know what I finally figured out? The people, the civilians . . . they're the ones with the power. They're living, man. Really living. We're just the ghosts they pass in the street.'

Her voice is filled with emotion, raw and electric, like a lightning storm.

'So you go to her, Columbus. You got a chance to shake off these chains and live. If you don't take it, you're a fool.'

It takes a moment for me to realize she's finished. My ears ring, her words chasing away the fog. The fear I pinpointed in her is equally rooted in me, but only now do I realize the depth of it. It's not a fear of dying anonymously, of dying painfully. The fear is that I'll die without having lived. Without really having lived.

When I speak, it's little more than a whisper.

'And if the life catches up to me? Or her?'

'Outrun it, Columbus. Make 'em think you're already dead.'

For the first time, maybe for the first *real* time, I can see it. Not a mirage, not a vaporizing dream, but a tangible, reachable image. I can take a cue from Coulfret, get our names on a list of dead travelers and disappear. Vanish to a place in the country, a place away from the trappings of the professional life. A place devoid of contracts and violence and death.

And why did Ruby tell me this? Does she see a strength in me she doesn't possess herself? Does she want to walk away but can't get her feet to move? Or is it because she hasn't found someone to walk away with?

'You got a suitcase somewhere you need for your flight?'

'Nah. Archie takes care of all that.'

'Then hop on. I'll give you a ride to the Florence airport.'

'I got a car coming . . . should be here any minute.'

'We'll cancel it.'

'Is this your way of kissing off my advice?'

'It's my way of saying thank you.'

She half-grins and rolls her eyes. Maybe she believes me and maybe she doesn't.

I step off the bike to fetch her the spare helmet I keep underneath the seat when a bullet whizzes by my head and hits Ruby square in the face. Her forehead caves and her body falls like the earth reached up and yanked her down.

For a split second I think I should just stay here, just let it happen, let Svoboda take me out too. I could step off the plank, walk into the quicksand, let *this* be my escape. Not fake my death . . . hell, make it real, make it count.

And just as quickly, instinct kicks in and I am diving and wheeling in the direction the bullet came and another shot rips the ground next to my head and I scramble away from where Ruby fell, keeping low, another shot explodes closer and I slither my way to the relative safety of a bus bench.

I can't stay here, though, stay in one place. I have to keep moving, fend him off before he gains position on me. I take a quick peek but can't find anything to target, and if he's expecting me to break for my motorcycle or try to help Ruby, then he should have shot her somewhere besides the bridge of her nose. She's beyond needing help; Ruby was dead before her body touched the ground.

I discharge a full clip, including the bullet I have racked in the chamber, and then break for the alleyway to my left, dropping my clip and re-racking while on a dead sprint.

A fourth bullet ricochets off a stone edifice within an inch of my ear and please don't let this be a dead end and please get me through the next two minutes so I can pay this goddamn bastard back.

I run hunched over, trying to make myself smaller, providing the narrowest possible target, and the alley funnels out to a cobblestone street. I feign left and break right and as soon as I'm clear of the alley, I slam on the brakes and press my back into the wall.

I don't want to think, not now, not about Ruby pleading with me to get out of this life, to escape it in a way she knew she couldn't, and her face disintegrated by a bullet intended for me. Shut it down, block it out, bite it back, and focus.

A half a second to scan the alley and he's there, at the opposite end, a thin man with simian arms and dark features clutching a pair of pistols and I swing out and we squeeze triggers at the same time, two ships steering into each other.

A bullet kicks up gravel behind me, and I see Svoboda whirl around and maybe I clipped him, but I'm not sure. He disappears around the entrance, the way he came in, and if he's playing possum then I'm going to run headlong into his ruse. I sprint up the alley, and there's no sign of blood, and I hear an engine catch and roar, and when I peek around the side, my motorcycle shoots away.

I look down at the rubble. Ruby lies where she fell, a dark halo congealing around her head.

This is how you die. Faceless and, before long, forgotten.

Not any more. Not Ruby. A car is pulling to the curb, a black Audi, the driver Archie had ordered to carry his sister to the Florence airport.

A plump man opens the door and steps out, looks around, wiping sleep from his eyes, and then spies Ruby's body on the pavement.

'My God,' he says in Italian, and the next thing he hears is his car screeching away behind him.

I've been on the wrong end of the hunt for far too long and it's past time to flip the switch. Svoboda's running now, and that means I must have wounded him. Maybe just a nick, but enough to toss him off his plans, and if there's an advantage I can wring out of this sorry mess, then I plan to make the most of it.

I duck my chin and blitz through the gears, redlining the tachometer, as up ahead the motorcycle takes a corner without slowing, Svoboda's knee practically scraping the street. He slingshots out and up at a ninety-degree angle, managing the corner without forfeiting speed. He can handle a bike better than I can, damn him.

I sweep into the same turn, throwing up the parking brake as I downshift and slide out. The Audi drifts into the turn and careens off a parked Smart Car before straightening again. I'm on his tail, but he's got six blocks on me and I'm not sure if the Audi's got the engine to catch a motorcycle.

Svoboda doesn't give me the chance.

He swings the bike around like it's on a turntable, points it in my direction and throttles the engine. Before I'm sure what's happening, an avalanche of bullets peppers my windshield, shattering the glass. I only have a half second to duck as this madman, this medieval fucking jouster, unloads an entire clip into my interior. The seat behind me explodes like a hand-grenade went off, and I jerk the wheel involuntarily as I bury my head in the floorboard.

The car lurches to the left like a horse stumbling out of the gate and smashes into God knows what and whatever advantage I had is gone. I hear the motorcycle's engine buzzing past somewhere out on the street, or maybe that's just my ears ringing.

He's better than me. This realization bangs around inside my head like a bullet. *This son-of-a-bitch is actually better at this than I am. He turned the tables on me before I knew what was coming, went from defense to offense in the blink of an eye, rope-a-doped me like a three-dollar stooge on amateur night at the county fair.*

I have to make a move now or it's over, and, goddammit, I will not let it be over. Not hiding in the floorboard of a fucking car in Siena while he drops the bike, walks up, and shoots me through the empty windshield. Not while Ruby lies dead in the street. My engine is still running; I can hear the Audi's purr even as my ears try to pick up the sound of approaching footsteps.

Without poking my head up, I throw the car into reverse and slam the palm of my hand on top of the accelerator, pushing it down flat. The car responds, lurching backward and just when it gets up to speed, it slams into something else and I knock my shoulder into the dashboard, but if there's ever going to be a time for a peek, this is it. I pop my head up like a gopher coming out of its hole, and quickly look left and right.

Gunfire flashes in front of me, forty yards down the street, but the bullets whiz harmlessly over my head, and I see my backward maneuver surprised him. He has to change out his clip and now it's my turn to grab momentum.

I throw the car into drive, spin the wheel, and race at him while he's reloading. Even while I close the distance, he sits on his bike, *my* bike, in the middle of the road like a goddam matador. Fuck, I thought I was calm under duress but this guy sure as hell doesn't rattle.

I realize my car isn't going to get to him before he has his ammunition locked in place and clearly he's thinking the same thing . . . I'm delivering myself right to him.

At the last possible moment, I open the driver's door and dive out, abandoning the car to complete the mission for me. I hit the pavement hard and roll up onto a knee.

The motorcycle is roaring away, out in front of the car, easily evading it as the Audi starts to lose momentum and slowly comes to a stop without actually crashing into anything, weak and ineffectual. I stay on the sidewalk a long time, but he never comes back.

16

The end is rarely final. It is ingrained in us from birth: the end of a day leads to tomorrow; the end of winter leads to spring; the end of a year begets a newborn, pale and innocent and vulnerable. The notion permeates our literature and culture: the end of a phoenix gives way to a new bird; the end of a king signals the coronation of his offspring; the end of a savior leads to a miraculous resurrection.

It is this singular idea, perhaps more than any other, that there *are* no endings, that there is *always* another sun coming up, another day dawning, a life beyond this life that keeps the machinery of the earth turning. The peasants toil in the fields, the workers grind for their paychecks, the soldiers sacrifice in battle in the hope that the end is rarely final, that they will have given of themselves so that others will continue on in a somehow changed world.

And what if the end *is* just the end? What if once you're caught on the hook and pulled into the boat, and you flop around on the deck before breathing your last breath, what if the world never knew you existed, what if you did nothing to benefit this place, what if it is just the same as it was before you came? What if the end is rarely the end, but it is for you and you're the one erased?

Or what if when you close your eyes, when your heart stops and your neurons quit firing, what if in that moment, the world simply ceases to be?

The sun sits high in the cloudless sky, alone, imperious. The heat is oppressive, like it's coming both down from the sky and up from the street. Pedestrians move around languidly, like there are weights tied to their ankles. Ladies fan themselves with magazines in a futile attempt to push air away from them, but the heat clings like ticks. Dogs lie in the meager shade of shop doorways, tongues out, panting. It is a hell of a May day in Rome.

Five of them have passed since Ruby died in Siena, and Italian police are looking for two men fleeing the scene, one on a motorcycle and one in a stolen black Audi. Details are sketchy; no one got a good look at the killers so early in the morning.

I spent the last five days on the coast, sitting in a hotel room, staring at the gray ocean, clearing my mind. I'm pissed about the motorcycle; that bike had treated me well. The only treasure of mine Svoboda can puzzle over is a first-edition copy of *The Compleat Angler,* which I'm sure he'll find in my saddlebag. Maybe he's flipping through it now. I purchased another copy, a paperback edition, from an English-language bookstore named Feltrinelli in Florence before I fled for the coast. In the five days prior to arriving in Rome, I read the book through twice.

Archibald waits at a tiny table, eyes covered by dark glasses, dressed in black. His expression is as sober and grave as a funeral director's. The first thing I notice is how gaunt his face looks when his smile is gone. When I take my seat across from him, his fingers stop drumming the table.

'I'm sorry,' I tell him.

'When I told you before I didn't have any uncles or aunts or relatives I gave a fuck about, I was lying.'

'I know.'

'She was there—' he stops, like he's having a hard time getting his mouth around the words. He steadies himself, then takes another stab. 'She was there every moment I needed her, every inch of the way.'

'I know.'

'Was he gunning for her, or did she catch one intended for you?'

'I have no idea.'

'Why didn't she leave when I told her she was off? Why'd she stick around?'

'She wanted to tell me something.'

He levels his eyes in my direction. They spill over with pain. 'What?'

'She told me I should quit the business. Disappear.'

'Now why the fuck would she tell you that?'

'She knew I have a woman waiting for me.'

He takes that in, and, like when he let me in on the secret that he had a sister, he knows I didn't release that information lightly.

'Tied on that same string, Columbus.'

'Yeah.'

It is true. There is no use denying it. Archibald Grant and I will forever be tied on that same string. A man who goes by Svoboda made sure of that on a quiet street in Siena.

Archibald slides a file to me underneath the table. I place it in my lap and the same weight hits me, the same heaviness I felt when William Ryan handed me a similar file with Jiri Dolezal's name at the top of the page. When will it be too much? When will the stack of rocks on my chest finally overcome me?

'I haven't slept in five days,' Archibald says. 'Save a nod here or a wink there. Everything I got, I put into that file.'

'Okay.'

'I visited Doriot in a Belgian prison. He turned me on to three other European fences. I've been to Madrid, Prague, and Munich. I got tongues to loosen and I got memories to be recalled. Every bit of knowledge about Svoboda is found in those pages. The only one who knows more about him is the Lord Almighty.'

'You know this makes you a target as well. He'll find out you've been sniffing around his background.'

'Let him come.'

I nod. 'Well, thank you. You did well.'

Archibald stands like he's going to leave, then drops his hands in his pockets. He suddenly looks old, like twenty years have passed since I saw him in that subterranean restaurant in Siena.

'Drop him, Columbus. Drop him and then get the hell out like Ruby said. I'll make sure no one comes for you.'

For a moment, he stands there, a ghost, like these words sucked out the last bit of his energy, like it's not me who has been crushed by the stones, but him. Then he turns and disappears into the crowd.

I open the file. Tomas Petr Kolar grew up an only child in eastern Czechoslovakia, in a village named Krasnik, long before the country split into two. His father, Petr, was an avid hunter when he wasn't serving the party in the factories, assembling railroad machine parts to be shipped to Poland. By the age of four, Petr had taught his son how to take apart and reassemble a VZ-24 rifle. Together, they shot wild hares and pheasants and roe deer and the occasional mouflon in the hills surrounding their village.

Kolar's mother was diagnosed with lung cancer when he was eight years old. He and his father watched her wither away until her face looked like a tight sheet stretched across a skull. She died fourteen weeks after her diagnosis, in a hospital bed, mumbling gibberish.

For two weeks, his father ignored him. For two weeks, he made his own bed, fixed his own dinner, bathed himself, and cleaned the house while his father sat in a chair staring out the window.

At the end of those fourteen days, his father shot himself in the head with the VZ-24 rifle. The man was thirty-eight years old. There is no indication Kolar was there when his old man placed the gun between his knees and pulled the trigger. But no one can say for sure.

There is a large gap of knowledge in the file from that point. No one knows where Kolar was taken after his father's suicide, where he was raised, where he received his education, who trained him in the art of assassination, when he changed his name to Svoboda. Archibald speculates he was in the military, but wasn't able to confirm it. However, Svoboda's early work involved the use of a CZ-2000 short assault rifle, a rarity left over from the Czech army's special forces missions behind NATO lines in the late nineties. He also carried a CZ-100 handgun, another weapon first introduced to the Czech army in 1995. It's convincing evidence the boy was scooped up in the military machine soon after his father's suicide. Maybe he bunked with another soldier named Svoboda and assumed his identity after the man fell in battle? Any guesses would just be speculation, but I'll pocket the name Tomas Kolar. Knowing it could very well come in handy.

The first true knowledge of Svoboda's whereabouts as an adult came in March 1999. He completed two contract killings that month, five days apart. One in Prague, one in Amsterdam. The assignments were distributed by two different fences. Two completely unique, unrelated targets.

This information is staggering. Two jobs within five days? Putting aside the psychological ramifications, this act teeters on recklessness, if not outright insanity. How could he plan his hit, or, even more importantly, his escape? How could he be sure he'd get to his target and get away with the kill?

I flip through the file just counting up the hits Archibald was able to uncover. From the three fences plus Doriot, Svoboda has averaged fourteen kills a year for the last half-dozen years. Fourteen! More than one a month. And that's just the ones Archibald found out about.

I flip further and focus in on one kill Archibald coaxed out of the Spanish fence. The assignment was to eliminate another professional contract killer, a British hit man named Ogle. The two came together in a hotel corridor in Carlisle, in northern England. For some reason, both men lost their guns and ended up fighting hand to hand. Svoboda gained leverage and bit into the larger man's neck, severing his carotid artery and ripping it out with his teeth. All while hanging on to his back like a lion taking down an elephant.

I flip through dozens of hits for which Archibald was able to carve out a few details, and an interesting story emerges. At least ten of his kills involve contracts on other assassins, maybe more. It seems he's developed a niche for himself, a specialty, an area where there appears to be steady work. It seems Svoboda has forged a business out of hunting hunters.

I study these closely, the hits specific to taking down men like me. Nearly all of these kills involve close, contact murder, without weaponry. Strangulation, choking, biting, beating, eye-gouging, cracking necks. This must be intentional. He doesn't want to shoot these men from a distance; he wants to destroy them with his hands. If I can figure out why, maybe I can crack the code on how to defeat him.

Another one of his kills leaps out at me. In 2006, he was hired to eliminate a French hit man named Garrigus. The hit took place at an apartment in Toulouse, a hideaway belonging to the French assassin's mistress. When the two bodies were discovered, the police made note that the girl was most likely killed first, by a bullet wound to the back of the head, before Garrigus drowned to death in the apartment's bathtub, his hands restrained behind him with plastic ties.

In one other instance, Svoboda killed a woman along with the mark. Again, she was killed first, by gunshot, and then he disposed of the target with his hands, choking the man to death behind a pub in London. That's all the information Archibald collected on the kill, but it speaks volumes.

Svoboda is more than a professional hit man. He may be very good at what he does, he may be a top earner, he may never default on a job, but he is no Silver Bear. He's a goddamn serial killer. He doesn't care about the contracts, the hunt, the getaway, the strategy, the creation of a connection that can be severed. He gets off on the actual killing.

Svoboda and I are nothing alike. We may have the same job, but we perform it in two different worlds. I thought he was better at this business than me, but now I know that simply isn't true. He might have skills and courage, but the skills are reckless and the courage is fueled by some sort of tortured madness. He can be beaten. I'm sure of it.

I devour the file, reading it and re-reading it until I have every page memorized. Archibald has outdone himself again. The file is as thorough as any I've been given. And all the information leads to one conclusion: Tomas Petr Kolar, also known as Svoboda, wants to work in close so he can kill me with his bare hands.

I think I'll let him try.

I know the question before it is asked. Why would I go see her? Why am I so heartless, so depraved, so selfish, that I would put her in harm's way, at this moment, when a killer who lusts for blood is hunting me, has already killed in front of me? A killer who I know likes to rack up as many bodies as possible, who actually thrives on leaving a mess?

She is in the middle of a sale when I enter Zodelli on the Via Poli. Risina's face lights up as soon as she spots me, her cheeks flushing with blood. If it's possible, she's grown even more radiant since I last saw her, like the recent sunny days have knocked out the underlying sadness and brought her beauty right to the surface.

I take a seat in a stuffed leather chair and watch her work.

'. . . a five-volume first edition we will only sell as a set. It contains 367 hand-colored folio lithographs, all produced by Joseph Wolf, who was the leading ornithological artist at the time. You see? Gould personally selected him. Beautiful.'

The man she is speaking with is the size of a bear and has a thick Russian accent. 'Remind me about the binding?'

'Of course. Contemporary full green levant morocco, with elaborate decorated spines . . . yes? Marvelous. They contain raised bands, marbled endpapers, and as you can see, all the edges are gilt.'

'The price is still one-fifty euro?'

'Yes, Mr. Bembatov.'

'Hmmph. Thank you.'

He turns, measures me for a moment, then shuffles toward the door like one of those old weeble-wobbles, like his weight needs to list side to side before it can move forward.

The bell above the door is still jingling when she crosses the room and is in my lap, in my arms.

'One-fifty?' I say, eyebrows raised.

'Thousand. It is one of the finest book sets we own. This is the fourth time Mr. Bembatov has been in to look at the complete set. He asks the same questions each time. But I'm beginning to think he's a fish who won't bite.'

'Oh, then I'll buy the set first. Would you like a credit card or . . . ?'

She slaps my chest playfully, then kisses my neck, my cheek, my head, my lips. Finally, she rests her forehead against mine.

'I don't like this, Jack. Not at all. I don't like it when you're away and I can't talk to you. I envision the worst. And if something were to happen to you, I would never know. No one would come tell me.'

'I won't put you through this much longer.'

'That sounds ominous.'

'I didn't mean it to be. I told you I was looking to make a change.'

She untangles herself from me and stands, a smile on her face. 'I choose to still believe you. I do think you mean it.'

'I do. I mean it.'

Her face abruptly changes, like she just remembered something disheartening.

'I have some disappointing news. I'm sorry, I just thought of it . . .'

'Oh?'

'I consulted all over regarding your story, the one of the boy in the silver wagon. I even contacted three people in the United States who specialize in children's literature. But no one has knowledge of this book.'

I nod, and for some inexplicable reason, this saddens me. I guess it shows on my face.

'I'm sorry. I don't know who else to contact . . .'

'Forget it. Like I said, I'm not sure where I read it. For all I know, someone may have made it up and told it to me as a child. I spent some time in some rough places. Maybe somebody told me the story as a form of escape. I don't know why, but it stuck with me.'

'If you had the author's name or knew one of the character's names . . .'

'I wish I did. I just . . . don't.'

She looks chagrined.

'Honestly, don't worry about it.'

She nods, and then her face brightens, like she's glad the bad news is out of the way. 'How long will you be in Rome?'

'For a while. Let's have dinner tonight.'

'Yes! Where should we go?'

'Do you know a place that is quiet, dark? A place where no tourists go?'

'Yes, a block from my building. A restaurant with four tables. It is called Dar Filettaro a Santa Barbara. Should I write that down?'

I laugh. 'No, I can remember it.'

'I'm off work at six. Please tell me you'll be there at six fifteen.'

'I'll be there at six fifteen.'

'I missed you, Jack.'

'I missed you too, Risina. More than you realize.'

He can be beaten, I tell myself on the way out the door. *I'm sure of it.*

She is dressed in a soft green gown, the color of mint leaves, and her hair is up, tied in the back, so her shoulders are exposed. I notice a freckle there I hadn't noticed before, and I think *there is still so much to discover*.

'You must order the fried baccala. It is their specialty. The best in Italy.'

'I will. Thank you for the recommendation.'

I have my back to the wall in the corner, and a glance over Risina's shoulder gives me an unobstructed view of the door. We are the only ones in the restaurant at this hour.

She leans forward, a glass of wine in her hand flirting with the candlelight.

'You told me that when you returned, Jack, you'd tell me your story. You'd tell me everything.'

'I plan to.'

'I won't force it out of you.'

'I will tell you. But not yet. I need a few days to arrange some things. Then I promise I'll lay everything out for you.'

'Ahhh . . .'

'You should know . . . my story . . . it's not pretty. It's not tidy.'

'The best stories are rarely symmetrical.'

'I'm not sure you'll like it.'

'I wish you wouldn't make a judgment as to what I will or won't like.'

'Fair enough. Let's just say I'm not sure my story has a happy ending.'

She grimaces and, for a moment, doesn't reply. I have a feeling there have been very few happy endings for Risina. 'Does this mean you'll be leaving Rome again?'

My eyes don't leave her face, but she senses my hesitation. She leans back, takes a sip of the wine.

'Never mind. It doesn't matter. Let's enjoy your time here.'

'Risina . . .'

'I told you I would not judge you, Jack. I won't.'

The waiter emerges from the kitchen and takes our order and Risina looks down at the table. If she is biting back emotion, she won't show it to me.

He can be beaten, I think again. *I know I can beat him.*

'The arrangements I have to make . . . are for both of us.'

'What do you mean?'

'This is going to come across . . . truth is, I don't know how this is going to come across.' I stop, chewing over what I want to say before plowing forward. 'What I do . . . I was serious when I said I don't want to do it any more. I want to escape it. I want to get out and never look back.

'My father . . . I know this is coming out of left field . . . but my father thought there was only one way out for him. I'm sure it seemed like an easy way out, but it never is. For a long time, I believed that route was the way for me too. But since I met you, Risina . . . since I met you, my thinking changed. I want to escape and live. I *choose* to escape. But I don't want to do it alone. I want to escape with you.'

Before she can respond, I press on, locking my eyes on hers. 'I have money, enough money so neither of us would ever have to work again. We can live on a beach somewhere. Or the woods if you prefer it. Or a farm. Or a hut in Africa for all I care. I know it's not fair to ask, I know you barely know me, but I know this is right. Maybe for the first time in my life, I know what is right.'

She hesitates, making sure I am finished, and in that moment's hesitation, I think I've lost. I played my cards, my best hand, and I came up short. But then she utters one word packed with hope.

'When?'

'As soon as possible.'

'And where would we go?'

'Wherever you want, as long as it's away. Away from congestion and traffic and people.'

'And I would leave everything behind? Say no goodbyes?'

'Yes.'

'And we would be together?'

'Yes.'

She looks up and her eyes shine, though no moisture spills out from the lids, no tears fall down her cheeks.

'Okay.'

'Okay?'

'Yes. Okay.' She reaches across the table and takes my hand. Hers is trembling. She is barely breathing.

'If after a week, a month, a year you decide this is no life for you, that I'm not the man you thought I was, I'll never stop you from returning. But I promise to you, Risina, I'll do my best to be the man you want me to be.'

The food arrives, but after nudging it with her fork, she looks up at me. 'Do you mind if we go to my apartment? Forget dinner and we just . . . you just hold me?'

I can beat him. I know I can. I can beat him.

'Let's go.'

For three nights we meet after the bookstore closes, at various small restaurants near her apartment. For three nights, we leave without eating and lie in her bed, holding on to each other as if we are afraid to let go, afraid if we loosen our grip, the other will vanish like smoke. For three nights, we say very little. For three nights, we live, and breathe, and love.

On the fourth night, Svoboda comes.

17

If I were Svoboda, here's how I would get inside. I would scout Columbus before he disappears into that basement restaurant in Siena, and I would watch after he leaves to see who else comes out.

Then I would follow the black girl, the other assassin, out of the building to see where she is headed. I would watch her, excited, as she waits around town instead of leaving. I would instinctively know she wants to meet with my target once more, that she has some unfinished business she wants to get off her chest. I would read it all over her face.

When she makes contact with my mark, I would jump at the chance to shoot her from a distance. My goal is not just to kill my target, because where is the satisfaction, the inherent thrill in that? No, my real aim is to make my target suffer before I end his life. Before I make him look me in the eye while I destroy him with my hands.

I've done it before. I've killed those close to my mark. My contracts are supposed to be for men like me, but these men are nothing. They are weak. The first rule of being an assassin is that a professional hit man cannot afford relationships of any kind. These relationships can and will be exploited. It is the staple of our business: to hit the target where he or she is weakest.

So I have. I followed one to his mistress. I shot the whore first, causing my mark to lose his edge, to give in to anger, to come at me wildly. I used his rage against him, kept him off balance until I was able to force him down, force his hands behind his back, force his wrists into restraints. From there,

I filled his bathtub with water and watched him drown a hundred miles away from any ocean.

So many of these men, these debasers of my profession, I've found to have chinks in their armor, found to have an affinity for the opposite sex. I've taken pleasure in proving to them just how foolish they are, how selfish, how infantile their decisions are to bring women into their lives. These men are not unlike my father, my stupid fool of a father, who couldn't see a life for himself after his own wife passed away. Who stared out a window for two weeks before blowing his head into the wall. How weak he was! How dumb!

How goddamn selfish and stupid and sad.

Imagine my surprise when this target, the one called Columbus, did not hesitate after I shot the black woman. How he immediately abandoned her. How he only cared for himself. I thought he might double back to help the woman, at least hesitate when her head exploded, but I was wrong.

Here, finally, is a formidable opponent. Here, finally, is a man like me, a Silver Bear, a man who puts his profession, his own life, first. I take his motorcycle and ride off with no helmet because I want to feel like him, to become Columbus. I turn and face him in the street like a gladiator, like a warrior, and only when I realize I have no more bullets, my reloaded clip is empty, do I retreat.

If I were Svoboda, in the hold of the motorcycle I would find a curious book, a four-centuries-old text by Izaak Walton titled *The Compleat Angler*. An ancient fucking book about fishing, of all god-damn things. Why this worthy opponent would choose this book, why he would leave an object like this behind, would be beyond me.

And then my fingers would alight on something maybe the owner didn't realize was there. Maybe the person from whom Columbus bought the rare book had tucked it in there without his knowledge, or maybe he had used it as a bookmark and forgotten about it. For inside the book, tucked between the last page and the cover, is a business card. It reads: Zodelli Rare Books, with an address on the Via Poli in Rome. And a name is printed underneath the embossed logo for the store: Risina Lorenzana, Chief Acquisitions Agent.

If I were Svoboda, I would flip the card over on the back and read Risina's home phone number, printed in black ink with a steady feminine hand.

If I were Svoboda, I would steer the motorcycle toward Rome. I would find this bookstore, locate this Risina Lorenzana, and wait.

I am sure Svoboda was disappointed to find that I, after all he'd heard and witnessed, was like so many of the others he had killed. That I had a relationship with a woman. That the black woman he shot in Siena was only an unfortunate associate while the real prize waited in Rome.

At the same time, I'm sure he was thrilled to have another chance to wound me, to make me suffer before he got his hands around my throat.

He must've been watching. Either that first night, or the second, or the third, he watched us meet at a public restaurant, and he watched us leave without eating, and he watched us walk the short distance to Risina's apartment. He marked the building and the window that lit up on the second floor shortly after we entered.

On the fourth night, he must've slipped inside her building and waited for us to come home.

I hold Risina's hand, her fingers locked in mine. We're feeling more comfortable now, like the idea has settled in and we're actually going to do this, going to just leave and not tell anyone where we're headed.

We've decided on a tropical location in a country where few people speak English. It's remote, but not so isolated it doesn't have Internet service, doesn't have a way for Risina to receive Italian language books. I think her trepidation has given way to excitement, that what four days ago seemed so foreign now seems attainable.

We enter her building and head inside the elevator. It is barely large enough to fit both of us, and she leans into me as it rises, her back to my front. Her hair is right under my nose and it smells like cedar.

There have been no warning signs, no bad omens. I haven't lost my wallet or had coffee spilled in my lap or bumped my shin into a bench. We ate dinner without incident and talked warmly throughout the meal. And now we stand in the elevator, fitting together perfectly, two halves of the same circle, like we've done this all our lives.

She opens her apartment door, scoops up the mail, and moves to her sofa, taking a seat on one end, tucking her feet underneath her as she starts to sort through the envelopes.

'I need to use the bathroom,' I say and head through a small door just off the main room.

There are three things I'm sure Svoboda doesn't know. One, I'm sure he doesn't know that I've marked the doors and windows with tape, similar to the way I marked my crawl space in Positano. If an outsider entered the apartment, I'd be able to tell in the first three seconds I'm in the room with just a casual sweep of my eyes.

Two, I'm sure he doesn't know that the bathroom I am moving toward has a second door, one that leads back around through the bedroom and enters the living room from the opposite side.

And three, I'm sure he didn't read *The Compleat Angler* carefully, if at all. Otherwise, he might have come across a passage in the fifth chapter. A passage I read over and over. A passage I memorized. It reads: 'for you are to know that a dead worm is but a dead bait, and like to catch nothing, compared to a lively, quick stirring worm.'

Risina looks up to see Svoboda coming at her with his gun out, his finger on the trigger. He has his free hand with his index finger covering his lips, signaling not to make a sound.

On his face is a grim satisfaction, the look of a fisherman who first feels a tug on his line.

'Tomas Kolar!' I scream from his left, where he's not expecting me, and he stutters for just a moment, the surprise of that name and the surprise that I know it and the surprise of where I'm coming from all combine to provide a half second's hesitation. He pulls the trigger, just as I launch at him, and the shot goes off wildly, plugging into the opposite side of the sofa from where Risina is perched.

Now she does scream as I take him down to the floor and pound his gun hand into the wood, once, twice, and he gives it up, letting it go while swinging his elbow around in an attempt to shift the leverage.

I should've shot this fucker when I rounded the corner and saw him with his gun hand out and up but I couldn't be sure I'd force him to miss unless I took out his arm with my bare hands.

He wallops me in the cheek with that loose elbow, and this is the fighting in which Archibald's report said he excels, close-contact grappling, and again he smashes me in the ribs. Before I can get my hands around him, he sees an opening and flips me over onto my back and in seconds, I can feel his teeth breaking through the skin of my neck. He's a street fighter, a dirty fucking lunatic, and everything is fair game.

The smell of blood fills my nose, and I just have a second to think *my blood, goddammit,* and I'm going to have to do something drastic and do it quickly. I use all of my strength to buck up like a Brahma bull, flipping my entire body over and my defensive move does the trick, his teeth come off my neck and he slides across the wood toward the door, toward his gun.

Just as he reaches for it, Risina's boot kicks out, sending the pistol flying toward the bathroom, and both Svoboda and my eyes track it all the way till it comes to a stop equidistant from both of us. Our eyes lock once more and I can see him make the calculations instantly . . . can he get to the gun before I do?

Risina jumps away, pushing her back against the wall like she's trying to disappear through it. She holds her breath, watching, waiting.

Svoboda's expression turns to fire as he decides against going for the gun. Instead, he springs around and throws open the front door, fleeing, just like he did when his bullets ran out.

Without thinking, without looking at Risina, I leap after him, bursting into the hallway like a missile and I close the gap between us in what seems like seconds. There won't be a chance to regroup, a chance to play this tragic drama out on another stage. This ends here, tonight, and so help me God, it only ends one way.

He jumps inside the open elevator a half step before I do and turns to receive me and I plow into him with the full force of my weight, lowering my shoulder like a ram and hitting him square in the chest.

His back smashes into the wall of the car, but he absorbs the blow and tries to get his fingers into my eyes as we lock together in the three feet of space.

I shake my eyes free and am able to ball my fist and throw a blow directly into his stomach with everything I have. The air rushes out of his lungs and in that instant, I have him. My hands immediately clamp on to his throat like a vise, and no matter how much he thrashes, and how wildly he kicks, and how desperately he paws, I do not loosen my Beowulfian grip.

I can feel the elevator car descending as Svoboda continues to claw at my fingers, trying desperately to pry them off his throat. Maybe we bumped into the button during the initial impact or maybe someone below is waiting on the car, but my concentration on the task at hand doesn't flag. I am not going to let go and he knows it.

It won't take long now. I wonder what his final thoughts are as I watch his eyes begin to roll backward. Is he thinking it is fitting he's going to die not by gunshot, but with a man's fingers clasped around his throat? Is he thinking about all the times he's been on the other end of this situation, that he's been the one to kill a rival assassin with his bare hands? Is he thinking about where he must have gone wrong? Is he thinking about Risina, about how I used her as living bait?

If I were Svoboda, I know what I'd be thinking. I'd be thinking I shouldn't have taken this job.

Risina's face is as white as a gravestone when I enter her apartment. I was going to tell her everything. Maybe I should have done it sooner. Maybe it would have made a difference.

She crosses the room and has her arms around me and her face buried in my chest before I can react, squeezing with all her strength. I hold her as tightly as I can, losing myself in it, my mind blank.

When she finally loosens her grip and leans back, her face has regained its color. Her voice is strong, though there is a slight quiver in it.

'Is he . . . ?'

'Yes.'

She nods. 'I think we should leave now.'

'Are you sure?'

'I'm sure.'

Outside her apartment, Rome is at once both quiet and alive. We walk up the sidewalk in the general direction of the train station, my arm around her waist, leaving the body, leaving that life behind.

I wonder how soon Italy will call to Risina after we leave. I wonder if she'll find it difficult not to answer.

EPILOGUE

We've come to look forward to the afternoon showers, when gray clouds gather over the mountain like mischievous schoolchildren before heading down the hill to drop buckets on our heads.

The air cools as the wind picks up, blanketing the village in a thick sheet of mist. Then, just as quickly, the sun emerges as though from a short nap, and chases the clouds out to sea. Shunned, abandoned, they thin out and fade to nothing.

The only outsider I've talked to since coming here is Archibald, once, soon after we arrived. I took a bus to a distant town and purchased a pre paid mobile phone.

'You gone, Columbus?'

'I'm gone.'

'Good. Your tracks are covered. So stay gone.' And he hung up.

I've had a few months since then to tell my story, and I've spooled it out for Risina slowly, afraid too many details about my life would lead to a conflagration, burning down the relationship before it had a chance to build. After the showers, when the beach is at its coolest, we lie in the sand, and she lets me talk. Usually, her knees are up by her chest, her arms wrapped around them, her eyes focused on mine. She nods encouragement when I hesitate, or asks for clarification when I leave out details, or presses me to repeat something if I recount it too quickly. Never once does she flinch, though I can sometimes see grief in her eyes.

I tell her of my mother, and Abe Mann. Of Pooley and Mr. Cox. Of Vespucci and the man who called himself Hap

Blowenfeld. I tell her of two men named Ponts and Gorti, of a bookmaker named Levien, and a girl I once loved named Jake Owens. I tell her of all my assignments, all my jobs, all my fences, from Vespucci to Ponts to William Ryan to Archibald Grant. I tell her of Anton Noel, of Leary, of Llanos, of Svoboda. Finally, I tell her of Ruby.

She asks me about the end, the incident in her apartment. I explain to her about getting inside my target's head, about trying to see the world as he sees it. That I have used this technique throughout my killing career as a psychological mechanism, that once I am inside my target's head, connected to him, then I can sever the connection and continue to do what I do. I tell her how I applied that to Svoboda, that by being his target, he became mine.

When I discovered that Svoboda on several occasions killed the girlfriend, mistress, lover, or wife of his targets, I knew the best play was to use Risina as bait. To settle into a routine, meeting her after work each night, going to dinner in a conspicuous restaurant, retiring to her apartment, until Svoboda picked up on the pattern and attempted to exploit it. From Archibald's file, I knew I was better than him. That I could beat him. I *knew* it.

When he stole the motorcycle and had the book, I knew it wouldn't take long for him to find her. I couldn't leave until he did. If we ran, he would follow. So while he stalked, I planned the trap. Dangled the living bait, let it wiggle in front of him, and then pulled the line when he struck.

Risina takes this information the same way she's taken everything I've told her: as stoically as Epictetus. I don't know if I was expecting her to get angry, abusive, maybe to slap me for admitting I used her as bait, but she does none of these. Instead, she closes the distance between us and presses her lips to mine. When night comes, we cross the beach to our home and go to bed without eating. Sometime in the night, I hear the shower going. How long she's been in there, I have no idea.

She appears in the doorway, her hair wet, swept back from her forehead, framing her face. She is naked, and with the moonlight snaking through the window, her body is exposed, vulnerable.

'I know your name isn't Columbus,' she says softly, swallowing, gathering her strength. 'And I know it isn't Jack Walker. You didn't know me when you met me, and I realize now you would have never given me your name. I understand . . . I realize I don't know your name, your real name.'

She folds her arms across her body. Her eyes never lower, never leave my face.

'So what I want to know . . . what I have to know . . . what is your name?'

And I tell her.

DARK MEN

Derek Haas

For Bruno, who premiered.
And for Augie, the sequel.

I

Would you listen to a story told by a dying man? Would you listen to me tell it in the present, like it is happening now? It seems I've been telling my story and living my story for so long, the two have mixed, and I'm no longer sure which is accurate, which informs the other: the story or the life. I try to tell it the way it happened, as it is happening, but how close am I to the truth?

I'll do my best to finish, to give you closure. You've been with me this long; I owe you that. But at some point, forgive me if my story suddenly ends.

In Fresno, California, in 2007, a tiger mauled a woman. The tiger was six years old and had arrived in the United States as a pet purchased by Lori Nagel through dubious channels in the Far East. Her friends told investigators the tiger was quite docile toward Lori, even affectionate, right up to the moment its five-inch dew claw severed an artery in Lori's left leg. She survived, but her leg didn't. She insisted the unfortunate incident was her fault; it was her carelessness, her inattentiveness that was the cause. Nevertheless, at the behest of animal control, a veterinarian euthanized the beast a few weeks after the incident.

The tiger's only crime was being a goddamn tiger.

A little over two years has passed since Risina Lorenzana and I moved to the little village on the sea. I am still here. It is the longest I have lived in one place, and I have almost stopped looking over my shoulder. Instincts die hard, however, and for most of my life, I've survived by keeping my guard up, my defenses engaged. I spent my youth incarcerated in a juvenile detention center named Waxham outside of Boston, Massachusetts; my adult life I spent as a contract killer, and a damned good one at that. I was what the Russians call a Silver Bear, a hit man who never defaults on a job, who takes any assignment no matter how difficult, and who commands top fees for his work. As such, I survived this professional life by honing my peripheral vision. I killed, I escaped, and when hunters came for me, I put them down.

Risina changed everything. She gave me a glimpse of what my life could be without a Glock in my hand, and when the opportunity arose to break free, I leapt at it.

She's the only one who knows my complete story, the only one alive who knows my true name.

I crack an egg, and the yolk spills out whole into a white bowl. A little salt, a little milk, a quick stir with a fork, and I pour the contents on to a pan set on low heat. Risina walks out of the bedroom, yawning, tying her black hair up so I can see all of her neck. When she puts her hands up, her pajama top pulls away from the bottoms, exposing her stomach, and something in me stirs. It's been over two years, and something in me always stirs.

'You've finally given up on my cooking.' Her Italian accent has softened, but only a bit, like the hint of spice in a pot of strong coffee. She pours herself some juice and plops down in a mismatched sofa chair we bought off a yard in a neighboring town.

'I'm just giving you a breather.'

'Ha. You can tell me the truth.'

'I'd rather not.'

She laughs. 'I'm terrible, I know. But I'm getting better.'

Risina has forged a relationship with a fisherman's wife, Kaimi, one of the few village natives to venture to our house after we settled. Kaimi's a plump woman, with a broad forehead and a broad smile. She's been teaching Risina the basics of cooking – how to season the meat before grilling it, how to add spices to the pot before boiling the water – but it's a bit like teaching music to a deaf man. Risina can get the mechanics right, but for some reason, the end result is as flavorless as cardboard.

Still, she continues to try, undaunted. Her inability to get frustrated fascinates me. Maybe it's an indigenous side effect to this place, where the rhythm of the day is always a few beats slower, a few notes softer. Or maybe it's just Risina, whose beauty has grown even more pronounced since we arrived. Something unnamed has relaxed inside her, and her inner calm now wafts off her in waves. She always had an underlying sadness just below the surface on her face, in her eyes, but it seems to have diminished like her accent. The sun has brought out the gold in her skin, and the simple dresses and the longer way she wears her hair combine to make her look even more radiant and alive.

I look decent. I've kept in shape by running on the beach and swimming in the water. My body's not as hard as it was, but I'm far from sluggish.

Kaimi's husband Ariki heads to his boat six days a week. He leaves his home before the sun rises, and walks into the town center before descending the cobblestone path to the bamboo huts that dot the dock. Here he cuts bait until 5:45, and then he pilots his long boat out to deeper water, alone, waiting for the sun to arrive and the fish to start biting.

I followed him from the shadows for five days once. I tracked him carefully, noting points that held the highest probability of success. I could kill him shortly after he leaves his house, drag his body to the jungle and have him buried before anyone else awakens. I could lie in wait at one of his favorite fishing spots, have him come to me, then shoot him and weigh his body down so it never floats to the surface. I could wait until Kaimi leaves to do her laundry and waylay him in his own shower after a long day on the water, when the man is at his most vulnerable.

I have no intention of killing Ariki, ever. But I'm keeping in shape in other ways, too.

Once every three months, I head to the only city of any size on this side of the country. I amass several things we're lacking: clothes, batteries, light bulbs and other assorted knick-knacks. But the true purpose of these trips is to stock up on the one necessity Risina can't do without: books. She's given up so much of her life to escape with me. Literature is like a lifeline for her, a connection with everything she left behind. When I met her, she was acquiring rare books for a small shop named Zodelli on the Via Poli in Rome, and the job was more than an occupation to her; it was a passion, a necessity, a fix. Something I understand well. Her dark eyes dance whenever I return with a few dozen hard covers, half written in her native Italian, half written in English. She makes a list of ten authors she wants me to find before I set out – Goethe and Poe and Dickens and Twain and Moravia – and leaves the rest of the purchases to my discretion. It takes me hours to make my selections, ranging from contemporary authors like Wolfe and Mailer and King, to my favorite writer, Steinbeck. I get no greater pleasure than opening the boxes for Risina when I return and then watch the color rise in her cheeks. In minutes, she is curled in a chair, her feet tucked under her, absorbed in the fresh pages.

I am near the front of the bookstore, a half-dozen classics in my hand, when I first notice a man marking me. He's a black guy with a wide face and a freshly purchased linen shirt. I can still make out the starched fold lines, since the shirt hasn't been washed.

The city attracts its share of tourists, but this man is no vacationer. I can see it in his hard eyes and the stiff way he holds his shoulders. He's watching me, only me, in the glass across the street, I'm sure of it. If he's trying to be stealthy, he's not very practiced at it.

My heartbeat slowly rises, and I have to admit, it's a welcome feeling, like finding an old jacket in the closet and discovering it still fits. Fuck, this is not right . . . I should be angry, worried, embarrassed I've been discovered, that my hard-fought-for independence has suddenly been compromised without warning. So why am I feeling the complete opposite? Why do I feel elated?

Over a year ago, Risina and I lit out for a remote sanctuary following an assignment in which I killed an innocent bystander along with my target. The unfortunate man had a brother who hired a host of assassins to track me down – to hunt the hunter – and when I killed the brother too and disposed of the final assassin, I thought I was free. I fled that world, persuading the girl I loved to escape with me.

But did I convince myself? Did I really want to escape?

The tiger is still a tiger.

I move out of the cashier's line and head back over to the classics shelf in the rear of the store to see if my movements elicit a response.

Like I thought, he's an amateur; he jerks his head to track my position, as conspicuous as if he'd rung a bell. I pull out my cell phone, pretend to check who is phoning me, then put the phone to my ear and pantomime a conversation while I really snap photos of the man through the window. They may not be perfect shots, but they should be enough.

A clerk stands near the back, sorting new arrivals.

'Bathroom?' I ask in her language and she points me to a short hallway. I quickly pass it and duck out the delivery entrance, slipping into an alley. I hurry to the nearest intersection where the alley meets the driveway and wait.

I don't have a weapon, so I'm going to have to use his.

I hear his hurried footsteps approaching, and I am right, he's an amateur, no doubt about that. If he's been in this line of work, he hasn't been doing it long. He's making as much noise as a fireworks display. In another minute, he won't be making any noise at all.

He swings around the corner in a dead sprint, and it only takes a solid kick to his trailing leg to send him sprawling, limbs akimbo, like a skier tumbling down a mountain. Before he can right himself, I am on him, pinning him to the cement with my knee in the small of his back. A quick sweep of his waist and I have his gun, a cheap chrome pistol I'm sure he bought in the last day or two, after arriving in the country. A second later, it is out and up and pointed at the back of his head.

Before I can pull the trigger, he shouts 'Columbus!'

I roll him over and have the gun under his chin. His eyes in that wide face are wild, feral, like a cornered wolf. No, whatever he is, he's no professional.

'What do you want?' I spit through clenched teeth. I like him scared and I mean to keep him that way.

'I came to find you . . .'

'No shit,' and I thumb the hammer back, cocking the pistol. I hope the gun isn't so cheap as to spring before I'm ready to pull the trigger. I want to find out who the hell this guy is who knows my name and how on earth he found me before I plant him.

He winces, his face screwing up like he tasted a lemon, and then he bellows, 'For Archie. For Archibald Grant . . . your old fence!'

Whatever I was expecting, it wasn't that.

'Archie?'

'Yeah man, that's what I'm trying to tell you. Archie's been taken.'

We sit in the back of a chicken-and-pork restaurant, drinking San Miguels.

'What's your name?'

'I go by Smoke.'

And as if the mention of his name turns his thoughts, he pulls out a pack of Fortunes, pops free a cigarette, and lights it with a shaky hand. I guess he hasn't quite calmed his nerves after having his own gun cocked beneath his chin.

'Then tell me something straight, Smoke ... you're no bagman.'

He blows a thin stream out of the side of his mouth. 'No ... shit no. I just handled things for Archie ... a "my-man-Friday" type setup. Whatever he needed me to track down, that was my job.'

'A fence in training.'

He nods. 'I thought about trying my hand at the killing business, but I wasn't sure I had the chops for it.'

'Now you know.'

'You're right about that.'

'How'd you find me?'

'Archie liked to tell stories about you, said you were the best he'd ever seen. Said if he ever got in a tight spot, I's to open an envelope he kept in a safety deposit box at Harris Bank on Wabash. That'd tell me where to find you. He told me this pretty soon after I started there ...'

'How long ... ?'

'Over a year. After his sister died, he came back to Chicago a bit lost. I knew him from his prison days.'

Ruby. His sister's name was Ruby, and she was one of the good ones. I had a real fondness for her; I like to think we were cut from the same cloth. Then Ruby had caught a bullet in that mess in Italy two years ago that made me want to leave the game forever. And here it was, all coming back.

'I meant, how long has Archie been missing?'

'Not missing. Taken. There's a note.'

He shifts to reach into his pants pocket and withdraws a single sheet of paper, folded into quarters, then hands it over without the slightest hesitation. As I unfold it, he takes another drag, squinting his left eye as the smoke blows past it, toward the ceiling.

'Goddamn, it's nice to smoke indoors. They don't let us do that shit in Chicago no more.'

The sheet is standard white typing paper, the kind found

jamming copy machines throughout the world. Block letters, written in a masculine hand with a black Sharpie:

BRING COLUMBUS HOME. OR YOU'LL GET GRANT BACK IN A WAY YOU WON'T LIKE.

I look up, and Smoke is studying my face.

'Why didn't you tell me this was about me?'

Smoke shrugs. 'I'm telling you now.'

When I level my eyes, he puts his palms up like a victim in a robbery. 'I didn't mean nothing by it. Just didn't know how you'd react. They ask for you and I immediately come find you. I wasn't looking to do an investigation . . . wouldn't know where to begin. But your name was on there clear as crystal and this seemed like a straight-up emergency, so here I am. Didn't want you to have the wrong idea.'

'When was the last time you saw Archie?'

'I was at his place the night before . . . wasn't unusual for us to be up 'til eleven-thirty, twelve, goin' over all the goin's on, but mostly talking shit, you know? I think I left around midnight, but I don't remember looking at a clock. It was late, though.

'Next day I was supposed to meet him for eggs and bacon at Sam & George's on North Lincoln, but Archie never showed.'

'That unusual?'

'First time ever. I knew something was up before the waitress set down the menus. He always beat me there. Always. Say what you want about Archibald Grant, but he's a punctual son-of-a-cuss.'

I couldn't argue with that. 'So what'd you do?'

'I got up, left a buck on the table for coffee, and headed to Archie's place. Banged on the door, but no answer. The lock wasn't forced or nothing, so I opened it and poked my head in.'

'You have a key?'

'Yeah. Archie gave me one.' He says it defensively, but I shake him off like a pitcher shaking off a sign from the plate.

'Keep going.'

'Not a sound in the joint. Air as still as a morgue.'

'No sign of a struggle?'

'Not in the front room, no.' He leans forward, lowers his voice. 'But in the bedroom, he must've put up a hell of a fight. Blood everywhere, lamps knocked over, mirror broke, bed knocked to shit. I knew it was bad, bad, bad. My first thought was he was dead, truth be told. All that blood. Someone must've stuck him and dragged the body away. But then I saw the note.'

'Where?'

'Living room table.' He tamps out another cigarette from his pack and lights it off the end of the first, dropping the original into a plastic ashtray when he's done.

'You think the note was put there for you to find it?'

'Don't know who else it'd be for. I'm the only one he lets into his house.'

'And you have absolutely no idea who did this or why they want me?'

'Swear on every single family member's name, living and dead.'

As a professional killer, I have to read faces the way a surgeon examines x-rays. A purse of the lips, a downward glance of the eyes, a nervous tap of the knee, there are dozens of tells that give away when a man is playing fast and loose with the truth. Smoke is skittish, no mistake, but his voice is steady and his eyes are focused. He's afraid of me, but he's telling the truth.

The air is dry and stale and the cigarette smoke hangs under the ceiling like a gas cloud, thick and poisoned.

I tap the note with my index finger. 'And you have no idea why they want me?'

'I hung around that place for two days, hoping someone would show up and explain things further, but not a creature was stirring, you know what I'm saying? On the third day, I went looking in that safety deposit box.'

'No one followed you to the bank?'

A look sweeps over his face like the thought never crossed his mind. His adam's apple dips like a yo-yo.

'No. I mean . . . no . . . I don't think so.' Like he's trying to convince himself.

'Doesn't matter,' I say so he'll get back on track.

'Anyway, that's where I found the file on you.'

'What's your plan from here?'

Smoke shrugs as he starts on his third cigarette. 'Man, I wish I knew. Like I said, Archie told me if he's ever in a tight spot, to set out to find you. And then your name's on this here note. I don't know what to tell you, but you gotta admit, this qualifies as a pretty goddamned tight spot, so I did what Archie asked. Beyond that . . .'

He lets his voice spool out, joining the smoke near the ceiling like he never intended to finish the sentence.

An image pops into my head, a highway in Nevada I drove a lifetime ago. The sky was clear, the desert calm, and the blacktop was an infinite line across the landscape, a shapeless, endless mirage. Each time I'd crest a bit of a slope or round a slight bend, the line would reemerge before me, stretching out to the horizon, teasing me, sentient, like it knew I could never reach its end.

I am about to drive that road again. I knew it the moment Smoke called me by name. The real question, the one I'm not sure I want to answer: did I ever truly leave it in the first place?

Risina is folding clothes in the back room when I enter, and her face lights up when she sees me coming through the door.

'What'd you bring me?'

Then she spots it in my face, and I guess she's believed this day would come since we first arrived.

'Someone found you.'

I nod.

'How much time do we have?'

I swallow, my mouth chalky. 'We leave tonight.'

'Where?'

'I have to go to the U.S. for a while.'

'What's a while?'

'I don't know.'

'And me?'

'I don't know.'

She folds her arms across her chest and raises her chin. She's never been one to lower her eyes, and she's not going to start now. 'Tell me what happened.'

I paint the picture of Smoke, about the way he found me and what he had to say about Archibald Grant and the note left behind that called me out by name.

'You told me you were out . . . that Archie wanted you out, was covering for you, he said. I don't understand this. His problems are not your problems.'

'I was out. I am. But he stitched me up when I needed stitching and I can't turn my back on him.'

Risina collapses into a chair, but still she doesn't lower her eyes.

'I want you to know . . .' I start but she cuts me off.

'Give me a moment to think, dammit.' This might be the first time she's ever snapped at me, and I can't say I blame her. 'Can you bring me some water?'

I move to the kitchen and pour some filtered water out of a jug we keep in the refrigerator. This might be the last time I'm in this kitchen, the last time I open this fridge, and even though this place isn't much, it has been good to us. Better not to think this way. This is no time for sentiment. Better to rip the bandage off quickly.

I return with the water. She takes it absently and drinks the entire glass without taking it from her lips. I'm not sure she even knows I'm in the room. I can see her eyes darting as her mind catches up to what I told her.

After a moment, she finally raises her eyes and focuses on me, maybe to keep the room from spinning. She blushes, blood rising in her cheeks.

'I'm sorry . . . this is new to me. I thought I was prepared, had prepared myself for something like this, but . . .'

She swallows and bites her lip. I know she is sorting her thoughts the way a contract bridge player organizes playing cards, bringing all the suits together before laying down the next play.

'Are you going to have to kill someone?'

'I don't know.'

'What if once you enter this life, you don't want to stop again?'

She's trying to read my face, less interested in what I say than how I look when I say it. It's a skill she's picked up from me. I answer with the truth.

'I don't know.'

She absorbs this like a physical blow. Just when I don't think she's going to say anything, she finds her voice. There is a strength there that shouldn't surprise me, though it does.

'I'm coming with you.'

'I don't—'

'It's not a question. I'm not asking for permission. I'm coming with you. You offered me a life with you and I won't run away just because the past caught up with us. *Us*. Not you. Us.'

'Risina—'

'You can't send me away. You can't kick me in the stomach like you did the first girl you loved.' Her eyes are hot now. 'I'm coming.'

I turn my voice to gravel. She hasn't heard this voice from me, but I want the weight behind my words to be clear. 'It's one thing to hear these stories about me and another to live them, to see them with your own eyes. I can't get back into this and have to worry about—'

She interrupts, fearlessly, her voice matching mine. If I

thought I could outgravel her, I misjudged the woman I love. 'Yes, you will. You'll learn to do it *and* worry about me at the same time. I'm not giving you the choice.'

'You'll see a side of me you won't recognize.'

'Don't you understand a damn thing I'm saying? I want to know *every* side of you. I must know! I've wanted *all* of you since I first met you. Not just one side or the other. Not just the mask you choose to show me.'

'And what if you hate what you see?'

'I won't.'

'And what if you die standing next to me?'

'Then I'll die. People do it every day.'

I start to ask another question and stop myself. There's a reason I fell in love with Risina the first time I saw her; it's here before me now. Defiance, ambition, determination, passion . . . the qualities of confidence. The qualities of a professional assassin. A tiger is a goddamned tiger. The beasts are born that way, and no matter how they are *nurtured*, their *nature* always emerges eventually.

'So when do we leave?' she asks.

'Now,' I whisper.

2

It takes us a few days to buy passports. Although Smoke failed spectacularly as a bagman, he's not a bad fence.

He's been with Archie Grant long enough to know how to scrounge the right information, ask the right questions, navigate the world beneath the world, the one where money exchanges hands and lips stay tight.

This is all new to Risina, and she adjusts, acting normally, with just a hint of boredom, the way she must've negotiated competitively for a rare book. An Italian fence named Vespucci once told me, 'no matter the situation, act like you've been there before.' Risina says little and keeps her face emotionless, neutral. Even as we're engaged in something as simple as obtaining illegal papers, she looks like she's done it a thousand times. Maybe she's a natural. I won't deny that I feel, well, proud of her. Maybe that's irrational, but I don't care.

In a hotel near the airport, we lie in bed, waiting on a morning flight.

'I don't want you to get too confident. We haven't done anything yet.'

'How do you want me to be?'

'Observant.'

She widens her eyes. 'Like this?' She holds it for a moment before breaking into a smile.

'I'm serious.'

'Yes, babe. I know. You're going to be tense and I understand that. This is the new man. The one who has to worry about someone besides himself. But when we're alone, then I'm going to want *you* back. Not Columbus.'

She pulls close to me and buries her nose in my neck.

'I wasn't aware this was a democracy.'

'Well, now you are.'

'As long as you understand that when we leave this room, or any room, I'm in charge. You look to me. You learn from me.'

'I understand.'

'I mean it, Risina.'

'I know you do. And I answered you that I understand.'

She sleeps peacefully, as though this is just another night in the fishing village. Maybe she's going to be okay in this world. Maybe she'll learn quickly and take direction and thrive. Maybe if I keep telling myself that over and over, I'll believe it.

Chicago is warm but stale, like a mausoleum releasing hundreds of years of trapped air after the front stone is rolled away. It must be the exhaust from the traffic in the city or the wind off the lake, or maybe the smell is just in my head. My temples throb like someone is tapping my head with a hammer.

Risina sits next to me in the rental sedan – a dark blue economy car – staring out the window, smiling absently.

I let her come. She insisted, but the decision was, is, mine. I could have blown off Smoke, protested I was out, truly out, that Archie's problems were Archie's problems, taken Risina and fled to another isolated country, but the truth is . . . I didn't want to. I'm like Eve staring at the picked apple, but that's not quite the right metaphor. I've already tasted the apple and instead of facing banishment, I've been offered passage back into Eden, or into my definition of paradise anyway. But at what price? There is always a price.

'I'm going to say something and I don't want you to protest or argue or answer. Just nod your head that you agree when I finish.'

She waits, and I can feel her eyes.

'This is my decision to have you with me. To teach you what I do. To bring you into this world. Okay? I take responsibility for it. I own it.'

She waits until I turn my head her way before she nods. Whether or not she agrees with me, I think I see understanding in her eyes. Regardless, I had to say it.

I've never had a charge before, and I want it defined and out in the open, as much for me as for her. I have to teach her, protect her, and lead her all at once, and I will not take these obligations lightly.

Straight from the airport, Smoke leads us to Archie's apartment. I check the side-view mirrors, looking for patterns in the traffic behind us, but I don't think anyone knows about our arrival. If the plan of the kidnappers was to tail Smoke and strike as soon as he found me, then they've done a lousy job. There's no tail from what I can see, and I didn't clock anyone back at the bookstore or restaurant before we left our hiding spot.

I've been inside Archie's building a couple of times before, once after killing a couple of his rival fences, and another time after I was shot in the ribs in a Chicago Public Library. Grant hired a private surgeon to stitch me up, and his sister Ruby took care of me until I got back on my feet. That was years ago, before I quit and before Ruby took a bullet to the face and died in front of a church in Siena as I stood next to her.

The apartment is as I remember it and as Smoke described. There's dried blood in the bedroom, the color of rust, and several pieces of furniture – a lamp, a nightstand – are overturned.

'I didn't touch nothing,' Smoke says. 'This is just as I found it.'

I scan the room, then zero in on a chest of drawers and put my finger in a smooth hole.

'Shit. Is that a bullet hole? I didn't *even* see that.' He hits the word 'even' to make sure I hear the truth in his voice.

'Can you help me move this?'

The back of the chest and the wall behind it have the same hole. Risina watches, fascinated.

'You got a little knife on you?' I say to Smoke.

He immediately shakes his head, but then thinks. 'Hold on a second . . .'

He scampers back to the kitchen and Risina smiles and nods, rocking forward on her toes. 'I'm impressed.'

'In this job, you have to look at a scene of violence, the aftermath, and read it like a book. I want you to try to visualize what happened in this room. On your own, no help from me.'

I hear Smoke rummaging around in kitchen drawers, but I focus on Risina. Her eyes trace the room, drinking it in, and I can see her gears turning.

'I don't know. There was a fight, and someone was shot.'

'Not shot. I don't think so. We'd see a different blood pattern on the floor, on the walls. When someone takes a bullet, a part of his insides usually comes out. So you'd see some other matter besides blood.'

'Then what do you think? He was stabbed?'

Before I can answer, Smoke returns holding a small kitchen knife, a screwdriver, and a letter opener, presenting all three items like a kid excited to please his teacher.

'The opener,' I say. A few minutes later and I fish the bullet out of the wall, then toss it to Risina. 'That's a .22 slug. Look at the size of it and try to commit it to memory. It's a low caliber round out of a small gun. An assassin's weapon. I'll get ahold of some other calibers so you can compare them.'

I turn to Smoke. 'Archie have a .22?'

'Yeah.'

'He keep it under the mattress?'

'Yeah.'

I lift it up, but the gun isn't there.

'Well, he got one shot off before they fought over the pistol. I'm saying "they" 'cause I'm guessing it was at least two guys.'

'Why?'

'Well, I could be wrong, but I think one held him up while the other one went to work on his face. That's why you have the blood here, in a circle, after they broke his nose and most likely knocked him out. They held him up while his head hung. It's hard to hold an unconscious guy still, and his head lolled a bit. That accounts for why there is so much blood on the floor. A stab wound would pour straight down and soak the victim's clothes. A broken nose? That's a gusher, and if they're holding him upright, it's just going to get everywhere.'

It's Smoke's turn to ask a question. 'Why would they do that?'

I shrug. 'They wanted information on me and the muscle went too far? They wanted to beat on him for putting up a fight, pulling a gun? Who knows? But they were careful not to step in the blood, which means the fist work happened after the initial fight. Anyway, none of this matters all that much until we figure out who's holding Archie and why they want me.'

Risina turns the bullet over in her fingers and holds it up close to her eye like a jeweler examining a diamond. 'But we know now it was more than one guy.'

'We know it was more than one guy here in the room. But maybe they were only hired muscle . . . not necessarily the guy looking for me. Either way, the person who wanted Archie snuck two or more guys into this place, which is no easy feat, I know from experience, and got them out of the building while transporting an unconscious resident.'

'They're professionals. Like you.'

I nod and chew my lip. I had come to that conclusion within five seconds of entering the room, but I wanted Risina to arrive at it on her own.

'So what now?'

'Now we bang on a door.'

* * *

Bo Willis is a big man, not quite forty, who looks like his monthly trip to the pharmacy includes a permanent prescription for Lipitor. He was a Chicago cop for twelve years but quit when he didn't make detective the second year in a row. Being a cop means taking a lot of ribbing from your fellow officers, and I'm sure he received his fair share after failing his detective exams or getting passed over. Bo joined a private security firm, the kind that requires short-sleeve blue uniforms and patches with names on them. He was content to punch the clock and collect his sixty-five a year, though he did it with a scowl on his face. His first couple of years he spent on a bench at an airport warehouse. The last three, he held down an Aero chair behind a security console in Archibald Grant's building.

We didn't have to knock on his door; Bo eats breakfast each morning at a place called Willard's Diner, occupying a booth near the front where he can spread out his newspaper. He looks up for a moment when Risina walks by, and follows her with his eyes until she passes. I want her to hear my conversation with the security guard, but I make a mental note that I'm going to have to talk to her about her appearance. In a business where invisibility is a weapon, I can't afford to have Risina turning heads by simply walking into the room.

I give Bo a few minutes to settle into the sports page and then slide into the booth opposite him. He starts, unused to having his territory invaded, and that's a good place to put him: uncomfortable, on defense before he even knows he's entered the arena.

'This is my booth, guy,' he says when I just stare at him. He has a flat Midwestern accent, and his voice comes out a little pinched, like air escaping a punctured tire.

'I know it's your booth, Bo. It's your booth every goddamned morning.'

'Do we know each other?' He's somewhere between puzzled and pissed. For a big guy, that voice is high, and does his tough guy stance a disservice. I wonder if it cut into his effectiveness as a cop. I wonder if he's been battling it his whole life.

'You don't know me, but I know you.'

'Listen, if this—'

'Shut up, Bo. Shut up and use your ears. You're going to have the opportunity to open your mouth again, and when you do, I want it to be to tell the truth.'

'I don't—'

'Who paid you to look the other way on March 25th?'

He blinks once, twice, swallowing hard. He's a headline in large type, as easy to read as the newspaper in front of him. 'I don't—'

'I'm going to describe your sister's house to you, Bo. It's on Wilmette Avenue, about thirty minutes from here, a white clapboard two-story number with a green mailbox out front. Your nephew, Mike, occupies the bedroom in the upper right corner and your niece, Kate, right? She sleeps in the lower left below a pink Hannah Montana poster. Your sister, Laura, she's been living alone now for what? Two years?'

Bo's face turns bright red, like a brake light. His voice rattles now. 'I don't know who you think you are—'

I cut him off. 'I'll tell you. I think I'm the guy who will kill your sister, your niece, and your nephew in the next hour if you don't tell me exactly what I want to know. And when I get done killing them, I'll head to your parents' house in Glen Ellyn. The brick number set back from the street with the two-door garage? Eventually I'll come back for you, Bo.'

He starts to open his mouth, but I'm quicker. 'I know you were a cop. I know you still have friends on the force. But I'm going to tell you as directly as you'll ever hear anything in your life: you and your friends have never dealt with someone like me. There's already a file on your family that will read "unsolved homicide" if you don't tell me exactly what I want to know.'

He lowers his eyes, and I've got him. I growl through clenched teeth, 'Who paid you to look the other way?'

For a moment, he doesn't say anything, just pushes waffle crumbs around the table. Then, so softly I almost don't hear him, 'Not look the other way . . .'

'Speak up.'

'Not look the other way. He paid me to leave. To get up and head out. Said he'd only need an hour. Gave me two thousand bucks. I didn't know what he was up to, I swear.'

'What'd he look like?'

'White guy, little dumpy to tell you the truth. Shaved head . . . just a regular guy, you know?'

'Accent?'

'I don't know. East Coast, I'd say, but I don't know. He didn't say much. Just said "two grand, walk away, one hour." That was it. He handed me the money and I took off, you know? I don't need any Mafia trouble if you know what I'm saying. Cooled my heels in Sharky's down the street. Looked at my watch and the hour was up. Gave it an extra half hour just to make sure I didn't walk in on something I didn't want to see. But when I came back, everything was the same.'

'Video?'

'That was the thing. Of course, I looked over the last hour's video. Or I was going to. But it was all erased, like the hour didn't happen. I don't even know how to work the console other than to hit rewind and play, but he knew how to do it. And there was nothing there.'

He shakes his head, remembering. 'I held my breath the next day, expecting to hear about some big theft, but nothing. No one ever complained, and no one came to me and said anything illegal happened, so I just . . .' He glides his hand out like an airplane taking off and says, 'pssssh.'

'Until today.'

'Yeah.' Now he looks up and meets my eyes. His expression is resigned, like a kid caught stealing, sitting in the store manager's office, waiting for his parents to show up and mete out some punishment.

I stand, and he can't help but exhale, relieved. Curiosity gets the best of him, though. 'So what was taken?' He looks up with expectant eyes.

I don't answer and head for the door.

'So that's why you had Smoke put a file together on the security guard.' I had asked him to do so a few days before, and he had come through quickly. The file was green but not bad; it contained what I needed to make an effective threat.

Risina walks next to me as we move north up State Street. We stop in a sporting goods store, and I move to a rack of ball caps.

'Yeah. Like in most businesses, information is key. The more you have, the more specific you can get, the more effective your threats are. What you have to do is plant images in your mark's mind and let the threat spread like a virus. Let his imagination do the job for you. You don't have to be particularly intimidating, you just have to know a few pointed facts about his family, about their names, about their houses, and the mark wilts like a picked flower. That's what a good fence does . . . gives you the information that gives you the power.'

I pick out a blue Cubs hat and then move over to women's clothing where I select a pair of baggy warm-ups and a large, plain T-shirt. 'Try these on.'

'You're shopping for me now?'

'Until you figure out how to blend in a little better, yes.'

She looks over the clothes I hand her, wrinkles her nose, and heads to the changing booths. If she thought being a female contract killer meant leather pants and stiletto heels, she's learning the opposite now. That shit looks good on a silver screen, but'll get you killed in Chicago.

After a minute, she exits, and it's all I can do to keep from laughing. Her hair is tucked up under the cap and the clothes fit like a kid trying on her dad's softball uniform. But the effect works: it's impossible to see what kind of a body she has under the clothes, and with the cap lowered, the top half of her face is in shadow. It's not perfect – you don't want to go too far the other way so that someone thinks 'why's a beauty like her wearing dumpy clothes?' – but it'll do for now.

Archie's office is in an old aluminum manufacturing plant on Harrison. Risina, Smoke, and I sit in a conference room, a stack of files on a long wooden table.

'This is everything, Smoke?'

'All the files in the last six months, plus a few Archie was putting together.'

'Okay, each of us takes a third. Sing out if you read anything that jumps out at you.'

'Meaning?'

'I don't know. We're tracking breadcrumbs looking for red flags. I don't know why someone wants to find me, so we have to work off the assumption that Archie's abduction is a factor. There are plenty of ways to try to find someone, but they chose to rough up Archie, which makes me think there's a personal connection between the kidnapper and him. Maybe it has something to do with a hit he fenced, and usually these types of things are immediate, so I thought we'd narrow it down to the last six months. He keeps thick files. Just look for anything that . . . anything that looks abnormal. That's the best I can think of to do to get started.'

Risina nods as Smoke divides the folders and slides her a stack. If she's surprised by the amount of professional killings contracted in the last six months just by this one fence, she doesn't show it. I think I know why. Here is something she can relate to, something in which she excels: literature. She opens the first file and burrows into it like a mole. I watch for a moment, thinking about that first time I saw her on the Via Poli in Rome, surrounded by all those austere books. This is a different kind of reading – a long way from Dickens and Walpole and Dante – but compelling just the same. After a moment of watching her, I pull a file off the top of my stack and get to work.

The first few files are typical assignments: eight-week jobs in various corners of the country. One shooter was assigned to each, and the jobs were all completed on time. Nothing remarkable about the marks: a lawyer, a construction contractor, a horse jockey. Guys who had no idea death was coming for them until the moment their bells were rung.

The fourth file is interesting. Archibald used one of his contract killers – a woman named Carla – to settle an old personal score back in Boston. Archie took down a rival fence who had set him up on an aiding and abetting charge.

'Tell me about Carla?' I say to Smoke.

Smoke shrugs. 'Dumpy woman. Nothing special. Archie borrowed her from another fence, wasn't in his regular stable. I don't think she worked much. Burned out or got burned or something.'

'You ever meet her?'

'I did. On that job you're holding now. She needed a scrounger to get her a bunch of equipment, and I helped facilitate.'

'What's a scrounger?' Risina asks.

'A fella who gets you any props you need while working a job – a delivery truck, a uniform, a wheelchair, an ID badge . . .'

'Weapons?'

Smoke shakes his head. 'Your fence'll supply those.'

'Yeah, scroungers are mainly for everyday things. They get paid well to work quietly and quickly.' Then, to Smoke, 'What was your vibe off Carla?'

Smoke shrugs. 'Not much to look at. Had a dog-face if you want me to get specific. Not sure what breed, but definitely canine. She didn't say much either, all business. A little jumpy, to tell you the truth. Why? What's in the file?'

'Nothing . . . just . . . a personal gig for Archie. File says it went down the way it was supposed to go down. It shouldn't be suspicious; but if I were looking for a reason to kidnap a fence, I'd start with the jobs he instigated himself. I might want to talk to this Carla.'

'Archie didn't have a problem with her. Like I said . . . that was the only time he used her.'

'Okay.'

I set the file aside and plow into the next one. An hour goes by with no further anomalies, no red flags waving at me. Shaky clients called off a few hits before the assassinations took place, but this is not uncommon. Clients buckle under the weight of what they've set into motion, and they'll pay extra to cancel the order, trying to salvage their conscience, afraid to wake up with blood on their hands. Fences can make a pretty good business on canceled hits.

I just open the last file in my stack – the execution of a pit boss at Harrah's Casino in Joliet – when Risina speaks up.

'I think I found something.'

And she did.

It's rare, but occasionally in this business there are incomplete hits. Not canceled hits . . . incomplete ones. An assassin might get killed while on the job, or the mark goes into hiding and just can't be found, or the police or FBI catch wind and sting the bagman in the act. The fence is forced into an awkward position; he has to turn the money back over to the client, which is a substantial sum, half of which, subtracting his fees, he paid to the hit man on commencement of the assignment. So personally he's on the hook for the total, unless he can barter with his hired gun to return a portion of the commencement fee. If his hired gun is alive and not in jail, that is. Worse, the fence takes a shot to his reputation by failing to execute the assignment. Clients get jumpy, rival fences swoop in like vultures to fill the void. A few dings like that, and the contracts dry up.

Four months ago, Archie put a file together on a Kansas City man named Rich Bacino. This is the file Risina found, the file I'm absorbing now. On the surface, it doesn't look like a difficult kill. Rich started an internet software company in the boom of the nineties and was prescient enough to sell it before the bust of the aught-years. He netted eighty million dollars before he turned forty. A bachelor, he bought up properties on both coasts and added an apartment in Paris. He spent a little money on the usual accoutrements of the rich: cars, boats, real estate. But Rich saved the majority of his cash for a newfound passion.

Rich started collecting.

Over the years, I've seen a lot of marks involved with an assortment of illegal activities. I've killed crime bosses, money launderers, numbers runners, low-level bagmen. I've killed corrupt politicians or judges taking bribes on the side. I've hit businessmen with mistresses and Sunday school teachers who were buried in gambling debts. I've also come across a few assholes involved in illegal collecting: kiddie porn or Nazi memorabilia or stolen art. You dabble with that stuff, it's just a matter of time before a guy like me shows up on your doorstep. You sit in slime long enough, you make enemies and you get dropped.

But Rich's collection is a first.

Rich Bacino collects skulls.

He has over fifty, all famous people, all acquired after the bodies were laid to rest without the heirs or families knowing about the exhumation. DNA tests and documentation prove their authenticity, though very few people will ever see the paperwork to confirm it. Collections like this aren't gathered for display; it's hard to describe, but they're built on a perverse sense of getting over on everyone else. It's like Poe's telltale heart beating underneath the floorboards while the constable stands obliviously above it – except instead of driving the collector mad, the beating, the *knowing* excites him. While his friends, family, and acquaintances visit in his living room, they have no idea that the skulls of say, Ronald Reagan or Jeffrey Dahmer or Gianni Versace are stored in the basement beneath them. It's a big secret fuck-you to everyone, an 'I'm more powerful than you'll ever know' high.

Exactly how much he pays for the skulls, I have no idea. Archie estimates millions of dollars exchange hands for each purchase. The more famous the person, the more public the grave, the higher the price.

So Rich either crossed someone he shouldn't have, or someone's loved ones found out about his hobby, because a price tag was put on *his* skull. Archie was hired to facilitate the kill, which was an eight-week job assigned ten weeks ago. And yet, Rich Bacino is still alive.

The bagman assigned to kill him was a native Chicagoan named Flagler. Next to his name, Archie had written a single word in red ink.

Missing.

I don't know if this odd file has anything to do with the abduction of Archie or the note asking to bring me home, but it's an unresolved issue in Archie's professional life, and it seems like a good place to start.

3

Risina and I are eating burgers at Blackie's on South Clark. The joint has been here for most of a century, and in a town that knows how to cook meat, it's a standout.

Smoke settles in across from us in the booth, looking a bit twitchy.

'What's up?'

'Nothing. I'm just not good at this, is all.'

'You did solid work on the security guard.'

Smoke shakes his head. 'That was a piece of pumpkin pie. This . . . I don't know if I helped much. I wish Archie were here.' He takes out a file and slides it furtively across the table.

I put my hands on top of the manila envelope but don't open it, just level my gaze at Smoke. 'Give me the highlights.'

'Well, looks like we've used Flagler twice before this job, but Archie didn't know him too well. Like that Carla you mentioned, he wasn't in the regular stable. He came on a rec from an East Coast fence named Talbott.'

'That who you talked to?'

'That's who I *tried* to talk to. He gave me the Heisman.' Smoke strikes the trophy pose before dropping his hands back to his lap.

'You gotta work him . . .'

'I don't have the tongue Archie has . . . you've seen that.'

'I think you're selling yourself short.'

'Man, I don't know.'

Risina pulls the file out from under my hands and starts skimming it. 'There's a lot of solid information here, Smoke.'

Smoke shrugs, his eyes downcast. 'I need a cigarette. Excuse me.' He climbs out of the booth and heads for the exit.

Risina starts to read the first page in the file, then stops. 'You don't think Smoke . . . ?' She pauses, trying to figure out the best way to say it. 'You don't think someone maybe got to Smoke, do you? Or that he's been involved from the get-go? I mean, this note says to bring you to Chicago, and here you sit.'

I shake my head. 'I think he needs to find his footing. Gain some confidence. This job is . . . it's not for everyone. It's one thing to watch Archie put files together, another to get out and beat the streets all by your lonesome. I'm sure I rattled him in that alley in Manila. Maybe he's putting one toe in the pool and finding out the water's a little too deep. Being a fence is a lot harder than it looks. Psychologically, I mean.'

'Hmmm.' Risina goes back to reading, her eyes floating over the page. I like the way she's thinking now, even if I don't agree with her. She's starting to engage her intuition, a weapon as important to a hit man as his gun. She's asking the right questions, at least.

After a moment, Smoke returns to the booth, smelling like his namesake. 'Sorry 'bout that. I tried to quit smoking once, but that didn't work out for me. Anyway, while I was out there I was thinking there was a nugget I found in this Flagler file that stuck with me. It's in there and you'll come across it, but I'll tell you anyway. This cat didn't pick up his money himself. Both times, the commencement pay and the completion – he gave instructions where to drop it. Now, most of Archie's regular guys on the payroll, Archie pays 'em direct. They're tight, you know? They're . . . like I said before . . .'

'In the stable.'

'Yeah. Not this guy.'

'You know where the drop-off was?'

'Yep. I took the duffel myself. Trailer park goes by "Little Arizona" near the Indiana border.'

'And you handed it to him?'

'No, that's the thing. I never met him.'

Smoke's file gave me part of Flagler's story, but it had holes in it big enough to drop a body through. He started as a bagman in Maryland, Virginia, and DC, and stayed mostly in that area up until about a year ago. Smoke didn't know what he looked like . . . and if Archie did, he didn't put it in his file. Archie was good about keeping notes on all his contractors, but for some reason, hadn't gotten around to recording much on Flagler. Smoke was sure *Flagler* wasn't his real name, but didn't know where, when, or why he chose it.

There was scant information regarding the jobs he'd worked on the East Coast, just that he had a fence named Spellman who died of colon cancer, allowing Flagler to become a free agent. He must've pulled a few jobs for the other fence named Talbott, who gave the recommendation to Archie, but like Smoke said, Talbott wasn't talking.

What Smoke did find were details on the two jobs he pulled for Archie prior to the one that went sour.

The first was the owner of a bar in Minneapolis, a sixty-year-old lothario. From the file Archie cobbled, the man was juggling six different women in various parts of the city. Three of them were married. I have no idea who ordered the killing: a jealous woman or a cuckolded husband, but the barkeep's Don Juan lifestyle caught up with him. He was shot in his car at one-fifteen in the morning after he closed down the bar and put his key in the ignition of his Cadillac. Robbery was the police department's initial suspicion; the safe inside the bar's back office was open and empty. But as details of the bar owner's social life emerged, the police shifted their attention to his spate of lovers. A dozen people were brought in for questioning, but all the suspects seemed to have strong alibis. The case remains unsolved and open.

The second assignment was a bit of a high-profile case. It involved the violent death of a professional athlete. Again,

Flagler used the robbery angle to throw the police off the scent. This is not an uncommon tactic; hired killers have been utilizing it for centuries. Make it look like a petty theft gone wrong and the cops will spin their wheels for weeks, staking out pawnshops and flea markets, trying to find the killer by tracking what was stolen. All the while, the trail grows as cold as a frozen pond. Robberies are supposed to be about money; the goods *have* to be fenced at some point. So nothing drives a detective more insane than when the stolen items simply vanish.

In this case, the athlete was a cornerback for the Bears, a guy who mostly worked on the punt and kick-off teams, but occasionally made it on to the field in nickel packages or long-yardage situations. He was in his sixth year in the league, and hadn't made a fortune, but had done all right for himself. He lived in a decent-sized house in Cabrini and was into guns, amassing dozens of handguns and rifles.

He was shot in the foyer of his house, just inside his front door, while wearing a bathrobe. He lived alone and his body wasn't discovered until he missed his second day of practice. Most of the athlete's weapon collection had been stolen from the home, and the police went the robbery/ homicide route.

The cops staked out gun shows and various shops around the city, but none of the weapons ever surfaced. Flagler was smart enough to bury them in the woods or drop them in the bottom of a lake, making the stolen guns a trail that would only lead to frustration. Half of a bagman's job is to escape cleanly after a mark is hit. A good killer's best weapon against the police is to behave illogically.

Contract killers know how homicide cops think. They want to keep their 'closed' case percentages up, and nine out of ten murderers are handed to them on a silver platter. A boyfriend kills his lover. A husband kills his wife. A drug dealer pops his rival. A couple of days of work, someone cracks, someone steps forward, and the homicide is solved. Case closed. A contract killer has no personal connection to the victim, and if he's good, he makes it look like the intention of the killing is something it's not. When the case goes infuriatingly cold, it's human nature for a homicide detective to move on to greener pastures.

Despite Smoke's misgivings, he had given me quite a bit to go on; in fact, Flagler's *modus operandi* helped fill in the blanks on why he went missing.

Flagler was contracted to kill a man who owned a strange, expensive collection of human skulls. I think Flagler finally found something worth stealing he didn't want to bury.

Little Arizona is located in Hegewisch, smack between Powder Horn and Wolf lakes, on top of an old landfill near the Indiana border. For being so near the city, it's a rural lifestyle, where fishermen can reel in a blue gill or a carp, and hunters can legally bag birds seeking a drink as they migrate south. For a trailer park and despite the occasional meth head, it's not a bad life.

I left Risina and Smoke back in the city to do further research on Flagler, to see if the two of them could sift through the silt of Archie's files and pan out any more gold. Risina was content to examine more of Archie's work, and didn't protest when I told her I'd like to make the run to the drop site alone. I have an ulterior motive for leaving her behind though: this is the first time I believe I might head into some violence, and I don't want to expose her. Not yet. Whether or not the violence is going to be directed toward me or dispensed by me doesn't make a difference.

The park is quiet and the plots for the trailers are spread out wider and more haphazard than I imagined, like someone dropped a box of matches and just left the sticks to lie as they fell. A black curtain of clouds is gathering in the north and heading this way, and I'd like to scope out the site and uncover any salient information before the skies open. Rain, so often thought of as a blessing, a life-giver, the washer of sins, is no friend to a hit man. It causes fingers to slip, vision to blur, and muddy ground to hold shoe prints in clear relief. Best to get in and get out before any complications.

Smoke had dropped Flagler's money off at the white and green pre-fabricated home in plot number 73. He said that both times, a middle-aged woman answered the door, took the duffel bag, and closed it in his face without saying a word. It's odd for Flagler to use such a method for receiving his kill fees . . . if he didn't want to collect his money himself, why use an immobile – rather than a fluid – location? Why use the same drop site twice?

When a lion is looking for a kill without having to expend too much energy, he follows the hyenas.

I knock on the door and paste a pleasant smile on my face, ready for the inevitable glance out the nearby window. After a moment, the door opens, and the middle-aged woman Smoke described grimaces down at me. She has meaty arms and a fleshy face, but with a layer of hungry menace in her eyes, like an alley cat who has found a home and no longer has to fight for its daily meal, but still keeps its fur up all the same.

'What'choo want?'

'Flagler.'

Her eyes flash for only a moment and then she leans into the frame, looking down at me. 'You ain't gonna buy it when I tell you I don't know no Flagler?'

I shake my head.

'I figgered. What'choo want with him?'

'I want to talk to him.'

'Well, if you find him, tell him I'm looking for him too. I haven't seen him in months.'

'How do you know him?'

'How does anyone know anyone?'

'You have a picture of him?'

'Wouldn't that be something. No . . .'

'All right then.' I start to leave, waiting for her to make the next move. Before I get ten steps from the door . . .

'You sure you jes' want to talk?'

I turn. 'Well, I have something for him, but I'd like to give it to him myself.'

'What?'

'None of your business, ma'am.'

'Money?'

I let her digest my hesitation. 'That's between me and Flagler. If you see him, tell him I'm staying at the South Shore Inn on South Brainerd.'

I head for my car and make a show of driving off.

Less than ten minutes later, she is in an old Celica hatchback that looks like it might roll over and die at any minute. She speeds out of the trailer park, tires throwing up dirt and gravel as she maneuvers on to the highway that cuts around the lake. The car is painted white and stands out nicely against the blacktop. Even as the rain hits, I can track it as easily as an elephant in short grass.

I settle in, not sure how far she's going to drive. She isn't making any evasive maneuvers, happy to roll down the highway like a homing beacon. I'm content to follow the hyena.

Forty-five minutes on the road and her blinker glows red as she exits into Edison Park, not far from O'Hare. Killers often live within a stone's throw of an airport, not just for convenience while on a job but for escape when things grow uncomfortable.

She parks in front of a hardware store, lumbers out of the Celica and hurries inside. I wait for a moment, gnawing on my lower lip. I thought she was going to break for his residence, so this detour to a retail shop has thrown me off. Does Flagler work here? Or more likely, own the place? Or is it a front for something else?

Five minutes have gone by and no sign of the hyena. I'm just going to have to go in after her. I'm starting to feel like the tables have flipped, and maybe I'm not the predator but the prey. Damn it, she just wasn't smart enough to pull it off, to bait me into the spider's web, was she? So why am I climbing out of my car now, exposed to the rain, heading toward the stand-alone store with the red awning marked, 'Wayne's Hardware'? Why am I in Chicago anyway, the moment someone puts my name in a note? If I've lost a step, I'm going to pay for it.

As I move quickly across the street, a new thought bangs around inside my head: *I'm glad Risina isn't here.*

And that's the crux of what has been dogging me since we left Manila. *I'm glad Risina isn't here.*

Can I do what I do and protect her? This moment, this situation reinforces that interrogative like the question mark at the end of the sentence. Should I force her to see it my way and explain it doesn't have to be the end for us? I know I'm not going to watch her die and I know I'm not going to leave her unprotected if something should happen to me. Not even a week into this assignment – I'm already thinking of it as an assignment, even if this is a rescue operation instead of killing someone – and the folly of the two of us working this as a tandem sweep starts to appear like cracks in a foundation. The question looms: is it better to recognize that folly now than to stand face to face with the ramifications under worse conditions?

Focus. Fuck. The hardware store has display windows in the front, the kind that let shoppers know of sale items but don't offer a view into the store. I quickly check the sides and the back but no windows. Only a gated rear door and a rolling receivables dock allow access into the place from the back alley. The neighborhood isn't the friendliest in Chicago and the proprietor has gone out of his way to make his shop impenetrable after hours. I guess I'm just going to have to waltz in the front goddamn door.

From the best I can gauge, the entire store is maybe three thousand square feet, but I don't know if it has low shelves so you can see across the length of it, or high shelves like a maze, or if the cash register is in the front or the back or how many workers or customers or . . . goddammit, I'm just going to have to play it like it lies, get my head on a swivel, keep my eyes peeled, and be ready.

I keep my gun tucked into my back since it's raining and I don't know if I'm walking into a store full of customers or a fortress full of killers, but my hand is at my hip and ready.

I throw open the door and nearly bump into the hyena before I can take one step inside the store. The woman gets a panicked look on her face and bellows, 'He's here!' a split second before I wallop her in the side of the head, dropping her like a stone, but her warning's enough, and whatever element of surprise I had evaporated with that shout like boiled water.

My eyes still haven't adjusted to the light and I hear the distinctive rack and eruption of a shotgun, a thick BOOM, BOOM. I jerk my head straight down on instinct and paint cans explode in the spot I vacated.

A double-barrel can be effective at close range but not from forty feet and it's a bitch of a gun to reload, and so I charge in the direction from which the cartridges were fired, my Glock leading the way, hoping I can stop him before he cocks the weapon again, and as I dash up the aisle, I just barely catch a flash of a red shirt barreling toward me, closing the distance, both of us with the same idea in mind. Before I can brace myself, he drives into me like a bull, sweeping me off my feet. We collide into a three-tiered shelf filled with paintbrushes, toppling it on top of us. I don't know where my gun went but it's not in my hand.

Even though the hyena came to warn him, I must've caught Flagler off-guard, unprepared, because his only line of defense was a shotgun and once both barrels fired, he resorted to grappling. I'm guessing she fed him the bit about someone with money asking around for him, someone who was staying at a motel nearby, and instead of realizing she'd led him right to me, he prepared to go on the offensive. Maybe I should have let that happen, played possum, rope-a-dope. Maybe that would've been better than lying on my back unarmed in an aisle of scattered paintbrushes.

He must've been taught somewhere how to street-fight. Before I gain my bearings, he goes right for my eyes, clawing with his fingers, trying to rake my lids with his nails, and when I move my arms up to block him, he immediately switches tactics, heads south and tries to pound my groin.

With all that time in a juvey home, I've learned a few dirty tricks myself, and flip my hips before he can land a sapping blow. Undaunted, he leaps up and off me. The high ground is always a good position to take, so I'm expecting him to try to stomp down on me but the blows don't come and when I look up, he's taking off for a different aisle.

As quickly as I can, I find my feet and sprint after him. Whatever he's going for, whatever he has stashed in this store, a hardware store for Chris'sakes, can't be good. The hyena is making mewing noises near the front door and if any customers with cell phones decide to come shopping right now, it won't be long until the cops are right behind them. I'm hoping the rain will keep them at bay. Who wants to look for lightbulbs and wingnuts in this shit?

I spot Flagler halfway down an aisle, and when he turns to face me, he's two-fisting a sledgehammer, the old fashioned kind with a steel mallet attached to the end of a hickory stick. I set my feet and prepare for the inevitable rush.

Before he makes his move, though, he wants to talk.

'What do you want?'

'Whatever you took.'

This causes a genuinely puzzled look to spring to his face. 'What're you talking about?'

'Rich Bacino. You were supposed to kill him but you didn't.'

His eyes flit now, like he's trying to calculate my play.

'What's it to you?'

'I think you took something from him instead. I think he either bought you off or you stole something out from under him. That's your play, take some shit so the cops think it's a robbery. Only this time, you took something worth a lot. And Bacino wants it back.'

'I don't . . .'

'Whose skull did you steal?'

His eyes narrow. My question landed. I can see it working out in his brain: does he try to deny it or just charge me?

The latter wins out and he raises the sledgehammer like a baseball bat, rushes in and swings in an upward arc, a homerun swing, a golf swing, aiming for my head. I duck backward and the mallet catches the shelf to my right, knocking it down and only too late do I realize this was also part of his feint. He released the tool as soon as he swung it, never really intending to catch me with it, and instead bum-rushes me while I'm still spilling backward, off-balance.

This time he crouches low and drives his shoulder into my sternum, lifting me off my feet so I can gain no traction before he pile-drives me into the cement floor.

Flagler is better than I thought, a professional hit man who is strong even without a gun in his mitts. He knows how to work over a body, knows how to get his knuckles bloody, and as I absorb the blow and try to keep air in my lungs, I start to think maybe I'm going to lose this fight, maybe he's better than I am. Maybe after all this time, it won't be a gun that brings me down but a brawl. I lost a few steps in my layoff and a man who never left the game is knocking more than my rust off.

He's hammering my ribs with his fists and I can't take much more before my wind is gone and then both of us hear the rack of a gun's chamber, my gun, and I twist my head to see the hyena, pointing the gun our way, terrified, out of her element, about to squeeze the trigger, trying to plug me while I'm on my back and compromised.

It's the distraction I'm looking for. I buck Flagler up as the hyena closes her eyes and squeezes the trigger and the gunshot is ear-splittingly loud as it echoes off the cement floor. The bullet catches Flagler in the upper arm, sending him sprawling. An amateur firing a Glock almost always hits a spot a couple of feet above the intended target as the pistol's kick is much stronger than anticipated.

She opens her eyes and her face blanches as she realizes what she's done. Before she can correct her mistake, I kick her legs out from under her, take the gun right out of her hands as she tumbles on to her back, and then drive an elbow into her nose, popping it and punching her lights out a second time. That crack should keep her down for a while.

Flagler does what I would have done . . . he tries to scramble away. I catch him easily and drive a fist right into the wound, and as he bites on that pain, his hand comes up in a feeble attempt to cover the bullet hole. I drive a second punch into his fingers, *through* his fingers, and he sprawls out on the floor, submissively throwing his hands up like a white flag.

After I do a quick search to make sure he doesn't have any blades stashed in his clothing, I move to the front door, flip the 'closed' sign around and lock it. We're going to have a longer conversation now, and I'm reluctant to share it with any new arrivals.

Flagler lives above the hardware store. It's a bizarre front for a professional hit man. Most killers prefer to deal with the public as little as possible, but here's this guy, welcoming them in and selling them circular saws and ceiling fans.

'My pop owned this place for forty-two years,' he offers by way of explanation. 'He left it to me when he croaked and I figured what the hell, I'll keep it open. He was a decent dude. Never did me wrong. She does more business than you'd think. Got to where I was only taking one or two contract gigs a year after I moved back. Should've just quit the game entirely. I definitely thought about it.'

'Who's the drop girl? The one who shot you downstairs?' I didn't really care, but I liked the way he was Mr. Chatty all of a sudden.

'My aunt Elaine. Elaine McCoy. I used to call her the Real McCoy because she always kept it real with me, you know? You didn't end her, did you?'

This guy. I shake my head once. 'Hogtied on aisle six.'

'The rope aisle.'

'Yep.'

He nods, 'Thanks for that. She knows what I do, and she knows she's in it, but still, it would've been a shame.'

'Where's the skull?'

'You gonna shoot me after I tell you? I don't care much, I'd just like to know if it's coming so I can get my mind right.'

I shake my head again. If he's relieved, he doesn't show it. If he doesn't believe me, he doesn't show it either.

'There's a floor safe under the lamp there. Combo's 24-34-24.'

I look over in the direction he indicated. 'You open the safe, fish out the skull and give it to me. Afterward, you can call whatever doctor you use and get 'im over here. I wasn't hired to kill you, so I'm not going to do any pro bono work. I just need the skull.'

He walks stiffly over to a straight black floor lamp near a television. Using his good hand, he rolls it along its base and exposes a recessed safe before he stoops over the lock. His face is white from the bullet wound; sweat has broken through and drips off his forehead. He forces himself to concentrate as he twists the dial on the safe's face, and then exhales when the door pops open.

I put the barrel of my pistol up against the middle of his back as he reaches inside with both hands. In movies, guns at close range are always pointed at victim's heads, but the head is the easiest part of the body to jerk suddenly, like I did when I heard the shotgun cock downstairs. But the middle of the back? The middle of the back is damn near impossible to spin out of the way in the time it takes for a skilled gunman to squeeze a trigger.

He doesn't flinch as he withdraws a bone-white human cranium from the safe and hands it to me.

'You gonna ask me whose skull it is?'

'I'm gonna ask you something else.'

'Yeah?'

'What would've happened if I would've dialed 24-34-24 into the safe like you told me?'

He swallows. His face blanches as white as the skull bones.

'I . . .'

'You told me 24-34-24. But when you popped open the safe just now, the combination you used was 10-20-10.'

He smiles weakly. 'You caught that?'

'Yeah. I have good eyes. Could've been a fighter pilot.'

He shrugs. 'It . . . uh . . . it would've blown up in your face.'

'I figured.'

'Does that mean . . .'

I fire into his back twice, through his skin and into his heart. He flops forward, dead before he can finish the sentence.

I wasn't lying when I told Flagler I wouldn't kill him. But attempting to trick me into tripping a bomb puts a foot on the throat of my mercy.

4

I walk into the warehouse, and for the first time, I realize I'm soaking wet. The cool air hits me as I step through the door, and I shudder as though a ghost walked on my grave. Like I said, though I haven't been on an assignment, not really, it *feels* like an assignment. The tiger is a tiger, and though some may forget, may think of the animal as domesticated, as tame, the beast remembers what it is, and watches, and waits. Instincts, though dulled, are resurrected like Lazarus. Smiles turn to screams. Familiarity turns to non-recognition. And love? Love inevitably turns to grief.

I played the game against a worthy opponent for the first time in over a year, and I came out on top. A feeling is growing inside me I'm not sure I can contain. I'm not sure I *want* to contain it.

The tiger is a goddamned tiger.

Risina has her back to me when I enter, and maybe she feels a change in the air, a charge, like an electric current ripping through the walls, because she bolts upright, nearly overturning her chair as she spins.

'You scared me,' she says breathlessly. Her eyes find what's in my hands. 'Is that . . . ?'

I nod at the skull, holding it up like the gravedigger in Hamlet.

'You know whose it is?'

I shake my head, and she laughs. The sound is like a hypnotist's snap, a bell ringing, because whatever foreboding premonition I brought into the room disappears in that sound. That laugh, that look on her face, that simple prism in her eyes sustained me through so much it almost seems surreal, absurd, that I questioned going on without her.

And maybe that's it, what I haven't been able to get my head around until now: maybe the key isn't absence but proximity. Maybe the key isn't sending her away, but pulling her closer. Maybe Risina is my battery, my power source.

'So we make the exchange with Bacino? That skull for whatever information he has on why your name is involved.'

'That's it.' And she's touched on the biggest problem in all this: if Bacino just wanted his skull back, and kidnapped Archie to get me to do the dirty work for him, why would he cite me specifically? It doesn't add up, it's not simple, there's a piece missing. That's the way of the killing game: it's a messy business.

'I'm looking forward to meeting him,' Risina says. Then, a second later . . . 'Archie, not Bacino.'

Smoke strolls into the room, his eyes downcast, his hands fidgety. I liked Smoke when I first met him, and I chalked his nervous disposition up to being a fish out of water, but now I'm suspicious. There's no doubt the time I spent out of the game dulled my skills; maybe it dulled my senses as well. I feel like a diver coming to the surface after a long time in the deep.

'Something wrong, Smoke?'

He meets my eyes, then quickly looks away, his head bobbing like a chicken looking for seed. 'Nah, just anxious is all.' I think that's all he's going to say, but he adds, 'I swear I feel like I'm being watched or followed or some shit.'

'You mark anyone? Same car in two different places, same eyes in a crowd, even if the face is different?'

Smoke shakes his head. 'Nah. I don't think so. Like I said, I'm anxious. Wanna get this over and done with. Get Archie back. It was just a feeling, was all. Maybe I been drinkin' too many sodas or some shit.'

I watch him twitch some more, like he doesn't know where to put his hands, so they stay in perpetual motion.

'In this world, you gotta trust your instincts, Smoke.'

His eyes shoot up and search mine to see if there's any malice behind my words. Am I talking *to* him or *about* him? Am I challenging him? I don't give him anything, my face as unreadable as a cipher.

There's something he's keeping from us, something that has him as skittish as a deer, and I'm sure Risina spots it too.

'So now we wait for the meet, I s'pose,' says Smoke.

'No.'

His eyes shoot up again. 'No?'

'Uh-uh. Playing defense is how you get backed into a corner, how you end up broken or dead.'

Risina offers, 'We take the fight to him?'

'That's right. Word of what happened to Flagler won't hit the streets until tomorrow at the earliest . . .'

'What happened to Flagler?'

I look at Risina carefully, and the question dies in the air.

'Oh,' is all she manages and her cheeks color. I have to remind myself how new she is to this life. It's another crack in the wall of my plans to keep her close, but that laugh. I have to concentrate on that laugh.

'So we hit him tonight before he has a chance to plan for our arrival. We meet him on our terms. If Archie's alive and Bacino has him, we'll get him back.'

Smoke nods, seeing it. He raises his eyebrows, and it looks like he's genuinely relieved. 'I s'pose you want to see the original file on Bacino again.'

'Yeah, we should all go over it and figure out the best place to hit him.'

I like to confront a man in his bed. It's the second most vulnerable place to hit a target, short of his shower or bath. It is where a mark's defenses are at his lowest – even if he's stashed a weapon under a pillow or beneath the mattress, the added effect of being groggy cancels any advantage. The romanticized notion of a hunted man sleeping with one eye open is bullshit. Once a mark is down for the night, it is exponentially easier to put him down permanently.

I don't need to kill Bacino; I just need him to know how easy it is for me to get to him. I need to embarrass him. I need to make him regret summoning a hit man named Columbus.

According to the file made up for Flagler, Bacino lives in a mansion in Highland Park. He's alone, except for a half-dozen bodyguards, the occasional woman, a pair of dogs, and his older brother, Ben, who collects a salary but does little to earn it. Ben is supposed to be some sort of chef, cooking for his brother, but the file mentions his real job is a gofer, an errand boy. Groceries need rounding up? Ben does it. Coffee needs brewing? Ben does it. Car needs a wash? Ben does it, but not much more than that. Whether or not he knows Rich collects skulls is not mentioned in the file. They live on opposite sides of the house, and Ben is a foot shorter and a hundred pounds heavier, so I'm not worried about confusing the two.

The bodyguards live at the house and rotate out, two-two-and-two in eight-hour shifts to cover the clock. The guys are ex-cops or ex-military, and they indicate Bacino isn't trifling with his detail, isn't just trying to create an exaggerated sense of security the way some people put security company signs in their yards even though they never turn on their alarms.

Archie's file is a good one, and if he makes it out of this alive, it'll be at least partly due to his meticulous work. Bacino sleeps in a second-story corner bedroom that faces away from the street. He usually stays up late, hitting the pillow around midnight and then sleeping through the morning.

'I'm going to get to him at two A.M., wake him up from sugarplum dreams by tapping my Glock to his forehead. And Risina?'

She raises her head, expectantly.

'You're coming with me.'

Outside, the moon is down and the sky is starless, as black as tar. We parked ten blocks away and hoofed the distance, both wearing dark shirts and pants. We stand in the expansive back yard of Bacino's neighbor, a Persian oil billionaire who is only in this country two months of the year. He pays a man to check on his property twice a day, but the caretaker cut that down to twice a week when he realized no one reported to the Persian about his performance. Risina and I have the yard to ourselves.

'Are you sure?' she whispers at about ten minutes to two.

I make certain she can see my eyes, even in the darkness. 'You were in it with me, even before you knew you were in it. And if something should happen to me, you're still in it. You understand?'

'I understand. You told me it was your choice to have me here, but it is my choice as well. Yes?'

'Yes.'

'The more prepared you are, the better I'll feel.'

'Then let's go wake up Bacino.'

We scale the brick wall separating the two yards as easily as steeplechase horses and stick to the shadows as we approach the back of the house. Archie's file is accurate: the night-shift bodyguards have joined up on the front patio to have a twenty-minute smoke. I imagine they've spent the last four years smoking together like this without incident, swapping stories about their lives away from this house, catching each other up on their wives or children or what the Cubs did the day before. I have a feeling they won't have these jobs much longer.

The alarm is a standard 10-zone system from a generic manufacturer, and since Bacino has a pair of golden retrievers who have free rein of the house, I'm confident he doesn't turn on the motion detectors. The sensor makers always say pets under forty pounds won't set 'em off, but they're full of shit. I'll know in a moment if I'm right.

We enter through a small rectangular pane of glass embedded in a set of French doors that lead from a den out to the pool. I don't break the pane – some alarms trigger just from the sound of glass shattering – so instead I use needlenose pliers to scrape away the wood putty and take out the glazier's points, starting at the center of the frame and working towards the edges. I only have a few minutes and have to move quickly. Once I pull the bottom of the wood apart, I gently slide the glass panel out and place it against the house. After we shimmy through the opening, I replace the wooden frame so to the casual eye, it looks like nothing is missing, though the pane is no longer there. The air is still, so I'm not worried about a breeze giving away our entry-point.

We sneak through an entertainment room, then a foyer, where we can just make out the soft voices of the two guards jawing away, and then we take a set of stairs to the top of the house before heading for the corner bedroom.

I feel Risina freeze even before I understand why, and then I hear the panting of a dog's breath, or two dogs' breaths, as I now make out their silhouettes in the doorframe of the nearby guest bedroom. They move forward, toward us, cautiously, their tails down, their ears pricked. If Bacino thought he owned guard dogs, thought they might bark a warning against intruders, he should have raised a different breed. Risina turns her hand palm upward and I do the same, holding it out toward the timid retrievers. Grateful for the acknowledgement, they mosey over and start licking our hands. A few quick pats to the head and they trot back to the guest room, mollified. Risina's grin is unmistakable, even in the dim light of the corridor.

As promised, I tap the barrel of my Glock on to Bacino's forehead. 'Tap' is probably the wrong word; I pop him hard. He bolts up like a snake bit his face and the first thing he sees is Risina at the foot of his bed. I wanted to disorient him and she does a hell of a job at that. He blinks a few times like he's still trying to swim to the surface, and then I slap him between the eyebrows again so he jumps, clamps his hand over his head and barks a sharp, 'No!' Not 'stop' or 'don't,' but 'no.' Under the circumstances, I think it's a decent reaction.

I rack the Glock so he knows there is a bullet in the chamber and a second 'no' dies in his throat. He starts to open his mouth, but I interrupt. 'We have what you want . . . you need to give us back what we want.'

'Who are you?'

'Columbus. Now where is Archie Grant?'

His eyes do that unmistakable thing where they squint as he searches his memory.

'I don't . . .'

I smack the hard polymer of the gun down on his nose. 'Ow, goddammit . . .' he manages as his hands flock to the spot.

'A bit harder and your nose breaks. And I'll pop it right through your fingers if you don't start talking.'

'Let me finish my goddamn sentence then,' he croaks, his voice muffled by his hands. I don't look over at Risina to see if she's startled by my aggression. She hangs in my periphery, immobile.

I nod and Bacino continues, his eyes watering. I gotta give him credit for keeping the tough-guy act going under the circumstances. Hell, maybe he *is* a tough guy. 'Mrs. Hauser. Kindergarten teacher. Craig Captain. Father's friend from college. Met him one time, when I was seven. John Mayfield. First man to ever cut my hair.'

He dabs his hands near his nostrils to check for blood, but his fingers are clean, and then he scrunches his nose a few times. His voice remains pinched. 'I have a thing for names. I remember names from before I could read or write. Guys I met only once. Guys my father brought around for a beer after work. Some people never forget a face . . . I never forget a name. Now you said this name, Archie Grant, like I should know it but I don't. You can pound on my nose until there's nothing left, but I don't know that name.'

He's telling the truth; it's unmistakable. How does he not know the name of the guy he kidnapped? There is only one answer. Bacino's a lot of things, but he's not the guy I'm looking for.

An idea starts to form in my mind. Maybe I got the end of this story right, but misread the beginning.

'You missing a skull?'

His eyes flash. 'Missing?'

'No one's stolen one of your skulls?'

'I . . .'

'You made a deal with a contract killer named Flagler.' It's not a question.

He looks back and forth from Risina to me. 'I . . .'

'He came to kill you, and you bought him off with a skull from your collection.'

Now he doesn't protest or stammer, just lets me continue my train of thought.

'He doesn't put a bullet in you, and you promise to give him one of your most expensive, rarest items. That's how it went down, right?'

Bacino folds his arms across his chest and pouts. 'I knew it wouldn't end there.'

I reach into my pack and pull out the skull, the one I thought was swiped by Flagler but was actually traded to him by Bacino. A skull for a life. Bacino looks at it with the eye of a practiced collector.

'Do you know how much that's worth?'

I shake my head.

'More than the contract on my life, I can assure you. You got it, you keep it. I know I'm not in a position to bargain, but I'll make the same deal with you I made with the other guy. Don't kill me and that skull's yours. You can make a fortune off of it. It's the head of—'

And right then, his brother opens the door holding a leather collar and wearing only a bathrobe. 'What talent you got up in here, bro?'

He's wearing a dopey grin and it takes a moment for his eyes to move from Risina to me. I can see the slow calculations take place in his head. He moves from lustfulness to confusion to understanding in the span of five seconds.

Good fences can get into a lot of places, discover a wealth of personal information, chronicle a life to a surprising degree. A pay-off to a talkative employee, a search through police records, a disguised visit to relatives or friends can prove indispensable in fleshing out a mark's file. And in areas that are off-limits, behind closed doors, an experienced fence will make educated assumptions.

Nothing in Bacino's file suggested he shared his late-night trysts with his sad-sack older brother. I thought we'd have another ten minutes before the bodyguards finished their smoke break, but now I understand why the guards take that break in the first place: to give these bastards some breathing room while they screw whores together. Who would want to listen to a pair of assholes slipping it to some one-night stand each night?

'Get help!' Bacino screams. It takes Ben a few seconds of blinking for the words to process. Then his lids pop open and his eyes widen as the pieces come together.

In a fistfight, the guy you're trading blows with will often try to land a haymaker to the jaw. The punch starts from somewhere near his belt and is as easy to spot coming as the headlight on the front of a train. An experienced dirty fighter will duck his chin and crouch so that the punch connects with the top of his head, almost always shattering the bones of the punching hand. It is the hardest part of the human body, the top of the skull.

Before Ben can flee, I hurl the stolen skull at his face with everything I have. The top of the cranium connects with his forehead, making a sound like a baseball bat thumping into a wooden support beam. Immediately, he drops to the floor as his legs turn to jelly.

Spying an opening, Bacino launches out of the bed and heads for Risina, roaring like a lion. I'm not going to be able to close the distance before he gets to her, but I'm going to make him sorry if he harms her in any way. He leaps for her throat, but she swings the gun around like she's unleashing a pair of brass knuckles, not taking the time to aim and pull the trigger, but nailing him in the side of the face with everything she has, the steel and polymer of the gun's barrel leading the way.

The blow connects with an audible crunch, a pistol-whip, and though it doesn't knock him out, it stuns him and shatters a few teeth in the process. Enraged, he blinks away tears and tries again, but I finish what Risina started, swinging for the back of his head with the butt of my gun, once, twice, until he falls face-down on the wooden floor.

The older brother Ben starts to groan.

'Time to go . . .'

'But?'

'He doesn't have Archie.'

'You believe him?'

I nod and that's all she needs from me. We're out the door, down the stairs, through the opening and over the wall before the bodyguards tamp out their cigarettes. We'll get a few more minutes as they mistake the moans of pain upstairs for something else. It'll be all we need.

5

Accidents don't exist in this business. A hit man dies, a fence goes missing, a mark wanders off the side of a building on his way to plummeting ten stories: none of this is surreptitious. This trade places a premium on precise planning, on exacting detail, and if a player has his ticket punched, more likely than not, a malevolent hand, not an act of God, is behind it.

The wind has grown belligerent throughout the day, racing around corners and smacking pedestrians in the face like a schoolyard bully. The sun is nothing more than a condemned man held in chains by a wall of dark gray clouds. The sky might rain, or it might just threaten the act, as though it gets some sort of twisted pleasure out of withholding the information. Every now and then, Chicago, as a city, likes to rise up and remind its citizens she won't be pushed to the background, she won't blend in behind them, she's a leading character in their life story and they'd be wise not to forget it.

The three of us, Smoke, Risina, and I, hurry under the scaffolding of some Gold Coast remodeling project and head toward a simple eatery named the Third Coast Café. 'Pardon our progress' signs have spread across the city like kudzu. Everywhere I look, another building constructed in the late-19th century aftermath of the Great Fire is in the middle of a facelift. After the housing crash, all those construction workers had to find something to do with their time, so the city funneled stimulus dollars into the hands of no-bid general contractors. Of course, it wouldn't be Chicago if evidence of kickbacks and greased palms hadn't already been hinted at by the *Times*.

The workers swarm the scaffolding like wasps, the wind only a nuisance. They raise equipment, bang away at walls, scrape, sand, and plaster, ignoring the weather. I guess anything becomes routine if you do it long enough.

The restaurant is half-full this time of day and customers hunch over coffee and pieces of pie, reluctant to give up their table and head back out into the wind. We slide into a booth in the back corner and order some food. Smoke's nervousness has reached a new apex; his leg shakes up and down like a piston.

'We're in a jam now,' he says. 'We're up against it.'

'Yeah, we're at square zero. We haven't even reached square one. The skull collector was an anomaly in Archie's files, but not the one who nabbed him or wanted me.'

'We chased the wrong dog up the wrong tree.'

'I suppose we could take a look at the file again, see if we can figure out who the client was, see if he's upset the mark is still alive.'

'Seems like it wouldn't have nothing to do with you, though?' He's asking more than he's telling. He has a point, but his fidgeting grows even more exaggerated.

'What aren't you telling me, Smoke?'

When Smoke looks up, I can't tell if he's surprised by my question or if I caught him by being direct. He swallows and wipes his mouth with his napkin. He looks to Risina for help, but she gives him a hard stare I didn't know she had in her. I'll admit it's disconcerting, coming from her. I wouldn't want to be on the receiving end of that look.

'What'd'you mean?'

'You've grown more fidgety than a prisoner walking toward the hangman.'

'I told you, I'm nervous 'bout this whole thing.'

'Yeah, you told me.'

'You know . . .' he tosses his napkin down on the table, then points his finger at me, 'this is exactly what I was worried about. *Exactly.*'

'What're you worried about, Smoke?'

His finger hasn't left the air. 'This! You turning on me, everyone looking at me like I had something to do with Archie disappearing. You think the first thing that crossed my mind when I saw that ransom note wasn't "uh-oh, you stepped in it now, Smoke?" I've been scared shitless since he was taken, and I could've run a thousand times. Hell, I didn't even have to come find you; I could've just caught the first bus to Frisco and forgot the whole damn thing. But I did because Archie said if he were ever in a pinch that's what I was supposed to do.'

His eyes focus, like he just now realizes his finger is jabbing the air toward me, that his voice is growing louder. He lowers his finger but doesn't lower his eyes.

'Let me tell you something about Archie and me. You won't understand this and I don't care if you do, but this is the truth and if that's a sound you've heard before then you'll recognize it now.

'I was twenty-eight years old before anyone believed in me. My whole life was spent with people telling me I wasn't good enough, wasn't smart enough, wasn't strong enough, wasn't solid enough, you know what I'm saying? My mom thought I looked like my father and never forgave me for that, even when I apologized. Can you imagine? Apologizing to your mom for the way you look? And all you get for it is your mother trying to beat your father's face off your neck.

'School stopped for me when I was fifteen. Just walked away and didn't go back. You think there were officers out there checking to see where I was? You think the school board or the principal or the teachers came around asking, "why isn't Leonard in school?" Let me let you in on a little secret: they don't care. No one gives a shit. Just one more drop-out, one more black boy out of our hallways, out of our detention hall, and good riddance.

'My first arrest was for boosting a car. I'd love to tell you a story about how some buddy of mine talked me into it, or how I wasn't going to do nothing but drive that car around and forget my life for a few hours, but that'd be a lie and you're here for the truth. The truth was I knew that Cam's Motorshop out by the airport would pay a couple thousand to strip down Hondas with no questions asked and that's where I was heading when I got stung. I wanted the money, plain and simple. I turned eighteen exactly three days before my arrest so I did a hundred days at Cook County instead of juvey. That was about as much fun as a punch in the dick. I'm sure you've seen your share of hellholes but you have no idea. You have no fucking idea, I assure you.

'The second time I got picked up was across state lines. I had grown pretty skillful at jacking cars by then and I had a regular thing going with six or seven chop shops all over Chicago. This one cat named Holmes I worked with a few times asked if I could drive a hot Nissan over to Boston where his brother Todd had a shop and drive back some other wheels to Indy. Said he'd pay five gees for the trouble and that cash sounded pretty damn good to me. I don't know what I was aiming to buy at the time, but I remember that the money would set me straight for a while. Needless to say, I saw the bubble lights go up behind me just crossing into Massachusetts, and I panicked, ended up with a helicopter spotlight over my head, six cruisers, and a set of those spikes stretched across the road to take me down to the rims. It was like a Hollywood movie except missing the ending where the good guy gets away. Or maybe I wasn't the good guy, come to think of it.

'Anyway, state lines is state lines and I ended up in Federal without a friend in the world. I tried to call Holmes and I'll be damned if the number done changed. I was staring three years in the face and the Fed House meant organized crime and drug traffickers and El Salvadoran gangs and Aryan brotherhoods and a whole mess of hard cases who wouldn't think twice about putting your insides on the outside of you if you know what I'm saying.

'The second day I'm locked up . . . the *second* damn day . . . I get sucker-punched in the walkway between the chapel and the restrooms. I'm walking along and WHAM! on my back, laid out flat. Didn't see the fist fly, didn't see the face, just a blast of pain, blinking white lights, and I'm looking up at the ceiling. I don't know who hit me or why they hit me or what I had to do to make it right . . . no one tells you that shit. Look at me, I'm all of five-ten and skin and bones and I was even thinner back then if you can dig that. No one helped me up and no one told me what the fuck I was supposed to do to keep from getting jawboned again.

'When I went to get my meal that afternoon, I saw some of the prisoners snickering at me and my fat lip and my purple cheek but I just ignored them best I could and sat down at one of the tables they had scattered in the cafeteria.

'That's where Archibald Grant found me, busted lip and busted flat, eating a dry hamburger in the cafeteria at Lewisburg. He asked me my name and he asked me my story and I don't know why I let everything out, but like I'm doing here, I did for him there. The words just poured out of me like water out of a busted bucket. I told him where I came from, where I'd been and why I was stuck up inside there.

'He looked at me, smiling that half smile of his, the way he does, you know, and didn't say nothing for a while. Then, he nodded like he'd known my story before I told it and he said I'd been stealing the wrong things. Cars, electronics, wallets, knicks and knacks, this place was full of people who boosted the wrong shit. Boosted it because they didn't know better. All that crap could only get you a little cash and what was the point in that? Risk versus reward was all upside down. Five thousand dollars worth five years in lockdown? In Federal? With these animals? Hell no. No fucking way.'

Smoke shakes his head vigorously, then swallows hard. He doesn't look at us, lost in his story, as he continues.

'Archie folded his hands and lowered his voice. He said what he stole, the only thing *worth* stealing, was information.

He said there was no greater commodity in the world. He said people laid down their lives for it since the dawn of man and they did it for good reason. Told me he stole information on the outside and he'd been stealing it on the inside, riding out his two-year term in comfort and security until he could resume business on the other side of the wall. Said he got thrown in here on purpose anyway, and though that claim had just the slightest ring of bullshit to it, I bought it like a fifty-cent bottle of beer. Looking back now, I'll just bet he did get himself thrown in there for whatever reason made sense at the time.'

I remember that time. My old fence Pooley went to visit Archie in that prison, and commented how he couldn't get to him to put a scare in him, get the information I needed at the time. Maybe Archie was in there to avoid my reach back then. It doesn't matter . . . I keep my mouth shut and listen to Smoke unfold his story.

'Anyway, I naturally said something along the lines of "why you telling me this?" And he said, "nobody ever believed in you, but I see a spark inside you maybe no one else saw before. Maybe it's buried deep down in there but I can see it." Of course I thought he was completely shining me but fuck if those words didn't sound like honey. Say what you want about Archibald Grant, but he's got a mouth on him that could sell scissors to a bald man. He told me he knew who waylayed me in the hall outside the chapel and he knew how to take care of that situation so I wouldn't be bothered again, not even looked at askew the whole time I was behind bars, but I needed to do something for him. "Could I do that?" he asked.

'I didn't know but I said I'd try. He said "good, good." Then he nodded to indicate a beefy prison guard standing behind the glass near the exit. "See that hack over there what looks like he ate too many dollar specials at the Taco Bell?"

Smoke stops and laughs to himself. 'You know how Archie do.'

I can't help but smile too, but signal with my hands tumbling over each other for him to get on with it. It doesn't do either of us any good to think of Archie in the past tense.

'He tells me the guard goes by the name of Nash. Archie says he's been able to crack the code on most of the hacks but this Nash has been a problem. Says he's tightlipped and none of the other guards'll spill on him.

'Now, as you can imagine, most bulls take a handout here or there for favors, but not this Nash. He's straight as an arrow and there was no chinks in the armor neither. He's one of those true blue badges you hear about but never expect to see. And those are the dangerous ones. Because nothing can fuck up a connected con's plans like a hack who won't play ball. Suddenly, you find yourself transferred to the wrong cell-block, or your pleasantries are confiscated, or you're eating at the wrong table in the cafeteria or worse. Balance of power is always a precarious thing in life, but in lock-down, it's hanging by tooth floss, I'll tell you that.

'Archie looks me over, and says, "get me *something*." "What'd'you mean, 'something'?" I ask back, and Archie gets that look in his eye he gets time to time that says "I'm smarter than you think I am." He looks down his nose at me and says, "What have we been talking about? Information, Smoke." He's the first one to call me that by the way cause I had this pack of Parliaments I pulled out and lit up in mid-conversation. That's the one good thing I'll say about L-burg . . . you can smoke inside that damn place. What happened to the world where we kicked all the smokers outdoors? Anyway, Archie keeps on, "Anything I can use on Nash to get what needs getting. One week. You find me some A-plus information and all your problems inside this box disappear like bad dreams in the morning light. Consider yourself off-limits for a week . . . nobody but nobody gonna be in your business, I *guarantee* that. And don't forget something, Smoke. I believe in you."'

Smoke fiddles with his unopened pack, turning the box over and over, occupying his hands. I have a feeling he'd like to pause the tale to step outside and light one up, but telling stories has a way of gaining a foothold on anything else you might want to do, planting its flag until it's over. He looks up at me.

'So what the fuck was I gonna do? I'm like three days into this shitbox and I'm going to find out information on a hack no one else has been able to procure? A bull with a clean certificate? How the fuck was I gonna do that? But those words were there, Columbus. He said 'em and I'll be damned if he didn't mean 'em. "I believe in you." Those words were like, I don't know, they had weight, man. You believe that?'

I nod and half of Smoke's mouth turns upward. His eyes start to shine, but he doesn't wipe at them.

'First thing I did was spend two days doing nothing but watching Nash. Marking his shift changes, seeing how he conducted himself, who he talked to, who he watched, hell, I even counted how many times he scratched his nuts. But there was nothing there. He just stood behind the glass and watched us with dark eyes.

'Now, he wasn't always behind the glass and that gave me a bit of hope. The bulls took various shifts, sometimes behind the glass, sometimes in the corridor outside the rec room, sometimes walking the block, and sometimes out in the yard.

'I watched him, I watched him, I watched him, and this cat Nash did not give me a goddamn inch. Believe that. I started thinking maybe he's a robot, like some android out of a space movie. C-3PO or some shit. Cons would try to talk to him and he'd just ignore their shit and give 'em a stare that stopped 'em cold.

'I was five days into my seven and I hadn't come up with jack squat. Not a plan, nothing. My mind was racing. Maybe I just make up a story and tell it to Archie, but what would that give me? Seemed like I might as well grab a shovel and start digging my own grave out in the yard. But damn if your mind don't play tricks on you in the box when you start running out of options. And those words were hanging over me the whole time . . . "I believe in you." I know it sounds corny as a holiday card, but I wanted that belief to be rewarded, made whole . . . that's the only way I can describe it. I wanted to justify his belief. This man I barely knew. Had only spoken to once.

'Then I saw an opening. The slimmest opening possible. An opening that would add some years on my sentence and would put the "hard" into "hard time" if I got caught.

'See, one thing I've come to learn about this job is you gotta look at things from a different angle. I was trying to shadow Nash and pick up on a mistake or a flaw or some way to get inside with him, but instead, I should've been watching where he wasn't. I didn't say that right. Let me explain.

'I noticed that the guards went into a locker room just off of A block when they checked in. Various guards would be in and out of there all day, Nash included. When he came in, he'd be wearing a pair of khakis and an oxford shirt, but when he walked out, he'd be wearing a different pair of pants and the blue dress shirt that all hacks wore, you know? It came to me then and there. I had to get inside that locker room and see if there was any clue, any *anything* he left behind in his locker when he went out on shift.

'So there it was. All my eggs in that basket. I only had a day left, and how the hell was I gonna get into that locker room? Prisoners weren't supposed to be out of A block at all, much less in the bullring.'

Smoke holds up one finger and flashes me a smile. 'Except one inmate. One guy, that's it. Little sawed off son-of-a-bitch named George Yackey. The Yack Attack, my ticket in. This con got the sweet gig of shining the bathrooms, sweeping the floors, picking up the dead bugs off the windowsills in the area called "A Extension" but what the cons called "the bullring" cause that's where the guards went for break and change. Yack was the only orange jumpsuit allowed back there, twice a day, to clean up the ring and make it look nice.

'Now understand, the bullring wasn't near the perimeter or even on the outskirts of the building, so it wasn't like you had shotguns trained on you or the hacks would think you were trying to escape if they caught you in there. In a lot of ways, it'd be worse for you, 'cause if you were in the ring unauthorized, the guards would assume you were trying to fuck 'em in some way. Steal from 'em or what-not. And here's a little fact about serving time no one talks about: if you make a legitimate attempt at escape . . . if you get caught climbing the side of a wall, or in a tunnel or gripping the undercarriage of a laundry truck as it drives off the site, the hacks don't beat the shit out of you. Hell, they're not even sore. They actually show you a little bit of respect. That's the truth! Don't ask me why it's so . . . best I can figure, they put themselves in the con's shoes and say, "why the hell wouldn't I want out of this dungeon any way I can? How'm I gonna blame this poor fool for trying?" Sure, they'll throw you in solitary for a month and take away privileges for a year, but when you walk down the block, they'll give you a nod like "not bad, you crazy son-of-a-bitch. Not bad."

'So if I was trying to escape, I might've had a bit of lenience if I was busted. But caught in their area? Caught in the ring? Those bulls'll go to town on your flesh until they catch bone, I guarantee that. That's lesson time to them. Gotta teach a lesson, right?

'Anyway, I went to Yackey's cell and I told him I needed a favor from him. I kept my eyes square and my hands spread like this, so he'd know I was in the *askin'* position, not the *tellin'* one, you know? He looked me up and down like I was dirt going down the shower room drain. So I made a play I had no idea would take, a play out of desperation, but what was I gonna do? I said, "Yack, let me tell you about your future. In the next day I'm going to be on the inside with Archibald Grant, and if you know what that's worth, then you should climb on my back now. Do me this favor, and we'll reap the rewards together. But if you choose to cross me, if you tell me to fuck off and go away, then put your money on the "don't pass" line and we'll see what happens.

'He thought about it for a long minute, maybe the longest of his life, certainly was of mine, and then looked up and asked me what I needed. "Five minutes of your time tomorrow," was my answer.

'I did my best to clean my jumper and shave my face and trim my hair and do everything I could to blend in, not stand out, not give the bulls a single thing that would call attention to myself if they happened to look my way as I approached the barrier between A block and the bullring. Five minutes, I told myself. Five minutes, in and out, get something, anything out of Nash's locker and run like hell back to the block.

'Now every day from two to three, that locker room in the bullring was empty. I clocked this for two straight days and this was the only pattern I could find. It had something to do with the rotation or the way they marked their shifts, but not once did a guard enter that locker room between two and three, and point of fact, the entire ring was empty during that time, save for George Yackey and his mop and bucket.

'At 2:15 on the last day, I walked from A block bathroom over to that barrier. Now, Yack Attack told me he'd meet me there at that time, swipe the card, get me inside, and that was that. But I'll be damned if he wasn't there.

'Now I'm standing next to the door and if a bull walks out of the cafeteria or out of the gym, I'm going to be looking like a big orange sign saying "this fucking con is up to no good." And I'm sweating and under my breath I'm cursing ol' Yack, this passive-aggressive motherfucker who told me what I wanted to hear but really placed his bet on the other side and the sad thing is he was right to do so. By noon tomorrow, I'd be powerless and he'd still have his sweet gig, so why the hell should he do me any favors?

'I'm stewing for a good couple of minutes, trying to figure out my next chess move, knowing that I need to vacate immediately, get the hell away from this barrier and get back to my cell and figure out what the hell I was gonna do in the next ten hours to get my ass out of this spot, and then I see the door to the locker room open inside the bullring and Yack shuffles out and heads to the barrier and opens the door to let me inside.

'He mutters something about wanting to make sure the coast was clear and for me to get the hell on with it, and if I don't start moving instead of gawking in the passageway, he's gonna slam the barrier back in my face.

'I move like a jackrabbit, into the bullring, one, two, three steps and I'm through the locker room door, my heart beating so hard I can feel it in my throat, and there I was feeling as exposed and vulnerable as a naked baby.

'The locker room was pretty much what you'd imagine, sort of in the shape of a domino, two rooms really, a half partition in the middle, with rows of lockers along each wall and wooden benches in the center so the bulls could change their socks or whatever needed changing.

'The clock in my head was already ticking as I stood dumbfounded in that off-limits room, and it hit me that I didn't know which fucking locker was Nash's. What the hell was I thinking? Walking in here blind like this. I moved around the front room looking for a clue, but all the lockers were the same, just steel outsides, shiny and clean, no tape or nothing marking whose was which. Fuck me, my head was telling me to just bail out now, slip back outside and through the barrier before I catch a beat-down the likes from which men don't come back normal, but my feet kept moving me on. I was between a rock and a bigger rock, I'll tell you that.

'So my feet walk me into the back part of the room, and there it is, a mop set right up against one particular locker. Yack Attack, who had no reason to do me any favors other than knowing I'd owe him if I did in fact find myself riding high after this, played me an ace. I moved the mop out of the way and even though the locker was locked, I slipped it open as easy as eating cake. I had one set of skills coming into this place and this baby lock wasn't going to stymie a man who knew his way around opening things up that needed opening.

'I get the locker unlocked and it makes more noise than I mean to make because I'm so fucking jumpy and my hands are a little sweat-soaked I have to admit, and I let the door slip and it bangs against the locker next to it. I hold my breath but no one comes a-calling, and I'm staring inside at his clothes, those same clothes I saw him come in with: a pair of khaki pants, neatly folded on a hanger, hanging next to a red striped oxford shirt and a blue blazer. Down in the bottom of the locker sit a pair of brown Cole Haan loafers. That's it. That's what I've risked my hide for . . . a set of clothes and nothing else.

'I fish through the pants pockets but they're empty, then I try the blazer but nothing in the inside pocket and I swear this headache springs up on me all of a sudden like when you drink something cold too fast, and I realize that my body's telling me emphatically and wholly that I've screwed the pooch and right then I notice some heavy coughing coming from outside the locker room door, like a fit, like Yack's out there choking on his lunch and through the murk of this headache I somehow realize this is a signal, a warning, and I shut the locker and dive behind the little half wall divider that separates the front part of the room from the back and press myself up against it as I hear the door open and a guard whose voice I recognize as this black bull named Propes is saying "You okay, prisoner?" to Yackey as he enters the room.

'I got a fifty-fifty shot, that's all I got. Either his locker's in the back part and he's going to catch me there looking like a fish out of the tank or his locker is in the front part and I might, just might, be okay if I can keep my teeth from chattering. You know how many times your life comes down to such a clear-cut, fifty-fifty chance? Maybe five, ten times, and there it was: white marble and I'm okay, black marble and I'm gone, baby, gone.

'I hear Propes take five, six steps into the room and he's close enough I can hear him breathing through his nose the way he does, and my heart's beating now like a donkey kicking the inside of my chest, and the bull sniffles a few times and opens up a locker in the front room on the right, no more than twenty feet from where I'm hiding, holding my breath.

'I hear Yack say, "you okay, boss?" and Propes says, "just forgot my damn Advil," and he must finally find the pills in whatever place he keeps 'em in his locker, because he closes the door and leaves without another word.

'Immediately, I'm back inside Nash's locker and I got one more place to look before I break down and cry, and so I stick my hand deep inside his shoes, and I'll be damned if I don't hit paydirt. He's got his wallet buried down in there and his keys and his sunglasses and some loose change, and I forget everything else and flip open the wallet. Forty seconds later, I'm out the door and Yack looks as sick with worry as I feel and another ten steps and he lets me out of the barrier and it is finished.'

Smoke looks up at me and he knows he has me. I'm a sucker for a good story, and most guys in the game know how to spin one. Archie was one of the best and Smoke must've picked up a thing or two sitting beside him. I don't interrupt because I'm enjoying this tale and because I know he's telling the truth.

'Next day, next *morning* even, Archibald Grant shows up in my cell as soon as the bars open and this is what he says to me. "Give me what you got." Not "did you get anything?" not "tell me you didn't blow this, Smoke," just "give me what you got." You see, he meant it when he said he believed in me. He knew I'd have something. He just knew it.

'I told him I had two things, actually. Nash's address on Las Palmas Street and that he had two little blond girls named Kahla and Mitty, ages 10 and 8, and that's all I could get. Archie smiled at me as big as Christmas and said "even better than I thought, Smoke. Even better than I thought."

'I'll tell you something, I don't know how he used that information to get over on Nash, but we've both been in this business long enough to know that if you got someone's address and you know his kids' names and what they look like, well, shiiiiiit. It don't take a mathematician to figure out what two plus two makes. Archie had that straight-shooting bull practically wiping his ass within a week. And Archie kept his word too . . . I didn't so much as have a con look at me sideways the rest of my time in Federal.

'Archie gained his release six months before me and I thought maybe that'd be my ass, but his grip on L-Burg stayed tight even after he shook tailfeathers. And the day I walked out of that cinderblock, he had a bus ticket waiting for me. Said I'd be working for him from now on and not to worry about nothing else. He said I'd still be in the stealing business, but stealing the most important shit of all: information. And he was right.'

Smoke stands up and that finger comes up again. This time his lips quiver as he pierces me with his eyes. 'That's my story. So don't sit here and tell me I had something to do with Archie getting kidnapped or that I might know who did it. Archibald Grant believed in me when no one else would. I'd give anything . . . check that, I'd give *everything* for him. You believe that, Columbus?'

I nod once. 'I do.' I can see Risina nodding too out of the corner of my eye.

'All right, then. Good. We on the same page and let's keep it that way.' He picks up his pack of cigarettes. 'I gotta go light one.'

Smoke leaves the booth and heads to the front door.

Risina exhales as he rolls out of hearing range. 'What do you think?'

'I think he gave it to us straight. What do *you* think?'

I can tell she's pleased that I reciprocated by asking for her opinion. 'I think he's closer to Archie than you are, closer than I'll ever be. I think he's scared for his friend. I think he'd do anything to get him back. And I think he told us the truth.'

I nod my agreement, pay the check, and Risina and I head for the door. I'm going to do something when I go outside that I rarely do. I'm going to apologize. Apologize to Smoke for doubting him. I need him with me on this, pulling in the same direction as me, and I need him to trust my decision-making, my instincts, even though those same instincts wanted to finger him as an accomplice or worse. The only way to accomplish that is to say I'm sorry.

Smoke is standing right outside the front door, under the construction scaffolding, his cigarette down to the filter, staring blankly across the street. I hold the door open for Risina and start to follow her outside.

Smoke looks our way, drops his cigarette to stamp it out, and his eyes search mine for, I don't know, understanding? Clarity? Acceptance?

I'll never know because the scaffolding crashes down like an avalanche, collapsing on top of his head, and kills him instantly.

6

We're in the kitchen, through it, heading out the back and I haven't let go of Risina's arm as I clench it in a vise grip. I only had a split second to react. I heard a sound like metal snapping and the whirr of a tension line releasing, all in the span of a crack of lightning, and as the scaffolding started to collapse, I shot my hand out, a miracle lunge, closed my fingers around Risina's arm and jerked her back into the café only a second before she would have been crushed. I didn't have time to warn Smoke, couldn't have shouted if I'd wanted to. The only thing I had time to do was watch him take the brunt of it, five stories of structure raining down on top of him like a machine press.

Accidents don't exist in this business.

Risina's natural instinct was to look back as the realization of what happened hit her. She wanted to help, to see if anyone could be rescued, to see if anyone was hurt but alive, but she's new to this world and I have to keep her moving, even if it means I bruise her arm because I will not let go.

Everyone hurries toward the front of the restaurant while we rush out the back.

'Wait, wait, wait,' she's saying but I'm not waiting, not allowing her to break stride. A half block down the alley I finally loosen my grip and she practically falls over as she jerks her arm away.

'What're you doing?' she shouts. Her Italian accent kicks in when she's angry. 'We have to see if—'

'We have to get out of here.'

'But what if we can—'

'He's dead, Risina. I saw the structure come down on top of him.'

'But how . . . how did it . . . ?'

'I don't know, but we need to keep moving—'

'It was an accident . . . we have to—'

'Listen to me! I told you when we started you have to follow my lead, and that's what I'm telling you now. We have to keep moving—'

'I'm not going to leave until—'

'That was no accident!' I say through clenched teeth.

My words hit her like an uppercut. Her whole face changes as the anger peels away. Her feet start up again and I don't need to grab her arm to lead the way. 'What do you mean?'

'I mean it was supposed to come down on *us*.'

We spill out of the alley onto Division Street and join a crowd that drifts out of a bar, then change our pace to match the jostling pedestrians, to get lost in them, and she doesn't say another word though I can see her face pulled tight in my periphery.

I don't think we're being followed.

Archibald Grant's office is deserted, but it won't be for long. Two forces are at play against us: word travels fast in this business, and power vacuums fill quickly. Some time in the next twenty-four hours, someone is going to find out Smoke died outside that Gold Coast restaurant. Without him around, a few of Archie's men are going to swoop in here like vultures and clean this place out, take the chairs, take the desks, take anything of value they can get their hands on and sell the lot to the highest bidder. The furniture isn't where they'll land the real money, though. Someone who guarded Archie or one of his bagmen will know the value in the files, the contracts, the information. A rival fence will pay handsomely for access to Archie's work, and some underling will soon attempt to provide it.

'So why are we here now?' Risina asks. 'You want the files for yourself?'

'Not the files. File.'

'I don't understand . . .'

I'm already ripping through the cabinets, looking for the stack Smoke slid over to me when we were trying to find an anomaly in the contracts over the last couple of years.

I had found an anomaly all right, but I didn't realize it at the time.

Accidents don't exist in this business.

'Help me find a file with the name "Hepper" at the top. First name was something like "Jan" or "Janet."'

We start pulling stacks out of the cabinet and blitz through them. I'm only looking at the names on the first page, the names of the targets. If it's not a match, I toss it to the floor and pick up the next.

None of the names in the initial stack look familiar, must not be ones I fished through the other day. I grab another batch and start flipping pages when Risina pipes up, 'Ann Hoeppner?'

'That's it!' I say, more excitement in my voice than I meant. She hands the dossier over and I open the cover. 'Yeah, this is the one.'

Risina blows a stray hair out of her face and places her hands on her hips. 'Can you please tell me what this is about?'

I hold up the file. 'Accidents don't exist in this business,' I tell her. And in a few minutes, to prove my point, I'm going to set this office on fire.

In the contract business, hit men employ various methods to kill marks. There are guys who specialize in long-range sniper rifles, guys who work in close with handguns or knives, guys who ply their trade with car bombs or poison or good old-fashioned ropes around the throat. There are experienced vendetta killers who'll carve up the target or take a piece of the body to bring back to the client, but Archie stayed away from that type of play. Vendetta killers leave an unseemly mess. Mafias like to contract these kinds of hits, but mafias have long memories and hold grudges. Archie knew it's best not to step into that particular sandbox unless you're prepared to get dirty.

But Ann Hoeppner's killer utilized a different method.

Ann was a thirty-eight-year-old college English professor in Columbus, Ohio. She wasn't married, had no kids, and lived alone just off the Ohio State campus. Normally, college professors don't make a lot of money, don't have fancy cars or houses, but Ann had a bank account that would make most Wall Street brokers buckle at the knees. Her grandfather had been a scientist and inventor whose most famous creation was the self-starter for automobile engines. When he retired, he held one-hundred-and-forty-three patents, owned two companies, and was one of the richest men in the Northeast. Ann gave her high school valedictorian speech in a crowded auditorium at the age of eighteen. She told her grandfather's life story to a bored audience, the exception being the ninety-four-year-old subject of the speech, who watched with moist eyes and rapt attention. He died seven days later.

When an attorney read the contents of the will the following week, everyone in the family was shocked to learn Ann was the sole beneficiary. Even as precocious as she was, the amount of the inheritance humbled and terrified her. Her parents, who had thought the old man senile, were genuinely delighted. Her cousins, aunts, and uncles were not.

Ann spread the money around to her extended family, though open hands were stretched in her direction for the rest of her life. She put most of the windfall into various investments and savings plans and bonds and retirement funds and went about her life as though nothing had happened. Sure, she paid for her tuition, room, board, and books, but never spent extravagantly. She drove a small SUV, lived on campus and ate in the dorm cafeteria. None of her fellow students knew she could have bought and sold the campus ten times over.

She wanted to be an English teacher and nothing, not even the kind of money that determined she'd never have to work a day in her life, deterred Ann from her goal. Nine years of school later, she received not only a doctorate degree but also an offer to teach at her alma mater.

Ann was in her tenth year of teaching when she died. The English building, Denney Hall, is a five-story glass and stone building on Seventeenth Avenue, not far from the football stadium. It has functioning elevators, but Ann liked to walk the stairs to get to her office on the top floor.

There were signs clearly indicating the stairs had recently been mopped, that pedestrians should be cautious, that the surface was slippery. The signs had graphics, too – the familiar yellow triangle accompanied by an exclamation point – 'caution' it said. 'Cuidado.' But Ann must have had her head in a book (a common occurrence, and a conclusion the police quickly reached). At the landing between the third and fourth floors lay a copy of John Donne's sonnets. Next to the open book lay Ann Hoeppner, a gash in her forehead and her neck snapped. She wasn't discovered until an hour after her fall. The death was ruled accidental after a cursory police investigation. Later, her estate was divided amongst her many family members – those same envious aunts, uncles, and cousins – as designated in her will.

But Ann Hoeppner's death was no more accidental than Smoke's. Her neck was snapped by a fall, but it didn't happen the way the police wrote it up, didn't happen because she had her nose buried in a book, didn't happen because she failed to pay attention to the caution signs placed at each stairwell entrance. A professional assassin named Spilatro, one of Archie's contract killers, performed the hit.

Like I said, bagmen use different methods to kill their marks, and Spilatro has a rare specialty: he makes his kills look like accidents. There has to be a direct line between this man's specialty and the way Smoke just died. Has to be. And I'm willing to bet you can connect the dots from Ann's file to Archie's abduction to the note that summoned me out of hiding.

'According to this, Archie used Spilatro three other times. Let's find those files and hustle out of here.'

We locate two of the three before a large man enters the office through the front door. I have my Glock up and pointed his way before he can step another inch into the room. He keeps his hands in his pockets and meets my stare with blank eyes.

'Who're you?' he asks, his face unreadable.

'Nobody.'

'Well, Nobody, what're you doing rifling through the boss's stuff?'

'The boss is gone.'

He greets this news with the same disaffected expression. His eyes flit to Risina, but I won't look her way.

'You gonna put that gun down?'

'No.'

He nods now, sniffs a few times. Despite his attempt to play it cool, I take the sniffs for what they are, a nervous tic.

'I think you and your lady friend best vacate.'

'I think you better watch your fucking mouth.'

Those words come from Risina, not me. Now I tilt my head around to look at her, and for the first time I see she has her pistol up too. I expect to see anxiousness on her face, but I see that she's sporting a half smile instead. It's unnerving for me; I have no doubt it's unsettling for the man staring down the barrel.

Slowly, he takes his empty hands out of his pockets and shows them to her . . .

'I apologize, ma'am . . .' he's saying, but she doesn't let him finish, interrupting—

'My friend and I are going to find the last thing we came to find and then you'll never see us again. Now you can do one of three things . . . you can sit in the corner and watch us until we go, you can leave and never come back, or you can make a play and see what happens. It's up to you.'

I'll be damned if I don't break into a smile. The big man looks at her one more time, back at me, and then makes his decision.

'Don't shoot me in the back on the way out the door.'

'Get the hell out of here.' Risina waves at the exit with the barrel of her gun. The man takes a last look at us, then nods, turns, and doesn't look back.

As soon as he's gone, Risina blows out a deep breath, like a kettle holding the pressure at bay as long as it can before it finally releases steam. When I look over at her, she ignores me and resumes her search for the files. I can see her hands shaking as she sorts through the stack.

'You okay?' I offer.

'What do you think?' she answers flatly.

I know not to push it from there.

It takes another twenty minutes to find the final file. When we leave the aluminum factory, Smoke's office is ablaze because, like I said, accidents don't exist in this business.

We sit on opposite ends of a couch, our backs to the armrests, our feet intertwined, facing each other. A pizza box is open on the small, glass coffee table and Risina digs into her third slice. We're in a two-bedroom suite in one of those corporate hotels that rent by the month to traveling executives. Smoke set us up before we got here, and I'm almost certain the information of where we're living while we're in Chicago died with him.

'It's natural to be nervous,' I offer as Risina polishes off a pepperoni.

'I know it is.' Her response is matter-of-fact, as though she's already chewed on her flaw for a bit and decided to approach it clinically. 'I thought I did a fine job of keeping it under control.'

I agree, but I don't say so. Instead, I ask, 'But for how long?'

'As long as was needed.'

'And if he'd've rushed you instead of backing away? What would you have done?'

'He didn't, so I don't know.'

'Would you have pulled the trigger?'

'I don't know. How should I know?'

'Because you need to already play it out in your head . . . decide what to do before it happens. You already have an analyst's eye and you're going to have to rely on that to see everything from all angles. Improvisation is a weapon too, but it's dangerous. Planning is key.'

She starts to interrupt but I hold up a finger. 'Planning doesn't mean you have to know everything before you walk into a room, though it helps. Planning means that as a situation emerges, your brain needs to immediately start calculating, "if this, then that. If that, then this." Rapid fire, as soon as it's happening.

'Take the guy today. He walks in unannounced, and you did the right thing, got your gun up and out and pointed in his direction before he could step a foot in the door. Put him on his heels and on the defense. It's like a chess match, you have to always be thrusting forward, on the offensive. But you can't just stop there; you can't think linearly. Immediately, your brain needs to kick in with . . . "if he runs, I follow. If he pulls a gun, I shoot. If he bum-rushes, I shoot. If he wants to talk, I give him some rope." All of those decisions at once, bam, bam, bam, bam, bam.

'Now by the size of him, I figured he was some low-level muscle Archie kept around for protection, but since Smoke wasn't there to tell us he was on the payroll, I wasn't going to take any chances. You follow me?'

'I'd follow you anywhere,' she says with a mock-seductive intonation.

'It's an expression. It means . . .'

'I *know* it's an expression. I just like to see you worked up.'

'Goddamn, Risina . . .'

'Awwww . . .' she tosses the pizza aside and reverses positions so her body falls on top of mine. 'I'm just having some fun.'

Before I can protest, she cuts me off. 'Kiss me.'

'What?'

'You're warm. Kiss me. You can teach me how to act like a killer later.'

And like with the man who walked into Archie's office, she doesn't leave me with much of a choice.

The three remaining files fill in some gaps on Spilatro. When he employs a new contract killer, Archie likes to first flesh out the file with information on the assassin himself, and then additional facts and opinions are added to the dossier after the initial hit is complete. Archie's sister Ruby once told me he put together a file on me, but I never asked for it, and he never gave it to me. Not that it really mattered. If it existed at one time, if it was in his office with all the others, it's nothing but ashes now.

Spilatro came to Archie as a recommendation from a Brooklyn fence named Jeffrey 'K-bomb' Kirschenbaum, a brilliant and feared player in the killing business, a man who wrote the book on how middlemen conduct their lives. Kirschenbaum grew up Jewish in the Bed-Stuy portion of the borough, which toughened him the way fire tempers steel. A gangly white kid in an all-black neighborhood, he had to learn to maneuver like an army strategist from the time he was in grade school, figure out how to manipulate opposing forces so he was never caught in the middle. Let the black kids have their turf wars and street fights. Deduce who was going to stand at the top of the hill, and make sure his allegiance fell in line. He was smart with numbers, but even better, he was smart with information, and a word here or a note there could swing a rivalry in a direction that most benefited 'K-bomb.' He liked playing the role of the man behind the curtain, the puller of strings, and as an adult fresh from a short stint at CUNY, he found his way into the killing business, constructing a stable of assassins out of his old contacts from the neighborhood and running his new venture like a CEO. He pioneered the idea of doing the grunt work for his hit men, of not just accepting a fee and doling out assignments, but of following a mark, of putting together a dossier on the target's life, of setting the table for his hired guns to make their hits. It was a real service operation, from top to bottom, soup to nuts. He provided each gunman with so much information, the shooter could plot myriad ways of killing his target while escaping cleanly. Consequently, a number of skilled assassins sought him out for their assignments, and his reputation grew. He treated his men fairly, and after thirty years, he remains a towering figure in the game.

Archie knew him, and he had exchanged resources with K-bomb from time to time. Five years ago, when a client hired Archie to specifically make a hit look like an accident, Archie reached out to Kirschenbaum to seek advice about whom he should bring in for the job. K-bomb said he had just the man, and farmed Spilatro out to Archie for a percentage. Unfortunately, Archie didn't collect much more information on Spilatro beyond who his fence was. This sticks out to me, a bit out of character for such a diligent fence. It speaks to how much Archie trusted or looked up to Kirschenbaum. It's awfully hard to see clearly when we have stars in our eyes.

That first hit was on a news reporter named Timothy O'Donnell, who also happened to be serving on a jury at the time of his death. *The New York Times* reported that on May 6, construction scaffolding collapsed on top of the middle-aged man while he was jogging his familiar route through downtown. It seems Spilatro isn't afraid to use old tricks for new assignments.

The other two files present similar kills . . . a bookkeeper died of asphyxiation in a building fire, and a police detective had his ticket punched when he slipped on a patch of ice and froze to death, unconscious, in an alley behind his local bar in

Boston. That particular job was worked as a tandem sweep: Spilatro and the same assassin who struck me as odd before, the woman named Carla who'd worked the personal kill for Archie. What role she played in this murder isn't mentioned, just that it was a success.

'Here's what's absent from all these files . . .'

'What's that?' Risina asks.

'Any personal information on Spilatro. What his real name is, where he lives, how he got his start, where he grew up.'

'And Archie usually has that?'

'Yes.'

'But no one knows any of that information about you, either.'

'Except Archie did at one point. And someone else does now.'

She starts to say something, then smiles. 'Yes, of course. *I* know.'

'So we need to find out if Spilatro has a "you" in his life.'

'I see. And how do we do that?'

'We go to New York and talk to his fence. Kirschenbaum.'

'He won't want to give up that information.'

'No, he won't.'

'But we're going to make him.'

'Yes, we are.'

'And he's good at this. So he's going to be protected.'

'That's right.'

I take her face in my hands, one palm on each cheek, and put our foreheads together.

'If you don't want to do this . . . if you have any concern at all, I won't think less of you.'

'Are you kidding? I think there's a bigger problem evolving that you need to consider.'

'What's that?'

'I'm starting to like this.'

7

Ridgefield, Connecticut is an affluent, three-hundred-year-old neighborhood settled at the foothills of the Berkshire Mountains. It boasts an historic district, an art museum, a small symphony hall, and two private high schools. Some sixty miles from New York City, it's a simple, ninety-minute train ride from the Branchville Metro North station, conveniently located in the southeast corner of town, all the way to Grand Central Station in Manhattan. And yet, it is a world away from Bedford-Stuyvesant, or 'Bed-Stuy.'

Kirschenbaum lives on a knoll in a five-bedroom brick house on four private acres in Ridgefield with vistas overlooking half the county. He has no wife, no children, no ties to the real world to be exploited. His house is a fortress, and he employs a regular staff of professional bodyguards, top-shelf guys who know how to handle a weapon and don't rattle.

There are several ways to reach a man who doesn't want to be reached. Usually, I focus on vices since most people who dip their toes into this pool have a few secrets they want kept in the deep end. They'll visit whores or buy narcotics or have a thing for guns or want to diddle boys, and this gives me a way to get to them. But I don't have time to plan a successful sneak attack, and I don't have a fence to help me figure out and explore his vices, and with Risina along for the ride, guns blazing might not be the best approach either. Navigating this world over the years, I've learned there's a time to explode, loud and aggressive, and there's a time to be supplicant, quiet and introspective.

Risina and I approach the brick columns bordering the gate leading to Kirschenbaum's property. There is a callbox but no button to press and no cameras visible even though I know they are there.

'Tell Kirschenbaum Columbus wants to see him,' I say to the gate. 'I don't have the time or resources to go through the proper channels. I'll be in room 202 tonight at the West Lane Inn for the ten minutes following midnight. If men come through the door with guns out, those men will be dropped. I have no problem with Kirschenbaum; I just need information.'

We turn and head down the path back to the street.

Kirschenbaum arrives on the hour and enters the room alone. If he's trying to set a tone, trying to signal he isn't intimidated, it works. I'm impressed. He doesn't need an entourage, doesn't bother with his retinue of bodyguards – he watched me on the tape at his gate and decided on this strategy, to come devoid of self-doubt.

From what I'd read about him, I knew he was tall, but his height is pronounced in person, or maybe it's accented by the way he almost has to stoop under the low ceilings of this old rustic inn. His hair is jet-black without a trace of gray, swept back from his forehead like he's wearing a helmet. He wears a tight navy sweater and black slacks. His eyes are pale, striking, alert. He has half of a robusto cigar jutting out of the corner of his mouth like an extension of his face, and the smoke hangs around his head like a wreath.

He stands just inside the doorway, and looks at me, seated in a wooden chair near the small table, then turns his neck without moving his body to pick up Risina, who hasn't moved from the corner near the door. I placed her there, in his blind spot, and she has her hands behind her back, leaning against the wall. A threat but not threatening.

'Where do you want to do this?' His voice is a lower register than I would have guessed. It seems to come from somewhere near his abdomen and has a raspy quality, like a frog croaking. He talks around the cigar like it isn't there.

'You want to have a seat?'

He heads for the only other chair in the room without nodding, sits and crosses one ankle on his knee, then folds his arms across his chest, comfortable as can be. After a moment, he takes the cigar out and holds it between his thumb and forefinger to use it as a pointer.

'She joining us?'

I shake my head.

He turns to her. 'What's your name, darling?'

That's something we hadn't yet discussed, and I curse myself for not thinking to do it sooner. There is an art to a fake name, and we should have decided on one a long time ago, before we entered the country. I'm hoping she doesn't answer, but one thing I've learned about Risina, she rarely does what I think she'll do. I may not have thought of a name for her, but she has.

'Tigre,' she says, not missing a beat, her accent thick.

I feel warmth rise up in my chest, though I keep my face blank. A tiger is a goddamned tiger. Since Smoke located me in that bookstore, I've thought *I* was the tiger, the hibernating predator who recognized the familiar scent of prey after a long lay-off. What I hadn't thought about, what I hadn't considered until just now, is that Risina, too, is a tiger. I'm not sure how I feel about this. Am I relieved she is more like me than I thought, or disappointed?

Kirschenbaum seems satisfied and spins back to me.

'You two working a tandem?'

'That's right.'

'How can I help you, Columbus?'

'You know my work?'

'I've been following you since your early days with Pooley. I never met the guy but his reputation was solid. It's too bad he had his ticket punched. You were with Bill Ryan after that?'

'Yeah.'

'Too bad about that one, too. And now Archibald Grant.'

'Yeah.'

'Anyone ever tell you you've had some bad luck with fences?' He says this matter-of-factly, and pops the cigar back in his mouth. I'm starting to understand how Kirschenbaum made such a name for himself. I feel like maybe I stepped under the ropes and into a ring, except we're going to spar with words instead of boxing gloves.

'That's why I'm here. Archie's been taken.'

'I heard. That's why you approached my gate. Where I live. With no appointment. No warning. Just walked up to my front gate.'

'Like I said, I want information.'

He spins to Risina again. 'Can you get me a glass of water, honey?'

She doesn't move, just smiles. He turns back to me, now grinning. He raises his eyebrows like he took a shot at shaking her, and no harm done. Then his face turns grave again. He's switching tones and moods and expressions so fast, it's dizzying.

'Information costs.'

'It always does.'

'What do you want to know?'

'I want to know everything about a contract killer you represent named Spilatro.'

He doesn't blink. 'I know quite a bit about him.'

'That's good. Now I know we're not wasting each other's time.'

'Here's a tidbit to wet your whistle. He doesn't do the work you think he does.'

He's telling me this so, like any salesman dangling a carrot, I'll bite. Instead I duck his jab . . .

'Do you know his real name?'

'As sure as I know your real name ain't Columbus. And you're originally from Boston. And your first fence wasn't Pooley but a dark Italian named Vespucci. And . . .'

Fuck, is he good. He's jabbing, jabbing, jabbing, trying to stagger me. To throw him off his rhythm, I interrupt. 'And if I were here to find out what you know about me, I'd be impressed, but I'm not, so I could give a shit. I want you to give up Spilatro.'

'So you can kill him.'

'Possibly.'

'How much you guesstimate giving him up is worth?'

'You tell me.'

'I'll take her.'

He jerks his thumb over his shoulder at Risina. The air in the room cools instantly, like a chill wind blew in through the vents. He puffs out a cloud of smoke and watches me through the haze.

I narrow my eyes but otherwise check my emotions. I hope Risina won't react, won't drop her wall, but Kirschenbaum doesn't give her the chance. He brays out laughter, a harsh, barking sound that, like his voice, seems to come from deep inside him.

'You should see your face right now. Jesus. I'm just fucking with you. Something tells me if I tried to take – what'd you call yourself again, babe? Tigre? – something tells me if I tried to take her, Tigre would stick a knife down my throat.'

'Try me,' Risina says, coolly.

'Nooooo, thank you.' He holds his hands up innocently, then turns back to me as his smile fades. 'Two hundred thousand.'

'How do you want the money?'

'Bank transfer. You have a cell phone?'

I shake my head. He fishes one out of his pants pocket, moving quickly and deliberately, not at all concerned that one of us is going to shoot him for putting his hands where we can't see them. He punches some numbers into the panel and then flips the phone to me.

'That's my accountant's number. Have your bank call him and work it out.'

'Okay. Transfer goes through in the morning . . . I'll pick up the information on Spilatro tomorrow night. Where do you want to make the exchange?'

'I'm sure as hell not going to write anything down for you. You know where I live, so come on over and we'll pour drinks, clink glasses, and have a powwow. You're invited this time.'

I flip him back the phone.

'Keep it,' he says and starts to toss it again my way.

'No thanks. I'll remember the number.'

'Of course you will, Columbus.' He bolts up quickly and, without shaking hands, heads for the door. 'Tomorrow night then. And like you said to me so colorfully, you come in with guns leading the way and you'll be dropped.' He takes one last look at Risina and says, 'That goes for you, too, honey. You mind if I call you "honey"?'

'You can call me whatever you want as long as you give us what we're looking for.'

'What part of Italy are you from?'

'The part that ends in an "a."'

He smiles at that – or it could be a sneer – shoots a finger-gun her way, turns the knob, and heads out, only a cloud of smoke left behind to let us know he was here.

'How'd I do?' Risina asks when we're sure he's gone.

'You're a natural,' I say, and I'll be damned if I don't mean it.

Eight minutes later, and we're out of the hotel without checking out, leaving Ridgefield until tomorrow night.

After breakfast at an all-night diner, we hole up in a chain bookstore in nearby Danbury, a two-story anchor to a shopping center. The place isn't crowded this time of day, and a clerk with 'Janine' on her nametag points us upstairs to the fiction shelves where we can get lost in the maze of bookcases, couches, and corners.

Risina flits among the titles like a butterfly, stooping over here or standing on her tiptoes there to read an author's name or a jacket blurb. She looks over the books, and I look over her.

Why aren't I more concerned? Or better yet . . . *why don't I feel guilty over what I've done?* I'm like a condemned prisoner who, instead of slinking off to a cell to live out his sentence, drags someone down the hole with him. I've lived sleeping with one eye open for so long, why would I ever wish wary nights and watchful days on someone else? But it's not that simple, and here's the part I have trouble admitting. This job is dangerous, yes, it is haunting, yes, and it exacts a moral toll, yes, but it also holds an allure that is almost impossible to understand until you've hunted a mark, ended his life, and escaped without a soul knowing you are the shooter. It's a drug, a high, a tonic. It's not a delusion of grandeur, because it is grandeur itself.

What I realize now is I want someone to share the experience with me. It's one thing to tell these details to a stranger, another to discuss everything with someone who is there, going through the same swings, the same highs with me.

Was I lying to myself when I justified bringing Risina along by saying she was already in the game so she might as well learn the rules? Or was I, once more, putting myself first?

'How much time do we have?' she asks, her finger inside a David Levien novel.

'All day.'

'Good.' She heads to an overstuffed chair at the end of an aisle, back to a faux-paneled wall, plops down, and starts reading.

Another answer is possible. The reason I found Risina, or maybe the reason she found me: she's been a tiger all along and only needed someone to unlock her cage. She's a natural. A predator.

And if that's the case, what happens when she first tastes blood?

The gate buzzes open, and Risina and I pull our sedan in and park near the front door. I'll admit, I'm troubled by the one sentence Kirschenbaum jabbed with: *He doesn't do the work you think he does.* I didn't know where he was going with that, but I didn't want to chase my tail either. He wasn't lying to me – he definitely knew something about Spilatro he didn't want to come right out and say. But what? *He doesn't do the work you think he does.* I did bite the carrot after all.

Smoke died in an accident the same way this contract killer operated in the past. I have the files that prove it. Spilatro killed Smoke, but he meant to kill me. He has to be the guy who put my name on the paper, the guy who kidnapped Archie. So why would Kirschenbaum say Spilatro doesn't do the work I think he does? What other work does Spilatro do?

Efficiently, Risina and I cross to the entrance and don't have long to wait as a mustachioed guard opens the door and points upstairs without saying a word. There's something familiar about him, but I can't place him and he has me wondering: did Kirschenbaum plant him somewhere else around us? Was he in the hotel? The bookstore? Have we been watched from the moment we left his front gate? And if this guy was trailing us and I didn't pick him up, then how many other men did K-bomb put on us? Kirschenbaum didn't have the career he had by flying by the seat of his pants, and maybe what I mistook for calm bravado in our hotel room was actually informed caution.

I've got a feeling of foreboding I've learned to trust over the years, but I don't want to look back at the guard and give away any hesitation, so I head up the staircase. Risina is in front of me and maybe that's what's making me jumpy . . . we've been on someone else's turf together before, but this is the first time that someone's known we were coming. My intuition told me that Kirschenbaum's play would be to give me what I want, that he's a bottom-line opportunist and the percentages were to give up information on Spilatro rather than risk a confrontation with me, but maybe my intuition is rusty and I'm going to find out I'm wrong the hard way.

We make it to a long hallway with wood floors and the first thing I notice is that the guard – where did I see him before? – didn't follow us up and, in fact, there are no other guards visible on the second floor. I know Kirschenbaum platoons his security but I don't know where they position themselves in the house, and the whole thing is starting to reek like a corpse.

Risina looks back at me for guidance. She knows instinctively not to ask questions aloud, and I nod her forward toward the cracked door that spills light at the end of the corridor. I think she picks up something on my face because she blanches a bit, swallows hard, and then keeps moving.

I'm acutely aware of our breathing, the only breathing I can hear in the house, and the front door opens and closes downstairs, I'm sure of it. What the hell are we walking into? If I could think of where I saw that guy, maybe without the mustache, maybe with different color hair or no hair, goddammit, I'm coming up blank . . . I can now glimpse a four-poster through the crack in the door, so this must be the master bedroom, and I touch Risina on the elbow to let me pass and enter first. She steps back and my heart pulses now, a welcome feeling, a fine feeling, and maybe Risina feels it too because she looks alert and spry.

The guard didn't frisk us, which is unusual but not unheard of in this situation, especially since we'd made contact and been invited here by the man we're meeting. I wouldn't have given up my gun anyway and we might have had a problem downstairs, but it doesn't matter now and I pull out my Glock from the small of my back and I don't look but I know Risina is doing the same.

Three more feet to the door, and there are voices, but they're television voices, two idiot anchormen blathering on about some reality star and that seems incongruous with the man in our hotel room, what he'd be watching on a weeknight, just one more square peg that doesn't fit. So much for not coming in with guns out . . .

I push the door open wider and the bedroom is empty, but there's an open set of French doors leading out to a deck on the right and maybe he's out there, but why wouldn't he have signaled us or had someone show us in?

This is not right and there's no use for pretense anymore.

'Kirshenbaum?'

No answer. As I move to the deck, I tell Risina to watch the door.

The deck has some patio furniture, the rustic kind of chairs with green cushions surrounding a slat-wood table, and Kirschenbaum is out here all right. He's wearing a plastic bag over his head, held tightly around his neck by an elastic cord, and his hands are tied behind his back and strapped to his feet. A lit cigar is in the ashtray in front of him.

I hear sirens in the distance headed our way and in that moment it hits me where I know the guard. I've seen him twice before, and goddammit, I should have recognized him. I used to be a fucking expert at breaking down a face, noting the eyes and the ears and the parts you cannot disguise, but I used to be a professional contract killer and now I don't know what the hell I am.

The first time I saw him was in a construction vest on scaffolding outside of the Third Coast Café, except he wore a dark beard and blond hair, and the second time was without facial hair, or any hair at all: the big bald guy who came into Archibald's office and asked us our business, the guy I fucking let go because I thought he was nobody important.

There can only be one answer. The man who let us in was Spilatro, and he's been playing me like a violin since I got to Chicago, or maybe before that, maybe since Smoke pulled a safety deposit box out of its slot and caught a flight to find me.

'What is it?' Risina calls from the doorway and I realize I need to snap out of it and move now if we're going to escape.

'K-bomb's dead.'

'What?' she asks, alarmed.

'Spilatro's framing us. Let's go.'

I take her by the elbow and just poke my head into the hallway when a pistol cracks and bullets pound the doorway next to my head. I feel Risina duck back and I spot blood fly and goddammit, if he hit her . . .

We spill backward into the room and her cheek is scratched to hell but not from a bullet, rather from splinters from the door and she looks angrier than I've ever seen her, like the blood on her cheek brought the tiger to the surface for good. Multiple pairs of feet pound up the stairs down the hall, and I catch a quick look at them as I fire a few rounds back, popping the first guy flush and stopping the rest, and maybe they don't know the boss is already dead, and maybe they don't hear the sirens as they close in on us.

Spilatro wasn't with them, though, I'm sure of it. The son of a bitch must've planned the whole thing. He framed us with both the cops and the bodyguards, hoping we'd get caught in the crossfire. He bolted out the front door as soon as we went up the stairs – that was the door opening and closing I heard – and he's probably a mile away by now.

I hear scuffles down the hall and maybe the guards hear the sirens outside, which grow nearer, louder by the second. Risina and I are going to have a chance, but it's going to be a slim one and we have to do it soon, we have to make our move in those moments of inevitable confusion as the cops make their way on to the scene but don't know exactly what they're rolling into.

I see the bubble lights now, a pair of cruisers, that's it, and they blitz through the gate, knocking it off its hinges, then roar up the driveway, pinning our rental sedan in front of them as both sets of doors fly open and uniformed police officers spill out, guns drawn.

I hear the front door open and one of the bodyguards shouts something and the cops yell back, and that's what I'm looking for . . . a little contact so I can change the pace.

I bust out the bedroom window glass and fire over the cops' heads, BAM, BAM, BAM, into their patrol cars, BAM, BAM, BAM and I hear the front door slam shut and a scared guard scream 'he's fucking shooting!' and then the downstairs explodes as the cops retaliate with indiscriminate, panicked firepower.

'Outside! Grab the cigar!' I scream at Risina and she dashes out and back in as quickly as a cat, the cigar held out to me.

I snatch it out of her hand, jam it in my mouth as I collect the sheets off the bed, puff, puff, wadding them up, puff, puff, getting the end of the heater to glow red like a coal in a stove, and then I hold it to the end of the sheets and it doesn't take long, they start to burn, and I toss them to the curtains, which catch fire and go up too as flames curl toward the ceiling and lick the molding.

Confusion is as big a weapon to a professional hit man as a gun, and the more obstacles you can throw at your pursuers the better your chances of survival.

We're out on the patio as the room goes up. We step past K-bomb's dead body and I plant both hands on the railing and hop it, drop from the second story to hit the grass and spring up without tumbling, and I don't have to look back to know Risina does the same.

'Don't shoot a cop unless you have to,' is all I have time to say, as we reach the front of the house, and I peek around the corner. The cops are out of their cars, and the two in the near sedan have moved up behind our rental to use it as cover. Smoke starts to pour out of the top floor, and the cops have their firearms pointed at the front door, waiting for the men inside to make a move.

I wait, wait, wait, and then I get the break I expect, the front door opens and one of Kirschenbaum's men shouts, 'We're unarmed! We're coming out! No one's firing! It's a goddamn inferno in here!'

'Keep your hands up or we *will* shoot!' shouts back the closest officer, more than a little distress in his voice.

'Don't shoot us, goddammit! We're unarmed! We're coming out! There are four of us!'

And the door swings open wide, as four hacking, wheezing guys make their way out on to the porch, black smoke trailing them. The cops' training kicks in right on cue and all of them bolt for the men. Each grabs a bodyguard and shoves him off the porch and on to the grass out in front as the house really starts to go up, a fireball.

The guys hack up smoke and the cops scream at them to stay the fuck down, to get their hands behind their backs and they pull out their plastic ties to secure the men's hands. It's now or never. I nod at Risina and we bolt for the near cruiser, the one with the engine still idling. Risina ducks for the passenger door, while I hop across the back trunk and swing around to the driver's side.

One of the cops, a young kid with a mop of red hair, must've caught our movement out of the corner of his eye. He swings around, his eyes as wide as plates, and fumbles for his gun.

In a flash, I aim, fire once, and knock him down, and I'm behind the wheel, hitting reverse, gunning the cop sedan out of there, roaring backwards, down the drive and out into the road.

'I thought you said not to shoot a cop!' Risina screams at me from the passenger seat.

'That applied to you, not me.'

'Oh man,' she starts to say, her hand up on her forehead, so I put a palm on her knee, firm.

'I didn't kill him. I just hit him in the thigh so he wouldn't pop a shot off at us as we fled. He's going to be fine.'

She gives me a sideways look to see if I'm fucking with her, but I'm not and I can see relief wash over her like an ocean wave.

We ditch the cruiser three blocks from a shopping center, but not before we wipe it down. The parking lot is full of cars, and I head to the furthest row, where the employees park and won't be out until closing time. I pick a small Honda – the make stolen most often – break in, and crack the ignition. Ten minutes later and we roll out of Ridgefield, headed south on Highway 33.

In the passenger seat, I believe I see Risina smile, but I'm already thinking of ditching this car and finding another one.

8

Risina and I are in New York, holed up in the St. Regis Hotel on East 55th Street. I have more money than I know what to do with and it might be safer to break my routine and stay somewhere with a little more polish than the usual unkempt inns I frequent when on assignment. Over the years, I collected staggering fees for completing my work. Since the money held no allure for me, I rarely spent any of it; instead, I socked it away in accounts all over the world. My fence kept credit cards up to date for me, and I have safety deposit boxes in over a dozen major cities containing the right plastic and right identities. Holding two of them in my wallet right now reminds me how important it is to find a new fence when this is over if Archie doesn't come out of it alive.

I like New York and its dense population. It's an easy city to get lost in; it's often advantageous to be a needle in a stack of needles.

I need to work out my thoughts. Usually, I'll just talk to myself, but it's nice to have someone to bounce ideas off of. 'I think Spilatro put the wheels in motion by kidnapping Archie and then watched them turn. He marked Smoke the whole way, and everything played out how he hoped. I get summoned out of hiding, delivered to his door. He doesn't want to negotiate though, doesn't want to talk, just wants to kill me. Hence the collapsed scaffolding. But that didn't work.'

'Then why didn't he pop you with a bullet when we walked through Kirschenbaum's front door? When he could've surprised us?'

'You think I'd've let him? I don't get surprised, Risina. I was prepared for a bodyguard to pull a gun. I just wasn't prepared for that bodyguard to be Spilatro.'

She considers that for a moment, then, 'But why? Why does he want to kill you? You've never encountered him before. He hasn't been linked to any of your past jobs, has he?'

'I don't know yet. If I had a good fence like Archie, or even a half-decent one like Smoke, at my disposal, he could be gathering information on Spilatro right now to help me figure out the connection between him and me. But I don't.'

She runs her hands through her hair, a habit that gives away when she's stumped. She opens her mouth but I interrupt, 'There is one thing we have to do now . . .'

'What?'

'In response to a kidnapping, the family usually follows a playbook. They get a ransom note and focus on what the kidnapper wants. They look at the ask and the risks and make a decision whether or not to give the kidnapper his demands, hoping for some sort of break after the exchange, after their loved one is returned safely. But they're looking at it backwards.

'If Archie is still alive – and that's a big "if" as far as I'm concerned – then giving me up isn't going to get us anywhere. He'll kill me, then kill Archie. There's only one way to take down a kidnapper . . . you have to find something or someone *he* loves and take it from him. Flip the game on his head.'

Her eyes track and her head nods as she sees it. 'We kidnap something of his right back.'

'That's right. Then see if he wants to talk to *us* about making an exchange. Not Archibald Grant for me. Those are his terms, his playbook. We take something or someone Spilatro holds precious and make the exchange about that. We have the leverage. Not him.'

'We stay on offense like you said before.'

'Exactly. But listen to me, Risina, this is going to get worse, much worse. It's going to get brutal, it's going to get ugly, and we're probably going to have to spill some blood in order to get Archie back. If Archie's already dead, we're going to destroy whomever or whatever Spilatro holds close to him, and then we're going to have to kill him.'

She swallows, but nods, then nods a second time as though to reinforce her acceptance. 'Remember that he brought us into this, he struck us first, and whatever we have to do is because of him. We didn't ask for this but we're damn sure going to end it. Messages are written in blood in this business.'

'A tiger is a tiger.'

'That's right. And he should have left me, should have left *us*, sleeping in the jungle.'

I go back to that final file, the fourth hit, that had Spilatro working a tandem with the woman named Carla, the same woman Archie then used later for his personal contract. When professional killers work a tandem sweep, when they're working together to accomplish a single hit, it usually indicates a certain closeness. The killers either came up together, or partnered for convenience purposes, or split the fees because they each had a specialty or strength that was necessary for the most effective hit. Rarely are they complete strangers. A degree of trust has to exist in order to execute an effective tandem.

Since all I have on Spilatro is his face, I'm going to need whatever information off of Carla I can get. I struck out with Kirschenbaum, so she's going to have to do.

She won't be on the lookout for me unless they're still tight, which I doubt based on those last three files, the hits Spilatro worked alone, plus the one she worked solo. They went their separate ways, and maybe the reason behind it will help me build a strategy for taking on the son-of-a-bitch who came after me.

Finding Carla is going to require calling in a favor. Looking at the clock, I'm going to have to wake up a fence in Belgium.

* * *

A shell game of pre-paid phones and intermediaries and appointment times and coded messages finally lands me a secure connection with Doriot, a Brussels-based fence I've crossed paths with a couple of times in Europe. Once when I went to his office so he could evaluate me, and a second time when I reached him in a prison in Lantin, where he thought he was safely hidden.

'Hello, Columbus. I heard you were dead, so this is a surprise.' His thick French accent sounds even rougher over the phone line.

'Still breathing.'

'Yes, I can hear that now.'

'And you're out of jail.'

'I couldn't afford to stay in.'

'And how's Brueggemann?'

'Unemployed, I'm afraid.'

Brueggemann was a German heavy who helped me find Doriot in that Lantin jail, against his will. I think I exposed his weakness as an employee.

'So you would not be calling me for any reason I can understand unless you need something from me, yes? So how may I help you?'

Belgians tend to get right to the point, a national trait I admire.

'I need you to do something for me.'

'I see. What is that something?'

'I need you to locate a New York female hitter who goes by Carla. I need you to hire her for a dummy job. Tell her she has to meet the fence and give her a fake address on Warren Street in Tribeca. I'll pick her up from there.'

'You going to put her down?'

'Nothing like that.'

'Who's her contracting fence?'

'I'm guessing Kirschenbaum, but he's dead so you'll have to figure out how to contact her.'

'I see.'

This is the part where he realizes he has me over a barrel and will ask for something. Either money or a favor or to pull a job for him for free. But Doriot is full of surprises.

'Okay, Columbus, how can I contact you?'

I give him the number on a prepaid phone and tell him to text me there with a secure number and then I'll call him back from a different line.

'Very well. I'll try to dial you in the next day or two.'

I decide to flush the quail if he's not going to attempt it. 'And what do you want in exchange?'

'Not a thing. I have a new outlook on life. I am trying to be accommodating to my friends and rely on providence to reward me with good fortune.'

'Uh-huh.'

'You are a cynic then. I understand. But my actions will turn you into a believer.'

'Okay . . . well, I'll talk to you soon.'

'Yes, soon.'

We hang up. If he's going to work out his personal issues on my behalf, I'm happy to accommodate.

Carla is in her late thirties, and looks the opposite of most female plugs I've encountered over the years. Professionals are always trying to get close to their marks in order to make the kill in private and get the hell away after business is done; as such, most of the women I've seen in this line of work are gorgeous. They work their way inside on the mark through suggestions of sex and pounce when the target is at his most vulnerable. By the time the mark figures out he's been conned, his bodyguards are outside the door, his pants are around his ankles, and his day is about to be ruined. Many a target has been popped at night, but not discovered until the next morning, naked, in bed, blood-dry.

Carla isn't talking too many men into the bedroom. She's dressed like she's used to towing around a couple of kids: knock-off designer jeans and an unflattering print shirt bearing a vague pattern of stripes. She's dowdy, about thirty pounds overweight, and has a face that wouldn't launch any ships out of Troy.

I smile when I spot her. She wouldn't stand out in any room, on any block, in any crowd, on any stage. She doesn't just blend into the background, she *is* the background. I almost didn't pick her out, even though she's the only woman walking down Warren Street at this time of morning. Her expression is neutral, as bland as her wardrobe and as unassuming as her gait. I like her already.

I approach Carla from behind so she'll have to turn. I want to see how she moves, see if I can spot where she keeps her weapons.

'Carla?'

She turns slowly, deliberately. Her eyes fix on my chest, unchallenging. Her voice is wheezy, like a trumpet with a faulty valve. Nothing about her is inviting.

'You Walker?'

'That's right. Let's move where we can talk.'

'You got an office around here?'

'I like to walk and talk.'

'You got muscle?'

'Just me.'

'You must be new to this.'

'I . . . how long I've been doing this is none of your business.'

She doesn't respond, just follows beside me as I head up the street toward the river. I think she's bought my newbie act, though I'm not certain.

I talk just above a whisper, 'You work tandem with a hitter named Spilatro?'

'Why's it matter?'

'I might need a two-fer and my client wants a team who've worked well together in the past.'

'Fsssh.' The trumpet hits another false note as she blows out a disappointed breath. 'I don't team anymore.'

'You guys have a falling-out?'

'Why's it matter?' she asks a second time.

'Just making conversation.'

'Now I know you haven't been doing this long.'

She stops in the street and this time lifts her eyes all the way to my face. 'You got a job? Give me a file and let me know when you want the account closed. Otherwise I'm going to walk in that direction, you're going to walk in that direction, and if we see each other again, we won't be shaking hands.'

During this, her face doesn't pinch or blacken. She just says it plainly, like we're discussing the Tribeca weather.

'All right, don't tighten up. I was just trying to get a feel for your style . . .'

'What you see is what you get,' she says.

'Fair enough. Let's stop right here.'

She obeys and folds her arms, impatient. I change tactics, hardening.

'We're going to have a conversation about Spilatro and you're going to tell me everything you know about him, or you'll be dead at my feet before you can take a step away. Your choice.'

This ambush catches her flush, off-guard. She blinks and swallows, not sure how control could have flipped so quickly.

Then her right eye flutters as a red laser shines into it, and we watch together as a small pinprick of red light slowly moves down her face until it stops square in the middle of her chest. Risina is high up on a rooftop working our own loose version of a tandem. Carla doesn't need to know that the red laser comes from an office pointer rather than a gunsight.

I hold my hand up. 'If I raise a finger, you drop. Nod if you understand.'

It takes her a moment to focus on me, and when she does, it is through defeated eyes. She nods. Her gaze flits back to the red dot on her chest.

'Who are you?'

'What's it matter?' I say, using her words. 'What do you know about Spilatro?'

'He . . .'

'Speak up.'

'He brought me into this business.'

'Oh yeah?'

'Yeah. I . . . uh . . .' She shakes her head slowly, like she can't believe what she's about to say. 'I was married to him.'

That's unexpected.

'Start from the beginning.'

It doesn't take long for the words to gush out of her like water from an overturned hydrant. I have the feeling Carla has been waiting a long time to tell her story, to get things off her chest. Most likely, she hasn't had anyone to talk to about what she does for a living. She just needs someone to whom she can confess her sins, both personal and professional, and I'm the first man to ask for it. That's unexpected, too.

For the first six years of their marriage, Carla Fogelman Spilatro had no idea her husband, Douglas, was a professional hit man. She thought he worked sales for a software company that specialized in creating computer programs for brokerages. He talked about programs for tracking stocks, programs for tracking sales, programs for tracking investments, and it all seemed, well, boring. She tuned him out. She didn't care. She worked too, as a speech pathologist for a hospital, assisting stroke patients who could no longer get their mouths around their words. It was stressful and grueling and demanding, and she came home each day exhausted, too tired to listen to her husband talk about quotas and sales leads.

Their marriage was comfortable if not comforting, and she was happy to have the television to herself when her husband went away on frequent business trips. They had no kids, confessing early in their courtship neither cared for children, and she never heard her biological clock tick the way so many other women did. Between her husband's commissions and her speech salary, they established themselves in the upper middle class and had a nice two-story home, the customary accoutrement of couples earning their income.

Her husband had one quirk. Miniatures. He had a basement full of miniatures – airplanes, trains, cars. In fact, he built elaborate cityscapes, with model skyscrapers and model traffic congestion and model construction equipment and sometimes little model pedestrians walking the model streets. She didn't mind him down in the basement, building his tiny worlds; she figured having him home when he was in town was better than having him out at bars or running around the way some husbands did. Besides, she could watch her shows while he was building and painting down there. She never had to fight him for the remote control.

A text changed her life. A simple text from her friend Michelle.

I DIDN'T KNOW DOUGLAS WAS IN CLEVELAND.
HE'S NOT.
OH. SWORE I SAW HIM. HOW R U?

She didn't respond, and when the TV suddenly sprang to life, she realized she'd been sitting there for the full thirty minutes it took TiVo to override the pause. She looked at her hand and realized she had chewed her thumbnail to the quick.

Doug wasn't in Cleveland. He was on a business trip, yes, but he said he was going to New York to see his client. What was the name he had said? Damn, why didn't she listen to him? Smith Barney? Something like that.

She was being silly. Why was her imagination running wild? Why did she watch stupid trash like *Desperate Housewives* and *Young and the Restless,* where every husband was philandering around like it was Roman times? People in real life didn't act like that, right?

She should just call him on his cell and see where he was. He'd probably said Cleveland anyway. Maybe she had mixed it up. Cleveland and New York?

'Hello?'

'Hey, hon, I can't talk right now.'

'Are you in a meeting?'

'Walking into one right now. I'll call you when it's over . . .'

'Are you in . . .' But he hung up before she could finish the question.

She got online and found a number for a Smith-Barney branch in Cleveland. There were three so she picked the first one and dialed the main line.

'Morgan Stanley Smith Barney Financial . . .'

'Yes, hello . . . my name is Carla Spilatro . . . I have to . . . is my husband Doug there right now?'

'I'm sorry?'

'Doug Spilatro with Valsoft?'

'Hold one moment.'

She waited, chewing that thumbnail down until she tasted blood.

A new voice came on the line. 'Hello, this is Matt Chapman, may I help you?'

'Hi, sorry to bother you. My husband works for Valsoft and I think he has a meeting with someone in your, uh, firm. His name is . . .'

'Don't know any Valsoft. You sure you have the right branch?'

Her heart beat harder. 'No, I guess I'm not sure.'

'Well, we have two other branches in Cleveland. I'll have Melanie come back on and give you the numbers . . .'

'Thank you . . . oh, wait. Mr. Chapman . . . ?'

'Yes?'

'You said you don't know Valsoft? It's my understanding they produce and manage the software you use on your computers?'

'Hmm. I don't think so. We use good ol' Microsoft.'

'Do all the branches use Microsoft?'

'I'm ninety-nine percent sure.'

She had moved her teeth off the thumb and on to the cuticles on her ring finger. 'Okay, sorry to bother you.'

'No problem.'

She looked up the Valsoft corporate webpage. It wasn't more than a few pages, but there was her husband's name and contact info under the 'outside sales' banner. Sure, the number listed was his cell phone, but he worked out of his car most days. The corporate office's main address was listed as Deerfield, Michigan, and she realized she had never been to Michigan, much less Deerfield. There was a main office phone number, so she picked up the phone to call again.

Then she stopped. What was she doing? One little text from her friend saying she'd seen Doug somewhere other than where he said he was – she was certain he had said New York – and she's running around checking on him like he's some sort of dual-life soap opera character. She put the phone down. She'd wait and talk to him when he returned and just ask him where he went and how the meetings went.

She plopped on to the couch but couldn't concentrate, so she ate an entire quart of Ben and Jerry's Cherry Garcia but still couldn't keep her thoughts straight. She flipped channels and all the networks were breaking in on the soaps to talk about a 'major accident' in Cleveland. The Cleveland of it caught her eye. Doug might be in Cleveland and there was an accident there too?

She grew up near there, in Shaker Heights, and knew the skyline well. It seemed a section of light rail track above a highway had collapsed and an RTA train hadn't been able to brake in time. It dove over the edge and killed fourteen people. Such a random, odd event. An act of God. One day you're riding a passenger train, maybe worried about making a meeting on time or concerned about the job interview you're headed to or wondering whether or not you're going to have time to pick up a snack on the way home from work and what stops you cold? A piece of track giving way and it's bye-bye to all those plans you made. Incredible.

A news camera in a helicopter was showing the accident under a 'LIVE' banner, a bird's-eye view of dozens of emergency vehicles surrounding the aftermath of the crash like moths circling a flame. As the chopper hovered, it settled on a particular angle, that view of God looking down from above on the carnage, and suddenly she felt as though she'd been jolted with electricity. She shot straight up on the couch and overturned her carton of ice cream as she sent the spoon clattering across the wooden floor.

That angle. The precise angle of the news footage. She'd seen that angle before. She'd seen this accident before.

She had gotten off her ass yesterday to do a bit of cleaning, and decided to vacuum the carpet in the basement when she wouldn't be under her husband's feet. The door was locked, which was odd, but she didn't think too much about it. She knew where her husband stored his keys, even if he had never outright told her. She imagined there wasn't a square inch of this house she didn't know intimately, and so had retrieved the key from its hiding place and gone down below so she could surprise Doug with a clean work area when he returned from New York. Or Cleveland.

She realized her tongue had turned to chalk, thinking about yesterday. She rose from the couch and headed to the basement door. Slowly, she descended the stairs as though she were in a dream, each step bringing her a better view of the table where Doug built his miniatures.

From the back, it looked like any of the dozens of skylines he'd built over the years, though this one had a familiarity to it she hadn't noticed yesterday.

She reached the basement floor without realizing it, her eyes fixed on the model city, crafted with such precise detail. Doug had grown into an accomplished designer; how had she not noticed it before? The level of detail. The precision of the streets and buildings. The photographs pulled from the internet and attached to the corkboard on the wall to serve as blueprints for the model.

She kept gliding around the model, following the path she'd taken with the vacuum cleaner, and her jaw dropped as her eyes led her around the cityscape.

The track was there . . . the light rail track. The exact place where the rail had collapsed according to the news footage was also collapsed here, and a miniature train was shown draped over the broken section, mimicking exactly what had happened.

Doug left on Wednesday. The last time he was in this basement was Tuesday night. The accident happened today? It was live, right? Or was she confused? It was all so . . .

She felt her stomach roll over and she bent at the middle, but nothing came out. Her body reacted before her mind could catch up. What the hell was going on? Why did the floor threaten to pull her down? She fought off the urge to collapse, to faint, and raced back up the stairs toward her computer. Maybe the news was old and it was a replay and she was confused. It only took a second to confirm on CNN.com that the accident was 'breaking news,' that it had happened today.

What the fuck was her husband up to? What the fuck was he involved in?

He came home the next afternoon. The basement door was wide open. If he was surprised about that, if he felt any moment of shame or regret about her discovery, she didn't know. She was waiting for him when he walked down the stairs, standing with the model between them.

'What did you do?' she barked.

'Carla . . .'

'Just tell me what this means!' She pointed at the model, at the collapsed miniature train. He circled around the table toward her, his arms outstretched, and she wanted to be hugged, needed to be hugged, but she wasn't ready to let him touch her yet. She realized tears were streaming down her face and she tried to blink them away. She had barely slept, had pictured this confrontation a million times since yesterday, but the reality never lines up with the way we imagine it. 'What did you do to those peop—'

The last word stuck in her throat as his hands closed around her neck. It took her a full five seconds to realize what had happened, was happening. So sure was she that he was coming around to placate her, to comfort her, to soothe her, that she never imagined he'd try to kill her. She flopped backward into the model, his precise model, and she felt a sting of pain as her back smashed through the light rail track and crushed the rest of the miniature train.

He was strong, much stronger than she would've thought. When did he get so strong? She kicked at him but her legs were on the wrong side and she couldn't gain any traction. Her fingers clawed at his hands but the grip was solid and his face, his horribly twisted face started to blur as tears soaked her eyes. She might have a chance for a couple of words, just a couple if she could get his fingers off her throat.

What had the self-defense expert said in that meeting at the hospital back when they had that rapist scare? Forget the neck. Thoughts whizzed around her head at a million miles an hour. Forget your neck and go for the eyes. His eyes.

She didn't think about it anymore, just went hard for his eyes as she grabbed the side of his head and dug in with her thumbnails. The effect was immediate; he flopped backward, never expecting her to fight back, and she sucked in air like a swimmer coming to the surface.

Recovering, he took a step forward and she managed to screech out: 'I took pictures!' The words sounded like they had been scratched with sandpaper, but they hit her husband flush and took hold. He stopped in mid-step, his feet rooted to the ground. His eyes darted back and forth as he tried to figure out his next move. Finally, he spoke. The calmness in his voice chilled her.

'Where?'

'Emailed to my hotmail account.'

He started to take another step, when her words stopped him again. 'Where do you think the police are going to look when I go missing? You don't know the password to that account, but all my friends have sent and received emails from me there. The cops'll figure out how to open it.'

His face was flush with anger. 'God. Dammit!' he spat, breaking it into two words so he could hammer the second.

'You stay away from me.'

'Just calm the fuck down.'

'I mean it.'

'I know you mean it, Carla. I know.' Then he moved over to a chair, sat down heavily, and rubbed his head in his hands. 'Just calm down and let me think.'

They went to breakfast. It seemed extraordinary at the time, and now even more so as she retold it to me. He told her everything. Everything. She had him by the balls, so he just came out with it. Maybe it had been weighing on his chest and he wanted to talk about it, just like she was doing now. Maybe he didn't know how to broach the subject with her before this tipping point . . . she didn't know. But over bacon and eggs at IHoP, he told her how he'd first gotten into the killing business after his discharge from the army; an infantryman in his unit had been taking contracts for a decade, and remembered Doug as having particular acumen for planning missions. Doug was adept at reading a map and conducting an ambush and presenting an almost geometrical strategy for accomplishing the squad's goals. You need to raid a building? Go find Doug. You need to take out an ammo dump? Go find Doug.

Ten years later, he was married to Carla and making eighty grand a year in middle-management sales when his old friend Decker knocked on the door and walked him through the business. Gave him the basics on fences and hits and kill fees and tandem sweeps and time commitments and hidden money and weapons caches, all one needed to know to become a professional contract killer. It wasn't much different than planning missions in Kabul, truth be told. Said if Doug were interested, then he'd introduce him to a fence and see how they did together. Said if he wasn't, he'd never see Decker again. It was a crossroads moment and the timing was right: Doug was bored out of his mind and looking for some spice.

The first hit was messy and personal and upsetting. Face to face with a guy in an elevator who never saw it coming, but the blood and the matter and the splatter were enough to make Doug gag every time he thought about it. He had seen violence in Iraq, but it was mostly at a distance, and he was never the one actually pulling the trigger.

But he liked the work. By God, he really did. It was like everything he had ever done in his life was designed to make him an effective killer: his love of statistics and science and numbers and percentages – the very things that pushed him into a computer science degree after his service – also helped him execute the perfect hit. He just didn't like the mess. Even when he was choking her hours before, he knew he wouldn't be able to go through with it. He was in the death business, but he didn't like the actual killing.

It was a paradox, but one to which he spent a month devoting his thinking time. Could he be an effective killer, but from a distance like in Iraq, where he wouldn't necessarily need to see the kill? And in doing so, could he create a new niche in the market?

It hit him in a flash, the way the best ideas most often do. Accidents.

The difficult part in executing a hit is getting away after the mark is murdered. So what if there isn't a murder? What if the death is ruled accidental? Would the client be willing to pay – possibly even pay a premium – if the hit appeared as though the mark were the victim of bad luck?

He floated the question to the fence Decker had secured for him. The man looked at Doug like his head had sprouted antennae. So he shut his mouth, took his next assignment, and started planning.

The mark was an Air Force colonel stationed in San Angelo, Texas. Doug didn't know why someone wanted him dead and he honestly didn't care. He just didn't have much sympathy for people – didn't value their lives; if he were being honest, he never did. Most people were assholes or stuck-up or inferior anyway. And no one lived forever, didn't matter who you were. Why should Doug give a shit if some stranger had his ticket punched?

He knew the colonel lived in a ratty one-story home near the base and so he rigged the building to collapse on him while he slept.

The plan worked, the roof fell in directly on top of the mark, and Doug even added a weight set in the attic so the death would be instantaneous. Except it wasn't. The colonel died, yes, but only after two weeks in the hospital in the ICU as doctors fought for his life. Spilatro sweated those two weeks like his own life hung in the balance. Maybe it did.

When he showed up to his fence after the mark finally died, Doug expected to be reprimanded. But Kirschenbaum clapped him on the back and asked him when he'd be ready to go again. It turned out the client was ecstatic with the way it went down, with the way the police and the press declared it to be a sad accident.

Kirschenbaum apologized for not recognizing what Spilatro brought to the table. He understood now the value in Doug's killing style. He'd like to increase his fee. He was seriously impressed with the innovation. He'd like to step up their relationship. Move Doug to the top of his stable.

Doug was pleased with himself. His father had never once complimented him like this. Nobody had.

So that's how he got into it and that's what he did. He hadn't worked in software sales in years. He was a contract killer, one of the most sought-after Silver Bears in the game. He told Carla how much money they really had, how much he had hidden away in cash, where no bank, no taxman, no creditor could get to it.

'But what about collateral damage?' she asked him. What about the other people who die in these accidents? What about the innocents on the train in Cleveland?

He shrugged. 'People die in accidents every day,' he told her. 'I don't care about them and I don't think about them.'

Then he put his hands out across the table, palms up, imploring her to hold hands, as if those same hands hadn't been around her throat two hours before.

'I overreacted,' he told her. 'But it was such a surprise to see you standing there . . . it was like a violation, I guess. I really apologize for that.'

'For trying to kill me?' she whispered as she tried her best not to raise her voice.

'That wasn't me. I promise. I was stressed out and off my game. I was seriously in shock. Nobody's ever thought to catch me before and I guess I hadn't prepared for it mentally. I saw you standing down there and an animal part of me took over. But I'm okay now. I see it now.'

Inexplicably, she softened and he pounced on it like a cat with a ball of string. 'I love you, honey. That's never changed. You mean more to me than anything. You tell me to stop, to get out, to drop this business and leave it in the sewer, then I will. We'll just move away and be done with it.'

And she believed him.

We sat on a stoop on Warren Street for hours while Carla laid it out for me. If she forewent details, I grilled her to fill them in. If I thought she was holding back, I turned up the heat. That laser sight on her chest would disappear for a time, then reappear at various intervals, so it stayed omnipresent in her mind. But I couldn't have pried half this information from her if she hadn't wanted to talk, hadn't *needed* to talk. I don't believe most of it, especially the parts where she presents herself in the best possible light. But the kernels of truth are there, and it is those kernels I can make pop.

'And instead of asking him to quit, you joined him?'

'Not at first. God, no. But you're right, I didn't ask him to quit either. The money was insane, and the job kept him busy. I just put my hands over my ears, hear no evil, see no evil, you know?'

'So when did you start working tandem?'

She gazes at her feet and that laser pinpoints her chest. Dark circles have formed around her eyes now, and her face has gone pallid, as if unburdening herself of this story has discarded her soul with it. 'I don't know. Years ago. He asked me if I wanted to help him out once and I guess I said yes. He figured he could charge more for two of us. So I ran interference and helped move a mark into place, but I . . . I never had the stomach for it.'

'Uh huh.'

She doesn't bother looking up to see the doubt in my expression, content to leave half-truths hanging in the ether like wisps of gossamer.

'You've worked at least one job that I know of on your own since you guys split.'

'I have bills to pay.'

She blows out a long breath.

'Look, you going to let me go now?'

'I need you to tell me where to find your husband.'

'Oh . . . that's right. You want to hire him for a tandem.'

I don't say anything. She picks at a piece of gravel on the pavement, crushes it into chalk between her thumb and forefinger.

'All you gotta do is give me one piece of information I can use to find him . . .' I point to that laser sight on her chest, 'and you'll never see that dot again.'

'The truth is . . .' and for this she looks up, clapping her hands together to wash the dust off. 'The truth is . . . you're going to have a very hard time finding him.'

'Yeah, why's that?'

'Because Doug's dead.'

9

Their last assignment together was the one Archie brokered. Did my name come up during that job? Did Archie mention me casually and Spilatro pounced on the name and came up with a plan to lure me out? Why would he want to?

The answer probably lies in the same reason I turned Archie's office into ash. I knew if those files were left behind, vultures would descend on them to pick over the pieces. There is value in those files, the same value Archie told Smoke about in a prison cafeteria. Information. I've pulled a lot of jobs over the years, some extremely prominent, some that changed the political landscape of this country. If someone knew where to find me, he could broker that information to the relatives of my marks who were looking for atonement. Maybe Archie mentioned he worked with me, and maybe Spilatro turned that into a job for himself, sold my name to the highest bidder while he promised he would be the instrument of revenge.

So why did Carla think Doug Spilatro was dead?

When I was a kid at Waxham Juvey in Western Mass, there was a board game we could check out as long as we played it in the library. It was called 'Mousetrap,' and it involved building an elaborate, Rube Goldbergian machine to catch a mouse. A crank rotated a gear that pushed an elastic lever that kicked over a bucket that sent a marble down a zig-zagging incline that fed into a chute and on and on until the cage fell on the unsuspecting mouse. But over the years, a few of the plastic pieces went missing and the trap wouldn't spring. We used straws and toothpicks and toothpaste caps to fill in the blanks, rigging it so the cage would drop. The mouse didn't know the real pieces weren't there, and it didn't matter as long as the trap sprung.

I think Spilatro has built his own mousetrap. Psychologically, he takes no pleasure in the kill itself; in fact, it repulses him. So he's thrown all of his passion, all of his expertise, into building elaborate killing machines, elaborate mousetraps. With a living, breathing target, the machine has to be able to contract or expand or adapt based on the movement of the prey. He can build miniatures and plan to his heart's content, but at some point toothpicks have to replace plastic pieces.

So the question is: how much has Spilatro been thrown off of his plan to kill me? Was I supposed to die in the construction accident that claimed Smoke? Was I supposed to get caught in the crossfire at Kirschenbaum's house, trapped between the bodyguards and the police? Or am I still scurrying my way through the mousetrap, tripping a rubber band instead of a crank?

And one more thing: Carla referred to Spilatro as a Silver Bear, even though he takes no pleasure in the actual kill. My first fence taught me that to do what I do, to live with what I do, I have to make the connection to my mark so I can sever the connection later. I have to get inside his head, exploit whatever evil I find there, so I can continue to the next job. What I'm missing from all this, what I still don't know, is *why* Spilatro singled me out. What connection do we have?

Carla and I move from the stoop on Warren Street to a coffee shop around the corner. I tell her she doesn't have to worry about getting shot, that I just want to hear the rest of her story, but my words don't seem to lift any weight off her shoulders. She sits like a prisoner in the corner of a cell, with no hope of rescue. I know Risina is out there watching, and I wonder if she can see the effects the killing business has on its participants.

'The last job. The one you did for Archie. Tell me about it.'

'Archie?'

'Archibald Grant. He was the fence.'

'Oh. Yes, Archie Grant. I only talked to him on the phone.'

'You never met him face-to-face?'

'I didn't meet anyone except for K-bomb. And he, I only met once.' She holds up one finger. 'He came to me after the job you're talking about, when I was still trying to figure out what the hell I was gonna do now that Doug was gone. I never knew the fence's name before that. I didn't even know what a fence was, to tell you the truth. He just showed up and asked me if I wanted to continue working. I'll be honest, I've only pulled a couple of jobs on my own. Today's call came in from a third party and I thought it was weird and my antenna went up, but I showed up anyway because I don't know what the hell I'm doing anymore. Should've known . . .'

'Yeah, well, here you are. If it makes you feel better, I'd've gotten to you one way or another.'

She shrugs. 'Maybe.'

'Tell me about that last tandem job. I want to hear every detail.'

'You have to understand, Doug only told me the bare minimum to keep me involved. I was the flash of light, the honking horn, you know what I mean?'

I shake my head.

'The distraction. The feint. The thing that causes the mark to look one way when death is coming from the other direction.'

'Bait?'

'Look at me. Do I look like bait?'

'I meant . . .'

'I know what you meant. Sure, I'd meet a few of the marks. Get 'em to a particular spot Doug would designate in the run-up. That was tough for me, I gotta say. It's one thing to see these targets from afar, another to shake their hands, hear them speak, watch 'em smile or what not.'

'The last job . . .'

'Yeah, I'm getting there. I'd been off for a while. I know Doug was taking contracts and fulfilling them without me.

Two or three in a row and truth be told, I didn't mind. I thought I'd like the adventure of it, the game, you know, but when I was lying in bed each night, I'd think about those men I helped put under, and I had a real hard time closing my eyes.'

She's checking my face, looking for a sympathetic nod, but I give her nothing. She blows a bit on the top of her coffee before taking a sip.

'Anyway, he'd been home for a while and I knew he must've gotten a new gig because he spent a lot of time down in the basement. I'm talking a good two months, only coming up for a meal, a smoke, a bathroom break, or bed. I figured he was going to work this one solo, but this particular Sunday, he calls me down there.

'This is a simple one, he tells me. Police detective in Boston who drinks too much. This cop must've tossed the wrong guy in the can, because there's a price on his head and Doug is collecting. The procuring fence wanted it to be a tandem, to make sure it went down on a certain day, and Doug convinced the acquiring fence that he'd supply the other contract killer. Me. So this fence . . .'

'Archie Grant,' I interrupt. I keep mentioning his name to see if it'll elicit a response, but so far, nothing.

'If you say so. Anyway, Doug tells me this fence is skeptical, but Doug insists on bringing me on, and we can kill two birds with one rock. We'll work the tandem and we'll make sure it looks like an accident. I guess that satisfied what's-his-name, because Doug got the gig and procured the down payment for both hitters.

'I remember thinking, *so this is why you want me to work with you now . . . so you can collect double fees on the same hit.* Say what you want about Doug, the man knew how to game a system no matter what it was. You thought you were pulling the strings? That's only cause he let you think so. He was the one working the puppets, didn't matter what the play was. It wasn't till I saw him doing it to others that I realized all these years, he'd been doing the same to me, you know? I guess that's neither here nor there now, but there it is.

'So getting back to this hit . . . Doug built this elaborate model of this alleyway in Boston. Painted and sanded and lit up to the very last detail. The bar where this detective liked to drown his sorrows was specially made with a flying roof so he could take it off and you could see inside. It was like nothing you ever saw. This one made the one he did for Cleveland look like a kindergartner's shitty homework assignment. Doug had little bartenders in there, little dishwashers, little beer mugs, even miniature peanut shells on the floor. The works.

'So he starts talking me through the plan. This mark comes in this joint every Saturday night like clockwork and stays not only till the bar closes, but after the owner locks the front door. The target is chummy with the owner or shaking him down or whatever but he gets special treatment, one last glass of whiskey on the house before the lights go out. The owner's a salty old Southey who fixes that last highball himself before running receipts in his office until the mark finally heads out the back door.

'So Doug has this plan. It involves me showing up just as the doors close, pretending to be a health inspector. I'm supposed to do a few hocus pocus maneuvers, you know, get the front door locked, slip a roofie in the mark's drink, keep the owner occupied in his office or the kitchen, wave our target out the back door, and that's just half of it. Doug's showing me this elaborate set up he's got worked out in the alley, real domino rally type stuff, ice on the steps, trip wire on the bottom, a lever that'll whack his feet out from under him so that he'll nail the back of his head on the ice, five other things I'm forgetting about. Complicated stuff and his eyes light up as he's telling me all about it.

'I tell him it's all too complicated and for just a moment, he looks at me the way he did when I confronted him in the basement when I first found the model. Oooh, boy, if the devil wears a face, that's what it looks like. I shut up quick and he catches himself like he stepped past the caution signs and straightens up right away but it was there and I saw it. He smiles and tells me how hard he's worked and how even if it's a small job getting a drunk to slip on some icy steps, he wants it done right. He's made a career out of getting it done right and I know better than to pop off again, so I button it and say however he wants to plug this guy is fine with me. I did not want to see that look again, I can assure you that.

'The night of the hit, everything is fine. I'm with Doug running lookout while he sets up the pieces of the trap in the alley. I haven't seen him work like this and I can tell he's excited about it, the way he's moving around, a smile on his face, all hopped up like a football player before a big game, you know? Like a kid on Christmas Eve? He's wearing a BWSC uniform – Boston Water and Sewer – and a fake beard and all that seemed *unnecessary* looking back but it made him happy so what the hell was I gonna say? He signals me when the trap is all set, and right on time, I hit the front door, just as the owner is cleaning up. Health Inspector is the best cover you can use with bars or restaurants because no one questions it – the manager or owner is mildly annoyed but always accommodating. This was no different and I got the mickey into the detective's drink while the owner and he looked up at a fire exit with a faulty light I pointed out. No big deal. It's amazing how many things people miss each day when they're made to look in a certain direction, you know? Look at the birdie over there while I take the wallet from your back pocket here. People, for the most part, are suckers.

'The plan goes exactly the way Doug drew it up. I took the owner to his office while he told the cop to head out back. I watched out of the corner of my eye, you know, as our target got up and stumbled off. I counted to a hundred in my mind, all while I was talking about grease traps and proper temperatures on the refrigeration system and where the "wash your hands" signs have to be displayed in the bathroom and I could see the owner's eyes glaze over.

'Abruptly, I get to a hundred and I tell him everything looks good and he can count on a top notch report and can he let me out the front? Doug had told me the probabilities were he would follow me out since he liked to park his Dodge Charger right out in front of his bar. Sure enough, he comes with me outside and I watch from across the street as he climbs into the muscle car and drives away.'

'So where's the complication?'

'There wasn't one, is what I'm saying. Not on this job . . .'

'So . . .'

'So I go to meet Doug at the rendezvous spot which is three blocks away, this street corner near a motel and he's got this smile big as summer on his face, you know? I'll never forget it. He's really happy. Says it went off without a hitch. Drunk detective stumbles down the stairs, the lever sweeps his feet, he cracks his skull, out cold. No way he won't freeze to death. Doug even rigged it so some water would spill off the gutter above him, ensuring the detective would be found as frozen as a popsicle. No other way to rule this one but straight up accidental death.'

'What about the lever?'

'Doug fixed it with a string so he could slide it away. Everything planned to the last detail, like I said. This is how his mind worked.

'He told me all about the kill as we walked toward the car. I remember thinking I hadn't seen him this happy since before we were married. And I was happy too, as weird as that sounds. I started seeing this life together, this future together. Me and Doug, a team. Other couples can sit on their asses watching the evening news while we'll be out – I don't know – changing the world. That's something you do, you know? You imagine the work you're doing is for the greater good although it's probably just settling some small-time scores. Maybe we can make this work, I thought. Maybe this partnership is all we need to make it work between us, better than it ever was before. It seems silly now, but that's what was going through my head.

'All of a sudden, this black van roars around the corner and I get the uneasy feeling it's coming up on us. You know that feeling? The kind that warms you up even though it's cold as balls outside? Doug puts his arm around me all protective like and I remember thinking that was kind of a sweet touch, you know? He wasn't much of an affectionate person, but he thought to put his arm on my shoulders and I thought that was nice.

'The van barrels up and skids to a stop and three sort of gangster looking guys get out, one black and two white and they call Doug by name. "You Spilatro?" the biggest one says. Doug doesn't answer, but I can hear his breathing stop and truth be told, I was scared to death. I hear another guy say, "yeah, he's Spilatro," and I see this guy's face as he steps into the light and he's looking a little familiar, like maybe I know him from somewhere, and I'll be damned if it isn't Decker, his old army buddy, the one who brought him into the killing life. After Doug told me about him, I looked him up in some of Doug's old army pictures, and this is the same guy, I'm sure of it. Doug realizes it at the same time as me and I can see him sigh heavily, like this is all just too much. The first guy, the muscle, raises his hand up and he's holding a gun, some kind of big automatic. Don't ask me what kind because I don't know. The last thing Doug says is "don't kill my wife," and crack, crack, the muscle shoots him twice in the chest. Blood flies on to me, I feel it hit the side of my face, and out of the corner of my eye I see Doug drop straight down. You know what I mean? Straight down like all his muscles shut down at once? Well, I just stood there like a jackass, you know, and the three guys pick up Doug's body and throw it in the van. Decker turns and looks at me and I think maybe he's deciding whether or not to drop me too, but he just gives me that hard stare men are so fond of, moves around to the driver's side, and varoom, they're gone. If this was retaliation for something Doug did, nobody said and I don't know. The van drove off as though nothing ever happened and I stood there, I swear for an hour or two, not in shock but not thinking either, you know?'

Her voice falls quiet and she takes a sip of her coffee, not raising her eyes. She doesn't have to blow on it this time.

I give her a moment to play it out, check to see if she's going to say more, and I have to give her an ounce of respect. She doesn't try to conjure up a tear or manage a sob.

I lean back and wait. Everything I do, every interaction hinges on the principle of dominance. Dominance can be physical, like cracking a man in the knee to drop him in front of you so he knows you're better than he is. Or it can be mental: a game of wits, a look, a gesture, a word – anything to gain an advantage over an adversary. Sometimes dominance can simply mean waiting.

After a couple of silent minutes, she looks up, eyes dry. There's resentment in her eyes, resentment for making her draw this out. Finally, when I have her broken, I speak up.

'You know he's not dead.'

'You want me to say it?'

'Why pretend?'

She moves the coffee cup back and forth in front of her, grimacing. 'He didn't have to do it for me. He could've just walked.'

'Didn't have to hire the guys, you mean.'

'Yeah. Plan the whole thing out. Tack it on to the end of the other job, you know?' She stops looking at me, at the inside of the diner, at anything. 'It was actually . . . well, it was the sweetest thing he did for me the whole time we were married.'

I nod, but this is not good. Not good at all.

'Can I get out of here now? I'm done with this.'

She's drained now, played out, bitter. If I squeeze her any more, she'll pop.

I nod and she hauls herself up, then hovers over me for a second as her shadow falls across half my face. 'It's a bad thing you've done, making me say it.' I don't look at her. 'It's a bad thing you've done.' When I feel the shadow move away, I know she's gone.

We meet in a pre-determined spot, a bench in Battery Park. It's quiet here this time of day. A patch of green. The water. An old man sits at a table by himself, moving chess pieces around while his lips move. Risina is already sitting when I arrive. For a moment, we don't speak. Anyone passing would think us two office drones meeting for a quiet date; the guy in sales with the girl from accounting.

'You let her leave.'

'Yeah. She was used up.'

I put my arm around Risina, and she leans into me. For just a few short breaths, we're back in that fishing village halfway around the world. Maybe this is all we'll have for a while.

'I thought the idea was to kidnap someone he loves . . .'

'It is. But he doesn't love her.'

'He didn't have to set it up for her like that. He could've run off.'

'That's true.'

'So that means something.'

'He loves the process, not her. He loves the mousetrap. He loves setting up all the pieces and knocking them down. He cooked up the dummy fall at the same time as he plotted out the actual kill. Brought her in on the tandem and made the whole thing one piece, you see? First the kill, then the fall . . . two parts of the same job. In his mind, they were always one. He doesn't care about her . . . he gets off on the complication.'

Risina frowns. 'But he thought to do it that way. It has to be a sign of . . . well, at least affection if not love.'

'Maybe. But it's not enough for what we need.'

She starts to speak, but I get there first. 'When I first understood which way this was breaking, I thought maybe I could enlist Carla to help us find Spilatro and hurt him. The way he treated her, faking his death, bringing this world into her life and then walking away? He left her holding the bag. I thought maybe she was bitter and we could use that bitterness. But she's not. And she's not the opposite either. She's not accepting. She's just . . . finished.'

Risina nods. The old man stands and collects his pieces. His lips move, but his words are lost in the wind.

'So we still have nothing. After all this?'

'I didn't say that. She gave us a great deal more than we had before we found her. We know Spilatro was married, we know he was in the army, we know he worked in software sales, at least for a while. We have ways to find him.'

'And we know how he thinks.'

I smile. Risina's intuition continues to surprise me. 'That's right. Now we know how he thinks.'

We're going to get to him through his friend, the army buddy who brought him into the game. I notice I'm thinking in plural pronouns again, 'we' instead of 'I,' and I like the way it sounds in my head. The tandem didn't work for Doug and Carla, but they're not us, not even close to us, and Carla served only as a convenience to him. He was using her for cover, that's it. That was her utility for him.

We're not like them at all. Carla said she saw a future for them in the moments before that future was wiped away, but he was the one who caused that plan to fail. It's different for Risina and me. We can pull jobs together, back each other's play, watch each other's back. I fell in love with Risina because of the animal inside her, just below the surface. She has more sand than I imagined back in Rome. She demonstrates it over and over. It's like I'm waiting for the other shoe to drop, even though she's not wearing any. We're not like them. We. Not I. We.

A tiny piece of information can be like a keyword to unravel a code. Based on Carla's story, I know approximately how old Spilatro is, and I know his army buddy's name, Decker, and I can guess a pretty accurate timeline of when they must have been in the service together. From there, it's a reasonable amount of digging to cross-reference the two names, and if the names are false, as I'm sure they will be, then it's a bit more cumbersome but not unconquerable to find similar names who served in the same unit. Most hit men aren't too creative in coming up with their aliases.

This is fence work, but most of the fences I know seem to be missing or dead. About that, K-bomb was right. I do have bad luck with fences.

Still, there is one I know who can be of service and is alive and free: the one in Belgium who has a new appreciation for handing out favors.

Doriot meets us two days later in a barbershop in the basement of the St. Regis. A pair of brothers own the joint, having taken over from their father, good guys, and when I reached out to them to use their place for an after-hours meeting, alone, they didn't hesitate to give me a key. A thousand-dollar tip on a shave and a trim didn't hurt to solidify the deal.

'I told you providence would smile on me for treating you respectfully, Columbus, and here I am in New York City, the Big Apple, so what can I do for you and how much can I be expected to earn? Not that I am only in it for the money since I like you so much, but business is business as I'm sure you understand.'

'I need a file on a guy.'

'Twenty thousand,' he says immediately.

'Give me a fucking break. Twenty thousand . . .'

'I have a ten percent relationship with my hitters, Columbus. This is what I make . . .'

'Bullshit.'

'Okay, fifteen . . .'

I could press him to twelve but I don't want to hurt his feelings before he goes to work for me. I'd rather cough up a few extra grand than have to worry about his effort.

'Fifteen's a deal but I don't want to decide on a play from your file and then find out the information is lacking.'

He shakes his head vigorously, feigning offense. 'I do this right for you, you maybe come back to me for more work. I see how this goes. You'll have a file so filled with truth you can lay it on top of the Bible.'

'All right then.'

'So who must I find for you?'

I give him everything I know about Decker and Spilatro as I regurgitate my conversation with Carla.

'How much time do I have?' he asks when I'm done.

'Three weeks enough?'

He frowns as though he's thinking about it. 'Are you sure you can't come up to eighteen?'

'Fifteen.'

'Okay, okay. I'm just asking the question. I'll start right away. You'll see. You have never worked with a fence like me. This file will be like Brussels chocolate.' He does that chef thing of kissing the tips of his fingers.

'I need one other thing.'

He pauses at the door, then surveys the barber implements surrounding us. 'If you tell me you need me to trim your hair, then I'm afraid you will have to come up with the twenty thousand after all.' He produces a short laugh that sounds more like a smoker's cough.

'I need to rent a house upstate until your file is ready. Somewhere in the country, somewhere back from a road, somewhere no one's gonna visit, even a mailman. Leave a key and an address for Jack Walker at reception tomorrow and you can have your twenty.'

He smacks his lips and raises his eyebrows.

'You sure you don't want a haircut too?'

'Just the keys.'

He smiles and heads out the door.

I want to see her kill something.

The house is a good find, a fifteen-minute drive inside the property line from a dirt road only marked by an unassuming gate. I walked the fence line on our first few days and it's over five miles from front to back and side to side. Doriot suspended mail service while we're renting the place, and I have yet to hear a car engine anywhere in the vicinity.

The woods surrounding the house are as thick as a blanket and teem with life. Deer, badgers, squirrels, woodchucks, robins, sparrows and quail go about their days foraging and fighting. I need to see her kill something. I don't care about the hunt or her ability to keep silent or her ability to hold the gun steady or her nerve in pulling the trigger. It's the *after* I'm worried about, the *after* I need to see. How she reacts to blood spilled by her own hand. Will she be like Spilatro and shy away from the mess? Or will she be like me and seek out another opportunity? And which do I really want?

'Why do you carry a Glock?'

'It's a good, lightweight semi-automatic that'll hold seventeen bullets in the clip and one in the chamber. It's made of polymer so it doesn't warp in bad weather and it takes just a second to slam in another clip if you're in a spot.'

She smirks and racks a round into the chamber. Her eyes narrow in a mock display of gravity, like she's playing a character in an action film, and then she laughs.

'You still think this is fun and games?'

'I think you need to break the tension sometimes or this would all be overwhelming.'

'Sometimes you have to rely on that tension, use it to heighten your senses.'

'Or break it to relax.'

'Who is teaching whom here?'

'Oh, come on. Don't look at me like that. You want me to say I'm scared, I'll say it without shame. I've been scared since the moment you came back from the bookstore with that look on your face. I haven't stopped being scared. If I paused to think about it, I'd probably start screaming and I don't know that I'd be able to stop. But I've always been good at learning and I've learned by watching you. I keep the fear inside and I make jokes and I laugh and I talk back and I try to look cool and all of that is to keep the fear choked down. So let me do this my way, please. I don't ask much of you and I pay attention, but you have to let me do this my way.'

I move in and pull her into me and we stand in the forest as the world falls silent. I'm not sure if I'm holding her or she's holding me, and when we break, her eyes are wet.

'Can you at least make the jokes better?'

She starts to react, then realizes I'm having fun with her. 'You shouldn't do that when I have a pistol in my hand.'

'You haven't even taken the safety off.'

She looks down at the grip and when she does I snatch the gun from her hand.

'Oldest trick in the book.'

She starts laughing, hard. The woods come to life again.

A squirrel darts into the path in front of us. It's a bit wary and cocks its head to the side to give us a once-over. It sniffs the air, hops twice more across the path, and rears on its hind legs again to gauge whether or not we present a threat.

Risina stops, levels her gun, and before I can say anything, she pulls the trigger, once, twice, three times, missing the first two shots low before she corrects and sends the creature pin-wheeling backward, tumbling end over end like a bowling pin, its hide a mess of blood and fur.

'Anything else you want me to kill?' she asks, unsmiling.

I study her face, and she breaks eye contact to saunter off. I'm starting to think I don't need to worry about the after. Maybe, instead, I should be worrying about what I've created.

He's waiting for us in the cabin.

That fucking bastard Doriot must've sold us out, and I never saw it coming. Didn't even have an inkling it was coming. I've grown too fucking seat-of-the-pants on this whole mission . . . except it's not really a mission, is it? Christ,

I should be shot in the head. Ever since I brought Risina into this and I didn't have a fence and I thought I could call in favors and I thought the name Columbus still meant something, it has been one thing after another and I still haven't learned. And that's the rubber meeting the road right there. Columbus. The name carries no weight. Not anymore.

When I was incarcerated in Waxham, I learned a term called 'chin-checking.' Roughly translated, it describes a gang leader who returns to his neighborhood after time in the joint. While he was gone, some young buck stepped in to fill his shoes in the power vacuum. The ex-con has to reassert his authority by walking up and punching the new kid right in the fucking mouth. Chin-checking. Hello, I'm back. I thought stepping back into this life would be like I never left, except I did leave, and memories are short. Doriot used to be afraid of me, but he's not anymore. If I get through this, Doriot's gonna learn a new term.

I open the cabin door and a cell phone is standing up on the table like a scar. Risina senses something is wrong the way animals perk up whenever a predator roams nearby. The phone rings before I can say anything to comfort her.

If he wanted to kill us, he could've shot us when we walked inside the door. If he wanted to plant a bomb in the phone, then we're already dead. But in my experience, people call when they want to talk.

Risina shakes her head but I press the green button on the phone.

'Hello.'

'You've been asking about me.'

'You wanted to flush me, here I am.'

'You presume to know my intentions?'

'I know a few things. I'll learn more.'

'I'll help you out. Here's a fact about me: I'm smarter than you.'

'That why you missed me outside the restaurant in Chicago?'

'Who says I missed?'

'It was sloppy.'

'Accidents are sloppy by nature. And sloppy by design.'

'And the police at Kirschenbaum's house?'

'Now looking for a murderer who happens to fit your description.'

'Not exactly the way you drew it up.'

He chuckles, and the sound is disturbing in its confidence. 'You don't sound sure about that.'

He's right. I don't. Even this conversation feels like I'm being spun whichever direction he wants me to go.

'You want—'

But I cut him off in a clumsy attempt to gain control. 'What's your play?'

'I don't—'

'Why kidnap Archie Grant? Why call me out by name?'

'You gonna let me finish?'

Is this how boxers feel as a round slips away? Right hooks coming but you're just too slow or tired or old or rusty to get out of the way?

'Is he alive?'

'Check the phone.'

The phone beeps in my hand, an incoming text message. I click on it without hanging up the line and there is a picture of Archie holding a *New York Times* with a photograph of a blazing inferno on the front page – fire trucks out and about, spraying the flames down, and I have no doubt if I drive to a newsstand, it'll be today's paper. Archie looks defiant in the photo, a *fuck you* face if I ever saw one. I put the phone to my ear again.

'Satisfied?'

'Let me talk to him.'

'He doesn't feel like talking.'

'What's this about? Why the games? You want me, here I am.'

'You contact my wife again and I'll blow Mr. Grant up in front of you. You'll walk around a corner or step off an elevator and he'll be tied up sitting in a chair. You'll barely have time to register what is happening before parts of your friend slap you in the face.'

'Come on. You wanted to flush me? You flushed me. Let's finish this out in the open.' Flailing. Too tired. Stumbling.

'You'll be out in the open, Columbus. You won't know where I'll be.'

'Just tell me what this is about. I don't mind spinning in circles, but at least tell me why I'm spinning.'

And right when I don't think he's going to say anything else, he surprises me. 'Dark men.'

I've heard that expression once before, in a hotel room in the Standard Hotel in Los Angeles, from the lips of the Speaker of the House of Representatives, the Democratic Nominee for President, Abe Mann, moments before I killed him. '*When I had my problem with your mother, some dark men made that problem disappear. You understand about dark men, I take it . . .*' he had said.

He went on to tell me about the men who were the real players behind the politicians, the dark men who moved the representative's mouths like ventriloquists, the dark men who wouldn't let their candidates, candidates like Abe Mann, leave the game. So the Speaker of the House hired a killer named Columbus and designated himself as the target. His only escape was death, and I was his suicide method.

The dark men must not have been happy about that decision. All this time I was worried about someone in law enforcement tracking me down, but now I see my anxiety was misplaced. I killed the man I was hired to kill, but I upset the dark men who wanted him alive so they could keep pulling his strings. It seems they've held his death against me all these years and now they've hired Spilatro to exact their revenge. He went to them with my name and they said 'bring us his head.' This changes everything.

Risina and I leave the house immediately, and instead of planning our next move, I just drive. The sun is heading west, dropping toward the horizon, so fuck it, I drive into it headlong, the light fierce in my eyes but maybe that's the way it's supposed to be. Maybe I deserve it. Maybe I've stuck to the shadows for too long and need to spend a little time with the sun in my eyes. Maybe some light will clean my fucking head.

Risina is pensive as she fights the urge to speak. Farms roll past the window, looking properly pastoral. After a moment, she pivots toward me. 'What did he mean by dark men?'

'An old job. I probably upset a few apple carts.'

'So these men want revenge?'

'Yes.'

'And they hired Spilatro to kill you?'

'I think so.'

She nods. 'Why him?'

'I think he went to them with my name.'

'You think Archie gave you up?'

I chew on the inside of my lower lip, and a new idea takes shape in my head.

'I don't believe so . . . I think there's a second explanation.'

'Give it to me.'

'What if these dark men work for the government? The CIA?'

'And . . .'

'And Spilatro was a soldier.'

'So?'

'So . . . what if he never left the military?'

We pull into a Hampton Inn somewhere outside the Berkshires. I switch cars at a used car lot, paying too much but not enough for the salesman to remember us. I choose a room at the inn on the first floor, in a corner with two windows and an outside door nearby in case we need to split in a hurry. I may not be all the way where I was three years ago, but I'm starting to take the smoothness off the edges.

After we make some bad coffee in the four-cup maker provided by the inn, Risina and I take a moment to sit and rest and think.

'You have that look in your eye.'

'What do you mean?'

'That same look you gave me that last day in our house before we headed to the U.S. You look like you want me to leave.'

'We're entering new territory here. I've spent my professional life in a world I understand. A world of outlaws. Government agents are a separate entity entirely. They have resources I don't have, access I can't imagine. We have to work around the law . . . they break laws with impunity.'

'It doesn't matter. We're in this together until the end. Spilatro knows about me. He's probably known about me since we landed in Chicago.'

I nod. She's right.

'If you tried to take care of this on your own, he'd find me and use me against you. There's no sending me away. No hiding me somewhere. If you're not watching me, then you won't know I'm safe. And he'll compromise you at a point when it'll matter.'

I keep nodding.

'I love you. I'll do whatever you tell me at this point. If you tell me to run, I'll run. If you tell me to hide, I'll do it. I'll wait for you to come back to me. But it's not the smart play, as you call it. He knows about me, and he knows you love me.'

'I do.'

'You'll just have to be your best with me dragging on your back.'

'No.'

Her eyes flash. 'What is this "no"?'

'No, I won't drag you on my back. You're going to have to step up and be the tiger I know you have inside you.'

She sets her jaw, and when she looks up, her eyes fill with resolve. 'I can be a tiger.'

'You're going to have to kill more than a squirrel.'

'I will pull the trigger when I have to.'

'Then let's find Lieutenant Decker.'

10

We backtracked through the four files we had on Spilatro, the four hits Archie assigned. And there it was. The connections between all those jobs that Risina and I and Archie himself had failed to catch. The first hit, the rich female English professor at Ohio State, had helped finance a PAC set up to block government land use for military training in Ohio. For the second, the TV reporter had been working on a story about bribes involving the top senator from Illinois. The unlucky bookkeeper in the third file had more than a few Washington clients on his ledgers. And the final file? The police detective in Boston? The one Carla helped knock over? He would've testified against two NSA officials who were caught with hookers and cocaine at the Intercontinental in downtown Boston if he hadn't slipped on the ice and had such an untimely accident. All Spilatro kills . . . all with government ties. And the fact that all those deaths looked like accidents was the icing on the cake. If they had looked like actual hits, actual assassinations, there would have been inquiries, scandal, attention paid. The dark men wanted these issues to disappear, not become headlines. Spilatro's killing style was perfect for these kinds of jobs.

I wonder if Archie knew he was a patsy for the government, and to what degree he was playing ball. I wonder if he slipped and accidentally gave Spilatro my name, or Spilatro discovered it and then sought out Archie, worked his way inside. Used Kirschenbaum to make himself available to Archie, then worked a few government jobs for him to gain trust. I wonder how extensively the Agency is involved in the private killing business and how many of my assignments over the years were actually financed by taxpayers.

Finally, I look up the light rail accident in Cleveland, the one Carla claims to have discovered in her basement, the one where a section of the rail collapsed, killing the fourteen passengers on board. Sure enough, three of the passengers worked for a top Defense contractor, McKnight International. Why the government wanted them dead, and what contract that helped to close, I have no idea.

But Spilatro works for Uncle Sam and has been all along, I'm now sure of it.

It takes her a week in DC. I remain uncertain on whether or not she's capable of shooting a man in the head, but as a researcher, she's extraordinary. This is an Ivy League-educated woman who built an impressive rare book collection by carefully researching titles, cross-referencing sources, compiling lists of potential dealers, wooing and cajoling and nudging reluctant sellers while she gathered the best information first, so she could swoop in and procure a title before her competition knew there was a deal to be made. My mistake, I'm beginning to realize, was grooming Risina to do what I do, to be a contract killer. I've been working with a natural fence the whole time.

She won't need to blend in, to hide in plain sight; in fact, she can use her beauty to secure what she needs, to make men *want* to help her. She can use an arrow I don't have in my quiver: she can be wholly unthreatening.

She made an appointment with the Assistant Secretary of Defense for Public Affairs at the Pentagon, posing as a freelance journalist. With the Presidential initiative for a more transparent government coupled with the Freedom of Information Act and countless journalistic precedents, it wasn't difficult for Risina to gain access to enlistment records. She charmed the ASOD as she explained she was writing a heartwarming article on Desert Storm veterans who had parlayed their time in the service into high-end jobs. So much of what is reported in the mainstream media focuses on the negative, she told him – the combat fatigue, the stress disorders, the disabilities – she was hoping to chronicle the positive effects on veterans who served their country well and made something of their lives after their tour of duty, using the skills they learned in the military to achieve civilian success. The assistant secretary damn near threw his spine out of alignment bending over backward to help her.

Roland Deckman, aka 'Decker,' and Aaron Spittrow, aka 'Spilatro,' both joined the army in 1988. Like I said, most hit men aren't too imaginative when they come up with their killing names, and Risina made short work of spotting two similar names in the same unit. They entered the 24th ID out of Fort Stewart, Georgia, one of the first units deployed to Saudi Arabia in the summer of 1990. When the Gulf War began, the 24th faced some of the fiercest resistance in the entire campaign, running up against the 6th Mechanized Division of the Iraqi Republican Guard. They still managed to capture the airfields at Jabbah and Tallil. Deckman and Spittrow worked as infantry grunts, nothing unusual in their service records.

The ASOD apologized to Risina profusely, but contact information on Deckman and Spittrow was sketchy following their military service. They both were honorably discharged in 1992, and where most soldiers would at least have a few files of contact and discharge information, those files seemed to be missing for Deckman and Spittrow. Risina asked if there was contact information from *before* they joined the army.

The ASOD smiled. That, he had. At least for one of them.

Northville, Michigan is a quiet slice of suburbia outside of Detroit, with modest homes peppered around mansions. Although many neighborhoods in Detroit look as though they've been abandoned and forgotten, Northville could just as easily be situated outside Kansas City, Chicago, or Dayton.

It is filled with regular folks making livings and raising families. Roland Deckman grew up here before he joined the army.

We drove straight to Michigan, taking shifts behind the wheel. Risina spent enough time driving in the States when she was in college that she isn't intimidated by the width of our highways. In fact, she handled our sedan like it was primed for the Indy 500.

'Do you know what the fastest car in the world is?' she asked as we blasted through Ohio.

'What?'

'A rental car.'

Well, at least her jokes have gotten better.

It's warm and rainy when we arrive, the kind of summer shower unique to Michigan that blows down like hell for fifteen minutes before it exhausts itself and retreats out to the lake.

We sit outside Deckman's parents' house. He's now a government assassin, I'm sure of it, a breed of animal I've been fortunate to avoid until recently. He's had training I've never had, supplies I can only dream of, access to targets that must be facilitated by entire teams of personnel and equipment, and a get-out-of-jail-free card that removes half the worry of making a kill.

But does he secretly despise his job? Does he question the political motivations behind his assignments? Does he rely too heavily on the system? Do his fortunes change with each new administration? And does this cement his loyalty to his friend Spilatro over his loyalty to his employers?

The real question, the only question that matters: is he a tiger?

No, I haven't had to worry about government hitters until now, until they sought me out, forced me back in when I was content enough to ride out my days in obscurity.

We sip coffee and wait for the rain to die.

'Decker's our key. He's who we're going to trade for Archie and how we're going to get them off me.'

'What makes you think Spilatro or Spittrow, or whatever his name is, will be more willing to deal for Decker than Carla?'

'Because these cover stories people tell are mostly lies but always have moments of truth. I think Decker has been Spilatro's friend and fellow soldier for twenty-plus years. I think they were already working jobs together when they were in the service. I think Decker went to the CIA first and rescued Spilatro from a dead-end life of middle-management and that formed a bond that is unbreakable.

'I could be wrong. He could mean nothing to Spilatro. But he helped him pull off that fake hit to fool his wife. After all that time, they were still together. My guess is the Agency isn't too keen on fostering or facilitating friendships . . . they'd want their officers working alone and anonymous. So these guys still pulling a job together has to mean more than blood . . . it has to. At least, that's what I'd like to believe.'

'Because it's the best plan?'

'Because it's all we have right now.'

The military is one thing, the CIA quite another. She couldn't get inside Langley the way she did the Pentagon, so the only chance we have of confronting Decker has to come from his past. Spilatro certainly covered his tracks, burning down the 'Aaron Spittrow' military records from both before and after his service, but Decker must've been comfortable no one would put the puzzle pieces together the way we did. He failed to erase the blackboard of his 'Deckman' upbringing, and the military kept a record of his home address.

His brother, Lance, now lives in the same home they grew up in. He's an alcoholic. He owes money to the bank, has sold the equity in the house, has tried unsuccessfully three times for a small business loan, and was rejected on the grounds of bad personal credit. All of this information, supposedly private, Risina pulled from the Internet during our ride west. A natural fence, like I said.

The rain abates, so we approach the house. After a minute, a man in his early forties opens the door. He holds a beer bottle in one hand, and his eyes are droopy, red-rimmed, like a basset hound's.

'Help you?' he says as he takes a glance at me and then lets his gaze linger on Risina.

'Mr. Deckman?'

He turns back to me. 'Yes?'

'Today's your lucky day.'

He leans into the doorframe as his expression turns suspicious. I'm holding a duffel bag, and he eyes it, then looks back at me. 'Hadn't had too many of those. What's the sale?'

'No sale. We're here to give you money. Can we come in?'

He folds his arms but doesn't budge.

'What's this about, pal?'

'It's about your brother.'

'My brother?'

'Roland Deckman's your brother, correct?'

His eyes dart back and forth between us now, the lids pulled open. 'Yes, but . . .'

'Well, he's made a significant amount of money over the last twenty years, and he wanted you to have most of it.'

'Is he . . . has something happened to him?'

'Can we come in, sir? We'd rather not do this on the doorstep.'

'Yes, of course.' He blinks down at himself, tries to smooth out the wrinkles in his shirt, then props the door open, stepping aside. 'Please, come in. Sorry . . . we get solicitors all the time here . . .'

'No problem.'

Risina moves in first, and I follow. The house is a craftsman, lots of wood and rustic furniture. The living room is cramped and messy, like it hasn't had a wipe-down in a while. The television is on, a video game in mid-pause on the screen.

'Can I get you guys a beer? Or a . . . or some water?'

'No, we're fine, thank you.'

We take seats on the sofa and Lance looks nervously at the screen and then presses a button on the remote so the television snaps to black.

After I let him stew for a moment, biting at the nail on his pinky finger, I lean forward. 'I'll cut right to it then, Mr. Deckman. I don't know if your brother told you, but he was working for Central Intelligence.'

'Yeah . . . he, uh, I don't know if I was supposed to know but he mentioned . . .'

'Good. It's certainly not against regulations.'

I pause a moment longer, then smile sadly. 'I'm sorry to say that your brother died in the line of duty.'

I watch Lance's eyes, and they continue to move back and forth between us but don't cloud over. It's easy to see inside his head: he doesn't give a damn about his brother, he just wants to know what is in it for him. I suspect his credit cards are maxed out, his bills are piling up, and the house we're sitting inside is one of the few possessions he owns outright, paid for by his parents before they croaked.

He catches himself and coughs into his fist. 'Oh . . . oh no. I . . . this is a shock, you know.'

'I understand.' I shift the duffel up to the coffee table, struggling for effect with the weight, and his eyes go to it like a prisoner looking at a key that fits his lock.

'Like I was saying, your brother socked away a significant sum during his employment, and his will states that he wants you to have it.'

'How much?' He catches himself again. 'I mean, wow, this is incredible. I'm . . .' He stops, coloring.

'Well, that's why we're here in person, Lance. This bag holds a hundred thousand dollars in cash . . .'

He's fun to watch. There's obvious disappointment at that amount – like it'll cover his debts but he isn't completely out of the woods. He won't be able to sit around playing video games for the rest of his life, all his bills paid. I keep playing with his emotions . . .

'. . . which represents five percent of his wealth.'

He swallows, and his lips purse and tremble like a baby with a pacifier. He's too dumb to do the math, but he knows the number has a lot of zeroes. I hand him the handles of the bag and he takes it in his lap. He wants to play it cool but he can't stop himself; he unzips the bag and looks over the stacks.

'Now here's the messy part.'

His eyes dart up, searching my face. 'Messy?'

'Yes, sir. See, we're authorized to release you the rest of the inheritance, but we need something from you before we can do that.'

He nods before he even knows he's doing it. 'Sure. What do you need?'

'Well, when an asset of ours dies, for national security reasons, we have to make sure all ties to him are erased. If an enemy were able to trace steps back to where he started, where he was living, where he kept personal possessions, files and such, we'd be . . . well, it would be bad for the country.'

I have zero idea what I'm talking about, but I've read enough Ludlum, Clancy, and Follet to impersonate a government handler. Well, at least conjure enough of a performance to manipulate a desperate man who doesn't know jack shit.

'Yeah, sure. I understand.' He stands up and absently wipes his hands on his shirt again. 'Let me see . . .' He heads to a back hallway, leaving us alone in the living room.

Risina eyes me, a half smile on her face. I shrug, and we wait. I can hear doors open and close somewhere in the house, and then the sound of paper shuffling.

After a moment, Lance returns, holding a small yellow legal pad. In his other hand is a cell phone. He exhales loudly . . . 'This is all I got. Umm . . . I haven't heard from Ro in years, shoot, I mean, had to be 2005 or so, after mom died. He had to sign some papers so I could, um, take over this place. He told me if I ever got in serious trouble, to, um . . . get ahold of him at this number.'

He hands me the legal pad and the only thing scrawled on it is an 888 number. He hands me the phone. 'He, uh, he said to use this phone so he'd know it was me. I guess it has a chip in it or something?' He hands me an old Nokia. 'I haven't, uh, charged it in a while.'

'Did you ever call him?'

'One time. I called him and some broad . . .' he looks over at Risina. 'Sorry, I mean, some woman answered and said she was with some bank or something. At first, I thought I'd dialed the wrong number, then I realized it was probably a cover or something? I told her to tell Roland that his brother needed him.

'I swear it wasn't another five minutes and the phone rang in my hand. He was all concerned, out-of-breath you know, asking if I was in trouble. I told him I was running out of funds, you know . . . maybe he could loan me some money? He told me to only call him if my life was in danger, if someone had threatened me, that was it. That's the last I heard from him. We were never close, but I guess he . . . uh, I guess he . . .' He looks down at the duffel. '. . . wanted me to have a better life or something.'

I stand up and Risina joins me. 'You sure this is everything you have that could lead back to him? No address in Washington or anything?'

He holds up his empty hands, then crosses his arms like he's hugging himself. 'No, nothing else. That's it. If he had a home address, he never gave it to me.'

I nod, and look into his eyes, like I'm checking to see if he's lying when I already know he's telling the truth.

'Okay, Mr. Deckman. Thank you.'

He looks at the duffel as we head to the door. 'Sure, no problem.' He follows us closely . . .

'So . . . the rest of the money?'

I stop, like I had forgotten about it. 'Yes, sorry. My associate here will deliver it when we make sure there isn't any other way to get to your brother's identity through you.'

'There isn't.'

'I'm sure there isn't. It's just a formality. You mind if we give it to you in cash? Makes it cleaner for us.'

'No, yeah, I mean, cash is great.'

'Karen here will get back to you shortly. We, uh, we know where you live,' I say with a laugh.

He laughs too, like he's relieved. As we step back off his stoop, 'How . . . how did he die if you don't mind my asking?'

'It's classified,' I offer, trying my best to look apologetic.

He nods again, then gives us a half wave, drops his hand like he was embarrassed about that, and then just shuts the door.

Risina and I climb in the car, and she chuckles. 'Okay, not all of this job is miserable.'

'No, not all of it,' I agree as I hold up the phone. 'Let's go find a place to call Decker and see if he might want to come say hello.'

We take him at the casino.

Downtown Detroit has three of them, one in Greektown, and two in the middle of downtown. The MGM is a Vegas-style complex, with a full floor of gaming tables, restaurants, nightclubs and a show theater attached to a forty-story hotel.

I call the number from his phone and know it's going to be recorded, so I evince my best impression of his brother's nasally whine when the woman picks up with 'National Investments.'

'It's Lance. I'm outta money. And these guys at the MGM, they're not messing around. Tell my bro . . . tell Ro I gotta . . . I'm going in at midnight to room 4001 to meet these guys . . . just tell him I love him.'

I hang up. The phone chirps in my hand three minutes later, but I ignore it. I don't remove the battery so they can pinpoint the location with whatever satellites do that type of thing. Since Risina and I are already checked into the hotel, it should paint a convincing picture.

I'm certain he'll come alone. He doesn't want his employers to know any more about his personal business than absolutely necessary, and certainly not about his deadbeat brother who got himself in a bad way with some casino heavies. No, my guess is he'll come in by himself, pissed off, armed but not ready to shoot, not ready to play defense. And as a man who understands the value of surprise, I'm betting he won't try to contact the casino owners ahead of time to straighten out this matter. If he does, my plan is sunk, but what better place to play the odds than right here in a gaming joint?

At eleven-thirty, Risina spots a man heading to the elevator, and after he gives it a cursory glance, he backtracks toward the reception area. His face is similar to his brother's, but better looking – a stronger jaw, brighter eyes – like the superior chromosomes bandied together to favor him and exclude his alcoholic brother. Still, the family resemblance is there.

The top floor requires an extra security card to trigger the elevator, so he'll have to request the floor, another indication this is our guy. Risina ducks in behind him, hears him request a room on the fortieth floor, and then listens to the receptionist give him room 4021.

He thanks her politely and heads back to the bank of elevators. I'm sure he's surging with grim energy, ready to confront the guys in room 4001 before his brother arrives, straighten out the situation, turn it ugly if he has to, whatever it takes to get his brother off the hook. After he presses the up button, the first doors to open are for the middle car in this deck of three, and as soon as he's in it, Risina calls up to me.

'Middle elevator, up now.'

I'm on the twentieth floor. Above the doors are LCD readouts displaying the floor number of each car's current position. I watch and hit my own 'up' button as the middle car passes the tenth floor. We tested this a few times and ten out of eleven, the elevator heading up is the one that stops; the only exception was when one of the other cars was already on the twentieth floor. But the right and left elevators are elsewhere and the one rising should be the correct choice, come on. Except now as I look, the elevator up on twenty-eight is heading down this direction and if it gets here first, I don't know what will happen, which door will open. The middle one continues to climb, please don't let someone else in the teens press 'up' and stop it. It's moving up steadily, 17, 18 . . . while the one on the right continues to fall, 22, 21, and then it hits 20 and I hold my breath, but it keeps heading down, 19, 18 on the way to the lobby and then the middle elevator door dings open. No one else is inside but Decker. I have a ball cap slung low so he won't get a good look at me. I doubt he knows my face but if he's working closely with Spilatro, I can't be sure.

I move in quickly, pull my card out to clear security for the top floor, then shrug since the 40 button is already lit up. I move to the back wall as the doors close, hoping he'll scoot up but he's experienced enough to keep his back to the wall. I have a burnt cigar in my mouth to mask the smell of what I'm about to do.

This is different from my usual work, an anomaly because I don't want Decker dead. If this had been an assignment, I would have popped him when the door opened. But I want him alive, unconscious. My left hand drops to my pocket, where the handkerchief soaked in chloroform rests. I can see him in my periphery, and he definitely checks me out as the elevator crosses 30 on its way to the top.

I have about ten more seconds to do this. I hope the smell doesn't give me away, but the cigar's scent is strong and should overpower the chemicals.

The elevator passes 34. I have eight more seconds, maybe five, but before I can pull out the rag, he says, 'Do I know you?' and I can feel the pressure of a handgun's barrel pressed against my temple. He's a professional, a *government* professional, and he's trained to spot anomalies like warning flags, so a guy on twenty pressing forty must stand out. He may not know I'm Columbus, but he knows I'm someone sent to shadow him, and he probably mistakes me for one of the guys who is about to hold his brother in room 4001.

The elevator chimes as the floor hits forty and in that little jostle elevator cars make when they come to a rest, I duck the gun and drive my forehead into his chin. He jerks back instinctively, and I pin his arm to the wall, the one fisting the gun, and I bang it one, two times into the back paneling and the gun drops. Unfortunately, by focusing my energy on the gun, my rib cage is vulnerable, and he takes advantage, pounding me in the side with his free fist, just as the door springs open.

He's a strong puncher, even in close quarters, and he connects in my kidney with a rabbit punch that doubles me over. He drops for the gun but I'm able to kick it out the open door onto the fortieth floor hallway and luckily, no one is up here waiting to catch a ride down. The door starts to shut on us, and he dives for the gun, but I grab his leg and the door bangs into him before springing open again. He kicks backward at me and connects with his heel to my chest before he dives for his gun in the hallway.

I leap for him. If he gets to that gun first, I'm sunk and this whole damn thing is for naught. I won't let that happen, can't let that happen. He's on the gun, but I'm on him, and before he can roll over and come up with it, I drive my fist into the crook of his elbow, snapping his arm backward. The elevator behind us closes and heads down again, leaving us to battle it out here in the fortieth floor foyer. I can see another car heading up this way, in the thirties and climbing. If it's coming to this floor, we're going to be spotted and who knows how quickly security will be here next. Somebody might have heard the scuffle and the hotel dicks are already on the way.

Unexpectedly, Deckman or Decker or whatever-the-fuck-his-name-is works his legs around my mid-section and squeezes my torso in a scissor-lock. I've seen mixed martial artists do this shit on TV, but it's a new one to me. Before I know it, he's forced me off of him, and I can barely breathe, barely move my arms as he squeezes the air out of my lungs. At the same time, he gropes with his hands, reaching behind him for the gun on the ground . . .

The elevator continues to climb toward our floor, 35, 36, but the numbers are going fuzzy, like I'm looking at them through a kaleidoscope. I pound my elbows into his thighs, but the muscles there are like rocks.

He keeps pulling us backward, just a few feet from his gun now, and if I'm going to make a move, it's going to have to be in that last instant, when he reaches for his pistol and releases just a little bit of pressure from my ribs.

We slide another few inches and I'm able to reach my hand into my pocket and withdraw that cloth. The numbers above the door pass 39 and that car is coming and whatever he or I plan to do, it's going to be in front of witnesses. He drags us the last few inches and his hands seize on that pistol, a little Colt .22, and the pressure from his legs around my waist loosens only a bit. We both twist around at the same time, toward each other, just as the elevator dings, and he swivels with the gun as I swivel with the cloth, but I'm a half-second faster and I mash that cloth into his face and hold it there, pin it there, up under his nose and mouth. He bucks wildly but doesn't fire that pistol and his eyes roll to the back of his head as his whole body goes slack, and his legs finally drop from my waist.

'You all right?' Risina says, stepping out of the elevator car, a Glock in her hand. I'm glad I was a half-second quicker or she might have witnessed something a bit bloodier when she emerged onto the floor.

'He's checked into 4021,' she says as she stoops over his limp body and withdraws his key card.

'Then let's show him to his room,' I grunt as I wrestle him up.

No sooner do we have him propped between us than a maid rounds the corner, pushing a cart. She barely glances our way as she moves down the hall. He's not the first semi-conscious guest she has encountered in the hallway and won't be the last, I'm sure. Probably not even tonight.

11

He comes out of it talking. My guess is he's been conscious long before he opened his eyes. He was hoping we would give something away while he pretended to be sawing logs, but his patience went unrewarded.

I sit in a metal folding chair in front of him. I hit him with a full wet rag of chloroform – hell, I almost passed out just soaking the cloth – so I estimated we had a couple of hours to make arrangements. We bribed a member of the hotel's security to take us down the service elevator and get us to our car in the garage. Five thousand dollars and a story about a Motown record producer who tripped himself stupid got us a wheelchair, an escort, and no questions. The lethargic guard might not have bought it from me, but one look at Risina sold the story.

It only took twenty minutes of driving around downtown for us to find what we were looking for: an abandoned warehouse. Shit, you could put on a blindfold and walk around downtown Detroit in any direction and find one. A cursory reconnaissance of the place yielded no derelicts and no security.

So when Deckman finally opens his eyes, it's the three of us alone, and with his arms and legs fastened tightly, like I said, he wants to talk.

'You have no idea who you guys are fucking with. If you touch one hair on my brother's head, I will open up a hurricane of destruction on you and your operation you can only dream of.'

I just stare at him with somnolent eyes, like I'm somewhere between amused and bored.

'Where is he? Where are you holding my brother?'

Still, I give him nothing, just let him get himself worked up.

'You might intimidate a lot of people with that thousand-yard-stare, tough guy, but I guarantee you are wasting it on me. We can talk and figure this business out together or you might as well pop me and get it over with, because the more you make me wait, the less lenient I'm going to be when we meet up later under different circumstances.'

'I could give two shits about your brother.'

He grins. 'That makes two of us. You got a cigarette I can bum?'

I just shake my head and he shrugs like it was worth a shot to ask for one. I wait for him to strain at his bindings again, testing out their tensile strength. He gives up after a moment, and I lean forward.

'I want to know how to contact Spilatro.'

Some hitters like to use their fists to elicit information, try to break a man so he'll pour out his secrets, like punching a hole in the bottom of a water bucket. Not me. Like Kirschenbaum did to me in that hotel room in Connecticut, I stagger Deckman by playing with his expectations.

The name 'Spilatro' floors him, like a driver who has to jerk the wheel suddenly when an animal darts into the road.

'I don't know what you're talking about.'

I let him dangle.

After a moment, he sighs and looks up at the ceiling. 'You're the guy, huh? The one he's gone on about?'

'I'm the guy.'

'Columbus.'

'That's right.'

'So you kidnapped me to get to him.'

'Means to an end.'

He nods. 'So now what?'

'A swap. You for my friend.'

'Oh, yeah. The pistol.'

'Pistol?'

'Black guy in Chicago. Pulled a .22 from under his mattress. Name was Grant but we'll always call him the Pistol after that.'

'That's right,' I say, and I'm oddly comforted that Archie impressed them enough to earn a new nickname. 'Spilatro had two guys there.'

'Three, actually. And Spilatro never left the lobby. Pretty straightforward snatch-and-grab except your friend pops up with that pea-shooter right as I get my knee into his back. He squeezed a round off at Bando but missed his head by six inches – I pried the gun away from him after that.' He spits on to the dirty cement next to his feet, making a clear mark in the dust. 'That scrawny dog could put up a fight. I'll give him that.'

'Who broke his nose?'

'Who cares?'

'Little payback from Bando?'

'Does it matter?'

I let that one sail by.

'How long have you and Spilatro been government guys?'

He looks at me sideways. 'Who sold you that dope?'

'Two and two makes four.'

'Except you put the wrong numbers into the calculator.'

'Did I?'

Deckman shrugs. 'Who's the chick?' he asks as he cranes his neck to get an eye on Risina.

'Man in your position might choose his words more carefully.'

'I haven't felt this terrified since my dad got out his belt,' he says flatly.

'Your dad in Northville?'

'My dad six feet under in Birmingham.'

'That's right. It's your brother in Northville.'

'You hurt him?'

I shake my head.

'Sure I can't have a smoke?'

I shake it again and he grins. 'How'd you get Lance to give me up?'

'I told him you were dead. Said you left him some money.'

He nods. 'Dollar signs was all it took, huh? Surprised you were the first to try it. He tell you I was a government man?'

'I already knew it.'

'Uh-huh. He's my kid brother. You think I'm gonna tell him I plug guys for money?'

'I don't care what you tell him.'

He falls silent for a moment. Then lifts his chin again, 'You gonna let me—'

I interrupt to throw a wrench in his tactics. 'How do we get ahold of your army buddy?'

He snickers, like this is all too much for him. 'You're not fishing. I can tell that. You must have a full file on me.'

'I had to pick up a new fence since you snatched mine.'

Risina smiles at that. She's behind Deckman, so he doesn't notice. I repeat, 'How do I contact Spilatro?'

'You got my phone?'

'What's the number?'

'Give me my phone and then give me my hands. I'll track him down for you.'

'Your phone is smashed and in a trash can in the parking garage at the MGM. Along with your two pistols and the knife you had in that cute little wrist sheath.'

This gets him to draw in his smirk. 'Doesn't matter. They'll know where I was last.'

'Who will?'

'You'll find out.'

'Will I? It's a big city.'

He shrugs, looks down at the floor. He tries to toe that spit mark he made in the dust, but can't get to it with his foot.

I haven't broken his confidence, but chipped at it, like a ship cracking through ice to get to the pole. I sit back and fold my hands behind my head. 'Tell me about the dark men.'

His eyelids flutter, slightly. Then, he offers, 'I gotta go to the can.'

I don't move, just keep the chain tethered between our eyes.

'You gonna make me piss myself?'

'You can earn trips to the bathroom.'

'You'd fit right in at Abu Ghraib.'

'I'll take your word for it.'

He takes another run at the bindings then settles again to see if he accomplished any slack. He grunts, unsatisfied, then does that thing people do when they're absently thinking. He sort of moves his lips over to the side of his face. After a moment, he looks up again. 'All right then. How you wanna play this? Because I'm getting bored and quite frankly, a little angry.'

'Tell us how to bring Spilatro out, and this can end licketysplit.'

'What if I don't?'

'I'm not going to shoot you, or beat you, or cut you, if that's what you're wondering. I always thought that was more of a weasel play, and I don't care for it, to tell you the truth. I mean, if you want immediate results, it's probably the way to go, cut a man up, get him to talk, but why go to the trouble when I have nothing but time? So what I'm going to do is sit behind you in the dark back there and watch you die of thirst.'

He stares at me evenly, his face hot, as he tries to gauge whether or not I mean what I say.

Risina walks over and hands me a fast-food bag. I take out a plastic bottle of water, take a swig, then set the remainder in my chair.

'I checked online, and the maximum someone can go without water is ten days. But the statistics say your body will pretty much shut down in three. Three days? Can you imagine? That's nothing. That's a weekend. That's a "hey, I've got plans on Tuesday so I'll see you on Wednesday."'

Risina pulls up a camera and takes a picture of him. Then we leave him there to think about that water bottle just out of his reach, Tantalus with his grapes.

This place must've once been some sort of manufacturing plant servicing the auto industry, but it has the look of a place run-down long before the Big Three started asking for government handouts.

An office adjacent to the room provides a window that looks out onto the front of the building so I can spot any unwelcome vehicles approaching. Whoever owns this warehouse doesn't keep a regular security guard here, but maybe he pays someone to come out and look around once a week or once a month, the way Bacino's neighbor did back in Chicago. It doesn't look like the front door has been cracked in years, and I'm happy to keep playing the percentages, but if someone does happen to roll snake eyes, I'd like to have a few minutes warning to get my money off the table.

The room has another window on the opposite wall that faces the back of Deckman's chair. He spent the first hour trying to tip the chair, and the second hour yelling just to yell. The next morning, he's stiff and sore and broken. It didn't take long.

'You kept in your piss. I'm proud of you.'

'Fuck you,' he croaks.

I start to stand again, and I can see the desperation in his eyes as clear as if I can read his thoughts. I'm going to guess he's never been tortured before, neither during the first Gulf War nor at any point in his professional life, because he doesn't have the mettle to test his own durability.

'Okay, listen. I don't know why we gotta play it like this.' His voice sounds scratchy, like a rake on the sidewalk.

'Tell me how to contact him.'

'Okay, but listen. Here's the thing.' His eyes ping-pong between my face and the water bottle in the chair. 'You're a dead man. You have to understand this. I say this not to be confrontational, but it's a fact, as sure as these walls are white or that floor is cement. As sure as I can admit you know what you're doing in tying a man to a chair. Spilatro is the smartest man I know, the smartest I've ever known. He thinks *differently*, you see? He sees the world as interconnected lines, or, or, dominoes toppling against each other . . . but *he* sets 'em up, you see? He cuts the lines. He knows exactly which pieces are going to fall when, because everything fits into the little designs, the patterns he creates. We're the dominoes, man. And he's the finger pushing 'em over.

'He was always better than me. It wasn't even a competition. He has this disconnect thing he can do where he just shuts it all off, any compassion, any concern for innocents, anything that stands in the way of the dominoes falling. He's already played this out, man. You just don't know it.'

'If that's true, then he gave you up like a pawn on a chessboard.'

'Did he? I don't know. You can't look at the micro with him. Just the macro.'

'So he's expecting my call?'

'I'm sure he is. Which is why I don't really feel like sticking out this "dying of thirst" scenario. Let's get on with it. Give me some water and I'll tell you how to get to him.'

'Was he expecting me to kill you?'

His throat bobs. 'What's that?'

I pull out my Glock and enunciate slowly. 'Was he expecting me to kill you?'

His mouth moves to the side of his face again. 'I don't think the percentage play is to do that if you want your friend back. I'm sure that's why we didn't dump what's-his name, Pistol, in the Chicago River. There's an exchange to be made. That's why we did it.'

'But if I shoot you now, it'll throw Spilatro off his game, right?'

'If you shoot me now, your friend is dead.'

I don't look at Risina. I told her she'd have to see this side of me and that she might not like it. But this is the game. This is the difference between talking about it and doing it, the difference between theory and application, the difference between looking at a photo of a crime scene and having another man's blood on your face, your hands. They brought the fight to us and that's where the truth lies. I hope she can see the difference. There is an entire universe in the difference.

'Maybe. All I know is if he was expecting me to take you and make an exchange, as you figure, then the best play for me is to kill you and disrupt his plans.'

'But you still don't know how to contact him.'

'Then tell me.'

His eyes dart wildly, like a wild animal that wants the food in your right hand but is worried about the left hand he can't see behind your back.

'If I tell you, how do I know you won't kill me?'

'You'll have to wait and see.'

'Not good enough.'

'I thought you wanted to end this. I thought Spilatro already knew how this was going to play out. One way or another, I'm going to confront him, either pretending I have you to trade, or physically having you to trade. Like I said, I have nothing but time.

'So we have three choices here. One, we can go back to the thirst scenario and see how you're doing tomorrow. Two, you can give me the number and hope for the best. And three, I can shoot you and figure out another way to contact Spilatro, maybe a way he hasn't figured yet.'

'That's what I'm telling you . . . he's figured all three plays! He knows what you're going to do. There's no free will here. Not with him!'

I pick up the water bottle, untwist the lid, and then take another swallow, so now the bottle is only half-full. 'All right then,' I say, setting the bottle back on the chair. 'See you tomorrow.'

I only take two steps before he says, 'Wait.'

Thirty seconds later, he gives me the number to reach Spilatro. I take off the lid to the water bottle and hold it to his lips. He gulps it down in three swallows. While the bottle is to his lips, I put my Glock to the side of his head and fire once.

I suppose there was a fourth play, the one where he tells me what I want to know, and I shoot him anyway.

She's in the bathroom, throwing up. I give her a lot of credit. She put up a brave face for a long time, but the reality of what I do for a living, what I've always done, caught up to her in this empty warehouse on the west side of downtown Detroit. I'm not going to try to talk to her through the closed bathroom door, though I have a lot to say. I do know the sooner we get out of here, the better I'll feel. While she jerked her head at the concussive sound of the pop, her face bloodless as she saw Deckman's head explode, and then turned on her heels to hightail it to the bathroom, I picked up the body and dragged it behind a rusted and forgotten drill press. Deckman kept his frame fit, so it wasn't too difficult to move him. I saw the bathroom door slam shut out of the corner of my eye as I finished disposing of the body.

I hear the water running in the sink. It hasn't stopped running. I imagine she's checking herself in the mirror, searching for a visible change in her face. After a moment, the door opens and she emerges, ashen.

'I'm sorry for this,' she says, chewing on a breath mint. 'I . . .'

'It had to be done, Risina.'

'I know. It's just . . .'

'We couldn't try to transport him. The longer you keep a prisoner around, the more chances he has to disrupt your assignment. And this is an assignment, Risina. I've been ducking that mentally for a while, but make no mistake about it, it's an assignment. The name at the top of the page is Spilatro. After we deal with him, we figure the rest of it out.'

'I understand. I need to get some air, if you don't mind, before I vomit again.'

I can't tell if she's agreeing with me because she processes what I'm saying or if she's trying to block it from her mind.

We find the side door and the crisp air envelops us, sweeping away the smell of dust and death in the warehouse. I parked our sedan around the side of the place so it wouldn't be visible from the street.

Before she can open the passenger door, I move over to hold her and she submits, burying her face in my chest.

'I was done, Risina. You know that. And then they came to us. They took Archie and penned a note with my name on it and forced me to answer it. These aren't innocent men.'

'I know,' she says, her face hidden. Her eyes weren't red when she emerged from the bathroom and she's not crying now.

'You going to be okay?'

'Yes.'

She reaches up and kisses me on the cheek, but it's perfunctory, devoid of feeling. 'We should leave, yes?'

'Yes.'

She slides into the passenger seat, and I get behind the wheel, crank the engine. In two minutes, we roll away from the broken chain link gate. Another ten and we're on the highway heading east. Another twenty and Risina's asleep, the last forty-eight hours sapping her energy like physical blows.

I don't know if her attitude toward me will change now that she's stepped behind the curtain and seen me unmasked. I told her once I was a bad man, but up until this morning, they were only words.

12

The blossoms have fallen off the cherry trees as we return to Washington. Discarded cotton candy mounds mark every few feet as sidewalk sweepers push the petals into piles. Trees we were admiring just a week ago now look bald and empty. It happens that quickly.

'Why didn't you tell me?'

'Tell you what?'

We've set up camp in a budget hotel on the outskirts of McLean, Virginia, near the location of the CIA headquarters. I'm looking to disrupt Spilatro's operating method any way I can. I've already put a bullet in the head of his oldest friend, now I'm going to approach him in his own back yard, see if I can shake the leaves from his trees.

'Tell me that you were going to shoot him after he gave you the number.'

'I knew it had to be done from the moment we kidnapped him in the hotel. You can't keep a wild dog chained to you for too long if you don't want to be bit. I didn't know how you'd react and honestly, didn't want to have an argument about it. I wanted you to be a part of it, but I didn't want you to give anything away if you knew. If he saw it in your eyes, I might not have gotten the information from him. It was a delicate tightrope—'

'You didn't trust me.'

'No, that's not it. Trust has nothing to do with it. It's only a matter of the unknown, and as a contract killer, you have to keep the unknown at bay every chance you get. That's the job. I didn't know how you'd react, and I knew what needed to happen. Once I killed him, it wouldn't matter how you reacted.'

'Well, you should have told me anyway. You should have dealt with my reaction up front instead of catching me by surprise.'

'I'm not going to apologize for this, Risina. I had to play the cards dealt to me.'

She folds her arms across her chest and glares at me, grimacing.

'I'm in this all the way with you,' she starts. 'You need to be in all the way with me.'

'I am.'

'No. You're lying to yourself about that. I've known it since Smoke died in Chicago and you saw you couldn't protect him. He died in the worst way possible, right in front of us. And since that moment—'

'Risina . . .'

'Let me finish. Since that moment, you've known it could happen to me too. So you won't let yourself be in all the way with me. You've been questioning bringing me with you from the beginning.'

I'm practiced at keeping my face blank, but it's as open as a book right now, and she reads it, reads that she's right.

Her voice catches, but she plows forward, her Italian accent thickening with every word. 'So listen to me and listen carefully. I'm not going away. I'm not leaving you. And you may not be able to protect me. I might get hurt or worse, but as you say, those are the cards we've been dealt. If the plan is to kill someone to get us to the point we need, then tell me. If the plan is to use me as bait the way you did in Rome with Svoboda, then tell me. Jesus Christ, just tell me. Quit trying to do everything alone. We're partners. We're a tandem, as you call it. Just tell me.'

'Okay.'

She starts to protest, so sure I am going to argue the point. 'Okay?'

'Yes. You're right. You're right about everything. I brought you along because you were in danger the moment Smoke found us. I thought there was a better chance I could keep you safe if you were with me than if I left you behind or stashed you somewhere. I didn't want you showing up in a photograph holding a newspaper with your mouth gagged and your hands tied behind your back, someone using you to break me.'

'I know what you are. I know your fearful symmetry, okay? I've known all along and I am a part of it, yes? The same hand that dared seize the fire to create you, created me.

'I've realized something about us. Something I think profound. Not because it's a clever thought, but just because it *is*. You walked into my bookshop in Rome and I didn't change you. You changed *me*. There is no changing you. Like a beast hibernating, you went dormant when we were on the island, but you didn't change.'

'I didn't mean for this to—'

'You don't understand what I'm saying. I want you to know you changed me, but I needed to change. Some of us don't find out who we are or what we are until another comes along to liberate us from the cages we build for ourselves. You did that to me. You liberated me.'

I stand up and move to her chair, hold out my hand and pull her into me. 'But what if you don't like the change? What if you discover you were happier before?'

'I was dead before.'

And then, as if to prove her point, she spends the next hour making us both feel alive.

He answers on the third ring.

'Hello?' It is unmistakably his voice, the same one I heard in the rented house in upstate New York. It has an enunciated sibilance to it that is as unique as a fingerprint.

'You have something I want.'

He stops breathing, presumably deciding whether he should hang up to regroup or plow forward. I've called him on his private phone, touched him when he thought he was the only one doing the touching. He pauses a moment, and that moment tells me everything – I have, in fact, disrupted his plan.

'Good. I was expecting your call. I'm surprised it took you this long.'

'You know, everyone keeps telling me how smart you are. Including you. But now I'm starting to wonder . . .'

'Okay. Okay,' he stammers.

Rattling him is easier than I imagined. I can picture him on the other end of the line, his face contorting the way it did when he found his wife standing next to his model of Cleveland. He doesn't care for surprises; that part of the story was true. I wonder what miniature mousetrap he's constructed for me and how worthless it is to him now.

'Okay,' he says for the third time. 'You come to me, and I'll release Mr. Grant.'

'Like a rat sniffing cheese while a steel bar snaps his neck?'

'You're starting to get the idea.'

'You want to exchange me for my friend?'

'I want you to come willingly. Your friend is immaterial.'

'You know who else is immaterial? A soldier you used to run with. Roland Deckman. He's gone by "Decker" for the last twenty years or so.'

Spilatro pauses, then starts laughing. There's an undercurrent to the sound though, like a stage laugh. It's strained, wrong. 'I assume that'd be the way you'd locate me. I tried to teach him, to give him advice, but he wouldn't listen. Some people in this game think they're invincible.'

'So now I have something you want.'

'I don't give a damn about Roland Deckman.'

'You have twelve hours or he dies.'

'Right.'

'Check your phone.'

I press 'send' on the picture that Risina took when Deckman was tied and alive.

'I'm not going to tell you you're bluffing, because I don't think you are. I just don't think you've thought this through. If you kill Decker . . .'

'What I haven't done is given you time to think it through. Twelve hours. I'll call you again on this phone with the meeting place two hours before. Have Archie ready to move.'

'You're making a mistake.'

'Just correcting one.'

'You'll have to give me more time if you want Mr. Grant in one piece.'

'Twelve hours.'

He hesitates again. Then, 'Where are you calling from?'

'Some place close.'

Walking to the car with Risina, I'm pleased. All conversations are about exchanging information, and when dealing with a mark, you try to get more than you give. Spilatro gave away something with his question at the end.

He's a government hitter all right, and he's working for these dark men, as he said, but this job isn't sanctioned. It isn't authorized. He doesn't have a support team or a gaggle of analysts helping him break it down. If he were working through proper channels, he would've immediately known where I was calling from, probably had it pinpointed within a few city blocks. The playing field is leveled in a way. Nonetheless, I place the phone under my right rear tire before I pull away from the hotel.

How do you disrupt someone who thinks he can game out every move? When Kasparov played Deep Blue in their infamous chess match of 1996, he beat the machine by charging illogically at the beginning of each match, then set up random traps to capitalize on the computer's hesitancy.

I'm going to charge illogically at Spilatro.

He's made a mistake: he thinks I care about Archie Grant. He thinks the kidnapping of my friend, of my fence, is why

I came back. He thinks that's why I'm holding Decker. He thinks I actually care about an exchange.

It was my *name*. He put my name on a sheet of paper and called me out. No matter who instructed him, who gave him the assignment to kill me, he's the one who put that note where Smoke would find it. He wrote my name on that paper and the machine was set into motion. It'll only stop moving when he's dead.

There's not going to be an exchange, a negotiation. Not because I've already killed Decker, but because I don't really care if Grant dies too. Sure, I'd rather he came out of this alive, but that would be a bonus, rather than the point.

I'm going to kill Spilatro as soon as I spot him. No talking, no give-and-take, just pull up my gun and shoot him in the head.

I tell this to Risina as we drive down a Virginia road, strip malls and shopping centers breaking up the horizon. Her hands are on her knees, knitted together.

'You said you wanted to know the plan. That's the plan.'

'You don't care about Archie? This has never been about Archie?'

'I like him. He's a good fence. A great one, even. And I liked his sister very much, too. But if he dies in the middle of this, or if he's already dead? I won't mourn him. I won't think about him. And he wouldn't mourn me either. You wanted to see me, Risina, to see the real me? This is who I am.'

She nods. 'You just shut off your feelings?'

'About everyone and everything except you. And I let my rage build for the man I have to kill. But don't let rage and rashness blend. My rage allows me to take a man's life and walk away from it cleanly, but I am never rash in executing the hit. Cold-blooded *and* cold-hearted, you have to be both.'

'And powerful, yes?'

'Power is the drug that hooks you to this job. Ending someone's life against his will – it's something you can't fathom until you do it. It takes an even greater hold of you when you know you do it well, when you plan it and execute it and get away with it. My first fence told me it was a power reserved for God, and there is an attraction in that power that is difficult to resist.'

'And Archie? How did he deal with this power?'

'If he does his job right, he sets up his hitters' successes. He compiles the information and hints at the best strategies. He lays out the evil in the target for his killers so they can stoke that rage. A hit man has to connect with the evil so he can sever the connection, and a good fence knows this, knows the importance of this. He does the plotting without the bloodshed. It's a different power the fence holds, but I'm sure the good ones share in it.'

'When we finish this, I want to be your fence.'

She says it in such a matter-of-fact way that I can tell she's been thinking about it for a while. 'Even if we get Archie out alive?'

'Even then.'

'But we could run again. Hide out. Find a new spot, somewhere even more remote.'

'No. You know we would just wait for the next man to come. There will always be a next man who comes.'

'I wanted to believe in a future without this.'

'You can't have it, any more than a tiger can lie in a cage and forget his instincts.'

She's right. She has a way of getting inside my head and saying things I won't let myself think.

'But why would you want to do this with me?'

'Because we are good together. Because I think I was born to do this work. Because I would like to know that you have every piece of information at your disposal to be successful. Because I can provide that, make the file come to life. Live, breathe. It's research, it's writing, but it has to have heart. For you to be the person you are, it has to have heart. I read all those files in Archie's office and it was like discovering a new library that no one knew existed. It was life and death and love and pain and beauty and horror in one place, in those pages, and it was riveting. Biblical. I can do that. I can put it all together for you. Only for you. And better than Archie. I need time to learn, but yes, better than Archie.'

'You sound certain.'

'I am.'

'Where would we live?'

'The place you and I both know best. Boston.'

'And how would you establish us there?'

'You still know a few people. Word will spread quickly that Columbus is back in the business.'

'And how will you protect yourself?'

'We'll protect each other. A pair of tigers, burning bright.'

She grins, pleased with her idea. Maybe it can work, if we survive the day.

I tell Spilatro an address near the Potomac just outside the District in an industrial area. Canneries rise out of the landscape, monstrous, noisy and bleak. It's as though men couldn't stand to look at the beauty of a river cutting through a fertile countryside and so did all in their power to poison the land.

I demanded the exchange take place at seven-thirty, when the sun hangs low and the commercial district will be primarily unpopulated. We might have to deal with security guards and cameras pointed at the street, but I don't care. I'm finishing it now.

I want to drop Risina off at a coffee shop and pick her up when it's over, but she refuses. I tell her that fences don't participate in kills, and she tells me she isn't my fence until this is over. The thought of not knowing what is happening while she sips on a decaf latte is more than she can bear. She's been in this one since the beginning and she'll be in it until the end, and if she sees the dark side of me again standing over Spilatro's dead body, then she welcomes it.

I told Spilatro the address and he tried to keep me on the line, but I didn't give him the opportunity. He's learned all he's going to learn about me, and now the preparation is over and the two killers have to take the field until one is dead.

A black Toyota Tercel with tinted windows slowly rolls to a nearby intersection, the address I gave him, and then turns right and speeds away. I expect to see the same car again soon . . . he came fifteen minutes early to get the lay of the land, do some reconnaissance. I haven't given him time to set up a mousetrap. He's in my world, the world of improvisation, a world he can't control, a world where he has to take advantage of the opportunities as they develop or die face-down in the street.

'This is it. I'm moving out. When you see the muzzle flash, race in and pick me up. Don't hesitate.'

She nods and I kiss her and I think she says 'be careful,' but it's lost in the wind as I duck low out of the passenger side and move to a row of shrubs. I didn't anticipate how quickly the wind could pick up this close to the river and there's an industrial smell to the air, that combination of gas and oil and chemicals that seems to linger around factories like a trip wire: 'Don't cross here or you'll cough up blood.'

The shrubs line a concrete barrier demarking the property of a sardine cannery, and I slip between the greenery and the wall to make my way down to the intersection.

The sky turns that deep sea green as the sun hides in the horizon, and the traffic on the street is minimal, a few trucks rolling out of factories and lumbering up the streets. I find a spot where the intersection is visible through a break in the branches, and here comes that Tercel. I'm going to show myself just long enough for him to step out of the car and ask about the exchange so I can pop him in the head.

Two hundred yards away and it's impossible to see if he has Archie in the car with him, and if he does, I'll do my best to save my old fence, but only once the job is done and Spilatro is down and I can get away clean. Only then.

One hundred yards now and my Glock is out and in my hand. The wind howls, whistling a dirge as it crests the concrete barrier and zips through the shrubbery. Fifty yards.

Out of nowhere, a taxi smashes into the side of the Tercel and drives it across the width of the street, up on to the opposite sidewalk. The section of the Tercel from the driver's side tire to the door is bent concave from the force of the taxi's bumper and the engine has caught fire and whatever play this is . . . I have no idea what he's up to, but it has to be a play.

I can feel the advantage shifting between us, or is that adrenaline in my system? I have to decide how to make a move and what move to make, goddamn him.

The taxi driver gets out of the car, a middle-easterner with a tight turban and a full beard, and he's yelling at the driver of the Tercel, and what the hell play can this be in the small amount of time I've given him? What am I walking into?

The door to the Tercel somehow swings open and a man climbs out but he isn't Spilatro, at least he doesn't look like Spilatro, not exactly, he looks too young from this angle, but can I be sure? He's dangling a gun at his side, and as the taxi driver registers this and starts to wave his hands and turn around saying 'no, no, no, no, no,' the driver shoots him in the back, BAM, dropping him in the road, just another piece of debris from the accident. Through the open door of the Tercel, I can see a figure slumped in the backseat, a dark figure, maybe it's Archie, fuck, this is not what I was expecting. The fire from the hood starts to vomit clouds of black smoke, whipped into a frenzy by the wind and someone nearby, some security guard or late-leaving lunch-bucket union douchebag must've heard the collision or is going to spot the smoke and dial 9-1-1 and then everything I've put into this moment is going to spoil like weeks-old bread. I'm going to have to bite, now.

When I kill, I don't like dropping anyone collaterally, anyone besides my target, because things get messy, but this isn't a target, not really, they targeted me, and if he enlisted some of these dark men, some other hitters the way he did Deckman with his wife's gambit, then they're going to join him lying on the pavement. What's real and what's not is what has had me on my heels this whole time but I have to move in and shift the advantage back to my favor.

I walk quickly from the shrubs and make my way toward the accident, toward the shooter who might be Spilatro but doesn't look like the man I saw two times, and he spots me coming.

'Where's Decker?' he says in a voice I don't recognize – he's not Spilatro – this only takes a moment to register, but he raises his weapon like a Western gunslinger and I already have mine up and fire from thirty yards away, catch him in the forehead and spin him like a top.

I step past the dead cab driver and the dead Tercel driver and head to the sedan, and the guy in the backseat, the one I thought was Archie blows a hole out the window. A bullet whizzes close enough to my ear to make my lobe flap like laundry drying in the wind, and I duck behind the car, lucky the bullet didn't rip my head off.

The man squirms in his seat as he tries to find me and when he turns to the back windshield, I'm already there, in his blind spot. I fire and the back windshield shatters along with half the man's face. He didn't adjust for the fraction of an inch the glass between us would make on his shot. I didn't make the same mistake.

'We have her!' says a voice to my right, and when I wheel, the cab driver is up off the pavement, up and alive and glaring at me, a pistol aimed my way. And now I see it. The beard is fake and the turban is covering a bald head and the bullet he took in the back was staged and the voice is that same prissy 'I'm smarter than you' whine I've heard before except there's a desperation anchoring it down to the pavement like an albatross around his neck.

I didn't give him time to prepare and the best he could come up with on the fly was a faux wreck attached to a shell game and his hitters were dealt the dummy hand and are dead before they even knew what game they were playing. I imagine Bando is one of them, the clown who broke Archie's nose for having the audacity to put up a fight in his own bedroom and now he's either the one dead on the pavement or the one dead in the backseat of the Tercel. Spilatro thought I'd walk up and talk and he could plug me from behind but he didn't count on my Glock speaking for me.

His words stop me though. His plan had a wild card, a joker. 'We have her' and I look up the street and sure enough, Risina is out of the driver's side with a gun to her head.

Holding the pistol is Carla.

Carla, who I listened to for hours as she poured her heart out regarding her husband's betrayal, whom I believed wholeheartedly, whose story I swallowed like a spoonful of fucking ice cream and maybe that's the part I misjudged the most about my rust, my diminished abilities. I thought my killing skills had dropped, the physical skills, but it's the mental part that has to be exercised to stay finely tuned . . . the ability to read faces, gestures, voices, lies. I thought I was in shape, but I'm faced with my failure now; I was played like a fool and my sand castle crashed down, stomped on by the ugly woman with the hound-dog face and the black heart.

She's too far away to attempt a shot and Spilatro sneers as he aims his gun in my direction.

'What say we all get in the car and take a trip?'

He gestures toward the taxi.

'I thought you didn't like confrontation up close and personal.'

'You shouldn't believe everything you hear from hostile witnesses.'

I nod, the Glock heavy in my hand.

Spilatro smiles, his voice hitting that fingernails-on-a-chalkboard pitch. 'I told you I was smarter than—'

I shoot him in the head, the bullet slamming into his right eye.

His gun goes off, a finger spasm, but I don't hear it, don't even wait to see Spilatro drop. My mental game may be lagging but my ability to hit a man at fifteen feet will never flag, and I sprint directly at Carla, my focus on only her, as everything else fades away. I don't feel the pavement under my feet, don't feel the wind in my face, don't feel the wetness searing the edges of my eyes. She's far away, too far away, why did I park so fucking far? Why did I bring Risina? Why didn't I—

Carla blanches, then shoves Risina into the car and is behind the wheel and I see her cold-cock Risina with the butt of her gun, one, two, three times, wham, wham, wham, a blur, a whipsaw, and Risina's face is bloody and out and she's slumped and the engine cranks and I shoot into the windshield which spiders but the car launches into a left turn, tires screaming, engine thundering.

Only then do I realize I'm bleeding, shot in the chest by Spilatro's involuntary finger jerk.

I don't know how to . . . won't know how to find her if she escapes with Risina.

Wheeling on a dime, I sprint back to the taxi with the damaged front end, the old Crown Vic that Spilatro drove into the Tercel, and I'm in the driver's seat and behind the wheel and the engine is still running. My breath is a bit shallow like I'm trying to suck air in through a straw but I'll be damned if I'm going to drop. I will not drop. Not now. Not when someone put a plug in me with a lucky shot after he was already dead.

I catch a flash of beige streaking through a gap in warehouses a block away and hear the bass blast of a big rig's horn followed by a screech of brakes and tires locking up as they cling to asphalt. Whatever happened slowed Carla's escape and may be my only hope because I don't have a plan anymore, certainly don't have one for Carla, and as soon as she shakes me she'll kill Risina, I know it, and I won't let that happen, can't let that happen. She might've thought better of holding a hostage and already finished the job, but fuck if I'm going to think about that . . .

I throw the taxi into a hard right to chase the sound of the semi's horn and as I whip behind the industrial plant, I just have time to see my rental car untangle itself from the left bumper of a cannery big rig.

I don't know what parts of Carla's story were bunk but I'm guessing she hasn't spent a lot of time as hunted rather than hunter, because she's panicking at the exact moment when she should have calmly made her getaway, disappeared around a corner and then I would have been lost.

The taxi has a fractured bumper and the alignment is pulling to the right but the engine is still functioning and the wheel responds to my jerks. I've spent the last few years with gunsights on me and despite the pain in my chest, despite the way my right arm is shutting down, hanging uselessly, the bullet wound worse than I thought, goddamn, I'm glad to be pursuing, chasing, closing, hunting. At least I have that. If I'm going to die, I'm going to die on offense.

I saw her knock Risina unconscious, and that image – that visual of this haggard woman repeatedly pounding Risina in the head with the butt of her gun – will sustain me until I catch Carla and kill her, bullet in my chest be damned.

The rental sedan blows through a red light and I don't hesitate, don't brake, just keep the accelerator pinned like I'm trying to stomp the pedal into the street. The taxi sways all over the road like a bird with a clipped wing and I hug the middle of the asphalt steadily, closing the distance with every swerve Carla makes.

She brakes into a hard right at the next intersection, swinging wide, and I'm able to cut the corner and narrow the gap between us to the length of a car. A UPS truck pulls out into our path and Carla swerves around it while I shoot the gap on the other side and when we bullet past the truck, I emerge right on her bumper.

Risina's head rises in the Taurus's passenger seat as she regains her senses.

No. *No no no no no no no.* Stay down, play dead, pretend to be out, don't call attention to yourself. Don't dangle bait in front of a desperate animal.

I wish these thoughts straight into Risina's brain, but she doesn't get the message. I see her head wobble and then her face turns towards Carla in the driver's seat. Even at eighty miles per hour, I can see this taking place through the back windshield as clearly as if I were in the front row of a stage play. Risina slowly comprehending her position. Carla quickly deciding she has a better chance of losing me if she doesn't have to deal with a living, breathing passenger. You can't keep a wild dog near by if you don't want to get bit. She raises her pistol to shoot Risina in the face at close range.

I upshift and tag her bumper just as she pulls the trigger. The gun jerks and fires, blowing out the rear passenger window. Startled into sobriety, Risina launches for Carla's face, going for her eyes with her fingernails leading the way.

I plow into the sedan's bumper again and this time our cars lock up and spin and twist and crumple and the world turns weightless before a blackness drops over me as suddenly as if a bag were thrown over my head.

The car is smoking and buckled but there are no emergency lights strobing through my eyelids, no sirens pounding my eardrums, so the collision must've just happened and though I was out momentarily, it must not have been for long. The taxi is upright, still centered on all four tires though it must've flipped at least once. The pain in my chest is pure heat, like someone is holding an iron to the spot, and I can't so much as raise my elbow or curl the fingers of my right hand. Whatever damage the bullet caused was exacerbated by the wreck, and patches of light swim in and out of my vision like a swarm of gnats.

Out. I have to climb out of the car.

My door won't budge, but the window is gone. Half the breakaway glass is in my hair, on my face, in my lap. With my good arm, I hoist myself through the opening while I bite my lip to keep from losing consciousness. Somehow, I pull myself into a sitting position, half in and half out of the car, then look around and spot the rental sedan on its back, tires up, rocking on its spine like a dog submissively showing its belly, overpowered.

Risina emerges from the passenger window and simultaneously, Carla crawls out of the driver's side, all elbows and knees, a clutch of metal in her right hand. She's managed to hold on to her pistol.

They both rise to their feet at the same time, body and shadow, mirror images, only the inverted wreck between them to throw off the symmetry.

Carla raises her pistol, a look of disbelief, of exasperation, of disgust on her face, and I spill out of the taxi, stumble, find my feet, no weapon, no gun, nothing, just an impossible gap, a gulf, the beginning and end of life between us. I charge Carla like a demon, and I don't hear my voice but I know I'm screaming, and I don't hear my footsteps but I know I'm running as fast as I've ever run, and the gun still points at Risina who stands like an offering waiting for the sacrifice, resigned to die fifteen feet from the barrel.

'Carla!' I shout as loud as a cannon, but I know I'll never reach her in time.

As though I willed it to be, the mutt-faced woman swings the revolver toward me and Risina anticipates the distraction and closes on her like a pouncing cat and the gun goes off, but the bullet ricochets off the pavement near my feet before it spins off to God knows where.

Risina tackles Carla to the ground and drives her elbow into the woman's jaw while her other hand wrenches the gun from her grasp.

I have thirty more feet to go before I can help. From my periphery, I see vans race up from various directions, insects swarming an open wound, black vans, unmarked, at least four of them but how can I be sure? I feel like I'm moving underwater now, swimming, hallucinating.

Twenty more feet and Risina straddles Carla and drives her elbow like a piston again and again into Carla's nose. Wham, wham, wham.

The vans blow past me and screech to a halt in the intersection.

Ten more feet and Risina levels Carla's gun. Men spill out of the van just as I arrive, suited men, dark men, and Risina points the weapon directly into Carla's face and pulls the trigger.

The concussive sound of the gunshot is like a bomb going off as two men sweep me off my feet in a dead run and my head hits the ground and the world snuffs out as dark as death.

13

Would you listen to a story told by a dying man? You've been with me this long. I owe you. I owe . . .

The bullet is out of my chest, and clean dressing and a suture are packed over the wound, but the right side of my body is numb. An oxygen mask covers my nose and mouth, but I still can't seem to suck in enough air. A light shines in my face, but I can't see past the bulb and whatever that damn machine is that pings with each heartbeat is pinging slowly, irregularly, a submarine's sonar that can't seem to locate an enemy.

It takes all my energy to twist my head to the side. I'm not in a hospital, that much is clear. This is a makeshift medical room that looks like it was cobbled together in a dilapidated warehouse. Piles of what appear to be sewing machines are stacked in a corner next to discarded reams of fabric. A few folding tables line the far wall. A leg is twisted on one and it leans over like a disabled man missing a crutch. Sewing machines seem fitting for some reason I can't quite put together. My thoughts are jumbled, like I'm trying to read the contents of a folded letter through an envelope held up to the light.

The bed I'm lying atop isn't a bed, just another folding table with a mattress stuck on it. The IV I'm hooked up to and the pinging machine look authentic but what do I know? I haven't spent much time in hospitals.

Risina. Did I see her shoot Carla in the face at close range? Did I pass out before that? Something keeps shaking my brain. She wrenched Carla's gun away, jammed it in the woman's face, pulled the trigger and then I was pitching sideways like a sailboat tossed in high winds and then ping, ping, ping, here in this warehouse doubling as a clinic and I can't catch my breath and Risina, ping, Risina, ping, Risina . . .

Footsteps approach and I don't have the energy to feign unconsciousness. I feel a thumb press my eyelids open and then a penlight shines into my eyes as a man with a tight beard frowns in my face. If I weren't so drained, if I could even lift my right hand from my side, I might try to wrestle that penlight from his hand and bury it into the side of his neck until his throat lit up like a fucking runway, but I can't seem to muster the strength.

'Can you talk?' he asks after he checks my pulse.

I shake my head, or at least I think I shake my head, and his frown grows more pronounced.

He turns to another man standing over his shoulder, a man I didn't realize was in the room. 'It's not good.'

'Chances?'

'Fifty-fifty.'

The other man bullies past the first and lowers himself inches from my nose. After a moment's inspection, he says, 'I'd take that bet,' then spins and exits my field of vision, if not the room.

I've never seen either man in my life.

I tried to change but I couldn't. Ping. I thought I'd evolved but I hadn't. Ping. I thought I could protect her but I couldn't. Ping. I thought I could end this but I didn't. Ping.

With each ping, my pulse seems louder, steadier. I can feel it in my throat, the ends of my fingers, my earlobes. I've never defaulted on a job, not one, and the only times I've failed to make a kill were by my own volition. This isn't a job, but the path was the same. Someone put my name on paper and I killed him for it. Someone else hired him to do it, 'dark men' he called them, and I'm going to kill them all. Every last one of them. If they hurt Risina, if they touched her, they're all going to die.

My fingertips. Ping.

I can feel the pulse there, yes, and now that I concentrate, I can flex the fingers. They don't do more than twitch, but they *do* twitch. It's not much but it's something. Maybe Spilatro's bullet didn't cause as much damage as I presumed, maybe I'm not paralyzed, maybe I'm not going to die.

I owe. I owe . . .

I know that focusing on a goal can increase your chances at recovery, that pledging to see one last relative, one last birthday, one last wedding, one last reunion can help the dying live for days, weeks, months longer than a doctor or surgeon thought possible.

Whatever they did to her, are doing to her, that's what I have to use to sustain me, to heal me. Hatred I can let grow inside me to replace the pain. Ping. Hatred I can let flow inside me as warm as medicine. Ping. I'm going to kill these motherfuckers, these dark men, and I'm not going to die before I get the chance to bury them.

I owe . . . I owe . . .

Can I bend my elbow? I concentrate solely on my right arm as I will it to flex. It responds, only a millimeter of movement, probably invisible to anyone but me. But it was there; I felt it. Ping.

A woman enters and breathes onions into my face while she checks my pulse, my blood pressure. I crack my eyes just enough to see that her face matches her breath.

'Back to the land of the living.'

I try to respond to that unimaginative opening but my throat feels like it is filled with sand.

She holds a cup of water to my lips and I start to gag, but when she withdraws the cup I manage to croak out 'more.'

She returns the water and it goes down better this time, like a sudden squall washing the dust from a dry creek bed.

'Your vitals are all solidly in the green,' she says. 'You look rough but you're gonna live for a bit.'

I cast my eyes about the room. We're alone but there are a couple of cameras affixed to the ceiling. The dark men may not be here, but they're watching.

I have to watch too. Wait and watch for a mistake. *I owe. I owe* . . . Ping.

It happens a week later. I can't be precisely sure of how much time passed, but it feels like a week. Nurse Onions has been in and out at regular intervals, what I'm guessing are eight-hour shifts, replaced by Orderly Tough Guy and Nurse Eyebrows. I did my best to extract some personal information out of each, but Onions is the only one who strung more than two words together. I haven't asked about Risina. I won't. If they already know I care for her, then I'll make them question how much. If they don't know, I'll make them think she was only my pawn.

My strength returns, slowly. I've been flexing my legs under the sheets and my arms, I've been swinging in small concentric circles just above the mattress. I hope it's unnoticeable to the cameras as I lie in the dark. I make barely enough movement to toggle a few pixels on their monitors or maybe they've figured out what I'm doing. A man named Mr. Cox used to lock me inside a house all day when I was a kid. While he was gone, I'd work on my strength until I was ready to confront him. I don't have the time or the freedom to do pushups, chin-ups, sit-ups like I did then. I'm just going to have to make a move with the strength I built from those little circles and flexes. They made a mistake not handcuffing me to the bedrail.

Onions enters carrying a steel tray of food. Some kind of protein shake, a peanut butter and jelly sandwich, a bowl of fruit. They haven't given me a single utensil, and that penlight hasn't made another appearance, but sometimes larger objects can do the trick. Ping. They should have brought everything in on a paper plate. Ping.

As she moves to set the tray in my lap, I spring up with more agility then they've seen out of me since they dragged me here. I grab the tray with both hands and as Onions leans in to restrain me, I slam the flat steel into her face with everything I have. She spills backward but doesn't drop as a metallic clang reverberates around the warehouse. Her nose is broken, and her hands go there instinctively, as I spin the tray around like I'm twirling a football and smack her with the flat end a second time, this time to the back of the head. She topples forward on to the bed now, a moan rising up like a foghorn from somewhere deep inside her.

I hear footsteps rushing in my direction from the darkness and I'm going to have to move quickly now. I charge the footsteps and just as Orderly Tough Guy steps into the light I hit him with the edge of the tray into the white of his throat and he falls to his knees, his strength sapped as he gasps for air. Twirling the tray again, I set my feet like a baseball batter and swing for the fences, the flat of the tray catching him in the temple. He capsizes the rest of the way to the floor and I'm into the darkness, looking for an exit.

I find an open doorway in the corner and enter a narrow corridor only lit by emergency lights. I move quickly now, the tray curled up in my arm. A man in a suit swings out from a doorway fifteen feet away, a gun in his hand, and this might've been the end of my escape, but as he pulls the trigger, I realize he's firing a stun-gun, one of those devices that shoots out an electrode along a connecting wire. This ignorant bastard thinks we're playing a game of capture or be captured instead of life and death. The electrode flies forward and I swat it away with the tray like I'm backhanding a tennis ball, and then I fling the tray at his head. It frisbees through the air, making the sound of a ringing bell as it slices into his forehead and nearly rips his scalp off. He drops instantaneously, as though his bones and muscles turned to jelly after the flying tomahawk nearly decapitated him. I scoop up the tray on the way through the door from which he just emerged.

The room is something akin to a break room, complete with a couple of vending machines, a long table lined with folding chairs, and a microwave. I flip through drawers along a row of cabinets, nothing, nothing, nothing and then jackpot: metal silverware. I take a handful of knives, start to leave my tray behind, then think better of it and retrieve it before heading through another door.

A new hallway, this one with a sign above a door at the end of it that reads 'exit,' but might as well say 'freedom.' I'm tired, sore, a little dizzy if I took the time to admit it, but all of that is just vague wisps at the back of my brain as I glide through the corridor and hit the door in full stride.

It slams open and slaps the outside wall with a bang and I'm surprised to find it overcast outside, like the beginning of a summer storm. It might be dawn, it might be dusk, impossible to tell.

Two cars are parked in an otherwise empty lot, a pair of foreign sedans and it won't take me long to jump one, get the hell out of here, and figure out where the fuck I am before I make my next move.

Just as I approach the driver's door of the black one, a familiar voice shouts from the doorway, jolting me as abruptly as if that guard's stun-gun had sent a thousand volts into my body.

'Columbus! Wait!'

I can't believe the voice I hear. I don't even have to turn around to know who it is. I start to shake my head, my hand poised inches from the sedan's door handle.

'Hold up just a second, now,' he calls out.

I turn, an about-face, and a wave of nausea suddenly springs up and threatens to cloud my vision. The first drops of rain prick my head, cold.

'Archie?'

It comes out more of a question than a statement, like he might disappear, a mirage.

'First thing I gotta say before you hit me with that silver tray, Columbus. I wasn't part of this. Not directly.'

He doesn't disappear. The rain starts to fall harder but he's really there, wet but not washing away.

'What the hell's going on, Archie?' In my mind I say this calmly, but I can hear it come out with a sharp edge.

'Well, I can answer that. I will, too. But what say you come back inside and we talk about it out of this mess.'

'What'd they do to you, Archie?'

'Come inside, Columbus.'

'If you think I'm walking back inside that warehouse, you've forgotten everything you know about me.'

He nods at that as the rain accumulates in his close-cropped afro. 'You gonna make me talk about this in the rain, aint'cha? Goddamn.'

He steps away from the warehouse door and approaches as cautiously as a bird looking for breadcrumbs under an occupied park bench.

'Second thing I gotta say is I didn't know.'

'What didn't you know?'

'Can we at least sit in that car to do this?'

'Only if we drive it away from here.'

'Sold.'

I ready my elbow to smash in the sedan's window. 'Wait!'

He holds up a set of keys. 'That's my rental.'

'Then you drive.'

'As long as you don't kill me before I tell you what for.'

'Depends on what your answers are, Archie.' I slide into the passenger seat and wait for the car to come to life. The rain patters the windshield like gunfire.

A back booth at Dunkin' Donuts admits us a place to talk and eat, two of Archie's favorite pastimes.

'It all played out how you know it. Some men put hands on me in the middle of the night. I put up a fight and they cracked me till I was flat. I didn't know it was Spilatro or the Agency or none of that. No one told me this was coming. You gotta believe that. I meant what I said when I said I'd help you stay gone.'

Archie doesn't smile as much as he used to. That was his trademark, flashing his teeth, making you feel comfortable, even when you thought maybe he was trying to pull one over on you. Maybe after his sister died, he couldn't bring himself to put on that show anymore. Or maybe this business with the government shook him up.

'How long have you been working for Uncle Sam?'

'Not working for. Working *with*. There's a continent of difference between those two prepositions.'

He bites into a cinnamon twist, but doesn't look down, his eyes stoic.

'Any fence worth a whit does some Agency shit time to time. They outsource the domestic bloodshed. It's their culture. They use their talent on foreign soil, but back home? They contract out the wetwork, same as everyone. You've done a job or two for them over the years, guaranteed.'

'I don't care.'

He holds up his palms defensively, like he wants me to let him finish. He hasn't dropped his hands below the table since we arrived.

'I know you don't, Columbus. You a Silver Bear and you don't look to know who hired you. A kill's a kill and it's all about the hunt. I get that. I'm just trying to put some background on this thing we're in.'

He coughs into his fist, like he's still sorting out his thoughts. 'Some people in the government found out you was the one what killed that senator . . .'

'Congressman.'

'Politician. Presidential candidate. Abe Mann. Whatever. We on the same page.'

'How'd they know it was me?'

'They got a name and that's all they got. Contractor named Columbus did it. There are only a few like you in the whole damn world, so the field was narrow. Who knows how the whisper became a fact, but they knew, and when they found out it was you, they found out about me.'

The cinnamon twist is gone and after he licks the sugar crystals off his fingers, he's on to an old-fashioned.

'They knew you'd given up the game, and they hired Spilatro to bring you back. He's the cat who came up with the kidnap plan, the ransom note, the bread crumb trail that would bring you out of hiding.'

'So these men could have revenge on me for killing their candidate, their puppet.'

Archie sets down his donut. 'Not exactly.'

I wait for more.

'They want you to work for them.'

I shake my head, my mouth twisted in a frown. 'Do I look like I have a bump on my head, Archie? Why would I buy that?'

'Because it's the truth. They saw the job you pulled in Los Angeles and wanted to know the man who could execute like that and walk away clean. They got beat by you, and dark men like them do one of two things when they get beat. They either fix the problem by plugging it up, or they recruit the son-of-a-bitch over to their side. Except with you, they figured best to do both.'

I don't think my head has stopped shaking.

Archie continues, undaunted, 'They went to their best hitter inside the company and said, "here's your assignment. You find this Columbus and you kill him." But what they were really saying was "let the best man win."'

'A test?'

'Something like that. *Competition*'s a better word. They want to run a stable with the best horses. And you just proved again you're the best in the game.'

'And you played along?'

'After the beatdown they put on me, they drove me to what they call a "secure location." Then the real players showed up and told me the what-all. They kept me fed, let me watch TV, but they made it clear they wasn't fucking around. Wanted to keep me alive and kicking so I could broker a deal if you bested Spilatro. And so here we are.'

'And Smoke is dead.'

His eyes cloud over. 'Yeah. It's a fuckin' shame Spilatro did him like that. Smoke was good people.'

I sit back and fold my arms. 'Call 'em over here.'

Archie gets that look on his face I've seen before, the one that says he forgot who he was dealing with. He wipes his fingers carefully with a napkin, then leans back and lets loose a long sigh. Finally, he cranes his neck and nods at the corner booth.

Two men wearing charcoal suits rise from the booth as they try unsuccessfully to keep their faces blank.

Archie slides around next to me, and they sit opposite.

'And the third. Call him over.'

The shorter of the two men – the one with bushy, black eyebrows that seem too large for his face – calls out to a third suited man perched at the counter. 'Grayson, you're made.'

A man at the counter slumps his shoulders, turns around, and pulls over a chair to the end of the table. The three men look approximately the same age – late forties – and all have hard eyes that indicate they've seen a lot of shit most people reserve for nightmares.

'You're the dark men, huh?'

Bushy Eyebrows speaks up. 'I'm Mitchells. This is Vancill. And Grayson's at the end there.'

'You ordered all this?'

Mitchells shrugs. 'I ordered your elimination. You cost us a great deal of time, effort and expense when you put our candidate in a bodybag.'

'He set it up.'

'But you killed him.'

'And now you want me to work for you?'

He smiles. 'We happen to have an opening.'

'Go fuck yourself.'

Mitchells sniffs the air like he just caught a whiff of something unpleasant.

'That's warranted, so I'll let it slide. But you're a very smart man, Columbus, so I won't let it slide twice. There are advantages to working for us that I know will be attractive to you. Namely, you'll get to keep doing what you love doing the most.'

'I was out.'

'Were you?' He says this without a smile. 'I'm trained to read people the way my colleagues are trained to crack code. I've watched your progress on this mission and before it . . . all over Europe for the preceding three years. Prague, Belgium, Spain, Paris. You're a killer, you're good at killing, and I'll be damned if you don't enjoy it. I don't know any plainer way to say it.'

He doesn't look like he's a man who flatters as a matter of course, and if this is an attempt at flattery, it's a clumsy one. Rather, he simply speaks the truth and says it plain. 'I would've sought you out sooner, would've tried to pull you in, but you stepped off the grid after you fell for the bookstore owner in Rome. That made it difficult to find you, and it would've been irresponsible for me not to make sure you hadn't lost a step once we did.'

He watches my eyes to see if his casual mention of Risina elicits a response.

'So this was all about pulling me in?'

'This was about making sure you were worth pulling in. My team here thinks you are. I think the jury's out.'

He says it levelly, a challenge there. Then to emphasize the point, 'You gonna ask about the girl?'

'You know her name. You can say it.'

'Risina Lorenzana. You gonna ask about her or you want to keep pretending she doesn't matter?'

'You want to keep poking me until you find out the answer?' I try to match his expression, but I'm not sure I pull it off.

He settles back. The other two haven't said a word and Archie just chews on his old-fashioned donut like it's the only thing in the room.

'All right,' I say after a charged moment. 'Let's hear your offer.'

Mitchells folds his fingers together. 'It's simple. You take your assignments from us. You give us a break on your rate. You keep working through Archie if you want, but we'll supplement his fieldwork with our intel. And if you get caught or captured, you put a bullet in your own head. Otherwise, your life won't change much. You won't be lying on a beach in a fishing village, but we won't overwork you either.'

'And there's no getting out?'

'You put a few years in and then we talk again. We're not inflexible.'

'And what about Risina?'

If he says 'what *about* her?' or cracks a smile, I'm going to leap across the table and kill him with my bare hands. But he must have told the truth when he said he was good at reading people because he adds no emotion to his voice when he says, 'She's free to go. You want to keep her in play, that's your decision.'

'I want her to be my fence.'

Archie stops in mid-bite and looks at me out of the tops of his eyes.

'Fine,' says Mitchells.

'You trying to cut me out after all we been through? Let me tell you something . . .'

'Don't get nervous. She's going to need some better training than I could give her. I know how to close a contract but I don't know shit about fence-work. I want you to show her the ropes.'

That seems to mollify Archie. He jabs his index finger into the table to make the point. 'I'll set her up square. I promise you that.'

I nod but I'm not ready to look him in the eye. It'll have to be enough.

Mitchells unfolds his hands. 'We have a deal then?'

'We have a deal.'

The dark men get up from the booth, including Archie, and start to shuffle away, satisfied.

Mitchells takes a step toward the door, then turns around and puts his hands on the table.

'And Columbus?'

'Yeah.'

'I also know your name,' he says.

EPILOGUE

I drive to a country house in rural Virginia, about twenty miles outside of Charlottesville. Mitchells gave me an address where Risina would be safe, and if he's lying, I'm hard pressed to figure out his play. They could've killed me in the aftermath of the Spilatro climax instead of freeing a bullet from my chest and sewing me up, instead of making me whole. They don't want me angry; there's no benefit to it. Right?

Farms with red barns, with tin silos, with white-post fences, with black cattle, with green grass in wide pastures pass outside my windshield like Ansel Adams photographs of a forgotten America. The sun hangs on the horizon and burns the clouds above it a malevolent red. The contrast between the farms and the sky is disquieting, as though doom hangs over placidity like a guillotine waiting to drop.

She is a tiger. She said it and she did the job and when the time came to pull the trigger, she fired the gun into a woman's face at point-blank range. She didn't shy away from the mess when it interfered with our life and everything she's done since Smoke showed up has been smart and efficient.

This could work. This could be better than how I imagined it. She'll have Archie to guide her and the intel of the Agency to supplement her, and I can't discount her innate passion and quick mind. She could be a great fence, the best I've had since Pooley. She'll surpass Archie in short order, I'm sure of it. I won't just be a horse in a stable to her, I'll be her only horse, and she'll do whatever it takes to ensure my success, the way Pooley used to perform the job when I first started. It can work. It will work.

Did the bloodshed change her? Did the battle sour her stomach? Will she want to disappear again, now that she's seen up close what a pistol can do to a human face? Will she want to run? Will she want to flee alone?

The road turns to gravel as the GPS tells me I have less than a mile to go. I'm nervous in a way I haven't been for a long time. We've been driving forward since this started, no time to catch our breath, no time to reflect, and now that she's had some moments apart, will she pull out of the spiral? Will she emerge like a repatriated prisoner, free from Stockholm Syndrome, with a fresh realization that this life was an illusion, a fantasy, and the reality is so much worse?

No. It can't be that way. I know her. Everything we've shared since I walked into that bookstore in Rome has been real, permanent, fervid. We were already solid, but now that we've been through the trenches together, we're unbreakable.

She can be a great fence. She proposed it and she meant it. She said I have to be all the way in with her and I am. I swear I am. We can do this together.

I reach a red mailbox with the address number stenciled in black on its side and turn the car through a gate, bump over a cattle guard, and head down a bumpy road through a forest. She proposed it. She knows my fearful symmetry. She always knew it.

The road clears and on a hill sits a simple white house.

She must hear me coming because she's through the front door, blinking away tears as soon as I'm out of the driver's side. We meet halfway up the sidewalk and are in each other's arms and it's as it was, as it will be. This can work. We can make it work. She can be my fence, and I'll be her assassin and we'll make it work.

She pulls back, her face wet, her eyes shiny.

'I'm pregnant,' she says.